THE BEHOLDEN

BEHOLDEN
THE

CASSANDRA ROSE CLARKE

EREWHON

THE BEHOLDEN
Copyright © 2022 by Cassandra Rose Clarke

First published in North America by Erewhon Books, LLC in 2022

Edited by Sarah T. Guan

Erewhon Books
2 W. 29th Street, Suite 3S
New York, NY 10001
www.erewhonbooks.com

Erewhon books are available at special discounts when purchased in bulk for premiums and sales promotions as well as for fund-raising or educational use. Special editions or book excerpts can also be created to specification. For details, send an email to specialmarkets@workman.com.

Library of Congress Cataloging-in-Publication data is available upon request.

ISBN 978-1-64566-025-5 (trade paperback)
ISBN 978-1-64566-035-4 (ebook)

Cover art by Kristina Carroll
Cover design by Dana Li
Interior design by Leah Marsh
Chapter head and line break image by vectortatu/Shutterstock

Printed in Canada

First US Edition: January 2022
10 9 8 7 6 5 4 3 2 1

THE BEHOLDEN

ONE

The riverboat glided through the black water of the lower Seraphine, a place where the trees were so thick they formed a ceiling overhead, blocking out the stars. Ico didn't like that, not seeing the stars. It was hard for a sailor to find his bearings in the darkness.

The door to the engine room slammed open, and Calix stomped out, his boots heavy on the boat's deck. One of the passengers startled, although the other, the pretty one, just turned her head toward him, her expression calm. Ico'd been watching her. She sat with her back straight, her chin lifted, her hands clasped in her lap. A proper lady, to be sure. But Ico had noticed her gown when they boarded back in Jaila-Seraphine, and although it was silk and lace, it was also worn out, threadbare. Opulence lost.

"We're approaching the turn off point." Calix stopped at Ico's side and stared out behind him. Ico glanced over his shoulder to see what Calix saw, but there was only the ink of the river, the ink of tree shadows.

Ico nodded. He stood with one hand at the wheel, directing the boat straight down the river. The paddle churned up the water behind him. "You think we'll even be able to find it?"

Calix grunted. "I'll bring up some extra lamps. Keep your eye on the two ladies. We don't know what we're going to see once we turn off."

The passengers didn't seem to have heard Calix. Good thing, too, since the last thing Ico needed was to steer the boat and try to comfort a pair of frightened noblewomen while Calix tended to the engines. At least he was paying him double. Ancestors knew Ico needed the money.

The passengers shifted in their seats. They'd insisted on sitting up on deck, even after the sun set and everything plunged into darkness. The pretty one leaned over and murmured something to the other, too low for Ico to hear. They were sisters, Calix had told him, although even he hadn't known much more than that.

Sisters who wanted passage to the Lady's Tributary.

Calix disappeared into the storage room down below. The boat slid forward, churning up the water, the little splashes of the paddles a quiet whisper in comparison to the shrieks of the insects and the nocturnal animals out in the forest. Ico stood in the murky light of the lanterns and guided the boat without much thought. Since leaving his old pirate life behind and going straight, he'd done this a thousand times, taken the riverboat down the main thoroughfare of the Seraphine. But usually there were other boats out on the river, fellow sailors who would shout the customary greetings over the water. But no one was out tonight.

"How much longer?" asked the pretty one. Her voice startled Ico, and he jumped, although practice kept him from knocking the wheel sideways.

"Not sure," he answered.

She turned toward him. Her brown skin was pristine, unmarred by lines or labor. Her eyes were large and dark and dewy, her hair a thick black cloud that she wore loose around her shoulders. Unmarried, then. A proper lady like that would keep to the customs.

"Could you ask the captain?" she said.

"You ask him," Ico said. "I'm not leaving the wheel, lest you want to get run aground." He tilted his head toward the shore. "Probably some beasties out tonight. I've heard tell that the bloodsucking tyzoti lives in this part of the forest. If you think you can stand up to that, then I'll be happy to end the journey now."

The pretty one glared at him, although her classic beauty tempered any sense of fierceness. The other one, though, the plain one, gave him a cold look and said, "There are no bloodsucking tyzotis in this part of the forest because the bloodsucking tyzoti does not exist. It's an Eirenese myth meant to disparage the Seraphine. Like the kajani."

Ico laughed. "You know so much about Eiren, lady?"

She lifted her chin. "More than you, I'm sure."

Ico doubted that. He spent time in Eiren back in his pirate days. Earned quite a bit of notoriety for himself up there, too, which was why he was attempting to go straight down here in the Seraphine. But beyond that, Eiren was an ancient place, set in its ways, with a long memory. Ico's ancestors had refused to take sides during a war five hundred years ago, and the Eirenese ability to hold a grudge was legendary.

The hatchway slammed open with a bang that reverberated through the night. Calix climbed up, a cluster of lanterns flung over one shoulder.

"The ladies were asking how much longer," Ico said.

Calix carried the lanterns over to the bow and then pulled a candle out of his pocket, which he lit on one of the already-burning lanterns. "Not sure," he answered, not looking up from his work. "Although it'll be soon."

"You told us you'd get us here before morning," the plain one said.

"And I will." Calix lit the first lantern and hung it on the hooks jutting out from the side of the boat.

"It's *imperative* that we arrive before daybreak."

"You mentioned that." Another lantern lit, another lantern hung. "Several times."

The plain one crossed her arms and huffed, and her sister touched her shoulder and said something comforting. The river revealed itself in the light of the lanterns. The current had picked up a ways back, but now he could see the ripples and eddies in the water, veering off to the left.

"Oh, we are close," he said.

"Mmmhmm." Calix hung the last lantern and straightened up. "Prepare yourself, ladies. Not sure what we're going to find once we turn off into the tributary."

Neither of the sisters answered.

The wheel jerked under Ico's hand; he gripped it tighter so the boat wouldn't swerve off to the shore. Water slapped up against the side. They were caught up in the current of the Lady's Tributary.

"Hold on, ladies!" Ico shouted. "Wouldn't want you to fall overboard."

That earned him a dark look from both of the women, but Calix laughed, a sound that echoed out through the darkness. He hung the last of the lanterns and came to the rear of the boat.

"Need any help?" he asked.

"I got it." Ico grabbed the wheel with both hands and leaned against it with his weight, turning the boat into the

4

current, trying to stay in control. The lantern light slid back and forth over the river. He caught sight of the shore, dark trees and long ropy vines, flashes of animal eyes.

"Think they're scared?" Calix whispered, jutting his head over at the two passengers.

"Hell, I'm scared," Ico answered. "Are you really going to let 'em wander into the woods alone?"

Calix laughed again. "What, didn't Biel tell you? That was part of their payment. They asked for a guide."

Ico jerked on the wheel again, a heavy stone in the pit of his stomach.

"I didn't agree to be a guide," he said. "Certainly not in the forest. At night." The lantern lights passed over a carved stone sign jutting out of the river. *Warning to travelers* was all Ico could see before darkness covered it.

One of the ladies gasped. Ico wasn't sure which one: when he looked over at them, both stared straight ahead, their spines rigid and their expressions blank. They could have been sitting on the Emperor's throne. Maybe he imagined their gasping. Maybe the Lady's magic was already starting to get to him.

"Well, I'm not leaving you with my boat," Calix said.

"Gods and monsters," Ico said. "You know I'm not in the mind to steal this shitheap."

"You've got that pirate's taint," Calix said.

Ico scowled. "I ain't a pirate anymore."

"Still. You're taking them."

They passed into the tributary. The river narrowed and the trees drooped down lower, their branches grazing across the top of the captain's quarters, making a dry, scratchy sound. Ico glared at the illuminated water of the boat. He was going to thrash Biel when he got back to Jaila-Seraphine. Drag him out of his favorite table at the inn and give him one good punch in the face, just to let him know Ico wasn't going to be made a fool of. Biel knew how hard it was to find honest sailor's work once you've been a pirate. And he also knew about the money Ico owed his old, less-than-savory associates.

Calix reached into his pocket and pulled out a slim metal flask. He started to take a drink, stopped, looked over at Ico. "You need this more than me, mate."

Ico swiped the flask away from him. "You know I'm gonna need more than a drink before I take those girls out there."

Calix sighed. "You're already getting half their fare."

"I want seventy percent."

Calix leaned over the edge of the boat and spat in the water. The passengers didn't look back at either of them— who the hell knew what they were up to? "Sixty," he said.

Ico kept his eyes on the back of the passengers' heads. For the last two days, as the boat had journeyed down the river from Jaila-Seraphine, he and Calix had avoided discussing where they were headed. Easier to pretend they were just taking the passengers to Nemia-Seraphine or the ship port on the open sea.

"Sixty-five," Ico said. "Or I'm stalling the boat out in the middle of the river and neither of us is getting paid."

Calix chuckled. "You wouldn't say that if you weren't from Akuran. We know not to trifle with the Airiana here." But then he slapped Ico hard on the back. "Deal. Sixty-five percent. And you can keep the flask."

Sixty-five percent. The girls had paid twice the usual fee, given their destination. Another two hundred coins to help pay off his debt. He was getting closer, at least.

Calix threw open the door to the steam room, splashing water on the fires to slow the boat down. Ico took a long pull from the flask, the liquor dark and crawling and potent. It slid down his throat and spread warmth through his extremities. Calix had gotten ahold of the expensive stuff, it seemed.

The water in the tributary was almost still. The boat drifted along, the steam from the engines a white ribbon against the darkness. The lanterns illuminated nothing but trees and the black water. The paddles slapped rhythmically against the water.

"Where will we know when to stop?" Ico said. He was talking to Calix, who was still hunched over the fires, but one of the passengers answered him instead.

"I'll tell you." It was the plain one.

"You'll tell me?" Ico laughed. "Right."

Calix pulled away from the fires, his body in silhouette against their red glow. "You'll tell me," he said to her. "I'm the captain here."

The plain one huffed and lifted her chin. She hadn't made the effort to look aristocratic the way her sister had, and her dress was made of the plain, thin-woven ramie fabric favored by the Empire's poor. Not even trying to hide their financial status, that one.

The plain one stood up and walked to the bow of the boat. The lantern lights poured around her, illuminating the burnished-gold highlights in her thick black hair and carving her brown skin into a mask of shadow and candlelight.

Ico kicked at Calix. "The hell is she doing?" he whispered.

"She's finding our stopping place." Now the pretty one was interrupting their conversation, too. She turned her cool lady's gaze to Ico. "Izara has been chosen to train as an acolyte at the Academy," she said. "She possesses Iomim's Treasure."

Ico rolled his eyes. "If she gets us lost in the jungle, know that I'm not risking my life to bring you back. Hopefully Iomim's Treasure will be enough to protect you from jaguars."

The pretty's ones eyes widened in anger, and Calix knocked Ico on the back of his head.

"Don't be threatening the passengers," he said.

The pretty one settled into her skirts, looking pleased.

"They're *paying* us," Calix hissed in Ico's ear. "You aren't a pirate anymore, and this is a respectable ferry. Don't forget it."

Ico glared at the dark water.

They sailed for a few moments more. The air grew thick with steam from the engines, and it filtered through the lantern light, making the night eerie and haunted. The plain one stood up at the bow of the boat, her hands on the railing. Didn't look like she was doing much. Just staring at the trees illuminated by the lanterns.

And then she pulled a scrap of parchment out of a pocket hidden away inside her skirts.

Ico frowned, watching her. She read over the parchment and then looked up at the river. She began to hum, an odd, haunting melody that sent chills rippling over Ico's body. He tightened his grip on the wheel, his muscles contracting, ready to spring into action. He knew danger when he heard it.

She glanced down at the parchment again, and this time she sang. Her voice wasn't very sweet—there was a smoky roughness to it, like a fire smoldering in the bowl of a pipe— but she could carry the unearthly tune. The pretty one watched her with her hands clenching the fabric of her dress. In the lantern lights her brown skin looked ashen.

"What the fuck is she doing?" Ico whispered to Calix.

Calix looked at him. "She's finding the entrance to the Lady's domain."

The wheel slipped out of Ico's hand, and the boat swung wildly to the left. The pretty one went sprawling across the passenger's bench, but the plain one (the acolyte, Ico thought), didn't move from her place at the bow. Calix cursed and wrenched the boat back into place.

"The hell?" he said. "Pay attention. You knew where we were going."

Ico took hold of the wheel again. He willed himself not to shake. Yes, he had known they were going to the Lady's Tributary, known the two women wanted to speak to her. But Ico was from Akuran, and he wasn't sure he'd ever really believed in the Lady of the Seraphine. But that singing was soaking into his bones, drawing his fears to the forefront.

Over on the passenger's bench, the pretty one had straightened herself up. She smoothed down her hair and her skirts, trying to look as if she wasn't afraid either.

The plain one was still singing.

Ico grabbed the wheel with his other hand, holding it tight, staring ahead at the darkness. The engine fires sparked and sputtered and threw off an arc of golden red light at his feet. He did his best not to look at the woman at the bow. Hearing her voice, beautiful and haunting and terrifying, was bad enough.

The singing stopped.

"You got something for me?" Calix called out. His voice trembled. Ico smirked.

The plain one turned around, one hand pressed against the railing. Her eyes were bright as stars. Ico's skin crawled. He jerked his gaze away from her, out to the forest.

The pretty one gasped. "Izara!" she cried.

"Stop the engines," she said. "We'll go to shore here."

Calix nodded and drifted over to the fires as if caught in a spell. The plain one sagged against the railing, and the pretty one ran over to her, wrapped her arm around her shoulders, muttered something in her ear.

Calix extinguished the fires.

"You heard the lady," he said. "Drop the anchor and prepare the rowboat."

Ico hesitated. A cold sickness swelled in his belly. He did not want to go to ashore.

"Dammit, Ico, do what I asked." Calix looked at him over

his shoulder. "I'll give you your seventy percent," he said softly. "Just get back here alive."

Ico sucked in a deep breath. "I can hold you to that?"

Calix glanced out at the woods. "Yeah," he said. "You can."

Ico yanked hard on the anchor, sending it splashing to the bottom of the Seraphine. Then he grabbed the tail of rope lashing the rowboat to the side of the riverboat and unwound it, his movements quick and sure. He knew if he stopped to think about it he might turn tail like a coward. The money, he told himself. Just focus on the money.

The rowboat dropped into the black water with a splash.

"Ladies," Ico said, turning to the two passengers. The plain one sagged against her sister, her eyes sunken. The pretty one lifted her gaze to meet Ico's. She nodded once. Then she guided her sister over to the side of the rowboat. Ico unfurled the rope ladder. The pretty one held out her hand expectantly. Ico sighed, and took it, and guided her over to the ladder. Her touch was cool and dry, as if she'd been sitting in a drawing room all this time.

The plain one threw her leg over the side of the boat without looking at him. She scrambled down the ladder. Ico followed, clutching the lantern between his teeth. The passengers huddled together on the boat, and the pretty one gave a little gasp when Ico boarded and the boat tilted to the left.

"Nothing to worry about," he said, a platitude he didn't mean, that slipped out because he was used to saying it to passengers. Ico dipped the oars into the water and pushed away from the riverboat. The shore was a silvery outline in the distance, starlight dancing off the water as it lapped against the eroded sand. Trees grew up thick and impenetrable. Once they passed into the forest proper, they wouldn't have the starlight to guide them anymore.

"When we hit land," the plain one said suddenly, jarring Ico out of his own thoughts, "we will need to go directly east. There will be a path for us to follow."

"A path? Here?" Ico turned to the thick tangle of trees. "You know we aren't in Jaila-Seraphine anymore."

"I am quite aware," the plain one snapped. "There will be a path."

Ico sighed. "Fine," he said. "We'll follow the path." Crazy broad. Or maybe it was the result of Iomim's Treasure—not even the strongest mage could really control magic, much as they liked to pretend.

The boat slipped quietly through the water. The shore loomed close. The pretty one kept squeezing her skirt, then smoothing out the fabric. Squeezing, smoothing. It was a movement as rhythmic as the oars dropping into the water. They rode the rest of the way to the shore in silence. Ico's thoughts were shaky and nervous, and he kept telling himself to focus on the money, that seventy percent Calix was promising him for sticking his neck out like this.

The boat scraped against the river bottom. Ico lifted one of the oars and jammed into the sand. "Give me a moment, ladies, I'll drag you ashore." He leered up at the pretty one. "Wouldn't want your shoes to get muddy."

"I don't care if my shoes get muddy," the pretty one shot back. "And there's no need to drag the boat with us in it. We can help."

Ico laughed. "Get out or stay in, but I don't need either of you touching my rowboat."

The pretty one lifted her chin. The plain one ignored the entire conversation, though—her gaze was on the forest. Ico didn't know how she could see anything. He certainly couldn't, not beyond the pale circle of light cast by the lantern.

"Quiet," she said suddenly. "If we make too much noise, it will spook the Lady."

A shiver wriggled down Ico's spine. The plain one stared out at the forest. Ico jumped out of the boat and grabbed it at the fore and dragged it up to the shore, the river's cold water lapping around his ankles. The lantern swung back and forth from its hook, the circle of light growing and shrinking. Without warning, the plain one jumped out of the boat.

"Izara!" the pretty one cried.

The plain one turned around and placed a finger to her lips. The pretty one frowned.

"Don't run off," Ico said to Izara, pitching his voice low. She ignored him, only moved along the shoreline, peering out at the forest. The boat wedged against the shore. Far enough. He grabbed the rope and stake out of the bottom of the boat. The pretty one stared after her sister, shadows moving across her face.

"You can climb on out," Ico said, still in that low whisper. "Keep watch on your sister there. I'm not getting paid to play bodyguard to you two."

"She knows what she's doing," the pretty one said, and then she lifted her skirts and stood up. The boat wobbled against the shore but she didn't even blink. It was only when she lifted her foot over the boat's edge that Ico remembered he was a riverboater now, not a scoundrel, and he ought to act the gentleman—if nothing else he didn't want to listen to Calix complain about it later, assuming the lady tattled on him. He held out his hand. The pretty one barely glanced at it as she rested her fingers against his. Second nature for a lady like that.

He guided her out of the boat and onto the shore. Izara was sniffing around the edge of the forest. Gonna get herself eaten by some nighttime predator if she didn't watch out.

Ico jammed the stake into the sand and tied off the boat. Then he grabbed the lantern and walked over to the pretty one, who stood with her arms wrapped under her chest. Her sister was a shadow in the distance.

"What's she doing?" Ico asked.

"Looking for the path," the pretty one answered.

Ico shook his head. Even he knew there weren't any footpaths around here. This was No Man's Land, a long swath of forest owned by No Man, may the ancestors bless him, and the forest grew thick and wild from disuse.

But then the plain one stopped. Ico raised the lantern to get a better look, but it did little to help. The darkness was too thick, even with the starlight. But he was fairly certain she was staring into the woods. His chest tightened. A predator? What stalked at night—jaguars, caimans? Calix would have his head if one of his passengers died under Ico's watch.

"Stay here," he muttered to the pretty one, and then he lunged forward, the lantern throwing oblong light over the river and the trees. Up ahead, the plain one turned to him, and the lantern caught her eyes and made them gleam. She held up one hand. Ico skidded to a stop.

The plain one, Izara, was moving her hand—gesturing to him. Gesturing to join her. Did she look scared? He couldn't tell in the darkness.

Ico reached down and slid the knife out of his belt, cursing Calix for not letting him carry a pistol. He moved toward the plain one. She was whispering something, her voice low and urgent—

"My sister," she said, stepping toward him. "Celestia. Bring her here—I've found it."

Ico stopped. "Found it?"

She nodded. "The path. Hurry, before we lose it!"

Ico looked to the forest. He saw nothing but thick ropy vines and tall black tree trunks.

"Hurry!" she said, a little more loudly, a little more urgently.

Ico sighed and turned around. He could just make out Celestia picking her way toward them.

"She's coming," he said, scowling. He'd told her to stay put. Good thing it wasn't a predator; otherwise, he'd have two dead noblewomen on his hands.

"Tell her to hurry," Izara whispered.

"She's hurrying." Ico lifted the lantern and waved it back and forth. Light spilled across the sand of the riverbed, making the rocks glint. Celestia lifted the hem of her skirt and scuttled forward. Ico glanced over at her sister. She stared into the darkness of the forest. Fucking unnatural.

"I'm here," Celestia said, breathless. Ico turned back to her. She stared up at him, her dark skin shining golden in the lantern-light.

"Hurry," Izara said. "It's fading. Hurry!"

Celestia pushed past Ico without hesitation. Ico spun around. Izara was halfway into the forest, shadows swallowing her whole. *Shit,* he thought, and plunged forward. The circle of light from the lantern seemed to be shrinking, squeezing around him. Celestia disappeared into the trees, and Izara stuck out her head and said, "Extinguish the light!"

"Are you insane?" Ico said.

"Do it!"

The lightpool hardly fell beyond his own feet. The water lapped at the shore, and for the first time Ico realized that the forest had gone silent. No shrieking of birds, no breaking of branches, no constant whining of insects. When the hell had that happened? Ico looked back to the boat, but the darkness was too thick for him to see anything.

And then there was a flash of movement, and the lantern light blinked out.

"What in the ancestors' names do you think you're doing?" he shouted. A hand clamped over his mouth.

"Silence!" Her voice was close to his ear, her breath hot and furious. "We don't need the light of men. *Come.*"

No light of men in No Man's Land. The girl's hand was on his wrist, yanking him forward. The trees seemed to open up before him. How could he see the trees, in this darkness? He couldn't see anything.

Lights.

Lights, up ahead, glimmering and faint.

There was a path too, an ancient one, the soil eroded down into a narrow ditch. Trees soared up on either side of them. The forest was still utterly silent, which made Ico's skin crawl. The lights floated among the trees, little pale spheres that danced and darted around each other. Ico fingered his knife, although he suspected, unease circling in his stomach, that a knife would do no good here.

The sisters walked ahead of him, side by side. Ico stared at the back of their heads. As long as he could see them—could see other humans—he wouldn't feel like he was walking into the most dangerous part of the forest.

When he gave up piracy, he thought he'd given up this kind of adventure shit, too. But apparently not.

Izara stopped. Ico nearly ran into her.

"What's going—" he started, but Celestia fixed an icy glare on him. Right. Keep quiet.

Izara tilted her head, as if she were listening to music.

"This way," Izara whispered, and then veered off to the left. Ico followed, realizing that the path split. Wonderful. He hoped Iomim's Treasure was enough to send them on the right way.

They walked, their footsteps rackety in the silent forest. Those eerie floating lights trailed along around them. The lights had multiplied, and they generated enough of a glow that the trees and the girls cast long shadows along the path. Ico reached up and wiped some of the sweat from his brow.

The night was balmy, almost cool, but he didn't know what they were going to find at the end of this path and that had him nervous. He thought about Calix sitting in the riverboat. Probably smoking his pipe, polishing that machete he was so damned proud of. Counting the payment from these two insane sisters.

Ico tapped Celestia on the shoulder. He didn't want to see what would happen if he disturbed the other one. Celestia glanced over at him. Her eyes gleamed from the floating lights.

"We there yet?" Ico asked.

"Don't ask that," said Izara, still staring straight ahead. "I have to concentrate to find the Lady."

"She has to *concentrate*," hissed Celestia before turning away from him. Ico sighed. Lights crowded among the tree branches. He wished he was back on the boat with Calix. Wished he was just ferrying passengers back and forth between Jaila-Seraphine and Kalen-Seraphine, like he'd been doing for the last month. Boring work but at least the forest there rustled with sound, at least you could hear the monkeys and the birds shrieking in the canopy. At least there you could find other people instead of these damned floating lights.

And then Ico heard something. A whisper, a babble—

No, he'd been a seaman long enough to know better. Water.

It wasn't the sound of the Seraphine proper. That Ico could recognize immediately, and anyway the Seraphine didn't babble. It roared. This sounded more like a stream, some little rivulet—or a tributary.

Cold sweat prickled over Ico's skin. The Lady's Tributary.

Izara slowed her walk and held up a hand. Ico and her sister stopped. Ico craned his head around the two sisters, trying to see the path up ahead. But the lights were swarming, blinding him.

The babbling of the water grew louder, sounding more and more like voices.

Izara gulped down deep breaths of air, her hands tugging nervously at her skirts. Celestia stared at her in alarm.

Ico pulled out his knife.

The babbling voices rose up around them. Ico thought he could make out words. He thought he heard his name, his full name, his Akuranian name, *Ishi Kui Ico*. He thought he heard pieces of the language he'd spoken as a child, a language he hadn't spoken for nearly ten years, ever since he left home. He could still understand it. *My Akuranian child*, the voice said. *Welcome to the Seraphine.*

One of the sisters let out a long, sharp gasp. Celestia stumbled backward, her hand over her mouth. She knocked into Ico. He immediately gripped her arms to steady her before stepping in front of her, knife out, ready to fight for her like a gentleman.

The knife landed with a powdery thud on the forest floor.

Standing in the path before him was a woman. Her skin was dark like river water, and water streamed out of her hair, running in shiny rivulets over her naked form. Ico looked at her for half a second and his eyes burned and he ripped his gaze away, down to the forest floor, where his vision crackled and sputtered llike he'd stared up at the sun.

"Welcome, daughters of the Seraphine," the woman said in her babbling voices.

With a strangled cry, Celestia fell to her knees, her head down, bowing like she'd come before the Emperor himself. Izara stayed standing, her gaze lifted. How could she look at that woman head on? Ico took a step back, dropped down to one knee. Better to do what Celestia did, he decided.

The woman laughed. It sounded like rain falling across the Seraphine.

"Those who can find me," she said, "do not need to bow to me. Stand. Both of you."

Ico's cheeks burned. He was reminded of his mother, chastising him in a garden. He stood, shakily. Peered up at the woman again. The water flowed and flowed over the lines of her body. She was dazzling. Too dazzling for someone like him. He looked away.

"Why do you come here?" the woman said.

No answer. Ico peered over at Celestia, who was staring down at the place where the woman rose from the earth. She barely looked at the woman, but Celestia's face was still slackened with awe, her eyes filled with stars. He glanced over at Izara. She hadn't moved once since the woman appeared, but now she stepped forward. Ico stared at her, trembling. She looked at the woman. Her hands gripped her skirts, the only disturbance in her calm exterior.

"Taja," she said.

Silence. Ico risked a glance at the woman. But that divine face was unreadable.

"You know my name," she said.

"Yes," said Izara.

"And how did you learn my name, Daughter of the Seraphine?"

Izara hesitated. Ico could hear a rushing in his ears—he didn't know if it was blood pumping into his brain or the forest finally reacting.

"I read it in a book," Izara said.

"A book?" More laughter. The floating lights bobbed around. "Quite a girl, to have access to a book which contains my name."

Izara dipped her head. "I suppose so, my Lady."

"My Lady Taja," the woman corrected. "If you know my name, you should speak it."

Ico reached up and wiped at the sweat forming on his

18

brow. The woman moved forward, her steps leaving damp imprints on the mulchy ground. Beside him, Celestia tensed, but Izara held her place, head lifted.

"You never answered my question," said the woman. *Taja.* But Ico couldn't bear to think of her in terms of her name. It felt like an abomination. "Why are you here? If you know my name, then I suppose you want something from me."

For the first time, Izara dropped her gaze. The woman smiled, an arc of light that spread out over the forest. Ico closed his eyes, fireworks dancing on his eyelids.

"We have a request, yes," said the plain one.

Ico's head throbbed. A request. This was why they'd come all this way, why they'd hired Calix and his riverboat, why Ico was cowering in the forest before one of the Airiana—because the two sisters wanted something.

"My sister has a request," Izara said.

Ico blinked. That, he hadn't expected. He looked over at Celestia, whose face had gone ashy in the unearthly light of the Lady's Tributary.

"Is that so?" the woman asked.

Ico kept his gaze on Celestia as she spoke. She didn't look away either. He didn't understand how she could look without their eyes burning. Did she have Iomim's Treasure, too, like her sister? Or maybe when her eyes burned, she just didn't care.

"Yes, my Lady," Celestia said.

"And what is your request?"

The entire forest held its breath. Ico watched Celestia's mouth, her lips cracked and dry. What could possibly be worth the journey, the magic, the risk of destruction?

"I would like a husband," she said.

Ico blinked.

"A husband?" said the woman.

"Yes," said Celestia.

"Shall he be handsome and kind, with a gentle touch and a way with animals?"

Celestia shook her head. She was dazed, Ico thought, delirious. And really, truly insane.

All this for a *husband*.

"No?" said the woman. A teasing lightness lifted the edges of her voice, still babbling like a brook. "You'd like him to be ugly and cruel?"

Celestia closed her eyes. Her sister was staring at her now, her expression dark. She was fucking it up, Ico realized.

"No," Celestia said, and her eyes opened and she drew up her shoulders. "He should be kind, yes, but most important he should be wealthy. My family—" Here she gestured at her sister "—We have kept our titles and our land but the coins are running out. Our wealth is gone. The lands still produce—" She took a deep breath and looked at her sister and her sister looked back and something flashed between them. Ico didn't know what, and he didn't care. He just wanted this terrifying farce to end.

"—But my sister and I cannot run the acreage on our own. We can't afford to pay workers, and we don't have the knowledge of trade necessary—"

Izara tugged sharply on her sister's gown, and Celestia stopped and took a deep breath.

"I would like a husband who will treat me with respect, and tend to our lands as they should be tended to. And he must have wealth of his own. Someone who can restore the glory of our family."

Silence. Ico lifted his gaze just enough to peer at the Lady of the Seraphine. Through the burning of his gaze he thought she looked amused.

"A wealthy husband," she said. "I suppose I can grant that request."

Both of the sisters sagged with relief. Celestia even smiled and grabbed her sister's hand. "Thank you," she said. "Thank you, Lady, I—"

"There will be a cost."

Celestia's smile vanished. Ice crept through Ico's limbs. A cost. No matter what the Seraphine nobility thought, a transaction with the Airiana was never a wise decision. Even he knew that.

He wished he could sneak away, run back through the forest and climb back aboard the riverboat. It wasn't his transaction but he was going to get caught up in it. He could just feel it, an energy sparking on the air.

"A cost, Lady Taja?" said Izara. Her eyes were wide— probably thought being of noble birth and knowing the name was enough. Silly girl. She should have known better.

"Of course. I can't simply grant wishes." The woman laughed. Ico wasn't sure he'd ever be able to stand the sound of rain again. "I will grant Celestia De Malena a kind and wealthy and competent husband, but you will be beholden to me for one favor." The woman moved forward. Ico resisted the urge to pull away. She put her hand on Celestia's face. "You are beholden," she said, and when she slipped her hand away she left a damp mark on the Celestia's cheek, a smear of silvery light that faded away in the span of a heartbeat. Then the woman turned to Izara, and she did the same thing, cupping her face in her hand. Izara closed her eyes. "And you are beholden."

Ico stepped back. His blood pumped. He could run. Screw his debt and run straight into the forest. He could survive in the wild; he'd done it before. Done it at sea, when the fresh water threatened to run dry.

The woman stepped toward him. He forced himself to look at her, his eyes streaming from the pain. She smiled. Her hair hung in wet, silky ropes over her shoulders, water

21

flowing over her body like a gown. Her eyes were as bright as suns.

"Please," Ico sputtered, "I'm just their guide. I'm not part of this."

"You are here," the woman said.

Ancestors damn it all, thought Ico, just as her hand pressed against her cheek. Her touch was cold and wet like the Seraphine itself. Ico sucked in breath. He wanted to tear away but he couldn't move. Her stony fingernails scraped against him, a warning, he thought, against protesting further.

"And you," she said, "are beholden."

It was done. It was over. It was lost. She pulled her hand away. Ico's skin tingled where she had touched him, and then it didn't anymore.

The woman stepped away from him.

"When I have need of you," the woman said, looking at each of them in turn, "I will call you."

"Thank you, my Lady," Celestia said.

"You'll meet your husband in three days' time," the woman said. "Through the aid of my river, you will meet him."

She stepped backwards, one foot behind the other, a careful and steady balance. The floating lights were blinking out.

"You are beholden," she said, but it was difficult to discern the words, because her voice had turned to the babble of the tributary again. And then she was gone, vanished into the darkness.

"Curse you both," Ico spat at the sisters. Izara ignored him, but Celestia tilted her head toward him in slight acknowledgement.

"May the ancestors rain poison on your heads," he said.

"You're right to be angry," Celestia said, not meeting his eye. "Thank you for this sacrifice."

Ico huffed. He bent to pick his knife off the ground and whirled away from the two sisters. The forest was alive, chittering with insects and nighttime creatures. Starlight filtered through the trees. Everything was ordinary again. As ordinary as it could be, with this Airiana price on his head.

He stalked back down the path. He didn't know if the sisters followed him or not. He didn't care.

TWO

Aurelia De Linza brought news of the electrification of Jaila-Seraphine when she arrived at Cross Winds acreage during her visiting tour of the great houses of the estuaries.

"It's a bit like Yusani alchemy," she said, sipping at the sparkling mango drink which was a Cross Winds specialty. "But without the dreadful side effects—the headaches and such."

"I never cared for Yusani alchemy," said Noreen, who was perched primly on the edge of the divan, as she always did when she stopped by for afternoon socializations. "But electricity seems so dangerous. As if we think we could control lightning!"

"We think we can control fire," said Celestia. "As soon as the sun goes down this place is blazing with torches."

The other two women nodded while Celestia drank her sparkling mango. Aurelia had arrived this morning, two days earlier than her letter had promised. Celestia'd had to rally the servants to prepare a proper luncheon despite the week's supplies being scheduled for delivery tomorrow. Cookie came through, though, the way she always did, with a rustic-style picnic out on the forest lawn. Now that the luncheon was over and they had retired to the sunroom, Celestia finally felt as she could relax. It was only a temporary relaxation, of course: this evening she would have other, non-Aurelia matters to attend to. But she wouldn't worry about them now.

"I found it terribly exciting," Aurelia was saying. "The lighting ceremony was really quite lovely—so many people, though! Fortunately, Father was able to secure a private viewing balcony." She set down her cup and then waved her fan half-heartedly a few times. "I do wish you had been there, Celestia, I think you would have found it marvelous. It was quite a sight when the lights went up—whoosh, all at once!" She laughed and gestured with her fan.

Noreen sniffed. "I still say it's not natural."

"Which buildings did they illuminate?" Celestia asked, hoping to head off another one of Noreen's screeds about the tyranny of progress before it could begin.

"The governor's mansion," said Aurelia. "And Soziri Square. Every window of the governor's mansion had a light in it, which was simply *breathtaking*. And within the square, they hung little strings of lights from the statues. Lovely, just lovely."

"And no one was sick?" Celestia asked.

"Not a soul, that's what the papers said the next day."

Celestia settled back in her chair, impressed. A way to light darkness without fire or magic—such an interesting proposition. They used fire here at Cross Winds, of course, as it was safer, and Lindon had that adventurer's distrust for magic, but Celestia had been in temples illuminated by Yusani alchemy, widely agreed to be the safest magical means of creating light. That light was very beautiful—a pale, diffuse glow, like sun-drenched mist—but after too long your forehead would throb from the strain. Beauty wasn't always worth it.

"I don't trust it," said Noreen.

"Of course you don't," said Celestia, smiling sweetly. "I think it sounds astonishing," she said to Aurelia. "Thank you for sharing."

"The governor said he hopes to electrify all of the major cities by the end of this year," Aurelia said. "And then he'll turn his attention to private homes. Can you imagine! No more woodsmoke or scorch marks or alchemy headaches. The light was *bright*, too, I didn't mention that. Much brighter than a candle." She reached out and touched Celestia's arm. "You'd be able to stay up all hours writing your poetry, dear."

"Oh, I don't have the time for that anymore," Celestia said. Now that she was married, there was no need for her to keep up her work in the arts.

"We were meant to sleep in the darkness," said Noreen. "And live our lives during the day."

Celestia kept her expression pleasant; she was used to dealing with Noreen. "Oh, I doubt electricity will change things that much."

"You're still young," Noreen said. "You haven't seen the things I've seen."

Aurelia shifted in her chair and fiddled with her cup. Noreen was an old-fashioned sort—behind her back Lindon was always saying she was as mossy as an ancient stone, and yes, there was some truth to it. But Celestia was fond of her nonetheless. She lived across the river, in a Kjaran-era manor that had been built nearly five hundred years ago. It possessed all those Kjaran details, the flying buttresses and black stonework and odd carvings on the roof. Celestia suspected that living amongst all that history had made Noreen resistant to change.

"What other houses will you be visiting?" Celestia asked Aurelia, before the conversation could turn too sour. It was a comfortable day, the northerly wind bringing an unseasonable coolness to the damp, sunny air. It would be a shame to waste it on unpleasant talk.

"Oh, Grimwood and May Lace and Jencox," Aurelia said, counting them off excitedly on her fingers. "And Wild Willow, off the Weeping Tributary—Mother is old friends with the Mistress De Dalmios. And Master De Dalmios has a working telegraph machine! He uses it for his business. I do hope someone sends him a message while I'm there."

Celestia smiled. "You sound like Izara. She was always as fascinated by machines as she was magic."

Aurelia beamed. "I'm nowhere near as clever as she is."

"How is Izara?" Noreen asked, mercifully keeping her own feelings about machines to herself.

"I haven't heard anything." Celestia looked down at her hands, folded neatly in the silky cloud of her skirts. "You know how the Academy is. So secretive. She can only send letters at certain times of the year."

"Of course," said Noreen, and Aurelia dipped her head a little, in embarrassment or acknowledgment Celestia wasn't sure. To serve as an acolyte of the Academy was to disappear from the ordinary world for a decade. It was necessary, claimed the dean that Celestia had spoken to the day her sister enrolled, for the students to immerse themselves in the magical sphere, so as to better connect with the Aetheric Realm. Even the briefest missive could be enough to undo years of effort. Celestia didn't pretend to understand it, but Izara was blessed by Iomim's Treasure—in great quantities, the dean had said—and it would be a shame to let that Treasure go to waste.

"I'm sure she's doing very well," said Aurelia.

"I'm sure she is, too," said Celestia, and Noreen nodded in agreement. There would be no disapproval here: magic was an ancient thing, worthy of her trust.

Aurelia then began to talk about the last house she had visited, Jasmine Night. It was a three days' trip by riverboat down the Seraphine, and Celestia had visited on a handful of occasions, mostly for holidays. It seemed Aurelia had been rather taken with Lady D'Corizen's pet cats, large, slinky creatures that, it was rumored, had the blood of jaguars running through their veins. Celestia half-listened, but her thoughts were still with Izara, secreted away somewhere high in the mountains. She'd been an acolyte for nearly three years, and so for three years Celestia had been without her sister. She thought then about the secret she was keeping from her friends, the secret she had planned to share with Lindon until Aurelia arrived early—perhaps she would still tell him tonight. She needed to. It was not the sort of thing she could keep to herself. Still, she wished Izara was here. It was the sort of thing more easily told to a sister.

A knock came at the door. Aurelia fell silent and looked at Celestia expectedly.

"Come in," Celestia called out.

It was Mr. Medulla, the butler. He scurried into the sunroom and gave a quick bow to each of the ladies. "Lady De Malena," he said. "I beg your pardon, but there is someone at the door."

Celestia frowned. Noreen peered over at her. "Oh, did you invite someone to join us? Lady De Buella, perhaps? Although I heard she was traveling—"

"No," said Celestia. "I didn't." She looked at Mr. Medulla. "Is it someone we know?"

Mr. Medulla coughed politely into his fist. He wore his darker linen today, a nod to the cool breezes drifting through the estate. "I'm afraid not, Lady. They're—" He paused, his small dark eyes flitting toward Celestia's guests. "They're adventurers."

"Adventurers!" cried Aurelia, just as Noreen pressed her fingers to her forehead.

"I see," said Celestia. She imagined her plans for revealing her secret to Lindon tonight as swaths of cheaply made fabric, the weave unravelling as she watched. If adventurers were here, Lindon would want to feast them, to stay up late drinking with them, listening to their stories and songs and reliving his own years as an adventurer before he met Celestia on the banks of the Seraphine five years ago.

"Oh, do invite them to stay," Aurelia said. "I haven't seen a single adventuring party since I started my travels, and they *never* come into Jaila-Seraphine." She gazed over at Celestia with doe-eyed naïveté. City girls had such romantic ideas about adventurers, having never dealt with them in close quarters.

"Show them to the sitting room." Celestia wished she could turn them away, but custom and Lindon dictated that wasn't an option. "See that they have water or sparkling lime—*no* ale."

"You're no fun," said Aurelia.

"Oh, she knows what she's doing," said Noreen.

"Of course, my lady. Will you speak to them about their arrangements or shall I fetch Master De Malena?"

Celestia hesitated. Lindon was out in the forest with the property manager Mr. Tili, overseeing the avocado planting. She hated to disturb him, and the thought of the adventurers sprawling out in her sitting room, with their filthy clothes and muddy boots, in the time it would take to bring him back, sent a shiver wriggling down her spine.

"I'll speak to them. Tell them I'll be there in a few moments. Get them settled, Mr. Medulla."

"Of course, my lady." He bowed, more deeply this time, and then slipped out of the room.

"This is exciting," said Aurelia, sitting up in her chair. "Do you think one of them will be handsome?"

"No," said Noreen.

Aurelia batted at her in annoyance, but Celestia just laughed. "She's right, you know. These men spend too long in the forest—"

"Master Lindon is handsome," said Aurelia coyly.

"He's the exception that proves the rule," said Celestia haughtily. Aurelia giggled, and Celestia couldn't hold that haughtiness for long, so she dissolved into laughter herself. Only Noreen didn't join in.

"At least they came here instead of my estate," she said.

"They always come here," said Celestia. "Lindon has a reputation among them. As you can imagine."

Noreen murmured a hum of acknowledgement. Celestia stood up and smoothed down her skirts. "I'm going to speak with them now. Feel free to ring Mr. Medulla if you need anything. The river lawn is lovely this time of day, if you feel like going for a constitutional." Celestia sighed. "I'm really not sure how long this is going to take."

"You never know with those brutes," said Noreen.

"Brutes," breathed Aurelia, before giggling again. Celestia smiled, but it was the smile of a married woman, of someone who knew better.

She left her guests in the sunroom. Noreen would likely disappear back across the river—with adventurers here she would be avoiding dinner tonight. And Aurelia needed time to explore the estate on her own anyway. The guided tour was planned for tomorrow morning, but there was more joy in sneaking around an estate unchaperoned—as Celestia had learned on her own visiting tour, many years ago, traveling on the last of her family's money, one last opportunity to save face before the wealth was gone for good.

The windows were open in the hallways, the sweet-scented wind of the forest billowing in with the curtains. Celestia's skirts blew around her ankles. A strange day, with this cool southerly breeze. She ought to enjoy it while she could—the afternoon rains would be starting soon, and in this weather they were likely to be chilly and unpleasant.

The sitting room doors were shut, but Celestia could hear the muffled voices of the adventurers anyway. One of them said something to make the others laugh, a riotous noise that made the hairs on her arm stand on end. Gods, if only the Lady of the Seraphine hadn't seen fit to marry her to an adventuring man.

Celestia took a deep breath and pushed open the doors. Her sitting room, with its meticulously dyed sofas and chairs, its expensive tapestries hanging from the walls, had been invaded. Three men and a woman, all of them dressed in the worn brown rags of all adventurers—no doubt their clothing had contained color at some point, but months of traipsing through the forest, or living at sea, or exploring the empty mountains, had done its damage. Their hair was filthy, greasy, and lank, and a trail of mud led around the floor of the room.

They were sitting in a clump near the window, sloshing their sparkling mangos around and laughing. They hadn't noticed her yet. She stepped into the room. Still nothing. She cleared her throat.

Finally, one of them, a man who looked more like a boy, glanced in her direction. He immediately leapt to his feet, spilling his sparkling mango in the process. The others took notice after that, twisting in their seats toward Celestia.

"Hello," she said.

"Lady De Malena." One of the men walked toward her, his arms spread out as if he expected an embrace. "Such a pleasure to meet you. We've heard nothing but good things. Isn't that right, boys?"

The others, even the woman, lifted their cups and cheered.

"That's lovely to hear," said Celestia, hoping her voice didn't sound too strained. If it did, the adventurers didn't notice, because they erupted into cheers again. Celestia suppressed a sigh. It was going to be a long, noisy evening.

"I wanted to show you to your accommodations myself," Celestia said. "We have some charming guest rooms in the river-facing wing. I hope you'll find them to your liking."

"Better than any place we've been sleeping the last three months," said the woman. "No doubt, no doubt at all."

"Well, 'cept for Spider," one of the men said, and he slapped the younger boy on his back. "That one knows how to wheedle his way into any whorehouse in the Seraphine, ain't that right?"

The adventurers roared with laughter. Celestia managed to keep her face dispassionate. Of course, it was all part of the fun for adventurers to play their brutish roles—most ladies delighted at the chance to hear a dirty joke or two in the great houses—but Celestia was simply not in the mood for it tonight.

"Dinner will be served at seven this evening," she said, raising her voice over the jeering of the adventurers. "I can ask Mr. Medulla to draw you baths, if you like."

"Baths?" shrieked one of the men. "Well, ain't that fancy."

Celestia resisted the urge to ask him to tone down his performance.

The woman flicked a concerned look at Celestia and shoved him hard on the shoulder. "You better take a bath if you're going to dine with the Lady De Malena." And then she gave a bow towards Celestia, swirling her hand like some noble in a play. Celestia smiled thinly.

"My husband will be joining us for dinner," she said. "I'm sure he'll be quite excited to hear about your travels."

"Lindon Asi!" shouted one of the adventurers, and that set them all to cheering again, and knocking their glasses of sparkling mango against one another. "Best adventurer in the Seraphine!"

It was always jarring to hear Lindon's old name. He'd taken hers so he could have the title that went along with it, rather than adding the contracted *D* that was a sign of a purchased title. Which wasn't, everyone agreed, much of a title at all.

"May he rest in peace," said the woman.

"Good riddance, more like," said the man. "More commissions for the rest of us!"

The adventurers roared with delight. Celestia couldn't stand it anymore. She surreptitiously reached over and rang the bell to call for Mr. Medulla. Custom be damned. He could tend to the adventurers' needs, the way he did any other guest in this house.

He appeared almost instantaneously, materializing at her side as if through some illicit magic. The adventurers laughed and jostled amongst themselves. "Shall I handle our guests for you, Lady De Malena?" he asked in a quiet, discreet voice.

"Yes, thank you very much." Celestia turned to the adventurers. "I'm afraid I've been called away."

They weren't listening to her. No matter; it made for an easier escape. She turned to Mr. Medulla and he said, "I will give them your apologies, my lady."

"Thank you." She flashed a bright, genuine smile at him and then slipped out of the room. The adventurer's voices followed her as she whisked down the hallway.

"I want to hear *everything*," Aurelia said.

The dinner table sparkled beneath the candles in the chandelier, light flickering and guttering across the room. A lovely effect, thought Celestia, and she wondered if it would be ruined by the electric lights from Jaila-Seraphine.

"Everything?" one of the adventurers asked, leaning forward over his plate. He had introduced himself to Lindon earlier as Orlando, and Celestia hardly recognized him from the drawing room. She hardly recognized any of the adventurers, now that their hair was washed and they wore clean clothes from the stores Celestia kept in one of the empty guest rooms. Another part of the custom of housing adventurers, and one that Celestia was certain had been devised by the wife of Lord De Nucci, the man who'd started the tradition.

"Agreed," said Lindon, lifting his glass. "We haven't had an adventuring party at Cross Winds in nearly six months. I miss the old stories."

"I imagine you do," said the young man, who had introduced himself as Spider during the aperitifs. The woman—Lucia—squawked with laughter, then immediately silenced herself. She wore men's clothes, trousers and a waistcoat, even though Celestia had offered her one of her old gowns. "Not interested, m'lady," she'd said. "Never could get used to skirts." Celestia had to admit the men's clothes suited her.

"Well," said Lindon, leaning back in his chair, "There's much to be said for settling down." He smiled over at Celestia and lifted his glass toward her. The golden glow of the candlelight illuminated the strong lines of his features, and Celestia was reminded of the first moment she had seen him, swimming across the Seraphine, a burning riverboat in his wake. It had been sunset, and the light had been the same, like liquid gold. She smiled back at him and hoped she would have a moment with him to herself later this evening. Even with Aurelia and the adventurers, her secret weighed heavily on her mind.

"Aye," said Orlando. "I could get used to this life." He gestured at the dining room, at the soup course steaming on the table. Then he winked at Aurelia, who covered her mouth and giggled. A proper lady.

"So where have you traveled?" Lindon asked. "Like the Lady Aurelia here, I want to know everything."

Everyone at the table laughed. The adventurers kept their laughter low-key and calm. These were higher-level adventurers, the sort hired out by nobility, and they knew the wild adventurer personas all needed to be tucked away during dinner.

"We actually just arrived back in the Seraphine," said Lucia, stirring at her soup. "About, oh, what was it—a week ago, maybe?"

"Mmhmm," said Orlando. "We've been up in Eiren, working a case for an Eirenese merchant."

"Eiren!" exclaimed Aurelia. "What was it like?"

"Cold." The fourth adventurer, Crell, sat beside Celestia. He hadn't spoken much at the aperitif. Only introduced himself as was proper and then stood over by the window, looking out at the dark forest.

"That it was," said Spider. "Cold like you can't possibly imagine. Seeps right into your bones."

"Hard country," said Lucia. "The country's as like to kill you as the people. Well, the wrong kind of people."

"The kind of people we're apt to run into," said Orlando, and Lindon chuckled knowingly before taking a spoonful of soup.

"What was your case?" Celestia asked.

"Oh, the usual kind of thing. The merchant's son had gone missing. Been kidnapped, in fact, by one of the northern warlords. Ransomed him for the merchant's wealth. Merchant hired us to go steal the kid back so he wouldn't have to pay."

"Pay the warlord anyway," said Lucia, and the adventurers laughed.

"Well, we didn't take his whole fortune," Orlando said. "We ain't crooks."

More laughter. Aurelia's eyes shimmered with delight, but Celestia only stirred at her soup and smiled politely. She'd heard these kinds of stories a million times over. From other adventurers who had taken advantage of the tradition and spent the night at Cross Winds, and from Lindon himself. How many merchants' children had he rescued from kidnappers, she wondered. She'd heard at least three similar stories from him, the details shifting and transmuting into one entangled epic.

"What was the warlord like?" Aurelia asked.

"Terrifying," said Orlando, leaning over the table toward her. She shrunk back, giggling. "Monstrous. A huge man—seven, eight foot tall." He lifted his hand. "Taller than me. And big around as a bear. Like a kajan from the old stories."

Lindon glanced over at Celestia, a knowing gleam in his eye. Aurelia stared at Orlando, transfixed, and Celestia prayed to the Airiana that she would take the proper precautions if she snuck into his room tonight.

"And pale, too," said Lucia. "A true Eiren man."

"Aye," said Spider. "Even his hair was pale. No color in him at all. Looked like he was carved out of snow and ice."

"How frightening!" said Aurelia.

"It wasn't so bad," said Spider.

Lucia laughed. "You weren't saying that when you were running away from his camp, screaming like a baby for his mother."

Spider glowered, but the rest of the adventurers broke into the raucous laughter Celestia had been bracing herself for. She spooned up her soup. Five more courses. Then, of course, they would retire to the smoking room, where Lindon would want to stay up all hours reliving the glory of his past. And she'd have to delay telling him her secret. Again. She'd already been delayed every night since deciding to finally share the secret with him a week ago. One more night shouldn't bother her—but it had been long enough. She was anxious for him to know.

Orlando launched into the story of the merchant's son and the northern warlord, with the other adventurers—save for Crell, who only listened as he ate his soup—throwing in details and corrections. Celestia had heard enough of these sorts of stories that she was able to predict, quite accurately, the twists and turns the tale would take. On the few occasions that Lindon had spoken honestly about his adventures, usually when he'd been drinking too much, Celestia had not been so quick to guess the route of the story. She would never have guessed, for instance, that one of his closest friends would die not during the heat of battle but from a snake in the forest that even children knew how to identify and avoid, because he was exhausted after walking for three months without proper food and shelter. She would never have guessed that men would eat biscuits riddled with worms as they rode across the sea to find their glories, or that Lindon had wept in the arms of a whore because he missed the sight of the Seraphine glittering in the sunlight. But this story, with its barbaric warlord and its frozen, windswept landscape, its battles and schemes—this was a story Celestia knew.

Aurelia, however, was enrapt, and she barely touched her food as the servants brought the courses out one after another. Even Lindon, who surely knew better than Celestia how false the story was, laughed and cheered at the appropriate parts. The story dragged on, twisting in improbable directions, and Celestia found herself watching Crell instead of Orlando and the others. Although he looked like the part of an adventurer, with his shaggy hair and unkempt beard and dirty fingernails, he ate in the mannered style, like a man who'd grown up in a great house. He cut his fish with delicacy, and he scooped up the last of his soup in the proper direction. Hours earlier he had been sloshing mango drink on the floor of her drawing room, roaring with laughter—now he was practically a gentleman. Old habits are not easily shaken.

Crell looked up at her.

Celestia immediately glanced away, cheeks hot.

"Yes, my lady?" Crell said.

Spoken like a true gentleman. Celestia lifted her eyes to him. He was staring at her, his gaze intense.

"Are you enjoying your meal?" Celestia said, scolding herself for staring so rudely.

"Haven't had food like this in a long time."

"I take it that's a good thing?"

At the other end of the table, Orlando reached a crescendo in the story, and everyone cheered in approval. Their table was becoming less and less like a table in a great house.

"Indeed, my lady. Tell your cook this fish is excellent." He gestured at the pile of bones on his plate.

"I'll do that. Thank you."

Spider interjected something into the tale of the northern warlord that made the other laugh riotously. Crell glared down at them.

"Fools," he muttered.

"Pardon?" said Celestia.

Crell grinned at her. "You're a curious one," he said.

"Oh, I wouldn't say that," Celestia responded, even though he was correct—she had been curious. "A lady is always concerned for the comfort of her guest. And you seem— uncomfortable, Mr. Crell."

He chuckled and took a drink of his wine. "I'm not uncomfortable, my lady, only bored."

"Well, the story's not for your entertainment, is it? You lived it, after all."

"The story's nothing but entertainment," he said. "Payment for letting us stay in your house."

Celestia smiled politely in response.

Crell leaned forward, pushing his empty plate aside. "Would you like to know what we really found in Eiren?" he asked in a low voice.

Celestia's skin prickled. She suspected he was trying to frighten her, but she was not easily frightened. Certainly not by stories. And she was bored, too. She wanted a story she could not predict.

"What did you find?" she asked.

"Something unnatural." Crell leaned back in his chair and swirled the wine around in his glass. "They call it a disease, but that's not what it is. A disease kills." He drained the last of his wine and set it on the table; one of the servants slid out of the shadows to refill it. Celestia stared at Crell, not sure what to say.

"I'm afraid I don't understand," she finally said.

He laughed, a hard and bitter laugh that blended in with the more mirthful laughter from the other end of the table. "Neither do we. Nor anyone in Eiren, much as they might claim otherwise. But I'm sure a lady of your standing isn't interested in hearing the details."

Celestia lifted her chin. "A lady of my standing might surprise you, Mr. Crell." Every time she said it, she became more certain that wasn't his true name, that his true name began with the nobleman's prefix.

"Well, in that case . . ." His eyes glittered. "Things in Eiren— they aren't dying."

Celestia blinked in surprise. "Come again?"

"I don't know how else to explain it." He turned toward Orlando, who was gesturing wildly above his place setting.

"Whatever it was, it was the real reason we were able to get the boy back. Warlord Eklund had killed him. But he wouldn't die."

Celestia let out a disbelieving laugh. "I'm afraid I'm not nearly as gullible as Aurelia."

"Good thing I'm not lying." Crell's eyes took on a hard glint. "I saw it with my own eyes. Eklund drew a knife across the boy's throat. He bled out. They tossed his corpse, and he stood up and walked right to us."

Celestia stared at him and listened to the excited staccato of Orlando's story.

"He wasn't really dead," she said. "He couldn't be."

"Lady De Malena, with all due respect," Crell said, "I've seen more corpses than you."

Celestia did not have a response to that.

"There were other rumors," he continued, taking a long sip of his wine. "About the grass growing underneath the snow. Trees not dropping their leaves. We didn't see any of that, though. Just the boy, striding toward us with his throat gaping open." He paused. "Whatever it is, I hope it doesn't come to the Seraphine."

Celestia shivered. She thought about her secret, and touched a hand to her stomach.

"Yes," she said. "I hope it doesn't come to the Seraphine, either."

<hr>

The door to Celestia's bedroom creaked open, and a long sliver of moonlight arced across her bed. She propped herself up on one elbow, blinking.

"Are you asleep?" It was Lindon, his voice a slurred whisper.

She sighed and flopped back down on her bed. "No, darling." This wasn't a lie. Although her bedroom was secluded and quiet, tucked away from the noise of their visitors, she hadn't been able to sleep. Her mind kept churning: Aurelia and the adventurers and all the needs they would have the next day. She'd have to make a list to give the servants. And then there was her secret, still weighing heavily on her, and the conversation with Crell about the strangeness in Eiren.

Lindon moved into her room, the door clicking shut behind him. His footsteps were heavy, and she listened to him in the dark, her heart fluttering in her chest.

"It's late," she said.

"I know," he said. "But I didn't get my goodnight kiss."

Celestia rolled her eyes, but she sat up in the bed as he slid in beside her. He smelled of palm wine and cigar smoke.

"I see you had a good time this evening," said Celestia.

"Mmm." Lindon leaned his head against the headboard. "It's always good to talk to men from the profession."

"And women," Celestia added.

Lindon laughed. "Yeah, and women. Not too often you see a woman living that life. But I knew a few in my time."

He fell quiet, and Celestia thought about those women that he had known, and wondered if they were like Lucia, brash and rough at the edges.

"How long are they planning on staying?" Celestia asked. She was stalling—she needed to tell him but she didn't want to, because she was afraid that speaking the secret aloud would undermine it somehow. They had been waiting for four years, since the night they were wed.

"Oh, a day or so. Orlando is chasing after a bounty for Aster D'Lillu down south—some cattle thief who's been impossible to catch."

Celestia smiled. "Do you think they'll catch him?"

"Those scoundrels?" Lindon squinted out into the shadows of the room. "Maybe. They're a rough bunch."

"Did they tell you about the—" She didn't know what to call it, and she understood then why the Eirenese were calling it a disease. "The disease? In Eiren?"

"The what?"

Celestia hesitated. She suspected that if she shared what Crell had told her, Lindon would laugh and take it for a joke. "There's a strange illness in Eiren. Crell said it was the reason they were able to save the merchant's son."

Lindon looked at her for a moment, his face blurred in the darkness. Then he threw back his head and laughed. "No," he said. "They didn't tell me that. Tricky bastards." He laughed again, shaking his head. "Should've known that story of theirs was too good to be true."

"It sounded awful," Celestia persisted. She couldn't get Crell's story out of her head. The boy walking toward them with a slashed throat. "Unnatural."

"Unnatural?" Lindon threw his arm around her shoulders and squeezed her in close. His body was warm and solid and she pressed against him, breathing him in. "I'm sure Crell made it worse than it was. But you mustn't trouble yourself. Whatever it is, it hasn't come to the Seraphine."

"That's an uncharitable thing to say."

"It's true, though." Lindon kissed the top of her head. "You've nothing to worry about."

Celestia rested her hands on her stomach. She thought about the secret she was carrying. She needed to tell him. The secret was part of him, too.

"Can I have my goodnight kiss now?" said Lindon, pressing his face close against hers. She tilted her head toward him, eyes closed, and pressed her lips to his. He cupped her face in his hands and kissed her more deeply than she expected. All she could taste was smoke.

"There," Lindon said, when he'd pulled away. He smiled down at her and tucked a strand of her hair behind her ear.

43

"My lovely wife. I might have stayed up all night talking to those brutes, but I am glad you stole me away from that life."

Celestia's cheeks warmed. She was lucky to have found such a man, his adventurer's wealth complemented by his charm and admiration for his wife. *Luck had nothing to do with it,* whispered a voice in the back of her head, the voice she always ignored.

Lindon moved to slide out of her bed, but she put her hand on his arm. He stopped and looked over at her, his eyes bright in the darkness. She took a deep breath. Part of her wanted to peel her nightgown away from her shoulders and pretend that was the reason she wanted him to stay. But no. It was too late, he had been drinking, and she had to tell him.

"What is it, dear?" he said.

"I'm pregnant."

Silence rang out through the room. Lindon didn't move. Celestia remembered the past four years, and all the times he asked her if this month was the month, and all the times she'd said no, her voice quavering. All the women's potions she had drunk down, hoping they would stimulate her fertility. All the prayers and offerings she made to Growth, the queen of all Airiana and the creatrix of all things. All the nights she waded into the river, terrified that this was how the Lady would have her repay the debt: that Celestia would have her husband, but no child. No heir. The end of the family line.

Izara had said it wasn't the repayment, that Celestia had not been specific enough in her request. "It'll happen eventually," she'd said, adding, in her clumsy way, "assuming neither of you are infertile."

But now, finally, Izara'd been proven correct. It *had* happened, and Celestia was sure, because the wandering alchemist had held a divining stone over her bare belly and said, "Would you like to know the sex, my lady?" And she had shook her head, because all that really mattered to her was the *yes* or the *no*.

"You're pregnant?" Lindon whispered.

Celestia nodded. This silence, this stillness, was not the reaction she had expected.

"Are you sure?"

"I saw the alchemist when he visited."

Lindon stared at her. Then he broke out into an enormous grin, and he wrapped his arms around her and pulled her up to his chest. "You're pregnant," he mumbled into her hair. "Gods and monsters, you're pregnant."

"I hope this is good news for you," she said into his shoulder, knowing full well that it was.

"Good news?" Lindon pulled her away and looked down at her. "This is *phenomenal* news! I wish you had told me earlier; we could have celebrated tonight."

"Oh, I didn't want to detract from the adventurers," Celestia said demurely.

Lindon scoffed. "A baby's more important than that lot." He splayed his hand against her belly. "I can't believe it," he said. "I'd almost given up hope."

Celestia's breath hitched at that.

"We'll need to get word to the staff," Lindon said. "You aren't to be on your feet until that baby's born. We'll raise ourselves a proper noble child."

Celestia laughed. "I don't have to start resting until I'm showing."

"I'm not taking any chances," he said, and he started to count off a list of assignments for the servants. But Celestia wasn't terribly bothered by it; she liked his tendency to fuss over her, as if a high-born lady was a delicate thing, and she liked him fussing over their baby. She settled back against the headboard and listened to his excited chatter—"We can leave an offering for Growth first thing tomorrow morning. The mangos are peaking right now, so that would be perfect. And we'll need to turn one of the guest rooms into a nursery, of course—my son's going to have every toy we can get him."

"We don't know if it's a boy," Celestia said.

"The alchemist didn't tell you the sex?"

She shook her head and smiled. "I wanted to be surprised."

Lindon laughed. "You're a tricky one, aren't you?" He gathered her up in his arms and kissed her again, long and lingering. Celestia let herself drift off on the kiss. She let herself be entangled in this lovely moment, and she did not think about the darkness creeping across Eiren.

High Mage Papazian swept into her office ten minutes late, according to the clock on the wall. Izara had been waiting for almost twenty. A mage could be late; an acolyte could not.

"I apologize, dear," Papazian said, scurrying over to her desk. "I was caught up with my practicum students. If the wards fall tonight, don't blame me." She shook her head and sank down in her chair. "Now, where did we leave off?"

"Decay," Izara said promptly. Her notebook already lay open in her lap, her notes from the last session scratching across the paper in neat, even lines. Papazian was an Airiana mage, one who did not enter into the Aetheric Realm and instead requested the Airiana to work magic on her behalf. It was a magical approach that Izara had no interest in, despite her aristocratic pedigree—she'd already seen the havoc making deals with the Airiana could wreak. Its practitioners all claimed the inherent danger of it was mitigated by being of noble birth, a lie that Izara had put her trust in five years ago. Now she knew better. And so she wanted to study alchemy, to step into the Aetheric Realm and uncover for herself the formulas that shaped reality.

Unfortunately, her first-hand experience with Airiana magic was the reason she now found herself sitting in Papazian's office once a week, taking notes over each of the Airiana and learning a style of magic that had frightened her so much five years ago that she had refused to touch it since. Papazian had insisted. And as much as Izara wanted to refuse, such things simply weren't allowed at the Academy.

"Ahh, Decay." Papazian leaned back in her chair, braided her fingers together on top of her round belly. "The dark twin. His magic can be very strong if you aren't afraid to dabble in it."

Izara wrote this down, not because she wanted to remember it, necessarily, but because she was too conscientious of an acolyte not to.

"The Exalted Twins have a reputation among mages of our strain," Papazian went on. "I'm sure you're aware of it, of course. Their power makes them exceedingly difficult to control, but that doesn't mean it can't be done." Papazian gave Izara a little wink, and Izara stared down at her notebook, not reading anything. "Now, as you know, dear, using the magic of the Airiana is a tricky proposition, even for us noble-born. But with the Exalted Twins—Decay and Growth—their magic is the literal root of the world, the seed of our creation, and using it incorrectly could cause the whole world to come undone."

Izara had stopped taking her dutiful notes. She stared down at her notebook, her thoughts stuck on that awful little wink. Papazian was the only person at the Academy who knew what had transpired between Izara and the Lady of the Seraphine. They had passed each other on the path to the dining hall sometime last year, and Papazian's hand had lashed out and grabbed Izara's arm. "You've been Beholden!" she had cried, her voice echoing through the rainy mountains.

"But that doesn't mean you can't dabble a bit, assuming you're under my protection," Papazian said.

"What!" Izara jerked her head up. "Dabble?"

"Why, yes." Papazian smiled at her from across her desk. "In the magic of the Exalted Twins. You're one of our most talented acolytes, and the dean and I agree that you are well-suited to channeling the Airiana, given your," she coughed a little, "history with the Lady. Shall we?"

Izara stared at Papazian. She had never been as talented with the rules of propriety as her sister, and she wished more than anything her sister was here right now, to tell her how to do this gracefully. But she was alone. "No," she said.

Papazian blinked. Frowned. "Excuse me?"

Izara jerked her gaze away, her face hot. "I want to focus on alchemy," she muttered, curling her fingers against the pages of her notebook. "I've already focused most of my efforts on Alchemist Venes' personal project and—"

"Alchemy?" Papazian made a sound like a broken wind-pipe. "Why would you want to do *alchemy*? Working with the Airiana has always been the purview of the Seraphine nobility, and you have such a clear *talent* for it, given what you accomplished without any training—"

Izara slammed her notebook shut and stood up. Her head was buzzing, but she couldn't stand to listen to this, not anymore. She had traded part of her life to the Lady of the Seraphine, and even now, five years later, she didn't know what that part would turn out to be.

It was said that working Airiana magic threw the chaotic side effects of magic onto the Airiana, but Izara didn't believe it. She would take the strange coincidences of alchemy or elemental sorcery over ever making deals with the Airiana again.

"I'm sorry, Grand Mage Papazian," Izara said, remembering to say her title, at least. "But I'm not comfortable with this."

Papazian stared at her for a moment, confusion twisting across her features. Then she broke out into a smile. Izara tensed. She didn't know how to read the situation anymore.

"Oh, my dear, there's nothing to be afraid of! I'll be here the entire time, and if anything gets outs of hand, I can put a stop to it, like this." She snapped her fingers. "We won't actually be *calling* on Decay. Simply getting a taste of his power."

She didn't understand. She thought Izara was scared of Decay, thought Izara didn't understand the whole point behind the Exalted Twins, that one was necessary for the other. Izara's fear subsided, replaced by a strain of annoyance. She wasn't some Eirenese peasant, terrified of the darkness inherent in the world.

"Fine," Izara spat. She didn't want to toy with the Airiana any more than she had to, but she wasn't about to let Papazian think she didn't understand them, either. She understood them better than any acolyte should.

"Excellent!" Papazian tapped her desk. "Sit, sit."

Izara slid back into her chair and watched Papazian clear an empty space on her desk. She felt something cold in the pit of her stomach. Papazian stood up and bustled over to her supply shelf, humming softly. Izara shoved the notebook into the gap between her hip and the chair. The Exalted Twins were not like the Lady of the Seraphine. She took human form, she controlled only the rivers and soft flowing streams. The Twins—their domain was the whole world. A world they had built together, when Decay ripped the universe to shreds, and Growth conjured it out of the chaos.

"Here we are." Papazian spread out a sheet of parchment and an ink jar and a dip pen. Izara stared down at the supplies. So far Papazian had not asked her to do any actual magic— only met with her, talked with her, sent her on her way. But it was typical Papazian style to have the first spell be with the most powerful of the Airiana, wasn't it? Whether they were calling on him or not.

"What's in that ink jar?" Izara said. It wasn't black, like ink should be.

Papazian peered up at her. "I think you can guess."

Izara closed her eyes. "I'm not supposed to do elemental blood magic until my fifth year."

"I received special permission from the dean. I just want you to experience this. We'll do a similar elemental spell with Growth next week."

Izara didn't want to do spells for any of the Airiana, whether they were just simple *tastes* or full-on conjurations. She knew where it led.

But Papazian was staring at her from across the desk, her expression vaguely challenging, as if she thought deep down Izara wasn't really capable. This was annoying enough that Izara picked up the ink jar and unscrewed the lid. The salty metallic tang of blood filled the air. She picked up the pen.

"Now, this is still elemental magic," Papazian said. "But it will help you to become comfortable with Decay's particular domain." She produced an old tattered book out of the pile of books on her desk and flipped open to a page with a drawing of a symbol that Izara recognized immediately from the temple at Jaila-Seraphine.

"You can call on the powers of Decay with blood and song," Papazian said.

It had been water and song for the Lady of the Seraphine. Izara shoved the thought aside.

"I'm sure you've learned one of his hymns at some point," Papazian said. "Any of them would do."

Izara nodded. All children learned the hymns of the Airiana. She remembered her tutor, in those years before the money dried up and her parents died, sitting in a patch of sun singing a song about the end of the world. The melody wormed its way into her head, low and haunting. She dipped her pen in the blood. The hymn started in the back of her throat, a separate voice from her own. She hummed it, softly, then sang the words, all those images of destruction flowing through her and into the cramped, airless space of Papazian's office. As she sang, she drew. An inverted triangle bisected by three straight lines. Drops of blood dripped from her pen. She sang, and as she sang she felt darkness building up in her chest: a kind of wild mania, an urge to reach out and destroy. She sang louder and dug her pen into the parchment, ripping it. Darkness came into the room and she smelled something too-sweet, like flowers drenched in perfume. The words of the song tore at her throat. Blood smeared against her hand.

In the distance, someone screamed, and it was like dropping coal onto a fire. The magic flared. Behind her eyelids Izara watched the world burn.

"Stop!" Papazian swatted the pen out of Izara's hand and everything stopped in an instant. Izara slammed back in her chair, blinking at the bright light of the room. Papazian was mopping up spilled blood—somehow the ink jar had fallen, and a line of blood crawled across the desk, threatening to drip over the side and onto the floor.

"You're stronger than I thought." Papazian tittered nervously. She glanced at Izara, her face ashen. Izara didn't say anything. She couldn't speak; her throat hurt too much from the singing. Papazian picked up the parchment and ripped it in half. "Are you with me?" she asked, looking at Izara with hard eyes.

Izara nodded. She croaked out, "It burned my throat," and Papazian sighed.

"I'm sorry, dear," she said. "I've done this with students before, and it usually just gives them a bit of a scare, nothing so—" She stopped. Her shoulders hitched. "I'm sorry."

Izara didn't want to be in this room any longer. She didn't want to smell that spilled blood, she didn't want to breathe in the lingering aftereffects of the magic she had brought in from the Aetheric Realm. And most of all, she didn't want to look at Papazian anymore. Papazian, who didn't understand anything that she had gone through; Papazian, who thought being Beholden was some kind of blessing.

Izara stumbled out of the office, Papazian yelling behind her but not following. She charged through the hallway, keeping her head down, refusing to make eye contact with anyone, until she banged through the doorways that led outside. The rush of cool mountain air flowed over her, and she felt then like she could breathe again. The path was empty, since classes and trainings were all in session right now, and for that Izara was grateful. She walked up the path, toward the herb garden that grew alongside the dormitories. Living plants were generally in Growth's domain, along with the Airiana of the earth and all the Laniana of each individual species. But Decay worked alone to create the soil out of dead animals and fallen leaves.

Still, you could not have one without the other.

But Izara had, back in Papazian's office. Growth had not been there when she drew that sign and sang that song. Only Decay. Only darkness. Only death.

⁓

It was snowing again.

Ico rolled over on his bed and pulled the blanket up around his neck. Xima was gone, which was not a surprise, considering the snow. He burrowed deeper into the blanket, trying to generate his own warmth. A fire burned in the corner, but it was not a natural fire, and so it cast a blue glow rather than red. Still, that blue fire let off a steady, shimmering heat.

"Icooooo." Xima's voice sounded like the wind howling outside the palace. "I need yooooooou."

Her voice billowed around the room, low and blustery. Ico pulled the blanket down from his face.

"Come up here!" he called out. "You made it too damn cold this morning."

Her laughter echoed through the walls. Perhaps it was eerie, the way it sounded so much like the wind—but to Ico that eeriness was part of its charm, and the sound of it right now, so soon after sleeping, stirred him.

"Come up here, and I'll give you a surprise!" he called out again. "Promise you'll like it."

More laughter, closer this time. Ico sat up, keeping the blanket wrapped snugly around his neck. The fire's blue light washed over the walls. The room was cavernous, carved out of ancient ice, like everything in the palace. When the sun was out, it shone through the walls, suffusing them with pale light. But the sun wasn't out today, and there was only the pinging of snow against the walls and roof.

Xima materialized in the door, bringing with her a swirl of snow that scattered across the floor and melted in the heat of the fire. Ico grinned at her.

"And what surprise is that, my dearest Ico?" She leaned against the doorway, the lines of her body sinuous and inviting. She wore a sheer gown that clung to her pale skin, revealing interesting shadows. Her hair was the color of snow and it cascaded around her shoulders in thick, wild curls.

"Come here and I'll show you," Ico said.

She laughed, and then she threw out her arms and launched herself across the room, leaving a trail of snow in her wake. She landed hard on the bed, straddling Ico over the blankets, and she leaned down so that their noses almost touched, her hair falling in a curtain around them.

"Gotta crawl under the blankets for your surprise," Ico said.

"Do I?" Her breath had a chill to it, like mint, but the closeness of her body, the strength of her legs and the soft pressure of her breasts, undid the cold. Ico lifted his head enough to kiss her, and as they kissed he shoved the blankets away. The heat of the blue fire brushed his bare skin, and Xima's gown was silky and luxuriant. He shoved the hem up her leg and ran his hand along her thigh.

"Oh, my north wind," she breathed into his ear, "all your surprises are the same."

Ico bit at the skin of her shoulder in response, and she gave a moan of pleasure and then sat up and pulled her gown away. It dissolved on the air, turning to steam that drifted up toward the ceiling. Her bare body gleamed blue. Ico traced the curve of her waist and then she settled onto him, gasping.

Ico didn't think he'd ever feel cold again.

He lasted long enough for Xima to achieve her own pleasure, which did not take long. Afterwards, she collapsed alongside him, her hand stroking his jawline. The snow struck against the walls of the palace.

"My north wind," she sighed. "My king-killer."

Ico grinned. She only called him that, *king-killer*, when she was pleased. He'd never killed a king before, of course, just pissed off King Oddvarr of the North when he was a pirate. He and his crew had taken a shining to Oddvarr's merchant ships. And somehow, the bounty on his head had caught the ear of one of the Airiana—Xima, who'd been slighted by Oddvarr in some way or another. Ico didn't completely understand it. But it was the first time one of the many bounties placed on him throughout the years actually worked in his favor.

"That was an expert distraction," Xima murmured.

"Distraction?" Ico ran his hand through her hair. "I was just cold."

She laughed. "You're always cold, dearest."

"That's what happens when the goddess of snow wants you to be her mortal lover."

"I've told you over and over," she purred. "I am not a goddess, and I'm born from all of the manifestations of the cold. *Not* just snow."

"Ah, of course. How could I forget? Ice and sleet get thrown in there too."

She laughed and then kissed him again, her touch cool against his hot skin. When she pulled away, Ico stared up at her, taking her in. He ran his fingers down the sharp plains of her face. She was incandescent in the snow-light filtering through the palace's ice walls.

"I won't allow you to distract me for long," she said softly. "I have a task for you."

Ico slumped back among the fluffy pillows. "But it's snowing."

"I'll stop the snow for you, and grant you clear skies and strong winds all the way to Sra Slarin."

Ico grinned. "A sailor could grow soft, conditions like that."

"Shall I send a tempest, then?"

"Not necessary." Ico rolled over onto his side, his head propped up on one hand. "So what needs done in Sra Slarin? Is your honor in need of defending? Or is there a rich man who desperately wishes to be relieved of the burden of his wealth? That was always my specialty."

Xima kissed him. "I'm afraid your talents will go to waste today. I only need a message delivered to my temple."

"Sounds easy enough.' He wrapped his arms around Xima's shoulders and rolled on top of her, the blankets wrapping around their bodies, cocooning them to the bed. Ico could stay here forever. To hell with Sra Slarin and messages to the temple. Xima was the only thing that mattered in Ico's world, ever since his ship had been destroyed during an autumn storm and he washed up on the frozen shores of her island, sea-battered and half-drowned. She mistook him for a hero.

"You're trying to distract me again," Xima mumbled against Ico's neck. Each word sent a shudder of pleasure down his spine. "But the message is important, my north wind. Important to *me*."

Ico peeled away from her and twisted a lock of her white hair around his finger. She gazed up at him, her eyes glinting. He couldn't say no to those eyes—couldn't say no to her, no matter what she asked. She claimed she was not a goddess, only a sister of the Airiana, but Ico knew better. He had never been the sort to worship women, and yet *worship* was the only way to describe what he felt for her.

He suspected that was his appeal to her. As much as she claimed she wasn't a goddess, she certainly enjoyed play-acting as one. Including taking on human nemeses and then bedding the pirate who, at least in her mind, had driven that nemesis to an early grave.

"I'll set sail as soon as the skies are clear," he said.

Xima had promised clear skies and strong winds, but those winds blew from the north, and they were laced through with ice and frost. Ico huddled inside his fur-lined coat, his eyes watering. The boat was an old sloop, powered by sails instead of steam, but Ico had sailed such boats as a boy, and the motions of wind-sail had come back to him when Xima first presented him with his new vessel. The roughness of rope in his palms had been comforting and familiar, as had the tight weight of the sails as they filled with wind. The old way of sailing, the harder way—but a way you felt with your whole body. Ico wasn't sure he'd ever go back to steam and paddles.

The sloop cut through the glassy water. Sra Slarin glimmered up ahead, rocky cliff faces shrouded in white mist. It was the closet outcropping of land to Xima's island, this far northern tip of Eiren, but it was still about a half-day's sail away.

Ico pulled away from the railing and sat down next to the brazier. The coal glowed orange-red, a natural fire that Ico had stoked himself. The wind was doing most of the sailing for him by now, and he held out his hands to the coals and thought of the heat of the Seraphine. It was heat as inescapable as the cold was, here on the top of the world, a heat that would steam against your skin, that you could feel like liquid inside your lungs. He couldn't say he missed it exactly. At least here, fires and furs could keep you warm: in the Seraphine, there was no escaping the wet heat.

Just like there was no escaping the Koza clan.

He thought he'd managed to make a life for himself as a sailor, not a pirate. In the Seraphine, he was free from his various northern bounty hunters, who would never travel so far south. And the Kozas, well, he just owed them money. He thought he could pay the debt off a bit at a time. But the Kozas tracked him down with mages. Men who could cast a spell and drag him out of an ordinary life and into a nightmare where he paid his debt in blood, not coin.

Ico reached into his coat and pulled out the pouches of salted fish and sweet wine he'd brought with him to stave off the hunger until he arrived at the temple. The priests always fed him, usually barley stew and crusty bread. Although it wasn't the otherworldly glittering feasts he ate on Xima's island, the priests' meals were warm and satisfying, and Ico could never speak a word against them.

He took a bite of salted fish and peered over the boat's edge. Still wasn't any closer to landfall.

So Ico settled back, moving close to the fire, and gnawed

on the salted fish. Of all the paths his life could have taken, this one was the most astounding. He should be dead.

A year ago, he had a place aboard a merchant ship that ran up and down the Seraphine, shipping crops and goods from the acreages along the shore. He'd been part of a crew; he'd been earning wages without thievery or blackmail. He set aside part of those wages to pay back his debts. But it wasn't fast enough.

One hot, endless night, the Kozas' magic had woken him up in his hammock swinging in the hull, stinging at him like insects. It was not long after that the screaming started.

The magic wasn't just for him. It compelled the entire crew, every soul aboard that boat, to drag themselves up to the top deck, where the Kozas had boarded, their faces hidden behind carved-bone masks. One by one, they tortured and slaughtered the crew that had welcomed Ico as family, using magic and knives and fire. He'd been lashed in place by the magic, his muscles screaming in pain but immovable, and the blood on the deck was so much that it sloshed around his ankles.

By sunrise, everyone was dead but him, their tattered bodies strewn like garlands from the masts and the stacks, the captain himself draped over the bow. And the Koza leader walked over to him, his hands crimson with blood, and leaned down to whisper in Ico's ear.

"Your debt's paid up," he said, his voice smooth and elegant, not the voice of a killer at all. "But I don't ever want to see your face in the Seraphine again. If you return here, we'll do worse than kill you. And we'll do it to anyone who dares help you."

The blood-soaked riverboat took Ico to the mouth of the Seraphine, his mind numb. He was too cold, too empty, to do anything proper for the crew, all of whom had died for his debts. He let the boat crash into a desolate stretch of forest and said a few words of prayer to Decay and then he stole away on a merchant ship headed to the north of Aesri.

They were almost to their destination when a winter storm came and ripped the boat apart. Ico was flung out into the churning black water, where he managed to climb aboard a hunk of shattered wood. He shivered in the cold rain as it pounded down on him. Lightning tore the sky into pieces. *This is it,* he thought. *I'm dying the death I deserve.*

But he didn't. Instead, he washed up on Xima's island, shivering and halfway to dead. One of her handmaidens found him, brought him to the palace. And Xima had recognized him.

"You're Ishi Kui Ico!" she cried.

He gaped at her.

"The famed human pirate," she trilled, delight radiating off her. "The one who drove that fiend Oddvarr to poverty and ruin and death!"

Before Ico could respond, Xima had him up in her embrace, blessing him with food and heat and her soft, supple body. She brought him into her palace and burned the cold out of him with her unnatural blue fires. She listened, enraptured, as he spun out his encounters with the Eirenese kingsguards and bounty hunters, her face always darkening at Oddvarr's name. He still didn't know what Oddvarr had done to her, and he didn't care.

He worshipped her for all of it, just as she wanted.

———◦———

Ico drew down the sails as he glided into the Sra Slarin docks. A few boats were bobbing in the water, although no one was on the docks themselves. Typical for the towns that worshipped Xima. They were all too far north, too far away from the seat of the Eirenese empire.

Ico tied off his boat and threw sand on the brazier. Black

smoke billowed up, and when it cleared, the coals were still burning.

"The fuck," he muttered.

He stared at the red glow shining up through the sand. He tossed on another handful, and another, until the coals were completely buried.

"There," he said, and went down below to the storage bay. He didn't keep much down there, mostly empty barrels in case he ever needed to bring back goods on one of his trips for Xima, but he had tucked Xima's message to the temple in the alcove near the roof. The message was folded and stamped and tucked away in a box carved of glittering ice that was cold to the touch but never melted. Ico slid the box out of its alcove and tossed it in his knapsack. He didn't like keeping the messages up above with him, on the chance that they might be damaged somehow, either by the elements or the fire in the brazier—Ico still wasn't sure how Xima's ice magic worked exactly. So he tucked her missives away instead.

He climbed back up top and then disembarked. The dockmaster's station was unattended. Ico didn't bother paying for his space. If the dockmaster wanted his money so badly, he could make himself available when Ico landed. Common courtesy, really.

The wind picked up as Ico made his way into town. It was damp and cold and it stirred up the powdery snow still lining the walkways in front of the buildings. No one was out. Ico pulled on the strap of his knapsack. The docks were one thing; not many people sailing in and out of Sra Slarin. But for all the shops to be closed up tight like this, for all the streets to be empty—

Ico didn't like it.

He pulled out his pistol and cocked it back, then shoved it into his belt at easy reach. His footsteps clattered against the stone walkways, their echoes bouncing off the buildings. The wind howled. Snow swirled up in front of him like a typhoon. Ico's shoulders were tense, like he was preparing for a fight. He kept moving in the direction of the temple, though. It didn't matter how unnerving this town was, Xima was expecting it of him.

Drop off the message and get the hell out, he thought. *Something's not right here.*

He turned off the main street, onto the path that led up to the Illiran temple. The road was lined with small, narrow houses in the Eirenese style, with tiny windows and cold weather gardens locked behind panes of glass. Ico had seen houses like these a hundred times before as he made his way up and down the coast.

"Good harvest," he said, his voice breaking the stillness of the town. The cold weather gardens were flourishing despite the drifts of snow, dark green leaves reaching toward the sky. But the further along he walked and the more houses he passed, the more uneasy he felt.

The gardens were so *lush*. Some had even broken the boundaries of their fences and sent pale shoots running across the ice-encased sidewalks. Thick, woody vines crawled up along the walls of the houses.

Ico stopped, his heart hammering in his chest. Snow tumbled around him. This was wrong. Those gardens should be frozen solid.

A figure moved in one of the windows, drawing the curtains shut.

Ico needed to get to the temple. The priests could explain what was going on. Maybe this was normal. Some invisible shift in the season.

He pushed on, trampling snow and fresh plants alike beneath his black boots. The snow turned green and the air smelled of soil and growth, not ice and metal. It smelled of the Seraphine, not Eiren.

When he passed the town square, he found it covered in bright, frozen flags, their color preserved in slabs of ice.

And then he saw the ice tree.

The ice tree was a fossil, a trunk turned to stone millennia ago. It had some relevance for the townspeople; Ico couldn't remember what it was. Only that the tree was dead with thick clawing branches that collected long daggers of icicles. The icicles were there today, as always.

But so were leaves. Green leaves, sprouting from the tree's dead branches in long, shimmering tufts. Ico stared, gape-jawed, his heart thudding.

The wind kicked up, pelting him with a blast of dry, powdery snow. Ico stumbled backwards, a tightness in the pit of his stomach. He couldn't stop staring at that dead tree and its bright leaves, growing so surely in the middle of winter.

Movement flickered up ahead. Ico whirled, kicking up old snow to reveal a patch of startingly green grass.

"Hello?" he shouted. "Who's there? I'm a friend of the temple."

His voice faded into the wind. He jogged forward. "Hello? Is anyone—"

He stopped.

A house was entirely overgrown with dark green vines. They had snaked their way to the roof and were pulling the bricks down into the snow. A ragged hole had already collapsed in the wall, snow piled up along the broken stone.

Ico moved forward, cautious. He remembered this house because it marked the place where the road branched off toward the temple; the last time he had been here, less than a month ago, it had been tidy and well cared for, with statues to the Airiana set up in the garden. Growth had been the largest of the statues, a buxom woman with flowers growing in her hair. He always noticed it when he walked by.

Now the statue of Growth was gone, and the house was

being pulled to the ground by vines that did not belong in this place.

"Hello?" he shouted again.

No answer.

Ico turned away from the collapsing house. He didn't want to stay in Sra Slarin any longer than he needed to.

He ran the rest of the way to the temple, his head ducked down to combat the chilling wind. He didn't look at any of the houses or their overgrown gardens, and he was relieved when they gave way to the open grasslands that surrounded the temple, even if it meant the wind blew more harshly and he had to see the tall, silvery grasses sticking out of the snow drifts. He slowed here, to catch his breath before he walked into the temple. It rose up before him, a glittering white-stone structure carved to look like slopes of snow. The priests, on his first visit here, not long after he washed ashore on Xima's island, had told him the temple had been built two thousand years earlier, from techniques that had since been lost. During the Last War it had served as a hospital, a fact the priests took great pride in, as it meant that their ancestors had provided comfort and aid during the fighting, and not harm.

Ico wondered if it was serving as a hospital now. If that was even what Sra Slarin needed.

The White Flames of Illira were still burning outside the gates, a sign Ico found encouraging. He checked the ice box in his bag to make sure that it hadn't been damaged and then followed the meandering path up to the temple. The White Flames guttered in the wind, and Ico caught the cold metal scent of their smoke. The temple gates ground open as he approached. Another good sign. Ico stepped into the court-yard.

Flowers bloomed everywhere.

A sick panic gripped Ico. Behind him, the temple gate groaned shut. The courtyard was covered in flowers, thousands of them. Pollen spun on the wind with the dry snow; Ico could smell it, he could feel it itching the back of his throat.

"Hello?" Ico called out. "It's the North Wind of Illira!"

The flowers seemed to swallow his voice. He waited, his heart pounding.

"Master Ico?"

The voice was thin and sounded far away, like it had been blown apart by the wind. Ico whirled around, the ice box in his knapsack hitting up against his thigh.

"Yeah?" he said. "I mean, yes? Where are you?"

"You should leave at once."

A chill tore down Ico's spine. "Can't," he said. "I have a message from Illira herself. Where *are* you?"

A faint echo of footsteps shuddered out into the courtyard. Ico turned around again, and this time he spotted one of the temple priests, swathed in the white robes of his order.

"Wait," Ico said. "Stop. I'll come to you."

"Not too close," the priest said. His cheeks were pink from the wind. "We don't know how it spreads."

Ico froze. "Are you sick?"

"I don't know what I am," the priest said. He did not look sick; if anything, he looked vibrant and healthy. Far younger than his grey hair would suggest.

"The message from our Goddess," the priest said. "Does it explain what's happening?"

Ico shook his head. "I don't know what it says."

The priest closed his eyes. "I thought I would see Her," he murmured, "in the cold embrace of death."

"What are you talking about?" Ico flicked his gaze around as he pulled the icebox out of his knapsack. The courtyard was empty, which just unnerved him further.

"Death has gone away!" the priest wailed. He jerked up the sleeves of his robe to reveal long red gashes running up the length of his forearms. They were the sort of cuts designed to open veins, and they were fresh wounds.

"Gods and monsters!" Ico shouted. "What did you do?"

"We had to test," the priest said. "We had to know for sure." He held up his arms. The wounds were fresh, red and angry-looking, but they were not bleeding as such wounds should bleed, only seeping blood, leaving dotted smears on the inside of the priest's robes that looked like flower petals.

"You did that to yourself?" Ico's hands trembled. The icebox's cold sides burned at his fingertips.

"Yes. It was the only way. But I did not sink into our lady's cold embrace." The priest stared into Ico's eyes, his expression manic. "I didn't even sink into the ocean of death. It is gone. All gone."

The man had clearly lost his mind. Ico held up the box and the sun caught in the ice, making the message inside glow. The priest gave as a sigh of contentment.

"I hope it's a message of hope," he murmured. "Please, North Wind, set it on the bench there. And then return to Illira. Tell her what you found here."

"What did I find here?" Ico spat out.

The priest pulled his sleeves back over his arms, hiding the ugly, screaming wounds. "We suspect—" He looked over at the flowers "We suspect the Dark Lord. His magic altered the Eirenese landscape before. Now it's doing it again."

"The Dark Lord?" Fragments of history fluttered at the edges of Ico's thought. The Dark Lord had been part of the Last War. Leader of the losing side—right? As a child he'd never studied the Last War. Akuran hadn't fought in it.

"Yes. Please. Tell Illira. She'll know what to do. Hurry!"

The last word was imbued with an urgency that cut Ico through to his core.

Ico set the box down on the bench, his skin crawling.

"Thank you, thank you," mumbled the man. "Now run, child. Flee, before the Dark Lord's aberrancy spreads to you. Go!"

Ico wasn't of a mind to stick around and play hero. He nodded once and then walked backwards up to the gate, which opened for him, dragging along inch by inch. The man plucked up the box from the bench.

The gate opened. A blast of north wind spilled in, smelling as sweet as summer.

Ico turned and ran.

———

Celestia dipped her pen into the pot of ink and then poised it above her paper. Already she had written *Dear Izara,* but that was the easy part.

Rain pattered outside, and the humidity drifted in through the open windows of Celestia's morning room, making the edges of the paper curl. She smoothed them down with her free hand. Touched her pen nub to the paper.

How are you? I hope this letter finds you well.

She paused and considered writing, *I hope it finds you at all,* but decided against it, as that sort of flippancy would decrease the letter's chances of ever making it through the readers at the Academy. They were known to burn letters that questioned the policies.

Things continue apace here at Cross Winds. Our mango crop this year was abundant, and we have recently begun shaping the sugar cane in preparation for a new crop next year—

It was easy to talk about Cross Winds, and safe besides. The pen scratched across the paper as if moved by some hand other than Celestia's. She told her sister about the visit from Aurelia and the adventurers, although she truncated their story about the northern warlord and left out mention of Crell's version of events entirely—that would *certainly* mark the letter as dangerous, and it would guarantee that Izara would never see it. When she finished, Celestia read over what she had written. Her hand dropped distractedly to her stomach. She had delayed telling Lindon out of anxiety, but her reticence in writing to Izara about her pregnancy grew out of the fact that she wished she could tell her face to face. Izara was her only sister—her only *family*, now that both of their parents had passed away. And yet she had to write the words on a letter that might not even make it through the Academy's absurd security protocols.

Sighing, Celestia dipped her in pen in the ink.

One last thing, she wrote, her handwriting quick and slanted, *I do wish I knew when you'd be free to come visit so I could tell you then, but I know it would be too late—I'm pregnant, sister. Pregnant, finally! An heir for Cross Winds. I don't know the sex, because I wish to be surprised. Lindon hopes it's a boy, but I of course want a girl. I hope she's as clever as you are, and as beautiful as the Empress. The world would be hers to command, don't you think?*

Celestia smiled, although she felt sad. She wished she could see Izara's face when she found out about Celestia's pregnancy. Izara was never one for wild displays of emotions—she kept everything close to her heart, tucked beneath the surface. Most people found her cold for it, but Celestia knew better. Her sister was far from cold; she only shared her feelings with the slightest of facial tics, the subtlest of tonal shifts. And Celestia knew how to interpret her.

I hope to see you soon, Celestia wrote, which was a safe phrase, guaranteed to make it past the readers. Anything too critical of the Academy and its policies would be confiscated. *I hope your studies are going well.* Another safe phrase, the closet she could come to asking about Izara's work at the Academy. Then she signed off the letter, flourishing her signature, and blew on the ink to dry it. In this weather, with that damp steam rising off the ground from the rain, it would take longer than usual. She carried the letter over to the opposite side of the room, away from the windows, and set it on her dresser.

Someone knocked at her door.

"Yes?" she called out.

Mr. Medulla entered. She glanced up at him, distracted, but then froze when she saw the expression on his face.

He seemed—worried.

"Yes?" she said, turning toward him. "Is—did something happen?"

"You have guests, Lady De Malena. Rather—important ones."

Celestia frowned. "What do you mean by important?"

Mr. Medulla glanced at the window, where the rain was still falling in a shimmery sun-lit mist.

"They say they're from the Emperor, my lady."

Celestia's entire body went numb. She pressed up against the dresser to steady herself. "The Emperor?" she whispered. "Did you—did you confirm?"

Mr. Medulla nodded, still looking out the window. "They carried the correct papers, my lady."

"Marked with the Emperor's alchemical seal?"

"Yes. I examined it myself." He paused. "They were officials, my lady. Not—sorcerers."

Celestia sucked in a deep breath. *Starless Mages,* he meant. The Emperor's army of dark magicians.

She ran her hands over her hair, smoothing out the wayward curls that always appeared in the humidity. She wasn't dressed to meet with the Emperor's men. She would need to change, as quickly as possible, and then deal with the matters of hospitality—

"They wish to speak to Master De Malena. They said it's a matter of great importance." Mr. Medulla turned from the window. His face was grave. "They wouldn't tell me anything beyond that. I've already sent Gregori out into the forest to fetch him."

Celestia nodded. "Yes, thank you. Have you told Cookie about their arrival? Will they be staying? At the very least they should sample the sparkling mango drink, or some of Cookie's pineapple cake."

"I'll tell her right away, my lady."

"And send up Alia. I'll need her help dressing."

"Of course." Mr. Medulla gave a shallow bow. Celestia still felt disoriented, certain she had forgotten something—

"Are they in the sitting room?" Celestia asked.

"Yes, my lady."

"Put them up in the drawing room, and be sure to pull the curtains back. I want them to have a view of the forest."

"Yes, my lady."

"Thank you, Mr. Medulla." Celestia sighed. "I'll be down as quickly as I can to entertain them while Master De Malena readies himself."

Another shallow bow, and then Mr. Medulla slipped out of the morning room. Celestia checked the letter to Izara, running her fingers over her signature—but the ink still smudged. *Curses,* she thought. She gathered up the letter and slid it into the drawer of her writing desk and then locked it, to avoid snooping from the staff. Then she bustled up to her room to change. Alia was waiting for her, a silk day dress stretched out on the bed.

"I chose the nicest thing in your closet, m'lady," Alia said, smoothing down the dress. "I do hope this works."

"It's perfect." Celestia stepped out of her thin cotton slippers and pulled on the sash tied around her waist. Alia immediately began undoing the buttons on the day dress. It was a lovely thing, a gift from Lindon from before they were married, the white silk hand-painted with delicate red hibiscus flowers. It was an appropriate thing for her to wear while she sat by her husband's side as he met with emissaries from the Emperor.

She slid out of her housedress and let it puddle on the floor. Alia helped her into the day dress and did up the buttons with deft fingers. Celestia stared at herself in the mirror. Her hair was still springing clear from the humidity, and she ran her hands together and then smoothed it over the side of her head. She had no time to rebraid it.

"A hat," she said to Alia, who was still looping up the buttons. "Something small and unobtrusive—my hair's a dreadful mess."

"What about flowers, m'lady? I can fetch some from the garden before you meet with your guests."

Celestia smiled at her reflection. Behind her, Alia squinted at the buttons. "That would be perfect," she said.

Alia finished the buttons and then draped the wide sash around Celestia's waist, crossing it in the front and then tying it off in the back. The effect pinched in Celestia's waist in the Jaila-Seraphine style.

"Perfect," Celestia said. "Run down and fetch the flowers. I'll meet you in the riverside hallway."

Alia dipped her head and then rushed out of the room. Celestia examined her reflection, looking for flaws. The hair would be taken care of, and it wouldn't be proper to apply makeup to meet with the emissaries. The dress worked well. She couldn't wear her old slippers, though; Celestia whirled away from the mirror and opened up her wardrobe and selected the thin white leather boots she'd had made at the cobbler down river. They slid on easily. Then she rushed out of her room, her skirt fluttering out around her ankles. The preparations had distracted her from the question of why these men where here, but as she made her way down the back staircase, different possibilities spun through her head. Lindon had often accepted assignments from the Emperor during his adventuring days. That was how he had earned his money. But he was no longer an adventurer.

Surely they weren't here to *arrest* him, then—

Celestia's chest constricted. She moved more quickly, skittering down the stairs and through the dappled forestside hallway. Her footsteps echoed against the walls of the house. The Emperor was not known for sending his representatives down into the river basin. He was too paranoid to let the court go roaming—that was what the rumors always claimed, all those stories Celestia had learned growing up, as all noble children did. He preferred to stay ensconced in his Palace in the Sky, cloaked in strange magics, hidden away from the eyes of his people. Even the landed gentry were rarely invited to court; it was rumored that such an invitation was not worth the isolation of that palace. Isolation or worse—the stories of the Starless Mages alone had been enough to wipe away any of Celestia's dreams of going to court when she was younger. Magic used to torture, the stories said, to murder. All at the behest of the Emperor. Supposedly the Emperor had even learned to keep the Airiana away from the palace.

Celestia turned the corner and found Alia waiting for her with a bouquet of red tasselflowers, still damp with rainwater. She sighed with relief.

"Here, m'lady," Alia said, plucking one of the flowers from the bouquet. She peered up at Celestia's hair. "Perhaps a crown styling?"

"Yes, perfect." Celestia glanced down the hallway. Around the corner waited the door to the drawing room, and inside the drawing room waited the emissaries of the emperor.

Alia stood on her tiptoes and waved the flower around. Celestia bent down, still looking to the end of the hallway. She couldn't hear anything—no voices, no laughter, no footsteps. Even the rain had stopped.

Alia hummed to herself, an old folksong of the poor, and one that Celestia had heard before. She couldn't say where. The melody was a haunting one, and it caught on Celestia's thoughts and stayed there. She did not like it as a backdrop to this meeting.

"There you are, m'lady," Alia stepped back and tilted her head. "Looks quite fetching, if I may be so bold."

"You may," said Celestia. "Did you bring a mirror?"

Alia reached into her pocket and produced the little round handheld mirror the cleaning girls were always using to admire their reflections. She held it up to Celestia and Celestia twisted her head right and left. Yes, the flowers did a good job of masking the wayward curls of her hair, and they matched the dress besides.

"Excellent work, Alia," Celestia said. "I'll ring if I need anything else."

Alia nodded and dropped the mirror to her side. Celestia turned and smoothed down her skirts. She took a deep breath.

And then she walked down the hallway.

Mr. Medulla was waiting outside the drawing room. He nodded as she approached and pulled the door open for her. A wisp of sweet-smelling smoke drifted out into the hallway. Celestia stepped inside.

There were two of them, both men. One was tall and thin, his thick black hair pulled back into a queue at the base of his neck. The other was older, and he wore his hair shorter, in the Nemia-Seraphine style. He was the source of the smoke, a cigarette burning between yellow-stained fingers.

"Lady De Malena," said the younger man, standing up to greet her. "My name is Juro, and this is my associate Anselm." He gestured at the older man, who tilted his head down. The cigarette burned white smoke. "We wish to speak to your husband. It's a matter of utmost importance to the empire."

Celestia watched him, trying to read his features for clues as to what could be so important that the emissaries traveled all this way. The older man was a blank: too well-trained for Celestia to read. He brought his cigarette to his lips and inhaled smoke.

"My husband oversees the work in the forest," Celestia said. "He'll be joining us briefly."

Juro nodded. Anselm smoked.

A knock at the door. Both men turned toward it, but it was Mr. Medulla who stepped inside, carrying a tray of sparkling mango drinks. He set it on the low-slung table in front of the sofa, bowed once, and then disappeared out into the hallway. Four drinks total. The men looked down at them, and Celestia reached forward and selected one and took a sip. "This is a Cross Winds specialty," she told them.

"Yes, your butler told us as much," said Juro. He picked up two cups and offered one to Anselm.

"I hope your travel was enjoyable."

"Yes," said Juro. "It was an uneventful trip, which is all we ask for. And the mountains are still warm this time of year."

"Of course." Celestia sipped from her sparkling mango. They would have traveled from the seat of the Empire, high up in the mountains, at the source of the Seraphine River. It was a difficult journey, even in the summer months.

Celestia's hand shook, the sparkling mango trembling in her cup. Two emissaries came all this way, traversing the same ancient path that had been built with the Emperor's palace a thousand years ago. Nothing ever changed in the mountains.

Anselm blew out a thick plume of smoke. It reminded Celestia of burning bougainvillea. "Your husband is taking his time, Lady De Malena."

Celestia put down her cup, grateful that she could steady her hand enough to set it smoothly against the table. "His work takes him deep into the forest, I'm afraid. I promise you he'll be here soon."

"It's rare for a lord to work his own land, isn't it?" said Juro.

"Yes." Celestia smiled. "But my husband is a rare man, as I'm sure you know, and he worked on an acreage like Cross Winds as a child."

Juro raised an eyebrow over his cup. "I did not know that. Did you, Anselm?" He turned to his companion, who scowled through his haze of smoke. "I take it this was before he came under the Emperor's employ as an adventurer."

"*Long* before," she agreed with a smile.

"It wouldn't surprise me, though, to learn that your husband was a child adventurer." Juro swirled his cup around. "With the stories I've heard about him."

Celestia gave another polite smile, but her thoughts whirred wildly. Juro was not talking like a man about to arrest Lindon, although the same could not be said of Anselm, who had not touched his sparkling mango and continued to scowl through his smoke. Perhaps Juro only hoped to put her at ease—or perhaps she was being paranoid.

Footsteps thudded in the hallway outside the drawing room. Celestia took a deep breath and settled back into her chair. She recognized the clomp of those footsteps. They belonged to Lindon, Lindon and his heavy wooden-soled workboots.

The door swung open, and there stood Lindon, his clothes still sweat-stained from working in the forest. His hair fell loose from its queue, and mud clumped on his boots and streaked across the bottom half of his trousers. At least his hands were clean.

Juro and Celestia both stood up in greeting. Anselm, however, stayed seated, staring at Lindon through the smoke.

"Your associate is more polite than you are, Anselm,"

Lindon said as he settled into his chair. Celestia sank down beside him.

"You are not a true lord," Anselm said darkly. "As much as you may have begged for it."

Juro coughed uncomfortably, and Celestia sat ramrod straight, keeping her expression blank. She knew Lindon had been eager for a title—it was the reason he had taken her name. And she had long suspected it was his reason for adventuring for the Emperor. It appeared her suspicions were correct.

Lindon, for his part, ignored Amselm's barb. "Emissaries of the Emperor," he said flatly. "I am honored, even if you pulled me away from tending to the new avocado trees we're planting this season."

Juro leaned forward, his eyes bright. "Master De Malena, thank you for seeing us on such short—"

Lindon held up one hand. "Forgive me for my rudeness, but I would like to see your credentials before we proceed."

Anselm let out a sharp laugh. "Hurt your feelings that I won't my lord you, did it?"

Lindon glared at him. "I haven't forgotten the old procedures. As it seems you have."

"No, Master De Malena, you're completely correct." Juro shot a dark look at Anselm, who puffed derisively on his cigarette before reaching into his coat and extracting a narrow paper document. He handed it to Lindon, who unfolded it, angling his body toward Celestia. It was a letter of identification, but what Celestia noticed first was the alchemical seal, glowing at the bottom of the paper with a dark crimson light. It hurt her eyes to look at it for too long.

"Very good. Glad to see you haven't gone rogue, Anselm." Lindon folded the paper back into thirds and handed it to Anselm, who smirked at him. "Thank you, gentlemen. Now. What is it you wish to speak with me about?"

"A matter of grave importance," said Juro. "The Emperor wishes to retain your services again."

His forthrightness made Celestia blink. All her fears about arrests and wrong-doing evaporated away, replaced by a new fear, something harder to place. "Your services?" she asked. "But you're retired!"

Lindon put his hand on her knee. "I'm sure the man is prepared to explain."

"Yes, Master De Malena. My lady." He dipped his head at Celestia. "The matter concerns our friends and allies in Eiren. They have noticed a dark occurrence on their shores."

Dark occurrence. Celestia thought of Crell, eating his dinner like a proper gentleman, telling her of a dead boy walking toward him through the snow.

"The land is changing again. Dramatically."

Celestia tensed. Changing? That seemed less concerning than what Crell had told her.

"It's winter there," Juro continued, "and yet beneath the snow, plants flower as if it's the middle of summer." Juro hesitated. Anselm just kept puffing on his cigarette, the smoke swirling thick around the ceiling of the drawing room. The scent was making Celestia woozy.

"If you'll recall your history lessons on the Last War," Juro said, "its beginning was marked by similar dramatic shifts in the Eirenese landscape."

Celestia felt dizzy.

"They have mages," Juro said, "who monitor the signs. And they believe these changes—" He did not look at Lindon or Celestia but off to the side, to one of the oil paintings of the forest hanging on the wall. "—are a portent. Of the return of Lord Kjari."

The last part he said in one rushed breath. It was met with a numb silence.

"Lord *Kjari?*" said Lindon.

Juro nodded.

"Are the mages of Eiren aware the man has been dead for five hundred years?" He laughed. "Are they aware they won the war? How long have these mages been cloistered away, exactly?"

Juro shifted uncomfortably. Celestia felt some pity for him, that he'd been ordered by the Emperor to make such an absurd claim.

"Tell me," Celestia said, making eye contact with him. "Do the mages have—proof of some sort?"

"These mages are specially trained to monitor for Lord Kjari's return," Juro said.

Lindon snorted. "Eiren," he muttered. "It's been five hundred years."

"It's one of many tasks they see to in the Eirenese kingdom," Juro said defensively. "Passing down everything learned about Lord Kjari during the war. These are scholars trained to look for the subtlest shifts in the Aetheric Realm. They know far more than you and I. And these changes in the landscape, they aren't natural."

Juro took a deep breath, but Anselm interrupted before he had a chance to continue. "It's not just the Eirenese mages," he said.

Celestia blinked in surprise, but Lindon physically recoiled, and his hand squeezed at Celestia's knee. "Don't tell me you're talking about—"

"The Starless Mages," said Anselm. He smiled through his smoke. "Still so skittish about them, Lindon."

Lindon said nothing. Anselm turned to Celestia.

"As I'm sure you're aware, my lady, the Starless Mages have an—affinity with the darker magics." His cigarette had burned down to an ember and he dropped it in the glass ashtray resting on the end table. The smoke still hadn't dissipated, though, and it hung in heavy clouds in the room. "Lord

Kjari's presence affected the Seraphine during his reign as it did Eiren. Not to the same extent, of course. But the after-effects of his tremendous magics changed the composition of the water, the habits of the animals, even the structure of the Aetheric Realm itself."

"And they're seeing those same after-effects?" asked Celestia.

Anselm fixed her with a dark look. A beat passed. "Yes," he said. "The Starless Mages have reported an unusual under-current in their magic. It seems to be affecting the Aetheric Realm."

"Lord Kjari is returning," said Juro. "There's no point in debating it. And that puts the Emperor in a dreadful bind. Obviously he does not wish to fight for his seat, but there's also the matter of our relationship with Eiren."

"Of course," said Lindon.

"If Lord Kjari does return, then the Empire must prove that our loyalties remain with Eiren, not the Dark One. We can't afford to refight a war from half a millennia ago."

Celestia thought of her studies on the Last War—a misnomer, of course, but at the time the world remained convinced that a war of that magnitude signaled an end to all wars to come. History had never terribly interested her, but she knew what all children of the Seraphine did: After the shattering of the Eiren peninsula into uninhabitable islands, the Eirenese blamed the infamous mage Lord Kjari. When Eiren marched southward to bind him, Lord Kjari gathered the nations of the south, before they were united as the Seraphine, to serve as his armies.

Millions of lives were lost in that war. It was said even now that Lord Kjari was a mage of immeasurable power, a conse-quence of unfettered magic. Eventually, he'd been defeated and driven away by some Eirenese hero, and the world set about the matter of repairing itself. The Academy was established to monitor all magic users. The Imperial family rose to power.

And now Eiren and the Seraphine were allies. These days, it was Aesri that was of concern, lurking in the west.

"What exactly do you want me to do?" Lindon asked.

Anselm reached into his jacket and extracted a cigarette case of burnished silver. He removed one of his cigarettes. Celestia moved to offer him a match, but he lit it with a snap of his fingers, some alchemist's party trick that left the scent of sulfur on the air.

"Lord Kjari cannot rise again," he said.

"Of course not," said Lindon. "No one wants to go to war, like he said." He tilted his head toward Juro.

"It's not just a matter of going to war with Eiren," said Anselm, "but of maintaining their allyship. We cannot, at this juncture, afford to lose them as—" A pause as he inhaled on his cigarette and then blew out smoke. "—as trading partners. Allowing Lord Kjari to rise shows bad faith on the part of the people of the Seraphine."

Lindon was still squeezing Celestia's knee. Lord Kjari! It was fanciful, this idea of him returning from the dead. A story told at the solstice festival, to send children shrieking and running into the darkness. But those men carried the alchemical seal of the Emperor. Celestia did not believe that they would lie.

"The Emperor sent us to you with an offer to return to his service," said Juro.

"I'm retired," Lindon said.

Anselm laughed sharply and inhaled the smoke from his cigarette. For a moment, Celestia wished she had Izara's disdain for propriety so she could say something biting. Or at least scowl at him.

"He's only asking you to complete this one assignment," Juro said. "Not seeking to keep you on retainer, as he did before."

Lindon tilted his head, and Celestia knew, with a sinking dread, that he was interested.

"If you accept our Emperor's offer," Juro said, "you will join with three Eirenese warriors to root out Lord Kjari and destroy him before he can gain control of the Seraphine a second time. You will be paid handsomely for your service, although neither I nor Anselm nor the Emperor himself can say how long this journey will take you. We cannot make any guarantees to your safety." Anselm bowed at Celestia. "For that I must apologize, my lady. I am sorry to take your husband away from you, but it's a matter of the Seraphine's survival."

Silence filled the room like the smoke from Anselm's cigarettes. Celestia was dizzy. She dropped her hand to her stomach without thinking. She was so close to providing an heir to Lindon's fortune and to Cross Winds both—what if she lost the baby, this small treasure that had taken her four years to unearth? She could only pray the Airiana wouldn't be so cruel.

"That's a big request," Lindon said.

Juro bowed his head apologetically, but Anselm just sucked on his cigarette and said, "It's nothing you can't handle, so stop pretending to dwell on it. There's no time for delay. The Eirenese warriors should have already arrived at the Imperial palace by now. You will need to leave today."

This time, Lindon did respond. His mouth opened and closed like a fish.

"Today?" whispered Celestia.

"Yes, my lady," said Juro. "We can't delay any more than we already have."

"May I talk to my wife about it?" Lindon asked, finally finding his voice. "She's landed gentry, that gives her some say in matters of the Empire—"

"I'm aware," said Anselm. "Else she would not have been allowed to stay as we explained the situation."

Celestia felt hot. A matter of grave importance, Juro had said at the very beginning. One that would take her husband away from her just as she entered into a pregnancy. Her husband gone, her sister gone—

A dark villain returning to the world.

She trembled. Did she really believe it, this story about Lord Kjari rising to power again?

"Gentlemen," she said. "Would you mind giving me a moment alone with my husband?"

"Yes," Lindon said quickly. "Please."

He was distracted. His eyes had a gleam to them, the same glean they took on whenever he told stories about his old adventures.

The two emissaries looked at each other. "Yes," said Juro, "that would be fine."

"But don't take long," said Anselm. "If we don't have your answer before sunset, we're riding off without you. Which," he added, blowing smoke, "you know is ill-advised."

"You're our first choice, Master De Malena," said Juro. "It would be difficult to travel to ask your replacement—"

Lindon waved his hand to stop Juro. "Understood. But please, let me speak to my wife."

The emissaries both nodded, stood, and shuffled out of the room. Anselm's smoke lingered on the air, sticking fast in Celestia's lungs. She looked at Lindon. He had already made up his mind. She couldn't even feel disappointed, because this decision was so expected of him.

"Please don't die," Celestia said.

Lindon laughed. "We all die eventually, my dear."

"I mean when you're on this assignment. Come back to us." She laid her hand on her stomach and Lindon's expression softened.

"Cellie, we can talk about this—"

"There's nothing to talk about." She wasn't angry, only

resigned, and her voice came out clear and earnest. "You had decided to go the moment they told you why they were here."

Lindon reached over and smoothed a wayward lock of hair away from her face. "The flowers," he said, "are a nice touch."

"I'm glad you noticed." Celestia turned toward the window. It looked out on the forest, shaped and molded by the De Malena family for fifty generations, long before Lord Kjari and his dark spells, long before the war that devastated half the world. "I can attend to matters here on my own. The forest workers don't *need* you working alongside them, and I can bring in a property manager to aid with the technicalities." She took a deep breath. "I'm quite capable of caring for myself, you know."

"Of course you are," Lindon said. "But the baby. You're a noblewoman, not some peasant who can handle all manner of misery. You *have* to rest, or else the baby will come out all wrong. Anxious and worried."

Celestia's hand dropped to her stomach. "Yes, well," she said, "the servants can worry for me."

Lindon fell silent. He looked out into the drawing room, and Celestia wondered what he saw exactly. He was not a man suited to this drawing room and never had been, no matter how badly he wanted a nobleman's title.

And of course there was the fact that his reasons for marrying her had not entirely been his own—but that was a secret she kept close to her heart. No one needed to know about her trip down the Seraphine five years ago, or her walk through the Lady's enchanted forest. Or the promise of a debt.

"Go," said Celestia. "If you need my permission, you have it. But I know this is what makes you happy."

Lindon looked back at her. "You make me happy, too, you know."

"Not in the same way." Celestia leaned forward and pressed her hands against his cheeks. "I'll be fine here, my darling, and all I ask is that you return to us."

"I've always walked away safe after an adventure," Lindon said.

"You don't have to walk away," said Celestia. "You can crawl back here on missing legs. I just want you to come home."

Then she kissed him, a fierce and protective kiss. Most days, she didn't know if she truly loved him, but today, in the smoky drawing room, a five-hundred-year-old threat looming on the horizon, she was certain she did.

THREE

zara followed the rocky path down to the public entrance of the Academy. The path was steep enough that steps had been carved into the rocks years ago, and she had to be mindful of the moss that grew over them, since it caught the morning dews and made the path slippery and treacherous. The mountain dropped off only a few paces to her left, into an enormous gorge filled with mist and tree canopies. It was the most dangerous path at the Academy—the walkways between the dormitories and the classrooms were fairly level and much wider, with tall stone fences to keep students from falling to their deaths. But picking your way down to the public entrance was terrifying. Even after three years, Izara still felt dizzy and unsure of her steps.

She'd heard the theories, whispered at night in the dormitories, that the Academy purposefully set the public entrance lower on the mountain, accessible only by a slippery, narrow path, as a way of discouraging students from visiting the public square there. Izara could believe it. The square was their link to the outside world, however tenuous that may be—the postal service had an office, and brave merchants would carry up sweets and trinkets to sell. Occasionally the tailor from the nearest village, nearly two days' travel away, would show up with bolts of fabric and a pair of shears, and students would rush down to the square for a chance to have coats and dresses and boots made, fine clothes to supplement the plain off-white uniforms of the Academy. Izara had no interest in clothes or jewelry—that sort of thing she left to her sister— but she had been known to brave the path for a chance at a box of bittersweet chocolates or sugared dolls.

Today, though, she didn't expect to find sweets waiting for her in the square.

The wind picked up, damp from the rains in the forest below, and she tensed and straightened her posture. The stone steps spiraled down. She wasn't close enough to see the gates of the square yet.

"Curse this wind," she muttered, moving closer to the flat edge of the mountain. Dirt swirled out with the wind, and a few pebbles fell in her path. She kept moving. A letter was waiting for her in the square. A coincidence, she suspected, from the blood elemental magic she had worked in High Mage Papazian's office last week. That magic had been haunting her, sending her uneasy dreams in the middle of the night. She missed her sister.

And now there was a letter.

It was a fluke that she even knew about it—another coincidence of the magic, most like. She had been applying some of her alchemical formulas in the laboratory when Nova and Heath came in, their arms wrapped around each other, giggling. They hadn't seen her at first, and Nova pushed Heath up against the wall and kissed him, her hand trailing down to the belt of his trousers. At that point, Izara had chimed a stirring rod against one of her beakers, and Heath and Nova pulled apart, their faces flushed and embarrassed.

"Oh," said Nova. "Hi, Izara."

They lived in the same dormitory, although Izara had never been friendly with her. Izara wasn't really friendly with anyone at the Academy.

"I'm working," said Izara, and gestured towards her stack of formulas. The soothing algorithms of alchemy had been the only thing to help her forget Decay's magic.

Nova grinned. "I'm not. By the way, love, Cas said they had a letter for you in the square. Lucky!" She'd grabbed Heath's hand and pulled him out of the laboratory, and their laughter had echoed down the hallway.

A letter. Letters were a rare sight at the Academy. Izara had cleaned up her work and immediately set out for the square. She hoped the coincidence brought forth by her spell would be a positive one. Sometimes they were. Sometimes they weren't.

The path twisted, revealing a flash of red up ahead—the gate. Izara sighed. Finally. She moved a bit more quickly now that the end was in sight. It was less steep here anyway. Izara passed through the gate and walked to the post office. It was strange to see the square so empty, without the bustle of students and the crush of merchants in their rickety, brightly colored carts. It looked abandoned, really, the sort of place haunted by ghosts.

The post office was a small clapboard hut sitting in a patch of pale grass. Izara stepped inside. Cas looked up from behind the counter, where he had been scribbling something on a sheet of paper. He was a student at the Academy, one of the older ones who had already begun to make his connections with the mage guilds of the Seraphine, looking for work.

Supposedly that was why he tended to the post office, because he could build connections from behind the counter.

"I'm Izara De Malena," she said, breathless from the hike down. "I was told you have a letter for me."

Cas blinked at her. His eyes were veiled from his soul being half in the Aetheric Realm, which made them bigger and darker than normal eyes. It was unnerving to look at him.

"I do," he said. "Wait here."

He leaned down from the counter and pulled out a reed-woven basket. It contained two letters, and Cas extracted one and handed it to her. She immediately flipped it over to look at the return address.

Celestia! Something good had come out of dabbling in Decay's realm after all.

Izara smiled, then glanced up at Cas, who was watching her with those eerie veiled eyes. She nodded once at him and then stepped back out into the cool wind of the square. She looked down at the letter again, at the neat script of Celestia's name. Izara ripped the envelope open and pulled out the letter. It was longer than usual, three pages of Celestia's delicate handwriting. Izara sat down in the cradle of branches at the base of the lone polylepis tree growing in the square. She read about Aurelia De Linza's touring visit, a tradition she had never experienced herself, partially so Celestia could use the money for her own touring visit but mostly because Izara would have been awful at it. She read about a visit from a group of adventurers—Celestia glossed over that, the way she always did. And then Izara found a line that made her eyes widen.

I'm pregnant, sister.

The letter fluttered in Izara's hand, paper snapping like a sail. Celestia was finally pregnant. Marriage, Izara thought, was like an alchemical transmutation. The right elements need only be introduced to change a person entirely. A baby, an heir: that was the last step of the process, the drop of crystallized smoke in a cauldron of prepared ice, turning water to fire.

Celestia had signed her name with a big flourish after the usual pleasantries, but then added an addendum to the letter, which was unlike her:

P.S. Lindon will be going away for several months, on business.

An odd thing for Celestia to add. Izara squinted at it. Ah, sure enough: the paper around the writing was distorted, wrinkled and thin. Izara lifted the letter to her nose and sniffed it. The paper smelled of copper. Celestia's addendum had been corrected by the Academy.

Izara sighed and skimmed back through the rest of the letter, to see if there was anything else that had been altered. No, only the bit about Lindon leaving. Izara wondered what had been there originally. Something important enough that Celestia would tack it on after her signature. Izara flipped back to the addendum. The distortion in the paper was large, almost half the page. Izara touched her fingers to it and felt that faint electric prickle that meant magic had occurred here. A powerful magic, one that neither Izara nor any of the students of the Academy could undo. It had happened to all their letters, however rare they were. Certain things they were not allowed to know. And the letters they wrote, on the designated days—it was the same thing. The Academy's magic sifted through their words and found the secrets and burned them out of the paper itself.

Izara folded the letter into thirds and tucked it into the envelope. A mystery, but it would have to wait until her time here was done, until she could see her sister again.

It didn't matter. Living and working at the Academy, Izara was used to mysteries. Particularly the unsolvable kind.

Izara stepped through fog, breathing in its acrid, charred-meat scent. Shadows moved in the distance, too distorted for her to see them clearly—denizens of this place, shadow-spirits who who moved parallel to any visitors and never showed their visages. Izara wasn't interested in them. She was interested in the stars spreading up in the black sky overhead, dotted in patterns that could unravel reality. She lay back, staring at them until her eyes watered, running the patterns she'd already teased out through her head. *Five by seven. Find the sine of thirty-seven. Solve for* x. *Solve for* x *and find the logarithmic function—*

"Have you worked out any of those formulas yet?"

Izara plummeted backwards through fog and emptiness and slammed into the light. It took her a moment to place herself, to pull away from her trance and reunite with the physical world instead of the Aetheric Realm: she was in Alchemist Vinsant's classroom. Pale sunlight filtered through the dusty windows. Only a few of the tables were occupied, students hunched over their own work. The Academy taught by expecting its students to *do*, and so each student was assigned a portion of an instructor's personal project as their practicum. None of them, save the instructor, knew the whole, and the instructors all seemed to delight in keeping them in the dark.

Alchemist Vinsant loomed over Izara, his arms crossed over his chest, his expression stern.

"Ah," started Izara, and looked down at the work she had done in the trance. Her handwriting was spiky and unfamiliar.

"You need to work on coming out of your trances quickly," Alchemist Vinsant said. "This delay is amateurish, the sort of thing you'd expect from a traveling mage." He tapped his foot. "Well?"

Izara rubbed her head. The physical world solidified around her, flat and dull in comparison to the Aetheric Realm, that place where knowledge dwelled. "Almost," she said.

"Almost?" Alchemist Vinsant raised one of his bushy white eyebrows. "Almost won't dismantle the fire-globes of Risidor. Or halt a shape-shifter before he slips out of your grasp." Alchemist Vinsant leaned down, peering at her work. Izara pressed herself against the back of her chair and held her breath. She *had* been close, before Alchemist Vinsant interrupted her and dragged away from the Aetheric Realm. The solution had shimmered on the horizon, just out of her grasp—

Alchemist Vinsant harrumphed and straightened up. "This is solid work, Lady De Malena."

Izara suppressed a smile—even that, Alchemist Vinsant would see as gloating, which he notoriously despised—and tilted her head down. "Thank you, Alchemist." The formula he had assigned her was one that had already made the rounds among his older students. It was rumored to be impossible, although Izara had recognized that it wasn't nearly three weeks ago. And she had been *so close*—

Underneath her desk, she wrapped her hands up in the fabric of her skirt, squeezing as tight as she could so she wouldn't say something she regretted.

"You're close," Alchemist Vinsant said.

I know, she thought.

He nodded. "I expect to see this solved within the next few days, Lady De Malena."

As if no fewer than five of the older students had told her he was punishing her, assigning her this particular formula.

"Yes, Alchemist," she said. She looked down at her work again. Read through her calculations. It was a matter of light, that was the trick, if she could only—

The bells at the dormitory clanged, jarring Izara out of her own head.

"Well, there it is," called out Alchemist Vinsant, stepping away from Izara's table. The other students were already shuffling their papers together. "Another opportunity to prove yourselves, and another day when you all choose food over intellectual enlightenment."

Izara sighed. Dinnertime. If she stayed here to work she wouldn't get to eat again until breakfast. She looked down at her calculations again, at the unfamiliar handwriting, the handwriting of one possessed. Could she get that deep into the Aetheric Realm again before bedtime? She didn't think so.

Izara slid her papers together into a neat a stack.

"Ah, you too, Lady De Malena?" Alchemist Vinsant glanced over at her. "I would have expected more from you."

"I'm afraid I'm hungry," said Izara, not meeting his eye. The other students left the stable together, their voices ringing out excitedly. In her three years, Izara had never left a stable like that.

Alchemist Vinsant made a show of rolling his eyes. "The restrictions of the physical world. If only we could survive on knowledge alone. Very well." He shooed her away with one hand. "But remember, Lady, I expect to see that solution in three days."

"I remember." Izara tucked her work into her bag and slung it over her shoulder. Alchemist Vinsant had turned away from her and wondered over to the windows, where he stared out at the overgrowth of trees and vines with his hands shoved in his pockets. Izara slipped out of the stable without saying anything more. Alchemist Vinsant wasn't much for courtesies, and in truth, neither was Izara.

The bells were still clanging, echoing out off the side of the mountain. Izara had dawdled enough that the paths were mostly empty now, with only a few stragglers up ahead, bounding into the warm glow of the dormitory's entrance. Izara could smell the smoke from the cooking fires, and above that, something pungent and spicy that probably meant they were serving curry today.

She ambled down the path. Her thoughts were still half in

the Aetheric Realm, still grasping at the formula she had come close to solving. Alchemy was the most exquisite of the magics, at least according to alchemists, because it required effort from all subjects in order to be understood. Maths and astronomy and philosophy all bowed at the feet of alchemy. Izara wasn't so convinced. The more she studied at the Academy, the more convinced she became that alchemy was in fact not understandable by humans, at least not completely, and that maths and astronomy and philosophy only gave them glimpses, like dappled sunlight falling in pieces through the thick foliage of the forest.

It began to rain.

Izara stopped, blinking in surprise. Rain? The sun had been shining only seconds ago—and in fact, it was still shining, even as the rain fell in thick sheets, obscuring the path and the dormitories up ahead.

"My papers!" Izara gasped, and she bolted forward, drawing the knapsack up close to her body. If the ink got wet, it would run.

The dormitory was a dark smear up ahead. Izara raced down the path as fast as she could. Rain pounded at her back and dripped into her eyes.

And then her foot caught on a loose stone in the path, and she fell.

She fell, and she kept falling.

At first, Izara could not register what was happening. The paths here were protected by stone fences and protective magic. No one fell off the side of the mountain.

And yet she was, right now. She was falling.

The rain fell with her, in long silvery streams. Izara screamed and the water fell into her mouth, tasting of silt and metal, like the Seraphine. Her knapsack slid off her shoulder and flew upwards, and her papers fanned out on the air, fluttering like birds.

Horror grasped at her stomach, stronger than the horror of dying.

"No!" she screamed, and then she slammed hard on the ground.

The world flickered. For a moment Izara couldn't breathe, and she rolled over onto her hands and knees and wheezed. The rain poured around her, puddling in patches on the ground. Izara looked up. She thought she saw the lights of the dormitory floating above her, half-buried in the vegetation on the side of the mountain.

Where *was* she?

Izara took a deep breath and pushed herself up to standing. She wobbled in place, her knees knocking up against each another. If she had fallen, she should have fallen farther than this, into the tangle of polylepis trees in the gorge. She should have died.

Maybe she had died.

Izara turned slowly, taking in her surroundings through the curtain of rain. She was in some sort of clearing. The ground was covered in thick black soil, like the sort you found on the forest floor, away from the mountain.

The rain water rushed over that black soil, forming a dark rivulet that flowed into the hazy trees in the distance. Izara followed it with her eyes, a tightness growing in her chest. Her ears buzzed. She could feel something in that river, the sharp charge of magic—not alchemical magic and not elemental magic. It was a magic she hadn't felt since she left the Seraphine Basin when she climbed up the side of the mountain in order to reach intellectual enlightenment.

"No," she whispered.

She stumbled backwards. The rain fell harder, the little river rushed faster. It was as dark as the Seraphine.

"No," Izara whispered. "No, please, no, no—"

The rain-river churned. Raindrops danced and jumped, higher and higher, until they began to move in unnatural ways, twining over and under one another, like a current flowing up instead of sideways.

Izara slipped on a patch of mud. Stumbled. Rainwater flowed into her eyes.

"Daughter of the Seraphine," said a voice in the rushing of the rain.

Izara cried out, then clapped her hand over her mouth. A hundred half-forgotten memories bubbled into the surface. A riverboat gliding through the black night. The lights of the forest guiding them closer and closer. A name. A *name*—

"Taja," gasped out Izara.

The woman in the water laughed. Her features flashed silver. "That will not work a second time, Daughter," she said. "You still owe me a debt."

Izara closed her eyes. She gasped at the air, trying to breathe, but it was as if she were being dragged down to the bottom of the Seraphine. The debt.

I will do anything, Celestia had said, sitting at the rickety table where they were eating overripe mangos from the untended forest. Her eyes had burned like the sun. Izara had been hungry, her stomach grumbling even though Celestia had given her one of her own mangos. *We need wealth. I will not let your talent go to waste. I won't let our* home *go to waste.*

The Lady of the Seraphine moved through the rain. Izara wanted to run but she was too petrified, and she knew she couldn't run, not in this choking rain. The Lady moved closer. She stopped a few handswidths away, close enough that Izara could see the forest on the other side of her, magnified by the water and the sunlight.

"You cannot let your debt lapse," the Lady said.

Izara found her voice. "I know," she whispered. Her tears fell with the rain.

"There is a fault line running through the center of the world," the Lady said. "A weakness that men from the north think they can repair. But they cannot. They will only shatter existence into pieces."

Izara trembled. "I don't understand."

"You will, in time. For now, you must leave the Academy."

Izara gasped in horror.

"I have brought you past their magic. You are free to leave unnoticed."

"No," Izara said without thinking.

The Lady tilted her head. "That is not an option, my Daughter. You must leave the Academy and sail downriver, to the Port of Istai-Seraphine."

Izara thought about her work, lost on the side of the mountain. She thought about the impossible formula she had almost solved. She thought about her future.

Gone, it was all gone.

"And that will fulfill the debt?" Izara said. "To give up the Academy?"

The Lady stared at her. "That is not the payment," she said. "The payment will be explained to you in Istai-Seraphine, with the others. I cannot speak freely here. Follow the water," and here the rain-river lit up in a spray of light, "to the Os'an River. You will find a boat waiting for you. It will take you to the Seraphine."

Izara shook her head. "I can't make that journey alone," she said. "Not without weapons, or food—"

"You will be protected," the Lady said. "As long as you stay on the water, you will be protected and fed."

Izara wrapped her arms around herself. She had known the cost of speaking the Lady's name and asking for a favor. But she had been young, and she hadn't understood it. Not really.

This was why no one should call up on the Airiana to work magic. The aristocracy thought far too highly of themselves that they had convinced themselves it was safe. But it wasn't.

Maybe Celestia's letter had not been the magical coincidence after all. Maybe this was, the Lady demanding her favor at the onset of Celestia's pregnancy.

"You know what will happen if you refuse," the Lady said. "You who spoke my name."

Izara nodded. Despite the waterfall of rain, her throat was as dry as the desert. When she uncovered the name in that ancient archive, she had uncovered the stories, too. Men compelled to drink water until it poisoned them. Men washed away by the river and devoured by shark-fish. Men drowned by rain.

"Go," the Lady said. "We must hurry, before the northern men break the world."

Izara couldn't move. She thought about Alchemist Vinsant's stable, the wooden desk where she worked her formulas and fell into her trances.

"Go!" screamed the Lady, her voice like the Emperor's Falls. "The debt must be repaid!"

Her voice pounded in Izara's ears. All thoughts of the Academy vanished.

Izara knew she had lost.

After Lindon's departure, a pallor fell over Cross Winds, although Celestia suspected it was her imagination: a melancholy from having to face her pregnancy without a husband. The enormity of the situation had first slammed into her as she watched Lindon depart up the river. He left on the emissaries' elegant Imperial boat, flags snapping in the wind. Night had fallen, a thick inkiness that seeped out of the trees. Lindon had stood at the railing, the crimson glow of the boat's engine illuminating him from behind. He raised one hand in goodbye. He was cast into silhouette by the fire, and so Celestia could not see his face as the boat pulled away—could not tell if he was sad or wistful or, more likely, thrilled.

In many ways, the everyday routines of the acreage continued uninterrupted. Like most high-profile adventurers, Lindon was a shrewd businessman, and so the forest-worker's labor ran like clockwork. The morning after Lindon's departure, Celestia dressed in cream-colored linen and heavy work boots and marched down to the forest-workers' village. They were only just beginning to stir, the breakfast cooking-fires just beginning to ignite. The air was already warm and muggy. As Celestia picked her way down the footpath, children burst out of one of the houses, their hair long and uncombed. They clutched chalkboards to their chests—they must be on their way to the village school.

Celestia smiled at the sight of them. They laughed and shrieked as they bounded to the tree-top house where classes were held. Celestia had hired the teacher herself, when they opened the school a year and a half ago, a new addition to the estate. She was the wife of a local merchant, clever and well-educated, and Celestia intended to send her child to her once she was old enough. A bit modern, but Celestia didn't mind being daring on occasion.

Celestia walked down to the village center. Faces appeared in the doorways as she passed, and whispers followed her through the village. She kept her head high, although inside she began to quake with anxiety. She hated to tell them that Lindon was gone. Perhaps she should work in the forests, alongside the workers, as Lindon had. But she had no knowledge of forest agriculture, no sense of when to prune back vines or where to plant amaranth to avoid overcrowding. Even when she and Izara had lived on the estate after their parents had died, stretching out the little remaining money as best they could, she had not been able to make the forest thrive the way Lindon had. She and Izara had eaten what they could find, harvesting from the outer edge of the forest, which at the time had spilled over onto the abandoned workers' village. It had been unrecognizable then.

Gregori was waiting for her at the dais at the village square. He waved when he saw her, and called out, "So you made it after all, my lady."

"Of course I did." Celestia stopped at the foot of the dais and smiled up at him. Lindon might be a shrewd businessman, but he still needed a man like Gregori, who possessed knowledge of the law and a keen financial sense. Gregori would keep the acreage running in Lindon's absence, although Celestia wanted to be at least partially involved. Not enough to affect the baby, of course, but enough that she would be aware of what was happening at Cross Winds.

The forest rustled around them, and Celestia could hear the monkeys shrieking in the distance and the birds calling out to one another. The sun poured down through the clearing. Already Celestia was starting to sweat.

Gregori checked his watch. "The morning bells will be ringing soon. Are you sure you'd like to make the announcement yourself?"

"Quite certain, thank you." Celestia stepped up onto the dais and turned to look at the square. It was covered with a thick, soft grass, as green as the forest. The path meandering through it was paved with white river stones. Lovely work, really.

Gregori flipped through the portfolio he'd carried out here with him, peering at it over the top of his glasses. It was too narrow to be a ledger.

"What are you reading?" Celestia asked.

Gregori glanced at her, then laughed. "Oh, nothing you need to worry about, my lady."

"Does it pertain to the acreage?"

Gregori blinked. A bead of sweat dripped down his temple. "Well, yes, of course—"

"Then it *is* something I need to worry about."

Gregori sighed, and Celestia prickled with annoyance that Gregori was so old-fashioned.

"I trust Lindon told you that I am to have final say on all business decisions in his absence?"

"Well, yes, of course." Gregori smiled thinly at her. "But surely, as lady of the house, you aren't interested in river rights—"

"Let me see the documents." Celestia held out one hand. It wasn't that she didn't *trust* Gregori, only that she took her duties quite seriously. If she let him keep this matter of river rights from her, he might find it beneficial to keep other matters from her as well, which was the sort of thing Celestia wanted to avoid. After all, Cross Winds was her ancestral home, not Lindon's. For the past four years, Celestia had tracked the progress of Cross Winds by cajoling Lindon to speak of its prospects as they lay in bed together, or when they dined at breakfast. But those methods weren't available to her anymore. She needed to be more forthright, even if it perturbed Gregori.

"Of course, my lady." Gregori gave a little bow and handed the portfolio over. Celestia glanced over it. He was correct in that it was a minor issue, a few notes on the passage of small-time merchants on the stretch of river in front of the acreage.

The bells clanged. Celestia gave a little jolt, nearly dropping the portfolio. At the house, the bells were musical, charming—but this close they were riotous and wild, with no music or melody at all. Gregori grinned. "Surprise you, my lady?"

"I've heard them before." Celestia handed back the portfolio and checked the hem of her blouse. It was still tucked neatly into the waistband of her skirt. "Thank you for allowing me to look over the river rights."

"Was everything in order, my lady?"

"Yes, thank you." The forest-workers were peeling away from their houses, moving in ones or two. Many of them were still eating breakfast, beans and bites of roasted goat wrapped up in flat bread, or fresh fish, charred over a fire and still stuck to its cooking stick. They spoke with each other in low voices, eyes darting up toward Celestia. Every now and then a group would erupt into laughter.

The square did not take long to fill. Soon that vivid green grass was hidden by the steps of hundreds of muddy boots. Gregori stepped forward, lifted one hand in the air. Voices died away to a faint murmur.

"There's been a change," Gregori said, his voice booming out over the square. "Lord De Malena has been called away."

Celestia scowled at him. He glanced over his shoulder at her, gave a weak smile, and then turned back to the crowd. They were still eating, watching with a vague curiosity. "Lady De Malena is here to speak to you in his stead."

The voices rose a little at that. Celestia took a deep breath. She smiled out at the crowd. They did not smile back, only bit at their breakfast and watched her with guarded, dark eyes.

"Master Gregori is right," she said. "I'm afraid my husband has been called away by the Empire."

Now *that* got people's attention. The workers turned to each to her, voices swelling again.

"Is it permanent?" someone shouted, from the back.

"Oh, no." Celestia shook her head. "No, not at all. I'm afraid I can't say much more than that, but rest assured, Lord De Malena is doing important work for the good of the Empire. In the interim, however, the estate has been placed under my control." And here Celestia touched a hand to her chest and lowered her eyes. "With Master Gregori overseeing the particulars. I'm afraid I'm not qualified to work alongside you, as my husband did—"

Laughter at that, loud and a bit mocking, but Celestia swallowed back her irritation and smiled pleasantly, as if she were not aware she was being made into a joke. "However, I appreciate your work as much as my husband, and I hope this season is one of our most prosperous yet. With your help, it can be."

The crowd applauded politely around their breakfasts. Celestia stepped back and nodded at Gregori, who began listing off the day's focus: taro bushes, to fill in the empty spaces, the clearing of the overgrown pumpkin vines. Celestia hardly registered what he said. Her heart thudded in her chest. She wasn't a woman of the people, the way her husband was. But she had spoken to the workers, she had promised them prosperity. All workers at Cross Winds took home a percentage of the forest's yield along with their wages, so prosperity was not simply a reward for Celestia, sitting up in the house while others toiled over her forest.

The sun was yellow. The air was damp. Cross Winds grew wild and controlled around her.

It would still be here, as successful as ever, when her husband returned.

～

The candles guttered, throwing scatters of light across the pages of *A Martial History of the Seraphine and Surrounding Principalities*. The paper was so thin that Celestia had torn a few narrow rips in it already, lines cracking across the history of her homeland. She wasn't sure when the book had last been opened—when she had pulled it off the shelf, a cloud of dust had exploded out with it, coating Celestia's dress with a faint layer of grime and setting her to coughing.

She flipped the page and skimmed through the dense text. She understood perhaps half of what was written—the history had been published nearly two hundred years ago by an

Akuranian scholar and then later translated into Sera. Still, she was able to glean a general sense of things. Although the history went more in depth than her own cursory under-standing of the Last War (a term the author found quaint), the author seemed far more fascinated by military maneuvers and tactical strategies than he was Lord Kjari as a person. The closest he came was an aside about Lord Kjari's practice of meeting with the widows of the officers he killed in battle. *It is unclear why he requested these meetings, if one could call them that— the wives were typically dragged to Kjari's palace by a troop of kajani and kept there against their will until he could speak with them. The commonly held belief among the Eirenese upper command at the time was that these meetings were a method of intimidation, a threat of what would happen to the living commanders' wives when they died.*

And that was all he said of it. Not even a mention of what happened to those wives, what stories they told when the left Kjari's palace. If they were even allowed to leave.

Celestia sighed and dropped her head back, the book hanging open in her lap. A hot, balmy wind blew in through the open window, curtains billowing out like ghosts. She could smell the forest and the distant scent of smoke from the workers' village. She wondered how far along the river Lindon was now, if he even was on the river anymore, given the fineness of that Imperial boat. Perhaps they had already arrived at the base of the Emperor's Mountain.

Celestia flipped another page, although she was still looking over at the billowing curtains. The air had the heavi-ness she associated with impending rain. She looked back to the book. Blinked in surprise.

There was a *picture*.

A woodcut portrait, really, depicting a harsh-looking man with long hair worn loose around his shoulders. Celestia's heart fluttered. She picked up the book and peered at the caption.

Artist's representation of Lord Kjari on the Eve of the Battle of the Os'un.

The candlelight moved over the walls. Celestia's face felt hot. Her heart thudded more heavily in her chest. She stared at the portrait. The ink was pale and faded, but the image was still clear. Lord Kjari looked like a man. A cold man, perhaps, a hard man—the lines of his face were sharp and cruel, and even in this faded image of a woodcutting, his eyes seemed to glitter. But a man who could live for five hundred years? Even the greatest wizards in the world couldn't manage that sort of longevity, nor could they raise themselves from the dead. And Lord Kjari had died. That was how Eiren had won the Last War.

Celestia glanced at the text surrounding the portrait, but it was concerned with the Battle of the Os'un. Of course. Celestia looked over to the portrait again. Lord Kjari glowered up at her.

Not Lord Kjari, she thought. *Just an artist's idea of him.* She wondered if the portrait had been carved on the actual night of the battle, by an artist in Lord Kjari's presence, or if it was merely an Akuranian version of him, created three hundred years after the fact. Celestia suspected the latter. Although the fierceness of those eyes did give her a shiver of doubt.

The wind gusted, and the curtains flew out over the floor. A soft misting of rain scattered across Celestia's bed. She sighed and slid the book aside and then walked over to the window. The night was hazy, and the forest rustled, the rain just starting to fall. She reached up and tugged on the window latch.

Somewhere in the darkness, a voice said, *Stop.*

Celestia yelped and dropped her hand. The wind howled around her. *Lord Kjari,* she thought stupidly, *come to drag me off to his castle.* She felt enough like a widow, certainly.

The wind blew through the forest. Celestia stood very still next to the window frame, listening for the voice again. She grew less certain she had heard something—maybe it was just her imagination running wild. Maybe that dull old text had more of an impact than she'd thought.

The rain fell harder, a soft patter against the side of the walls. Water blew into her room. She sighed and reached up for the latch again.

This time, the voice was clearer.

Daughter of the Seraphine. It is time.

Celestia froze, her arm extended. *Daughter of the Seraphine.* She had not heard that phrase in years.

"Y-yes?" she called out, her voice soft and weak. She peered out the window, rain sprinkling over her face.

May I come in?

Celestia trembled. She had known this day would come eventually. She had asked for a service, and offered payment on credit. But she hadn't thought it would come when she was finally pregnant, when Lindon was out adventuring on behalf of the Emperor.

"No," she whispered, and she felt a revulsion in the pit of her belly. She could not say no to the Airiana. She lifted her voice out to the night. "You may come in." The rain was like a sheen of silver over the estate. Water puddled at her feet. "Please, I know I owe a debt."

No answer but the wind and rain. Celestia pulled away from the window and wrapped her arms around her waist. The baby. What if the Lady had come for her baby? She stumbled away from the window, over to her bed. The picture of Lord Kjari stared up at her from the open book, and she reached down and flipped it shut.

What would she tell Lindon, if he returned, and their baby belonged to the Lady of the Seraphine?

A rain puddle gleaming by the still-open window began to move, inching over her floor, leaving a trail of wetness like a snail's.

"My Lady," Celestia whispered, pressing her hand against her stomach.

The water bubbled and then stretched, sliding up in a shining silver tower that slowly melted into the shape of a woman. It had been five years, but Celestia would never forget her face, nor the way her eyes burned when she looked too long upon it.

"Hello, Daughter of the Seraphine," the Lady said.

Celestia curtsied, dipping her head low. Her legs trembled.

"You owe me a favor," the Lady said. "I've already collected your sister."

Celestia jerked her gaze, meeting the Lady in the eye. It was haughty, impolite, but Celestia heard in the Lady's words a promise that her baby was safe, at least for the moment.

"I beg your pardon?" she whispered.

"I've collected your sister. She makes her way down my river now." The Lady smiled. She didn't stream water as she had that night on the tributary, but her skin was reflective like the river's surface, and Celestia could catch flashes of her own face: an eye, a corner of her mouth, a spray of black hair.

Celestia's eyes watered with pain, and she looked away.

"My sister was studying at the Academy," said Celestia, suddenly breathless. "She's not allowed to leave."

"But leave she must. She owes me a debt."

"No." Celestia shook her head. "No, that's not fair. It was *my* favor, and I should pay the cost." Just me, she added silently. Not Izara, not my baby.

"The three who stood before," the Lady said, "shall return my boon with a favor. I have need of a favor now."

"But did you have to—" Celestia threw up her hands in frustration. Izara's education at the Academy was one half of the reason they had defaulted to asking the Lady for aid at all. Celestia's dream was to see Cross Winds restored to glory; Izara's was to study with the scholars in the mountains. With a wealthy husband, they could do both.

Celestia's face burned. Tears formed on the edges of her eyes. "That's not *fair*," she said. "You can't simply take her away from the Academy!"

The Lady tilted her head. "Do you deny my call?"

"Of course not!" cried Celestia. "I always fulfill my bargains." Her hand went to her belly, but she quickly dropped it at her side and squeezed it into a fist. "But the price you ask of Izara is too much."

"I gave you want you wanted," the Lady said. "And you promised payment. I'm extracting my payment. It is exactly what the favor was worth."

Celestia closed her eyes. The day Izara left it had been raining, the sky dark with clouds, and they had embraced under the veranda before Izara darted out to the riverboat waiting at the end of the dock. She had been smiling so brightly that her smile cut through the rain clouds. Celestia had never seen her look so happy.

But it was true: that moment had never been paid for.

"What is the favor to be?" Celestia asked, breathless.

"The same one I asked of your sister." The Lady smiled and the water of her form glowed murkily in the candlelight. "You will need to travel by boat to the Port of Istai-Seraphine, where I can speak freely. There, I will explain your debt in full, when you meet with the others."

A tightness caught in Celestia's throat. "Travel?" she said. "But I can't—my husband just left for Imperial business, and I have to stay to run the acreage." She put her hand on her belly. "And—"

"And you're with child, yes." The Lady tilted her head. "You will have my protection on the water, Daughter of the Seraphine. As for your acreage—" She lifted one hand. Water slid down her forearm and dripped against the floor. "That is the business of the land. Not my concern."

Celestia took a deep breath. At least she had Gregori.

Lindon trusted him, so she supposed she did as well. It wasn't as if she had much choice. The Lady required a debt to be paid; Celestia would pay it. It would be like visiting Jaila-Seraphine for a season, she told herself. Gregori could manage the day-to-days. If anything, he'd prefer not to have her at home, demanding to be let in on the particulars.

"Prepare your boat," the Lady said. "You must leave at once."

Celestia nodded. She was trembling. A journey upriver, to meet the others. The others—Izara, of course. And the third. She didn't even remember his name, only that he had been from Akuran and the captain's first mate.

"Don't delay," the Lady said. "The northern men are coming."

The phrase snagged on Celestia's thoughts. "The northern men?" she said. "What do you—"

But the Lady splashed back into her puddle before Celestia could finish the question. Lindon was with northern men. It was too much of a coincidence, wasn't it, for him to be called away and then her only a few days later? An uneasiness grew in Celestia's belly. These were the sort of coincidences that came with magic. Izara had explained it to her once.

Izara had also told her what happened to those who denied the Airiana their requests. And so Celestia pulled open the drawers of the wardrobe and began pulling out clothing for the trip upriver.

~

Celestia planned to depart the next day, shortly after lunch. She wasn't certain if the Lady wanted her to slip away in the night, as Lindon had done, but unlike Lindon, Celestia had to see to the matter of the estate first.

She woke early the next morning, left offerings to Growth in the garden for the baby's protection, and skipped breakfast so she could thread down to the manager's bungalow where Gregori lived. The sun was just beginning to rise over the forest, and everything was tinted a pale pinkish green. She wore a simple cotton dress, appropriate for travel, as Alia would be packing her chosen pieces in a trunk soon enough. Celestia knocked on Gregori's door. She hoped she was early enough to catch him before he went down to the village.

Footsteps on the other side of the door. Celestia took a deep breath.

The door opened. Gregori blinked at her; he was already dressed for the day's work, but his hair was mussed and his cheeks were rough with stubble. "Lady De Malena," he stuttered. "I didn't expect to see you today."

"My apologies." Celestia smiled at him. "I'm afraid I need to speak with you."

Gregori nodded. "Would you like to come inside?" He pulled the door open wider and Celestia slipped inside. The bungalow was small and tidy, the air still cool from the previous night. "I was just making some coffee, if you would like any."

Celestia shook her head. "I'm afraid I don't have much time."

Gregori frowned.

"I will be leaving this afternoon. For a visit to Istai-Seraphine." Celestia spoke carefully, watching Gregori's face for a reaction.

"Istai-Seraphine?" Lines materialized in Gregori's brow. "But *why*, my lady?"

"I have some business to attend to there." Celestia had considered lying about her destination, but she wanted a place for Gregori to send communications if necessary. The port of Istai-Seraphine wasn't much of a tourist destination, to be sure. It wasn't much of a destination at all. "A friend," she added, "wishes me to visit her. She's fallen ill. A malignancy in her breast. I'm sure you understand."

"Oh, of course." Gregori fumbled around with his coat. "Yes, my lady, I do."

"I'll be leaving the acreage under your care." Celestia folded her hands in front of her. "I'm sure you'll do an excellent job. I hope to return before Lindon does, but I'm also not certain how long Lindon will be away, so perhaps not."

Gregori nodded. He was keeping himself calm and unflappable, which was an admirable quality.

"I'll write to you when I arrive at Istai-Seraphine," she said, "and let you know the best way to be in touch with me. I won't be staying with my friend."

"I see." Gregori gave no sign that he found this odd—and it was odd, for any friend of Celestia's should be familiar with the rules of hospitality, and as such would insist that Celestia stay with her. But Gregori was too polite to pry.

"I've asked the staff to close up the main wings of the house," Celestia added. "You won't need to worry about things in the house proper; the staff are equipped to run it on their own."

Gregori's brow wrinkled at this. "You're closing up the wings?" he asked. "How long do you think you'll be gone?"

Inwardly, Celestia cringed, but outwardly she only smiled at him, and gave a little tittering laugh. "I'm not certain, I told you! But I want to make things as easy on the staff as possible."

Gregori hesitated. Celestia gazed at him levelly, her heart thudding, waiting for him to protest, for him to ask a question she had not prepared for. But he only gave a quick, shallow bow and said, "Yes, my lady. That's quite thoughtful of you. I don't foresee any problems in the forest, not this time of year."

"I'm happy to hear that," Celestia said. "Now, I don't want to keep you from your coffee. I'll write to you as soon as I arrive. I'm sure you'll do wonderfully, Gregori."

Gregori smiled thinly. Celestia turned and ducked out of the house. When the door had closed behind her she stood on the porch and took a deep breath. The air was sticky and still, but the forest was alive, insects buzzing and monkeys shrieking, their cries echoing out against the sky. Celestia stepped off the porch. That was the matter of the acreage taken care of, then. Now she only had to see to the riverboat.

Like all of the great estates of the Seraphine, Cross Winds kept its own riverboat. This particular boat had been in the Da Malena family for two generations, a relic of the last days of her family's wealth. She hadn't the heart to get rid of it.

She walked to the boathouse even though it was on the edge of the estate. It was pleasant walking along the river despite the damp humidity of the air, and Celestia wanted a chance to see Cross Winds before she left to attend to the Lady's favor. The landscape had changed drastically in the time since Celestia had knelt on the ground and begged the Lady for a husband. The path was cleared and lined with stones, and the vines had been cut away from the trees, forming a tunnel through the forest that led down to the boathouse. The river sparked and flashed, and a boat slid silently past as Celestia walked, belching steam.

Cross Winds. Her home. She would see it again. Of that, Celestia was certain.

The path widened, revealing the boathouse through the trees. Adelric slammed out of the side door, waving his hand in greeting. "Lady De Malena!" he cried. "I heard you have need of my services."

"That I do." Adelric was an old acquaintance of Lindon's; he lived out here, keeping the riverboat in order and watching the telegram for reports of storms or flooding or animal attacks.

He bowed at Celestia, twisting his right hand in a flourish. "And I am happy to oblige. Where will we be sailing to?"

"The port of Istai-Seraphine." Celestia looked past the boathouse as she spoke, out at the river, wide and green in the sunlight.

"Istai-Seraphine?" Adelric made a choking sound that Celestia suspected was a strangled laugh. She shot him with a dark look. He pretended to cough into one hand. "Of course, my lady. Shame Master De Malena won't be able to accompany you."

"Yes," Celestia said, the sun shining into her eyes. "A shame."

"I'm still sore about not being able to take him upriver myself. All the way to the Mountain! Imagine that!" Adelric grinned. "Well, she's all fixed up for you, my lady. Ready to leave when you are." Adelric thumped against the side of the boathouse. "Just load her up and we'll be on her way." A shadow crossed over his face. Celestia stiffened; she knew a question she didn't want to answer was on its way.

"If you don't mind my asking," Adelric began, "who will be accompanying you? Just want to calculate the weight, of course."

"That won't be necessary," Celestia said. "I'll be making the trip alone."

Adelric's eyes widened. "Are you certain?"

"Yes." Celestia lifted her chin. She knew it wasn't proper, but the Lady expected only her to arrive at the port of Istai-Seraphine. "In fact, since I plan on staying for some time, I'll release you once we've landed."

Adelric blinked in surprise. "You know I don't mind waiting. Been to Istai before, back in your husband's adventuring days. A fine place for a bachelor." His grin vanished as quickly as it appeared. "I beg your pardon, my lady."

Celestia resisted the urge to roll her eyes. "I'm sure Cross

Winds is as fine a place for a bachelor as any. You'll return here after I'm settled. I'll send a message through telegram when I'm ready for the return trip."

She could see Adelric considering all this, rolling it around in his head. She could see the questions, the foremost of which must be *why*. Why would a landed lady travel alone? Why would she wish to be left in a place like the port of Istai-Seraphine, a place pirates were said to congregate? At least he didn't know about the baby; certainly that would engender even more questions. And Celestia had her answers. She just couldn't share them.

"I plan on leaving shortly after lunch," Celestia said. "Alia will bring my things once they're packed. How long will you expect the trip to take?"

The hot sun glared off the river. Adelric looked down at his feet, where he kicked at the dirt. "Three days," he said. "Unless we run into gridlock on the water."

Celestia nodded. Her heart was pounding. Three days. Three days until she learned what the price for all this—Lindon, her child, the acreage, the staff to pack her belongings, the house she was leaving behind—was going to cost her.

"It was fucking unnatural, I tell you." Ico paced back and forth across the shining floor of Xima's palace. His footsteps echoed and echoed and then vanished, the same as his voice. All that empty space had unnerved him when he first arrived here, after so long in the denseness of the Seraphine. "The man should have been dead. I've seen what cuts like that can do. And his were still seeping blood." He stopped and looked up at Xima, who had draped herself over her chair at the dining table, one leg dangling over the armrest. Her dress shimmered in the lights, the fabric so thin Ico could see her skin underneath it. Ordinarily the sight of her like that would have been enough for him to forget his troubles. But not today.

"What *is* it?" He stared at her, pleading. "Do you really think it's some Dark Lord?"

Xima frowned. "I don't know, my love."

"Which part?"

"What it is." She looked away from him. "Why it's here. I only know that you're safe, my north wind."

Ico pressed his hands over his eyes. Her words should have made him feel better but they didn't. The uncanniness of what he'd seen had burrowed itself into his memory. "The priests said you could tell me what's going on."

"The priests believe I am a goddess. But as I've told you, I'm not."

Ico sighed. He dropped his hands away from his face. Xima was watching him, her head tilted, her eyes dark with concern. She beckoned for him, one finger curling into a hook. He let himself be drawn forward. She straightened in her chair and Ico knelt before her and lay his head in her lap. She pushed a hand through his hair, her touch cold and comforting.

"You are safe," she said in a low voice. "The troubles of the outside world can't reach you within the confines of my palace."

"And when I leave your palace?"

Her hand kept raking through his hair, a rhythmic, soothing gesture. "Those troubles can't follow you here." She cupped his face with both hands and tilted it up toward her. She was dazzling as always, sunlight bouncing off snow. For a moment Ico was overwhelmed with his desire.

"And I won't send you away again, my north wind," she said. "Not until this matter has been settled."

Ico dropped his head in her lap. He kept thinking about

the red blossoms of blood on the priest's robe, and the house overgrown with the vines in the dead of winter. He kept thinking about the desperation in the priest's voice as he commanded Ico to send word to Xima, and yet she knew nothing of it. He hadn't expected anything to come of that dark lord nonsense—the Eirenese were always yammering about dark lords. Some seismic gash existed in their culture so that they would blame anything on a dark lord. But even Ico couldn't deny there was a whiff of magic after-effects in the unnaturalness he saw in Sra Slarin.

Xima's hand trailed down Ico's hair. "I swear, you'll be safe as long as you stay within my palace walls."

"Safe!" Ico looked up at her. "Should I be worried? Is this thing spreading?"

"I told you, you did not need to worry. Here, eat—having some food in your belly will make you feel better, won't it? That always seems to be the way with humans."

Ico knew Xima was avoiding answering his question. But as she stroked his hair, the scent of food filled up the room—a savory smokiness that made his mouth water and the back of his jaw ache. Over on the table, the food had appeared. Like all the feasts in Xima's palace, it didn't look like real food, like human food, but rather like pieces of ice sparkling in the sun. But Ico's stomach still grumbled at the sight of it. He knew how nourishing that food could be.

"See?" Xima said. "The fastest way to soothe a human. Go on."

"You still have a lot to learn about humans," Ico said, although her enticement worked, the way it always did. He stood up and then slid into the chair beside her. His platter of ice gleamed. He picked up a chunk of ice with his fingers and took a bite. It melted on his tongue, warm and substantial and tasting of the ginger and lemongrass of his homeland. "But this food is delicious. Thank you."

Xima smiled. A platter of food had appeared at her place, too, but she didn't bother to eat. Sometimes she did, when she was bored. Today, though, she slid the platter aside and leaned forward, watching Ico. She did that sometimes, too; she had such a fascination with ordinary human activities like eating. Her eyes sparkled. Ico crunched on another piece of ice. This one tasted like slow-braised goat meat, flavored with orange and spices. The memory of Sra Slarin faded to the background. Xima's lips curled up at the ends, her smile suggestive. Ico took another bite of ice. His body was warm from Xima's gaze.

"I know what you're doing," he said between bites.

"Do you, my north wind?"

"Trying to make me forget what I saw." Sra Slarin flashed in his memory. Winter gardens flourishing beneath snow, vines pulling down houses, a man who claimed to have died standing in front of him.

"Is it working?"

"Sure is." Ico licked at his fingers. "Though I still think you should, I dunno, *do* something about it." He broke off a piece of ice and set it on his tongue. It tasted of sweetened berries and soft cream.

"There's nothing I can do. I only control the snow and ice. Not plants. And certainly not humans."

"You can't, I don't know, talk to someone?" Ico wiped his mouth with the back of his hand. Ice water sparkled on his skin. He looked over at Xima.

"Talk to someone?" Xima frowned. "Who would I talk to?"

"One of the Airiana?" Ico shifted uncomfortably under Xima's gaze. "Growth, maybe? There was a lot of growth happening in that village." *Too much,* he thought uneasily.

"Growth?" Xima laughed, her voice sparkling like sunlight flashing on ice. "Oh, I'm sure she's aware of these happenings."

"Then why isn't she doing anything?"

Xima shrugged. "She keeps her distance. She sets processes into motion and watches them unfold."

"Seriously?" Ico thought of the shrines to Growth he'd seen in the Seraphine, the carved statues of a voluptuous woman growing wild with hyacinth and moonflowers. People left bottles of honey wine and sweet bread, pleading to her for fertility. And apparently she never even bothered to listen.

But Xima was doing the same, wasn't she? Sra Slarin had left offerings to Xima for centuries. She was supposed to protect them.

But the thoughts sparkled away as Ico bit into another piece of ice, as Xima brushed her hand against him. He was within the walls of the ice palace, its eerie blue light falling around him, and death was a far-off dream. He scooped up the last few shards of ice. More of the sweetened berries. It never mattered what order he ate the ice in, it always came out as a proper meal. Part of Xima's magic.

"Did you enjoy your meal?" Xima asked as he pushed his empty platter away.

"You know I did," Ico said.

"And yet you still seem upset."

He shook his head. Was he? Sra Slarin seemed far away, now that he was tucked inside the palace. It might as well have been on the other side of the world.

"Don't be upset," she purred, pressing one finger to his jawline, turning his face toward hers. "You're safe here."

When he looked at her, her eyes glittering with icy delight, her lips curled up in a seductive smile, he believed her. It was always that way. And as he stared at her, he knew: No unnatural magic could break through the walls here. He'd been living on ice for the last year.

He stood up and yanked Xima's chair out from the table and spun it around. Then he knelt before her again. She gazed down at him expectantly. He slid his hand up the inside of her thigh. Her skin was cold, like the sea. Her dress parted for him, falling like water on the either side of her. Ico kissed her. She tasted like ice, like true ice, clean and cold and pristine. She gave a moan and pressed her hand against the back of his head, and Ico touched himself through his trousers, pleasure spreading like fire.

Ico was her north wind. He carried her messages, he offered his body to her. And in return she protected him: from strange magic and the Koza clan, from fear and uncertainty and all the dangers of the outside world.

Ico woke with a start. He'd been dreaming—not of cool skin and iceberry breath, but of heat, muggy and thick and unmoving. The Seraphine.

He slid out of the bed, pulling the sheets around his naked waist. Xima was gone, and the room was cold, no blue fires burning in the corner. A tremor of fear slid down Ico's spine. She'd fucked him nice and hard after dinner, like she was trying to erase the memory of Sra Slarin completely—it was another one of the things she found so amusing about humans, how easily they were distracted by sex.

But this time it hadn't worked, much to her confusion. And shortly after he rolled away from her after she finished but he hadn't, Xima had wandered away.

He dressed in wool and furs and moved out into the hallway. It was colder here, his breath forming in frosted patterns on the air. That couldn't be right. Xima kept it warm for him. She kept him safe.

His footsteps bounced off the palace's walls and echoed into oblivion. When he reached the top of the big winding staircase, the ice transparent enough to see all the way down, he called out Xima's name. His voice was swallowed up by the cold. But then he heard an echo, a twin voice. Not his voice, though—Xima's, soft and musical. Ico leaned against the stair bannister and breathed a sigh of relief. She was somewhere in here. Hiding from him, playing some kind of game. Another one of her quirks.

Ico hurried down the stairs. At the landing he stopped and listened again. Her voice bounced around at strange angles, as the sound always did in the ice palace. He'd gotten used to it.

"Xima?" he called out again.

Her voice fell silent. The palace seemed to hum. Then:

"Ico? My north wind?"

Her voice was close, as if she stood beside him, whispering in his ear. But he was alone in the hallway.

"The hell are you doing, Xima?" Ico strode forward. "You know I like games as much as—"

"In the great hall, my love." Her voice still sounded next to his ear. "I'm sorry I didn't wake you."

Ico thought he heard a quaver in her words. Strange. He smoothed back his hair with both hands and then made his way to the great hall. Another strangeness. Xima never went into the great hall unless she had guests.

Ico shivered, not sure if it was the cold or not.

The doors to the great hall appeared up ahead, carved, like everything in the palace, out of shimmering ice. They swung open as Ico approached, and light flooded out, blue-white and blazing. Ico blinked and turned his head, his eyes watering.

"He's arrived," said Xima.

Ico lifted his head. Slowly, shapes materialized out of the wash of light. The columns of twisting ice. The patterns on the floor. The great throne dead ahead, jagged and sharp and huge as an iceberg. Xima sat upon it, shrouded in glowing white light, like moonlight reflecting off of snow.

"Come in, my north wind," said Xima. She didn't smile, the way she always did when she saw him.

Ico passed through the threshold, although his steps were cautious. He didn't carry weapons inside the palace. Never had a need for them. But right now—

Right now he wished for his knife, for his pistol.

"What's going on?" he asked. The room was empty save for a statue at the base of the throne: a statue of a woman, carved out of ice. "Has something happened?"

Xima looked away, and Ico moved closer to her. It was colder in the great hall than it had been out in the corridor, and Ico felt cold stings on his face. Not snow—sleet. Frozen rain.

"Xima?" He stopped halfway to the throne. His earlier fear returned, stronger this time. Her magic wasn't working the way it should. "Something's wrong."

Xima turned toward him again. She did not respond.

"Nothing's wrong, my Akuranian child."

That voice. It was not Xima's. But Ico had heard it before, nearly five years ago. It was a voice like the Seraphine, although here in the palace it was altered—slower, colder, as if the Seraphine had somehow iced over.

Ico screamed and leapt into a fighting stance, his hand going for a knife that wasn't there. He whipped his head around, looking for a woman pouring water.

"I'm here," the voice said. "Right in front of you."

And then the ice statue moved, a shower of ice falling in an arch as limbs rubbed against limbs. The statue's head turned. Her feature glinted like crystals, but Ico recognized her. He slumped down. She'd found him. Five years and she'd found him.

Xima watched them both, her expression sad.

"My Akuranian child," said the ice-woman, lurching toward him over the shining floor. "You left me."

"Had to," Ico said. He glanced up at Xima. She gave him a soft half-smile, but that sadness was still there. It made his chest hurt. He looked back to the woman. "Get tangled up with one of the pirate clans. If I'd stuck around, they would've killed me."

The woman stopped. Her expression was frozen into place, huge dark eyes and a placid mouth. When she spoke, her lips didn't move. Instead, her voice rang out from inside the ice. "I'm sorry to hear that."

Ico doubted that. He shoved his hands inside his coat, trying to warm them.

"It's troublesome news," she continued. "Considering that you still owe me a favor." A pause. Her frozen face watched him. Unnerving as hell. "A favor that must be granted in the Seraphine."

"No," Ico said. He moved sideways, circling back toward Xima. No harm could come to him within the palace walls. She fucking promised. "I can't go back there. They use alchemists as trackers. The minute I sail into the Seraphine Bay, they'll *know*." He edged closer to Xima's throne.

The woman's head turned to follow him. Her body did not, and so her neck twisted at an impossible angle. Ico's skin crawled.

"As long as you're on the water," the woman said, "I can offer you my protection."

"Or I can stay here," Ico said. "Help you out with some other favor." He grinned, trying to mask his fear. The memory of the bodies of his fellow crewmates strung from the masts. "I'm sure you can work something out with Xima. You're both Airiana, yeah?"

The woman stared at him. The ice of her form sparkled.

Ico bumped against the edge of Xima's throne. He tore his eyes away from the twisted form of the water-woman and found Xima staring down at him. The white glow of her hair and her dress hurt his eyes.

"You didn't tell me," she said, "that you had made an arrangement with Taja."

The name sparked at the edge of Ico's thoughts. He heard it in a different voice—one of the sisters, the weird one, that he'd taken into the woods that night. It was her damn fault, saying the woman's name. Let her deal with the favor.

"Didn't think it was worth mentioning," Ico said. The woman was uncoiling herself, her body slowly scraping around so that it faced the same way as her head. Powdered ice fell across the floor. "And I was forced into the arrangement anyway. She never granted me any favor."

"A human thing to say," Xima said. Her voice was harsh. Ico looked over at her in surprise. She stared straight ahead, her fingers digging into the armrests of the throne. Ico wanted to curl up inside himself. She was angry. Angry at him. That had never happened before. No wonder the fires were out. No wonder he could see his breath materializing on the air in front of him.

"The other two are making their way to the Port of Istai-Seraphine," the woman said. "You will have to meet them there to learn the exact nature of the favor."

"Or you could just tell me now," Ico said. "Save us all the trouble."

"Ico!" Xima's voice was the roar of an avalanche. Ico jerked away from the throne, stumbling over his feet. Xima stood up and turned to him. Her hair glowed brighter, and the sleet fell harder, stinging his bare face. "You cannot refuse to fulfill your favor. Don't you understand what you traffic in?" She gestured toward the woman. "She provided you with a service. And you must pay!"

The sleet whirled through the great hall. Ico cowered for a moment. Xima stared at him, her hands curling into fists.

"I told you, she didn't provide me with a service," Ico muttered. "It was for those two sisters." He glanced over at the woman. "Did you tell her that? That I was just leading them in through the woods? That you made me a part of something I didn't have anything to do with?"

In the silence Ico could hear the pinging of sleet against the icy floor.

"I laid out my terms that night," the woman said. "You should have refused then."

"I didn't have a chance to re—"

"Ico," Xima said sharply.

He turned to her, vaguely shocked. She never spoke to him like that.

"Can't you do something?" he said weakly.

Xima sighed and slumped back into her throne. The sleet stopped.

"You must go," she said softly, and this was the Xima that Ico had first seen when he was brought to her palace freezing to death, the Xima who had wrapped him in furs and lit a blue fire to keep him warm. "These rules were set long before humans even existed. A payment for a service." She lifted her face, but she did not look at Ico, only at the woman. "Will he be safe?"

"As long as he stays on the water," the woman said.

Xima smiled. "That will be easy for you, my north wind. My pirate."

Panic swelled in Ico's chest. "You're really not going to stop it? You said I was safe as long as I was within your palace walls. You said—"

"Safe from the dangers of the human world, yes." Xima stood and glided toward him. She drew him into her arms, and he fell against her cold breast. She didn't have a heartbeat, only a rushing like winter wind that echoed from deep inside her chest. "And Taja is not a danger." Xima closed her eyes. "She's a friend. An ally."

Ico peered over at the woman, who watched them in her frozen shell. "I'm not worried about her. I'm worried about the gods-damned Koza clan."

"They won't attack you on the water," the woman said.

"And off the water?" Ico snapped. "What happens when we stop for supplies? Or if this favor of yours takes us off the river? What then?" He pulled away from Xima and stalked up to the woman. "They can climb off their boats, too. Kill and torture those two sisters who got me into this mess."

The woman's empty face watched him. "The Koza clan mostly hunt in brackish waters," she said. "They pray to me at times, but mostly they pray to Ocean. They'll be unaware of your return, and once you've worked your way deep into the Seraphine, you won't need to worry."

Ico scowled. The Kozas had exiled him. They didn't want to catch him anywhere near the Seraphine—had murdered an entire boat of innocent people to drive that point home. Eventually, the Koza alchemists would cast a whiff of smoke or flame or whatever the fuck they used that would whisper his whereabouts. And then it'd be over for all of them.

"There's no point in protesting," Xima said. The sleet was falling again, although only lightly, a soft patter across the floor. "You can't refuse. The sooner you go, the sooner you can return to me."

"You can stop this," Ico whispered.

Xima gathered Ico in her arms again. Ico fell against her, his eyes closed. He had known this day was coming, deep down he'd known. He'd lied to himself about it for half a decade.

"I can't," Xima said, her voice soft against the top of his head. "This is my sister's business, and I can't interfere." She paused, stroking his hair, and Ico squeezed his eyes shut because he did not want to cry in front of Xima. "If I could help you, I would, but he's hidden himself from me."

"Who has?" Ico pulled away and looked up at her. "What are you talking about?"

"I can offer what little protection I can in those sweltering lands," Xima said. "High in the mountains, I will find you."

"You didn't answer my question." Ico curled his hands into fists. "Who's this *he*?"

"The one you're tasked with finding," Xima said. "He's hidden himself from all of us."

"You tell him too much," said the woman. Her voice sounded like a thunderstorm.

"My palace is safe, sister." Xima's arms were crossed over her chest, and she gazed at the frozen Lady of the Seraphine with an air of petulance. "You can tell him his task now."

"What task?" Ico said, hopelessness like a flame in his chest. "Xima, just tell me—who am I going to have to find?"

"You'll see, my love." She brushed a lock of Ico's hair away from his face. For one moment all that mattered was Xima, her touch, her closeness. "I wish I could give you more. But you'll be safe, my north wind. You've been kissed by the Airiana." And then, as if to prove it, she kissed him, her mouth hard against his. Ico's feet lifted off the ground. His head spun.

She pulled away, and he stumbled back, his breath forming snowflakes on the air.

"Go," Xima said. "I'll be waiting for your return."

Ico looked down at the floor, keeping his gaze away from either of them. The sloop was sturdy enough, he could claim he was sailing south and then go west, toward Aesri. Magic and the Airiana didn't have as much sway there, the rumors went. He could hide out for a few months and then return.

He lifted his gaze. Xima and the woman both stared at him, and a chill shot straight down his spine. His breath caught in his throat. Something was charging up on the air. The sleet picked up again, icing over the top of the fur of his coat. The room felt off-kilter. The two Airiana still stared at him. The hairs on the back of his neck stood on end.

Magic. Pure fucking magic.

"Don't you da—" he started.

"Goodbye, my north wind," said Xima.

The walls crashed into him like ocean waves. For a moment he was drowning. His whole body had become water.

And then he felt the warmth of the sun. He could smell the soil, mulchy and rich. He blinked, caught a glimpse of a bright blue sky, a swirl of white clouds, a spray of green leaves.

"No," he muttered, "No no no—"

Somewhere behind him, a voice shouted, in the lilted Sera tongue, "Oi, what have we got here? You drunk? We don't take kindly to drunkards 'round here."

"No." Ico sat up. The sunlight was bright and blazing. It burned his eyes. "No, no no no."

Someone shoved at him from behind, and Ico swatted them away. "I'm not drunk!" he shouted, and he struggled to his feet. He stood on a pier, rickety, built of ancient wood and ancient stone.

And at the end of the pier, glittering like diamonds, was the Seraphine.

FOUR

The first signs of the Port of Istai-Seraphine began to materialize along the shore. Little wooden houses, laundry hanging to dry from the branches of the nearby trees. A pen of goats, the creatures clumping at one end to watch the river. Eventually, a dirt path appeared alongside the shore, with hand-painted signs jutting out in intervals over the water. *Welcome to Istai,* one read. Another, *Beware aolde vipers. DANGER.*

Celestia sighed. She was leaning against the balcony, the breeze cooling the sweat on her skin.

"They warning us about the snakes yet?"

Celestia straightened and looked over her shoulder, lifting one hand to block out the glare of the sun. Adelric had stepped out of the main cabin, and he ran a rag over his glistening brow.

"They have," she said.

He grinned. "You might want to go down below, my lady."

Celestia turned away from him. The thought of going back to the belly of the riverboat, where the air was dank and hot, left her nauseated. "I'll take my chance with the aolde vipers," she called out. A spray of river water caught on the boat's draft and sprinkled across her face. She closed her eyes, relishing the coolness. "How much longer do you expect it to take?"

Adelric ambled up alongside her. "Not long at all," he said. "The docks should be around that bend up there." He gestured to a place where the river was swallowed up by trees. "They aren't kidding about the snakes, though. You be careful when you're out wandering through town."

"I know." Celestia fanned at herself with one hand; her actual fan she had left down in her cabin, and she wasn't of a mind to fetch it now. She'd grown up with stories about the aolde vipers, and other monsters too. Creatures that lived deep in the forest, in places where the vegetation grew too thick for proper cultivation. Some of the stories even claimed that the creatures had been crafted from magic by Lord Kjari during his reign, the way he crafted the kajani who fought in his armies.

That was all Lord Kjari was in Celestia's lifetime: a children's story.

"I can start bringing your trunk up on deck if you'd like," Adelric said. "Should have time before I'll need to dock the boat."

"I'd appreciate that very much."

He nodded and slipped away, disappearing down the ladder. Celestia pulled away from the railing and sat down on the viewing bench. The forest rolled by. Eyes flashed in the branches, even this close to the port—monkeys, most likely, who were smart enough to steal food when humans weren't looking.

Adelric was right; it didn't take long for the boat to glide along the bend in the river, at which point the dock of Istai-Seraphine appeared. Adelric unloaded Celestia's trunk beside the disembarkation ramp, and then he took up position at the wheel. Smoke puffed out of the stack as he quelled the fires, slowing the boat down. The docks were small and shabby. Only one boat was anchored at them, a weatherworn old thing with a garland of flowers draped over its stern. Some upper Seraphine tradition, Celestia suspected. Perhaps it warded off the aolde vipers. Izara would know.

A pang went through Celestia's chest. She had mostly avoided thinking of Izara on the way up the river, not because she didn't miss her sister but because thoughts of her brought on waves of guilt. This favor was Celestia's price to pay.

Celestia took a deep breath. No. It did no good to think of things that weren't meant to be. And anyway, the riverboat was sliding up to the docks. She'd be disembarking soon, which meant she would need to decide what to do next. The Lady hadn't given her any instructions beyond telling her to journey to the port of Istai-Seraphine. Now she was here, and as she stared over the railing of the boat, watching the shabby buildings appearing in the shadows of the trees, she wondered what was expected of her next. She stood and walked up the bow and gripped the railing. Istai was small and sleepy. The only human she saw was a man lounging in a chair beside the docks, smoke from a pipe puffing up into the air. Behind him the roads were empty save for a single rickety-looking cart leaning up against a palmito tree.

The riverboat bumped up against the shore. The man in the chair lifted his head and squinted at the boat. Then he pushed himself up to standing and disappeared into a little square building beside the docks. Celestia frowned.

A thump on the deck. She glanced over her shoulder; Adelric had picked up her trunk and was lugging it toward the ramp. "Where will I be taking this, then?" he asked.

Celestia pressed her hands against her skirts. "Ashore."

Adelric laughed. "Well, I know that, my lady. Where will you be staying? I bet the dockmaster will let us rent that cart there." He nodded at the cart, just as the man stepped out of the building, this time clutching a coin purse and a ledger book. "Ah, speak of the devil. Won't miss his chance to charge us, that's for sure." Adelric yanked on the rope tied to the disembarkation ramp and the ramp clattered down to the docks. "My lady," he said, with a half-bow.

Celestia gathered up her skirts and swept off the boat. She hadn't considered what she would do with her things when she arrived. After all, there was no sick friend, no reservations at a local inn—was there even an inn, in this falling apart little village by the river? Even any *people*?

"Five issls a day," the man called out as Celestia stepped onto the dirt path.

"Bullshit," said Adelric. He stepped up beside her and dropped the chest on the ground. "A dock like this, we ain't paying more than two a day."

"The boat will be leaving immediately," Celestia said. "How much will that cost me?"

The dockmaster narrowed his eyes at her, and Adelric leaned in close and whispered, "My lady, at least let me tend to your things first."

"That won't be necessary." Celestia's heart thudded against her ribcage. "I can transport them myself."

Adelric opened his mouth to protest, but Celestia shot him her haughtiest glare, and he lowered his gaze and nodded.

"That trunk looks awful heavy," the dockmaster said. "You sure you want to work yourself into a lather dragging it into town?"

"How much will it cost if the boat leaves immediately?" she asked, drawing up her spine.

The dockmaster's eyes glittered.

"Nothing," said Adelric. "It'll cost nothing for me to pull right on out of here. My lady, may I have a word?"

"No," Celestia said, because she knew already what he would tell her: that the dockmaster wasn't to be trusted, that the moment he left she'd be robbed and beaten, that a landed lady should not walk the streets of Istai-Seraphine on her own. And her own fear was shimmering inside of her. But the Lady had asked her to come here, and she'd asked her to be alone. And so Celestia would be alone.

"My lady—" Adelric said.

Celestia held up one hand and said, "Enough. I've made my decision. Return home and wait for my letter."

A silence fell over the three of them. Out in the forest birds shrieked at one another. An insect buzzed around Celestia's head. She didn't swat at it.

Adelric was the first to move. He nodded and backed away, eyes flitting back and forth between Celestia and the dockmaster. Celestia watched him go with a calm stillness, but inside her thoughts were whirring. She would make preparations to stay here until twilight, assuming the Lady hadn't contacted her. That only left the matter of the trunk.

"You're an interesting woman, Lady—?" The dockmaster's voice startled her. It was rough like sandpaper, as if his throat had been rubbed raw. She looked away from Adelric and fixed a steely gaze upon him.

"My name is of no concern to you," she said. "If you would accept five issls to keep a riverboat, could I pay the same amount for you to watch my trunk?"

The dockmaster's eyes widened. "Of course, Lady X." He smiled at her and then flipped open the ledger. Celestia caught a whiff of burning wood—the riverboat, she saw when she glanced over her shoulder. Smoke was billowing out of the smoke stack again.

"I just need you to sign here," the dockmaster said. Celestia turned back to him and took the quill and scrawled a large dark X on the signature line. Then she reached into her purse and extracted the five coins. The dockmaster jangled them in his cupped palm.

"Very nice, Lady X. You're much more generous than your riverman there." He jerked his chin out at the riverboat.

"Yes, well, I do expect you to carry it inside for me." She leveled her gaze at him. "And I expect nothing to be missing when I retrieve it."

"Of *course*, my lady." The dockmaster bowed deeply at the waist. "We're honest folk here in Istai-Seraphine." He slid the coin purse onto his belt and set the ledger in his chair. Then he picked up the handle of the trunk and dragged it inside the building where he'd fetched his things. It looked even more worn out up close. The paint was peeling off in long strips, and dirt and grime had caked over the windows. Celestia followed him inside. It was dim and hot and dusty, and the dockmaster shoved her trunk over into a corner. She wasn't really worried about him breaking into it. The thing was protected by an expensive alchemical-clockwork lock from Jaila-Seraphine. If he tried to pick the lock, it would send a shockwave of pain up his arm and leave him paralyzed for half a day.

"I thank you, sir," she said. "I'm sure my things will be well-protected under your care."

That earned her another bow and a leery grin. "Where will you be off to next, my lady?"

Celestia looked over at the doorway, bright with sunlight. "A place to eat," she said. "Perhaps a cafe." Really, she wanted a place to wait. The Lady could find her anywhere, of that Celestia was certain. But she wanted to be out of the sun and off the street, to protect herself as well as the baby. Adelric was right to worry.

"Ain't no cafes here, but you can find a public house down the road," the dockmaster said. "Called the River Star Inn. Best palm wine in the upper Seraphine, if you ask me." He nodded in satisfaction. "There's food, too."

"That sounds perfect," said Celestia. "Thank you."

"It's on the forest side of town," the dockmaster said. "A bit of a walk, but it's a straight shot."

Celestia nodded and thanked him and stepped out of the dockmaster's headquarters. The sun blazed off the river, although up ahead the road was shaded by tall swaying trees. Already the dust from the paths was coating the hem of her dress. Celestia told herself it didn't matter.

She walked down the road, into the forest.

———

The walk to the public house took longer than the dock-master implied. The main path led Celestia past more shabby buildings, the wood rotting away and the windows covered in ripped mosquito netting. She didn't see many people, even as she moved deeper into the town: a worker pushing a cart of black soil through the trees, a gang of old men playing stones in front of a general store. They all peered suspiciously at her as she glided past them, and Celestia lifted her head, her cheeks burning from their gazes. But they didn't say anything to her. For that, she was grateful.

Eventually the road narrowed and the shabby buildings became shabby houses that poked up around the roots of the forest trees like mushrooms. Like most towns along the river, Istai-Seraphine was built into the forest itself, which only made its streets seem more tangled and confusing. Celestia stopped, her stomach twisting up into knots. Had she passed the public house? She turned and looked at the road leading back into town. She hated the thought of having to retrace her steps. Already her feet were aching and the fabric of her dress was sticking to her sweat-soaked back. She turned to look back toward the houses. A face appeared in one of the windows, small and round, and then vanished. She thought she heard laughter.

Celestia took a deep breath. She did not understand why the Lady of the Seraphine had sent her to this place. She had said she needed to speak freely, but what was it about these falling-apart houses and this dusty road that was protecting her? Why not send them to her tributary? It felt like punishment unto itself, bringing Celestia here. Especially with the baby.

Lady, you can appear to me now, she thought, but she was answered only by the shrieks and rustle of the forests. She trudged forward. Maybe she hadn't passed the public house yet. She'd never been one to frequent anything like a public house, and so perhaps it was more of a house than a cafe.

Her shoes sank into the soft soil of the path. She looked over at each house as she passed them. A thought occurred to her that the dockmaster could have been lying, that there was no public house at all. He was probably laughing at her naivete now, maybe sharing the story with some fisherman who'd come in from the day's work. She could just see them, a group of crusty, filthy men, laughing so hard that tears came to their eyes. Celestia fumed. *Why* hadn't the Lady provided more instructions? Why couldn't Celestia have delayed her trip so that she would arrive when Izara did? Although perhaps Izara was already here. Perhaps this was all some cruel joke of the Lady's, to watch Celestia stumble and lurch though the center of a miserable little river town, her dress smeared with mud and her shoes ruined and her hair falling out of its bun and sticking in ribbons to her face. Perhaps this humiliation was the favor the Lady wanted.

And then Celestia saw a sign. Crude, hand-painted, like the signs that had directed Adelric to Istai itself when they were on the river. *Public House. Open to all.*

Celestia closed her eyes and let out a long sigh of relief. The public house *was* just a house, as worn-down as the others, with sagging porch and a roof thatched half with river reeds and half with patchy bushels of straw. Celestia stumbled up to the front door and pushed it open.

"Hello?" she called out, feeling strange about sauntering into someone's house, even if the sign had said it was open to all. She peered in and found one large room, the windows up high to let the heat out. A counter was set up against the far wall, and a woman sat behind it reading a book, a pair of glasses perched on the tip of her nose. The rest of the room was crammed with furniture—ratty old chairs and sofas and tables, the walls hung with cheap paintings of various Airiana—but it was empty save for a man hunched over an ale glass.

"Hello?" Celestia called out again, and she slipped into the house and shut the door behind her. At this, the woman finally looked up.

"Can I help you?" she snapped.

Celestia felt a surge of panic but she stifled it down. "I was told I could find something to eat here."

The woman set her book aside and slid her glasses up to the bridge of her nose. "You got coin?"

"Yes." Celestia's gaze darted around. The mismatched furniture and the eyes of the Airiana paintings made her dizzy. Or maybe it was the heat and her hunger.

"Well." The woman broke out into a bright smile. "In that case, welcome to the Istai Public House. Have a seat anywhere you like. We're cooking up river fish and palms today." She bustled around the corner. "Oh, you look hotter than a sunny patch in summer, my dear. You walk here from the docks?"

"Yes."

The woman clucked. "Worst part of the day for that. Don't get the rains till later in this part of the forest. Have a seat, dear. I'll bring you children's wine to go with your meal. It'll cool you down faster." She disappeared through a door beside the counter.

Celestia nodded and sank into the closest chair. Although she knew it was dreadfully uncouth, she still reached down and eased her feet out of her boots. She'd been suffering from a sharp shooting pain in her left heel during the last half of the walk, and once her foot was free the pain turned to a dull throb, easy to ignore. Celestia settled back into her chair and breathed.

The woman was fast with her drink. Celestia gulped the palm wine down, barely tasting it. The woman chuckled at the sight of that. "Should have hired Alo to bring you down here in his cart," she said. "Fancy lady like you."

"I thought the walk would be shorter." Celestia reached into her purse and extracted five coins, the amount a bit above the standard price for food and children's wine, and lay them on her table. "Might I have another drink?"

"Of course, m'lady." The woman gave a curtsy and slid the coins into her open palm. *M'lady*. Celestia hadn't identified her background to the woman, and yet she'd guessed at it anyway.

Gods, but what did the Lady want with her? And why did she want it in this place?

Celestia leaned back in her chair and looked up at the underside of the thatched roof. She could see little patches of tree canopy through the straw.

The woman returned with a fresh glass of palm wine and set it on the table. "Your meal should be ready shortly, m'lady."

"Hey! Housekeeper!"

The woman straightened up, scowling. It was the man drinking in the corner. He lifted his ale glass. "Could I get another, please?"

Celestia froze, her glass of palm wine halfway to her lips. She'd taken the man to be some Istai drunk, but he spoke with an unusual accent, one she'd only heard once before in her life.

May the ancestors rain poison on your heads.

The woman bustled over to him. "What were you drinking again? The house ale?"

The man grunted in response. He still had his back to Celestia, and so all she could see of him was a curved spine and wide shoulders and a wave of glossy black hair sticking in sweaty clumps to the back of his neck. The man who had accompanied her and Izara to the Lady's Tributary that night. He'd been there when the Lady appeared. He owed her a favor, too.

Celestia put on her boots and stood up. Her heart pounded. The woman gave her a sharp glance as she walked past, but she didn't say anything. The man leaned back in his chair, stretching his legs out beneath the table. She couldn't remember his name, the man who'd accompanied them. He might not ever have told them.

"Excuse me," she said, her voice soft and timid. The man didn't respond. She tried again, louder: "Um, excuse me? Sir?"

The man snorted with laughter. "Sir? Really?" He twisted around in his seat and looked at her, his hair falling into his eyes. He'd barely aged in the five years. The same dark eyes and high cheekbones. His gaze lingered on her for a moment, and then his eyes widened, and he said, "Holy shit."

Heat rushed into Celestia's cheeks. "You recognize me, don't you?"

"You're dressed a lot nicer than you were before." He

turned back to his table. Celestia glanced down at her dress. A simple thing, linen dyed with berries to turn it pale blue. It was a traveling dress, but she'd had it made after she married Lindon, which made it nicer and newer than the ball gown she'd worn, stupidly, to see the Lady.

"You get that wish of yours?"

Celestia hesitated. Glanced over at the doors leading into the kitchens. They didn't move. "Did she call you here, too?"

The man played with his empty ale glass, spinning it around on the tabletop. "What do you think?"

Had he been this rude that night five years ago? Celestia didn't think so—he'd been rough, yes, and had teased them. But he hadn't been so *harsh.*

She swished over to his table and slid down in the chair beside him. He peered up at her through his hair. His eyes burned.

"I'm dreadfully sorry this happened to you." Without thinking, she reached one hand across the table to lay on his arm, but she caught herself, and set her hand on the table instead, stretched out stupidly in front of her. He looked down at her hand and didn't say anything.

"It was never my intention—if either of us had known that you would be pulled into the price, I would never have allowed—"

The kitchen doors slammed open. Celestia snapped her hand away, not wanting to seem unpropitious, even here. The woman carried both of their drinks and she grinned as she made her way over to the table. "See you're making things easier for me," she said as she set the drinks down.

Celestia smiled politely in response. The man gulped at his ale.

The woman left their table and resumed her place at the counter. Celestia watched the man drink and then wipe his mouth with the back of his hand. He looked over at her.

"Why are you sitting here?" he said.

"I thought we should talk." Celestia sipped at her palm wine. The sweetness of it made her tongue fuzzy.

"What's there to talk about?"

"Quite a lot, I think." Celestia blinked. "Our names, to begin with. We're going to be working together."

The man snorted into his drink. "Whatever you say."

"The Lady told me she would tell me our task here in Istai-Seraphine. Our," she took another drink, "payment."

"Payment?" The man glared at her. "For what, exactly? Your fucking husband?"

Celestia's face flushed, but she didn't let herself look away. "Yes, my husband," she said. "I already said that I'm sorry you were involved—"

"Doesn't matter." He looked over at her. The sun beaming in through the windows caught the silvery-blue highlights in his hair. "Name's Ico. Don't remember yours."

Ico. An Akuranian name, she thought. "I'm Celestia De Malena," she said.

"De Malena." He accentuated the space between the words. "Got your title back?"

"I never lost my title." She glared at him.

"Right. Only the man." He knocked back the rest of his ale. "Hope it was worth it."

Celestia did not want to dignify his snideness with a response. It was worth it, yes, for her to have Cross Winds operating again, with visitors and staff and, soon, children. Once this business was over with, once Lindon returned from his trip for the Emperor. Their lives would settle back into place. She only hoped that Izara could do the same.

And this man. This Ico. He slumped back in his chair and drummed his fingers on the table.

"Where were you?" she said. "When you were—called?"

"Not in a great house on the river, I'll tell you that."

Footsteps thudded against the wooden floor. Celestia glanced over—it was the housekeeper, carrying a platter of steaming food.

"Your meal. Fresh caught this morning." She set the platter down. The fish rested on a bed of limp palms.

"Thank you," she said. The woman reached into her apron pocket and extracted a fork, which she handed over to Celestia. Ico gave a hard laugh.

"Not what you're used to, I bet," he said.

"It looks delicious," Celestia said, even though he was right. This was simple food, riverfolk food. Her first bite brought back memories of those years before the money had run out entirely, before her mother had died. She had treated frugality like a game. Like play-pretend. But Celestia eventually realized the truth.

Ico asked the woman for another ale. Celestia wondered how much he'd drank already. He seemed sober enough.

"My sister is supposed to join us as well," she said, when the woman had slipped back into the kitchen.

"The one that knew the goddess's name," he said. "Should I blame her or you for this shit heap?"

Celestia glared at him. "Me," she said. "I asked her to do it. I take it she hasn't arrived yet."

"Wouldn't know. I woke up on the docks this morning and I've been here ever since."

"You've been drinking since this morning?" Celestia said, a dull panic rising in her throat. She didn't want to be in the company of a drunk for the duration of this task, whatever it turned out to be. Not only would it be unpleasant, it would have an unfortunate effect on the baby.

Ico grinned. His eyes sparkled. "Maybe."

He hadn't. She was certain of it. A small relief, at least.

The woman brought another drink for Ico, and he nursed this one the way he hadn't the others. Celestia finished her meal in silence. Her thoughts wandered to her sister. It would be better when Izara was here. Izara knew the ways of magic, and therefore the ways of the Airiana. She could ensure that everything was taken care of as quickly as possible. Celestia would be home at Cross Winds before her stomach even began to swell beneath her clothes.

She finished her meal, laying her fork diagonally across her plate. Ico looked over at her. For all his bluster, he'd seemed deep in thought over the course of her meal, his gaze distant, his expression slack. She wondered again what he'd left behind. She suspected it was something more important than a cheap riverboat sailing passengers up and down the Seraphine. Woke up here this morning, he'd said. As if he'd been dropped here somehow.

"You gonna drink with me?" he said.

She opened her mouth to answer no. But the sun was starting to set. The light coming in through the windows was a sickly golden color. She should walk back into the town and find a place to sleep the night, since she still did not know when the Lady would appear to her. And it was that—the reality of the Lady's absence—which made her change her answer. She had traveled all this way, it felt, and been abandoned.

She nodded. Ico lifted his hand to catch the attention of the woman. "Two ales," he called out.

Celestia pushed her plate away and looked at the light falling across the floor. She wished it were water.

<hr />

Izara jolted awake. She'd been dreaming, something about the mountains and the damp mist that curled over the paths of the Academy. It was fading now, though, vanishing into darkness.

She sat up, disoriented. The room was moving, rocking back and forth.

The boat. She was still aboard the Lady's riverboat. As she had been for the last five days.

Izara fell back against her cot and rubbed at her head. Five days aboard this boat, alone. No captain, even. The fires stoked themselves, the paddle wheel turned of its own accord. The first day, Izara had watched the ship wheel jerking back and forth without human hands to guide it. The sight had left her feeling cold and hollowed out. No wizard could do this kind of magic. But this wasn't a wizard's boat.

She wondered what had woken her. The entire trip the boat had been dead silent save for the splash of the paddle. Half of the time she couldn't even hear the sounds of the rainforest. Only a buzzing silence, and the water.

Back and forth, went the room. The boat didn't normally rock this much.

Izara sat up again, her heart thudding. The little round window let in a pale beam of light, the way it always did, but this light, she realized, was too yellow to be moonlight. Too saturated. And it flickered unsteadily, like fire.

Had they stopped?

Izara slid off her cot and ran up to deck without bothering to put on her shoes. The boat creaked as she moved through it, a mournful noise she had, in the last day, begun to think of as the boat's voice. But if it was really speaking to her, she had no idea what the boat could be trying to say. She hadn't dared go into trance, not in a space so saturated with unfamiliar magic. She'd no idea what it might do to her.

She slammed open the hatchway and climbed up top. A hot night wind blew across the deck. Night birds screamed to one another deep in the forest. But there was a light, as she'd suspected: a tall lamp glowing at the shore. Which was where the boat was. Nestled up close to the shore.

A town, Izara realized, the darkness forming into shapes around her. Docks. Buildings. She took deep breaths, trying to steady herself. Then she darted back into her room and flung open the trunk that had been waiting in the captain's quarters when she boarded high up in the mountains. It replenished itself every morning, offering up clean clothes for her to wear.

She dug out a pair of boots, the leather worn and soft, a simple linen underdress, and, after a moment's consideration, a lady's traveling jacket, which she cinched in at the waist. Then she climbed back on deck and clambered over the railing, dropping herself on the closest dock. It swayed a little beneath her feet. She braced herself, although her thoughts still spun around and around. She tried to catch onto one, tried to decide what to do next: Was this the port of Istai-Seraphine? She should confirm. If it was, then Celestia would be here somewhere. At an inn, sleeping in a cheap bed. Izara felt a rush of calm at the thought of her sister. They'd survived the lean years at Cross Winds together. They could survive this.

She marched to the end of the dock. The night wind billowed her sleeping gown around her calves and tossed her hair into her eyes. There were no signs on any of these buildings, and as Izara moved closer to them she saw how shabby they were, how run-down. A panic constricted her chest. The port of Istai-Seraphine wasn't empty, was it? She'd heard the name before and always thought it inhabited, but perhaps the Lady had brought them to a ghost village.

Now there was a new urgency in her steps. Izara bounded up to the closest building—she assumed it was the dockmasters's office—and rapped sharply on the door. The wind gusted, stirring up the trees in a thick, rustling swell. They sounded like voices. The Airiana of the Forest, she thought. Grand Mage Papazian had told her that he spoke through the trees. He was beloved by certain elemental mages, who would harness the rushing of leaves and work magic from the earth.

Thinking of Papazian, of the Academy, sent a sharp pain through her chest. She hadn't thought of it much since she'd left. What was the point? The Lady had called her away to honor the debt. Izara couldn't say no. And now she couldn't go back to the Academy again. They would see her departure as a failure, as a desertion. If you went down the mountain, you could not come back up. And so she'd shoved the Academy aside, and focused on the journey downriver, trying to guess what the Lady would ask of them, not allowing herself to think of her future beyond that.

But she'd still dreamed of the Academy.

Izara knocked again. Nothing stirred inside the building. She turned away, frustrated, and stepped back onto the road. The wind blew up clouds of dirt that shimmered in the lamplight. The boat knocked up against the otherwise empty dock. Maybe Celestia wasn't here after all.

Izara's panic grew stronger. Despite the night's damp heat, her skin was clammy and cold. She wondered if the boat had brought her to the wrong place somehow. She hadn't done any magic during her trip, not wanting to risk interference, but perhaps she could cast some kind of interrogation spell, see if the boat could reveal anything to her.

No, not yet. She wasn't quite that desperate.

She stumbled down the road, peering up at the buildings. All of them seemed abandoned. It didn't take long before she'd left the sphere of light from the docklamp, and even with the buildings lining the road, the forest seemed to press in on her. She stopped and tilted back her head to look at the tree canopy blocking out the stars. Jaguars hunted at night. Asami birds, too, with their sharp, poison-tipped claws. And aolfe vipers. And other creatures, ones that hadn't yet been cataloged by Seraphine scientists.

Izara turned and ran back into the light. Even though it was pale and unsteady, she felt safer in its glow. She turned in place, suddenly terrified at the thought of interrogating the boat with magic. Toying with Airiana magic had landed her in this situation in the first place. She should have refused the Lady's call, somehow. Climbed her way back up to the Academy and run to the Headmaster and begged for his aid. But what good would that have done? Izara knew what his response would be: You are no longer an acolyte here. Pay your debt.

It was the maxim repeated every day among the halls of the Academy, in every class, by every teacher. Magic requires payment. Pay your debt.

Pay your debt.

Izara felt a tickle on her cheek. She gasped and brushed at her skin—but she was only crying. She sank down to her knees beside the lamp. The light fluttered over her. The tears dripped faster now, falling into dark spots on her lap. She hadn't cried on the riverboat. She had been numb ever since she saw the Lady in the rain, ever since she left the Academy for good. And now she was in a ghost village in the middle of the jungle, and she didn't even have her sister here to comfort her.

She wept, rubbing at her eyes with the sleeves of her traveling jacket. The wind died down, leaving the air sticky and still, and she could hear the river in distance, the soft susurration of its current.

The river. *Water.*

Izara looked up. The river was a shadow beyond the sphere of lamplight. She twisted up the fabric of her skirt, trying to wipe away the sweat on her palms. She didn't need to ask the boat at all. She could sing the melody, say her name—already Izara could feel the words of the song crawling up her throat. The tune spun around inside her head.

She was already beholden. Perhaps the Lady of the Seraphine expected this, for her to reach out to her. Surely they had to communicate somehow.

Izara stepped away from the lamp and walked quickly down to the end of one of the docks. She knelt and stared down at the water. Her breath came out short and panting. The water gleamed in the moonlight. She wished she could use the order and reason of alchemy to draw the Lady to her. It was so much easier to understand, so much easier to correct your mistakes.

She closed her eyes and began to sing. At first, the song came out stuttery like her breath, but the more she sang, the calmer she felt, until her voice was flowing out into the night like water. Iomim's Gift pulsed inside her.

Izara's eyes flew open. She kept singing. The river water was swirling around into a whirlpool. The boat, a few docks down, rocked up against the dock, sending out a hollow, empty rhythm that kept time with her singing. The song was an ancient hymn of the Airiana, and it felt like honey on her throat. She'd first uncovered it in a moldy old book in the library at Cross Winds, during that time moldy old legacies were all that remained of the estate.

The song ended. The river was still churning. Izara smiled.

"Taja," she cried out. "I call to you!"

A tension cracked on the air, like lightning. The water spun faster, flinging spray across Izara's face. "Taja!" she called.

The river fell still. In the sudden silence an animal cried out deep in the jungle.

Izara frowned.

"What are you doing?"

The voice came from behind her, and it sounded like a thunderstorm. Izara scrambled to her feet.

The Lady stood dripping on the dock. She was a dark as the river itself.

"Calling you." Izara gave a shallow little bow. "I arrived here, and—"

Now that she stood before the Lady, this magic felt like an intrusion. And she had a spark of insight—

It was bullying to control the Airiana, tradition of the nobility or not.

"And you were impatient?" the Lady asked. She glided closer to Izara, and Izara could smell the river on her, metallic and cold. "You thought I'd abandoned you?"

"No," Izara said, even though that was exactly what she'd thought. "I only—my sister isn't here, is she? I didn't know what to do next. The town's abandoned, and—"

The Lady lashed out one arm and curled her cold watery hand around Izara's throat. Izara let out a thick, gurgled scream. The Lady pulled her close. Izara could see the fish swimming through the Lady's veins. Her eyes glimmered like moonpools.

"You must trust me," she hissed. "And you mustn't call me like that ever again. Times are dangerous. I don't know which way the magic will flow. If he hears it, all could be lost." Her fingers slipped away from Izara's throat, and Izara fell to her knees, her head dropped down. Water dripped down the front of her jacket.

"I'm sorry," she stammered. "I panicked. I was frightened."

The Lady began to puddle, her body slowly sinking into the wood of the docks. She reached out her hand again, but this time she only lifted Izara's chin. The water flowed into her features. It was almost painful for Izara to look at her. She was too inhuman, like all Airiana.

"You can't be frightened anymore," the Lady said. "Not if you're to do as I demand." She drew her hand back and it blended in with the rest of her body. "And if you call me like that again, once you've set off on your journey—if you force me to attend to you during a time when it isn't safe,

147

or when he's listening—you will not be able to escape my waters."

Izara nodded, fear shuddering down her spine. Stupid, stupid, stupid. She'd never been one to be afraid of the dark, or of the forest. And yet she'd let it happen anyway.

"I have to remain hidden," the Lady said. "He can't know that I'm doing this."

"Who's he?" Izara spat out, her curiosity, her fear, getting the best of her.

"Go back to your boat," the Lady said. "Wait there. The others will be along shortly. And then I'll explain what you must do to repay my favor." The Lady drew herself up again. Izara stayed crouched on the dock. Up and up went the Lady, a tower of water. Izara trembled, although she no longer feared punishment. It was the favor, still nameless. A journey that could put them in danger? A reason for the Lady to hide herself? It was worse than she was expecting.

The Lady exploded into a shower of river water that soaked Izara's clothes and hair. She sat on the dock for a long time, the forest rustling around her. Her mind was numb. The thought of magic made her sick. So did the thought of the future.

~———

The sun rose, white-hot and shining like a diamond in the sky. Izara had not slept. She'd only sat aboard the deck of the boat, her clothes drying out in the warm night air, and waited.

Celestia didn't come.

The town did wake up, though. Workers trudged their way down the road, disappearing into the dilapidated buildings jutting out from the forest. At one point a man emerged from the building next to the dock—he turned out to be the dockmaster, which Izara learned when he marched up to the boat and demanded payment. She counted out his fee from a bag of coins produced by the boat's magic and handed it over. They must have been genuine, because he slipped them in his pocket before ambling back into the dockmaster's building.

Izara kept waiting, watching what few people came down to the shore. Children, mostly, with tangled hair and dirty feet. At one point, a priest in rotting robes emerged from the treeline, and Izara felt a coil of fear: those robes marked him as a priest of Decay. She watched him shuffle down to the water-line and kneel in the mud there, squeezing it with his fingers. The dockmaster stepped out, saw him, and whirled back inside.

The priest lifted his gaze and Izara knew he was staring at her from the darkness of his rotting robes. But he didn't speak. The priests of Decay never spoke.

Eventually, he disappeared back into the forest, and the air seemed lighter. Izara's stomach grumbled, and a plate of flat-breads appeared on deck a few moments later, along with a cask of fresh water. The boat provided food and drink along with clothing. As an alchemy acolyte, Izara knew food and drink of magical providence was perfectly safe in and of itself; a mage could poison it, of course, but she didn't have that concern here aboard the Lady's boat. Still, she could only eat a few bites. She was thinking on what the Lady had told her last night. Or rather, what the Lady had only hinted at. Not knowing, that made things worse.

Izara was sick of waiting. She shouldn't have called the Lady, but there were other ways she could gain insight.

She went below deck, slowed her breathing, slipped into her trance, and entered into the Aetheric Realm. Here, the mists were balmy and thick and the sky was the color of roses. She pushed the mists away to find small, smooth stones laid out in spirals: the formula defining the reality of Istai-

Seraphine. She only half-understood it, and so she sat about rearranging the stones, trying to decipher the formula. Numbers itched at her thoughts. But whatever was woven into the Realm here, it wasn't enough to reveal what the Lady needed from her.

Too close, she thought. *I have to look at the bigger picture.*

She closed her eyes, the Aetheric mists damp against her skin, and concentrated. She had done this a handful of times before, at the behest of Alchemist Visant, and it always exhausted her. But she forced herself to expand into the Realm. Aetheric spirits drifted past her, swirling in their unknowable patterns, as Izara looked out into the Realm, trying to find something—

The mist rippled.

Izara frowned. She felt it again, a strange rippling against her skin. The mist felt thicker than it should, almost viscous.

She lifted her hand to eyes and found her fingers twined with something like cobwebs. The alchemical formulas within it were like nothing she'd ever seen: densely layered, calculations woven into calculations. A constant fractaling of magic.

Suddenly, Izara didn't want this substance on her skin anymore. It felt *wrong*. An aberration. She pulled it away but the pulling seemed to make it grow and stretch. She screamed and felt her panic surge up inside her—

She slammed out of her trance, gasping. Her hands seemed clean, with no traces of that cobwebby substance, but she still ran up on deck and dropped the water bucket over the side and scrubbed her hands until they were red.

The sun had risen higher up in the sky; the air had grown hotter and stickier. The road, which hadn't been exactly bustling to start with, had begun to clear. Izara fought back tears and didn't quite know why. She kept thinking of those constantly multiplying formulas and wished she was at the

Academy, that she could take what she had seen to Alchemist Vinsant or to the headmaster or to anyone.

Someone stepped out of the forest.

This someone did not walk like the other people Izara had been watching earlier that morning; this someone moved with the grace of a dancer, her skirts swishing elegantly around her feet.

Celestia.

Izara tilted the water from the bucket into the chamber pot and leapt over the side of the boat and jogged down the dock, the strangeness she had seen in the Realm pushed into the back of her mind.

Someone was with Celestia. A man, stumbling a little in his steps.

Of course. There had been three of them. Izara, Celestia, the guide who took them into the forest.

Izara slowed her jog, the heat pressing against her lungs. She had gotten used to the cooler, thinner air in the mountains. But Celestia raised one hand in the air and called out, "Izzie!" Her voice was as bright as music after the endless silences of the riverboat.

"Celestia!" Izara pushed herself forward again. The heat buzzed around her. Celestia was too much of a lady to run, but she quickened her pace, leaving the stumbling man behind her. When she and Izara met in the road, Celestia threw her arms around Izara's shoulders and pulled her in tight. Izara blinked in surprise; Celestia tended to save overt displays of affection for the privacy of one's own home.

"It's so good to see you," she said, pressing her hands against Izara's face. When she spoke, Izara caught a faint whiff of palm wine.

"You've been *drinking*?" she sputtered.

Celestia laughed. "Only a little. Only to pass the time." She gazed up at Izara, her expression clear. She looked different, Izara thought. Her hair was longer and curlier and her skin looked like satin. The pregnancy. But there were still faint lines crossing over her forehead. "I'm so sorry," she whispered suddenly, and she pulled Izara into a hug again. "That you were dragged away from the Academy—I hope we can convince them to take you back—"

Izara's heart stung. "I knew it was a risk," she said stiffly. "When we decided to go to the Lady. I knew."

Celestia pulled away and looked at her again, her head tilted. Izara glanced away.

"We should go back to my boat," she said. "The Lady will probably be contacting us soon."

"Good." It was the man Celestia had been walking with. He wasn't Sera: his light skin gave that much away. He stomped up to the two sisters and pushed his black hair out of his eyes. "We can get this shit taken care of."

Celestia tittered. She was drunker than she let on. "Don't talk like that, Ico."

Ico. An Akuranian name. Izara looked at the man again. He was squinting past her. "That your boat?"

"You're the riverboat operator," Izara said. "The one who went with us into the forest."

"Worst mistake of my life," Ico grumbled. He pushed past her and made his way toward the docks. Izara watched him go. Magic was a strange thing. An unfair thing. This boon hadn't belonged to him.

"He's not happy about our predicament," Celestia murmured. "I had to hear about it all last night."

"I bet he's not," Izara said, still watching him. She blinked, shook her head. "We should wait onboard the boat, though. The Lady told me you'd be coming."

"The Lady!" Celestia turned toward her. "You saw her? I've been here since yesterday morning, and neither of us heard a peep."

Izara's cheeks burned. "I called her," she said, and turned away so she wouldn't have to see Celestia's reaction. She followed the trail of footprints Ico had left in the dirt.

"Izara De Malena!" Celestia called out. "What do you mean you *called* her?"

Izara kept walking. Celestia's feet pattered behind her. A hand gripped her shoulder. She stopped, sighed.

"Do we have to answer another boon?" Celestia's hissed. The alcohol turned her voice crueler than it would normally have been.

"I didn't ask for a favor," Izara said. "I just—I got here at night, and I panicked. You don't need to worry." She pulled away from Celestia and walked back to her boat. The threat that the Lady had shared, about never contacting her again, about the potential danger of their payment—that she kept to herself.

Ico was walking up and down the dock, admiring the boat with glassy drunkard's eyes. "It's a beauty," he said as Izara approached. "Part of the De Malena fleet?" He grinned at her. "Your sister told me all about Lindon De Malena and his wondrous exploits."

"It was a gift from the Lady," Izara said flatly. "And it's enchanted."

A dark expression crossed over Ico's features. "Enchanted?"

"Yes." She didn't feel like explaining further; he'd see soon enough. She pulled down the gangplank and walked aboard. The wind was up, hot and damp. Rains were on their way. In this weather, they'd just make the heat worse.

She walked to the stern of the boat so she could look out over the river instead of the town. Ico was on board; she could hear him stomping around, his steps as heavy and slurred as his words. And then another pair of footsteps, lighter, more delicate: Celestia. *Danger*, the Lady had said.

And with Celestia pregnant after trying for so long. It wasn't *fair.*

The water glimmered in the sun, green sparks flying up into the air. Izara sighed.

"How much longer do you think we'll be waiting for her?"

Izara turned toward Celestia, who stood a few paces away, her hands clasped in front of her waist. She looked so demure, so noble.

"I don't know," Izara said. "Not long, I hope."

"What do you think she wants us to do?" Celestia glided forward and stood beside Izara. Together they watched the river rushing past.

"Remember when we were children," Celestia said, "and we used to sneak out to go fishing?"

Izara smiled. She did remember. Fishing was a sport of the poor, a sign that a family didn't have enough to eat. When they were older and the money ran out, Celestia had refused to fish. She had already grown into her propriety by then. But as little girls, they had crept out of their rooms at dawn and used tree branches and embroidery thread to make fishing lines.

"It never worked," she said.

Celestia laughed. "Well, we didn't know what we were supposed to be doing." Her hand drifted down to her stomach and she stared out over the river, the wind blowing her hair into her eyes. Izara imagined the baby, too small even to be seen. *We'll do this fast,* she thought. *She'll be home before she even shows.*

Danger, the Lady had said.

"My trunk is in storage with the dockmaster," Celestia said. "Don't let me leave it here."

Izara was about to respond, to tell her that the Lady's riverboat could provide her with clothing and food, when the river water started churning. Celestia let out a gasp and stepped away from the railing, but Izara stayed in place. Watching.

The Lady didn't reveal herself with as much drama as she had the night before. She simply emerged out of the river and climbed over the side of the boat, splashing water onto the deck. Celestia lowered her head and touched her hand to her forehead. It was a sign of respect, the sort of thing a worker would do when he had need to apologize to a nobleman. She really was drunk.

"Hello, Daughters of the Seraphine," the Lady said.

Smoke belched out of the stack. Celestia looked up. "My trunk!" she cried. "Are we leaving?"

"Leave your things behind," the Lady said. "Finery will be of no use to you."

A crash came from inside the steam room, followed by a string of frightened cursing. Ico spilled out on deck, his eyes wild. He froze when he saw the Lady.

"You don't understand," Celestia said. "I have jewelry—it's irreplaceable—sentimental value—"

"You should not have brought it with you," the Lady said, and she glided past them, leaving a trail of water in her wake. The boat was already pulling away from the Port of Istai-Seraphine, turning slowly in place to push them back upriver.

Ico watched the Lady pass him, his eyes following her movement. Then he rushed over to Izara. "How the hell is this thing moving?" he asked softly.

"I told you," Izara said. "It's enchanted."

The Lady stood at the bow of the ship, sunlight making her sparkle. Celestia grasped the railing. "My silk dresses," she said softly. "I brought my finest—what if we have need of them? What if we have to meet the Emperor? And now they'll be lost!"

Izara's heart twisted. She looked down at her hands. This was her fault. Celestia may have asked her to do it, may have begged her to do it, but she could have said no. She could have spared them all this debt.

The wind picked up as the boat glided up the river. Izara could smell the rain on the air.

"Gather," the Lady said. "I must explain your task."

At first, none of them moved. And then Ico shuffled forward. He moved cautiously, as if he expected the Lady to attack. He glanced at Izara. "Don't you want to find out what shit we've gotten ourselves into?" he said.

"It's not shit," Izara said softly.

"You don't know that."

Celestia peeled herself away from the railing. The wind blew her hair across her face. She glided forward. "I'm curious, yes."

The Lady watched them all, sunlight glittering across her skin.

They approached the Lady side by side. The Lady's features were swallowed up by the streaming rush of water, and so Izara couldn't tell if she was irritated or pleased or apathetic. It was unnerving. At least with her teachers at the Academy she could read their faces.

"The task I have for you is an important one," the Lady said.

Ico shuffled beside Izara, muttered something under his breath. Izara skin's prickled with tension.

"In an ideal world," the Lady said, "I would do this myself. But alas, I cannot." She tilted her head down at this, water dripping across the deck of the boat. "I can't even speak of him outside of my domain, lest his allies hear my words and take them back to him." She brushed one arm out at the river, dotted with spangles of light, searing and almost painful to look at. "He has powerful friends. Only on the river can I hide from them completely."

He, he, he. Who was the Lady speaking about?

"So that's why you brought us to that shithole of a town?" Ico said. "That's your domain?"

Izara gasped in horror. Even Celestia looked scandalized. But the Lady just stared levelly at Ico.

"Istai–Seraphine has been blessed by Forest," the Lady said. "And he offered to keep you hidden from our common enemy as you gathered to face your task. He is on my side."

Celestia pressed up against Izara, fumbling to grab at her hand. Izara grabbed it and squeezed.

"Why do we need protection, my Lady?" Celestia asked, her voice wavering.

The Lady turned toward her. "He can't know you are looking for him," she said. "He can't know that I've gathered you, that I'm sending you to find him."

Who, screamed Izara inside her head.

"If he knew, he would destroy you," the Lady said. "He doesn't wish to be found."

"Will you just tell us who you're talking about?" Ico barked.

The Lady turned her cold, watery gaze upon him. She no longer glittered; the clouds had come up. The rains were almost here.

"Lord Isidore Kjari," she said.

Celestia gasped, covered her mouth with her hand. Izara felt dizzy.

"But Lord Kjari's dead," Izara whispered. The Last War. She had only just begun to study it at the Academy, study the way magic had been used by either side. Lord Kjari had been the most powerful mage of his time, strong enough that he irrevocably altered the terrain of Eiren, plunging it into cold and ice. He was a warning to all the mages who came after him in the five hundred years since an Eirenese warrior had killed him and ended the war. Gain too much power and you would become a madman.

"Not dead," the Lady said. Water streamed over her face and for a moment it looked as if she were crying. "Tucked away in his moving palace. You must find him. Draw him out so I can speak with him."

"But—but why?" Izara sputtered.

The Lady didn't answer. The rain started to fall, a soft whisper across the water and across the canopy of the trees.

"This can't be right," Celestia said, stepping toward the Lady. She spoke clearly, eloquently. She didn't seem to care that the rain was soaking her hair and her fine linen traveling dress.

"Celestia—" Izara started, but Celestia ignored her.

"Lord Kjari," she continued. "He's not hidden away anywhere. He's *returning*. The Emperor has sent men," her voice wavered here, and Izara knew then that one of them was Lindon, that was the business he'd been called away on, "to find him. To *kill* him. Because there's a—a darkness in Eiren, something—"

"You know about that?" Ico asked. He had gone paler than usual, his eyes dark with fear. "The dead walking again?"

"What?" squawked Izara.

Celestia nodded. "I heard about it from an adventurer—"

"I saw it," Ico said flatly.

"Enough," the Lady said. As the rain fell, her form grew taller and wider and more imposing. "That darkness you saw, the endless growth and revival of the dead, is an effect of Isidore's magic as he recedes into the isolation of his palace. He's using a tremendous amount of his power to stay hidden."

Endless growth, Izara thought, remembering the formulas she had seen in the Aetheric Realms, dense and endlessly multiplying. "I saw it too," she breathed. "In the Aetheric Realm—" She looked at the others. "It's because of his magic. It's affecting Eiren again, just as it had five hundred years ago."

When it sparked a war that killed millions.

"Yes," the Lady said. "It's one of many reasons why you must find him and bring him to me. Killing him will not stop his magic, only release it. He must stop his spells himself, or else it won't only be Eiren that is affected, but the entire world." The Lady reached out one hand and pressed it against Celestia's belly. Celestia froze, staring up at her.

"Your child," the Lady said, "will never emerge from your womb. He will only grow and grow inside you until he rips you to shreds. And that will only be the beginning of both of your suffering."

She drew her hand away. Celestia let out a frightened, choking sob.

"She's fucking pregnant?" Ico said.

"What do you want us to do?" Izara said. She stepped in front of her sister, who was still weeping, her arms wrapped around her stomach.

"Find him," the Lady said. The rain was stronger now, drops falling into Izara's eyes, and the Lady was little more than a tower of water. Her voice boomed out with the sound of the rain. "I do not know where he's hidden his palace, but it is in the land of the Seraphine Empire. I can tell you that much. Find him, lure him out, bring him to my domain. As quickly as you can."

The Lady was bleeding into the rain, dissipating into tiny, individual drops. Her voice pulled further and further apart. "Find him. Bring him to me. And tell him I'm soorrrry—"

The last word dragged out on a howl of wind, and the Lady was gone, vanished into rain drops and river water. Izara couldn't move. Celestia tried to smother her sobs.

"This is fucking insane!" Ico shouted

The rain poured around them. Ico turned to Izara. "I'm Akuranian!" he shouted. "My people didn't fight in that stupid war!"

"We don't have a choice," Izara said quietly.

"And you brought a fucking pregnant woman along?" He pointed at Celestia. "This is madness. I might expect this shit from the Eirenese, but here? In the Seraphine? You don't blame everything that goes wrong on some ancestors-damned dark lord." He whirled around on his heel and stalked into the engine room. The boat rocked along the river.

"Lindon," Celestia whispered. Izara turned to her. She had collapsed on the sitting bench, her hair plastered to her face from the rain. Izara couldn't tell what were tears and what were raindrops. Celestia wiped at her eyes. "The Lady must be wrong. The Emperor's mages wouldn't lie—"

Izara sank down next to Celestia and clutched her tight, staring out at the trees peeking through the humid fog of the rain. "No," she said. "They wouldn't lie. But they could read the signs wrong. Kjari's magic was always too powerful for most to understand." So powerful the Academy had formed to stop anyone from stumbling upon it again. And despite knowing it was wrong, Izara still felt a little quiver of excitement—if they did find Lord Kjari, might she have a chance to see his forbidden magic first hand? Magic so powerful it was raising the dead?

Celestia shook her head, weeping. But Izara had no doubt that the Lady was correct. She was Airiana. The Emperor, for all his power and all his claims of divinity, was only a man. It was a dangerous truth she had been taught at the Academy: the Imperial family had not risen to power because their ancestors were Airiana, as was accepted, but because one of the ancestors had exploited the chaos after the Last War, stepping in to fill the void of power left by the death of Lord Kjari.

Who wasn't, it turned out, dead after all.

⁓

The rain stopped not long after the Lady vanished back into the river, and the sun came out and turned all the moisture into steam. Celestia steadied herself against the railing, nausea rising in her stomach. She'd been lucky so far, with only a few bouts of pregnancy sickness in those weeks leading up to the confirmation from the traveling mage. But the Lady's instructions had brought the sickness on again.

She leaned over the railing and coughed up her breakfast into the river.

When the nausea passed, she slid down to sitting, her back pressed against the railing, the hot sun hurting her eyes. Her soaked-through traveling dress was heavy and uncomfortable, and she was sure she looked a mess. But her trunk was still in storage in Istai-Seraphine, and so she wasn't even given the dignity of maintaining her appearance.

Footsteps sounded on the deck, and Izara appeared around the corner. She was carrying, to Celestia's surprise, a change of clothes. And she had changed too, out of her coat and sleeping gown into a pair of men's trousers and a thin white shirt.

"Where did you get those?" Celestia asked.

"The boat." Izara held out the dress she carried like an offering. "There's a trunk in storage that is filled with whatever clothes you need. Here."

Celestia stared at the proffered dress. As uncomfortable as she was in her wet clothes, accepting that dress felt like making another bargain—what price would she have to pay for this new dress, with its cottony, diaphanous fabric, its stiff lace trim?

"It's fine," Izara said. "Magic just reshapes reality. The clothes are very much real. Very much safe."

"Yes, but will we have to pay for it somehow?"

Izara kept holding out the dress. "No. We didn't ask for a favor."

With a sigh, Celestia rose to her feet. Her stomach churned, but she managed not to spit up again. She gathered up the dress and went into the captain's quarters to change. Izara followed her, chattering about the boat's magic—"It gives us food, too, whenever we need it. That's the same. Perfectly safe."

"Even for the baby?" Celestia kicked the wet tangle of her dress into the corner and pulled on the dress from the boat. It felt lighter than air against her skin.

"Yes," Izara said. "I swear to you."

Celestia closed her eyes. The boat tugged forward. Her stomach roiled. "I'm not hungry right now. I still have pregnancy sickness."

"Ico's down there eating," Izara said. "I'm sure the boat can get you some milk and honey, to settle your stomach. He asked me to come fetch you, actually—we need to decide what we're going to do next."

Her voice seemed to fade away.

Celestia sighed. Milk and honey did sound good, despite her doubts about their origins. But if Izara said it was safe, then they were safe. She would know. "Fine. I'll join you."

Izara led Celestia into the boat's cramped dining room. It was up near the bow of the boat, with a narrow window that looked out at the river. A lantern dangled from the ceiling, moving slightly with the boat's rhythm, growing the light and then shrinking it. The lantern wasn't burning oil. It wasn't burning anything.

More magic.

Ico was already at the table, a plate of food steaming in

front of him: mashed plantains and grilled river shark steaks and a salad of forest greens. The pungent scent rose up in the air and pulled at Celestia's stomach.

"Sit down," Izara said. "The table will give you whatever you want."

"Are you sure she should be eating magic food?" Ico asked.

Celestia stopped and stared at him. Her stomach lurched again.

"It's perfectly safe," Izara told him. "And you certainly don't seem too worried."

Ico took a drink of the palm wine sitting next to his plate. Celestia sighed; did the boat's magic really have to give him more alcohol?

"It's *fine*," Izara told her, sitting down at the table. "Please. You need to have something."

Celestia nodded. She drifted over to the empty chair. Another plate of food was on the table, in front of Izara— when had that happened? She hadn't seen it materialize. A chill shuddered up her spine as she sank down into her chair. She glanced over at Izara, picking up her fork to eat her own grilled river shark. When she looked back at the table, a glass of milk was waiting for her.

Ico and Izara ate their food in gulping, impolite bites. Celestia thought of the baby existing as a tiny speck inside her. Her mouth watered, looking at the milk. She knew she should trust Izara. She had studied at the Academy; she understood magic better than anyone else on this boat. Except perhaps for the boat itself.

Celestia felt a touch on her arm, feather-soft. She looked up. Izara watched her, the fork laid diagonally across her plate.

"I promise you," she whispered. "It's safe. And you need the nourishment. *Both* of you."

Ico snorted. "Yeah, we're gonna need to talk about that—"

"Not now," Izara snapped. She nodded at Celestia. "Please. Drink. You have to keep your strength up."

Celestia rubbed at her forehead. Her stomach churned, and there was the sour taste of vomit in her mouth. She reached over and picked up the milk and took a sip. The honeyed sweetness coated her throat.

"Good," said Izara, who settled back in her chair. "We don't know when we're going to be called on to act. We should eat when we can."

Ico's fork clattered against his plate. "We don't even know what the hell we're going to be doing," he said. "I wouldn't get ahead of yourself, missy."

Izara glared at him. Celestia just sipped at her milk. It calmed her, and settled her stomach besides. Some dark part of her brain whispered about the dangers of magic, but she didn't stop.

"We know exactly what we're doing," Izara said. "We're to find Lord Kjari and convince him to speak with the Lady of the Seraphine."

"Lord Kjari is some Eirenese nightmare," Ico said. "He's dead. He died five hundred years ago."

"Clearly," Izara said, "he didn't."

Celestia set her glass down. "The Lady isn't the only one who's claimed Lord Kjari is still alive," she said. "The Emperor believes it as well."

Izara glanced over at her. "We don't have to discuss this," she said softly.

"Why not?" Celestia looked across the table at Ico. The lantern illuminated his skin. He was listening, although his arms were crossed over his chest, as if to ward them both away. "My husband is already looking for Lord Kjari."

"Yeah," Ico said. "You mentioned that. You also mentioned he's trying to kill him. So not exactly a huge help, is he?"

"He could be," Celestia said softly.

"You're all crazy." Ico tossed his fork to his empty plate with a clatter. "This Kjari person is fucking dead. I don't care how powerful a magician he is, no one lives for five hundred years."

"The changes in Eiren are real enough," Celestia said.

Ico went quiet, his expression dark.

"If the dead are coming back to life," Izara said, "if that's really what you saw, Ico—"

"I don't know what I saw," he muttered.

Celestia sighed, exasperated. "It's what the adventurer saw," she said. "And I believe him."

Izara nodded. "That could be the after-effect of Kjari—resurrecting himself." She swallowed. "I saw something, too. In the Aetheric Realm. There's certainly something happening. And necromancy of that sort is *theoretically* possible."

"Fine, something's happening," Ico snapped. "But what the hell are the three of us supposed to do about it?" Ico's face twisted into a snarl, and Celestia had to look away from him, her heart thudding. "What if this is just some game? Isn't that what the Airiana do? Play games with us mere mortals?"

Silence hung heavy in the room. The milk seemed to curdle in Celestia's stomach. She'd read the stories about the Airiana. She'd known the risks when they rode down the river to find her tributary.

Izara ran a hand through her hair. It was loose around her shoulders, as usual—she was always too distracted to style it properly. "I do think we have to consider why she wants us to find him—do you think the Lady is trying to engineer a war with Eiren? Another Last War?"

Another dreadful possibility. Another way of playing games.

"What happens if we don't do it?" Ico asked. "If we don't find him?"

Izara shook her head. The lantern light cast strange shadows over her face, and Celestia felt as if she were far away from them, as if she'd slipped into one of her magical trances. "Then we will never be released. We'll keep searching for him until we die."

Ico cursed, leaned back in his chair.

"Not fulfilling the task is not an option," Celestia said, more sternly than she intended. "We have to find Lord Kjari. Lindon is already looking for him. If we find Lindon, we'll be able to find Kjari."

"How do you know Lindon's going to find him?" Ico snapped.

Celestia glared at him. "Because my husband is one of the greatest adventurers in the Seraphine. There's a reason he was called into service by the Emperor. And since you don't seem to have any suggestions other than trying to wriggle out of your debt like a pirate, I don't know why I should listen to your opinion on the matter."

Ico grinned at her, his mouth stretching wide. "My *lady*," he said, "I was a pirate. A very good one, at that."

Heat flushed in Celestia's cheeks. This was the last thing she wanted to hear. It was bad enough that she was riding on the river during her pregnancy like some poor fisherman's wife—now she had a pirate's influence looming over her child? She twisted the fabric of her dress up in her hands, underneath the table where the others couldn't see. "All the more reason to ask for Lindon's help," she snapped. "Izara, what do you think?"

Izara stirred her leftover plantains around, fork tines scraping against the ceramic of the plate. "Where's Lindon searching? Did he go to Eiren?"

Celestia shook her head. "No. Two Eirenese adventurers

came here to aid him. They believe Kjari to be in the Seraphine as well, same as what the Lady said."

"Then why are the after-effects, or whatever the fuck they are, happening in Eiren?" Ico said.

Celestia turned to Izara, but she only shook her head.

"That was where they had the most effect five hundred years ago," she said, although she sounded uncertain. "It's not happening in all of Eiren, presumably—we would have heard about it here in the Seraphine." Her voice changed as she spoke, her words spilling out more quickly. Celestia always loved watching her sister work through a problem. "I bet it's only affecting the places that were distorted by his magic during the war. Places steeped in his magic."

"Will it spread?" Celestia asked, touching her stomach. "The Lady made it sound as if it would."

Izara looked over at her with wide, frightened eyes. "I honestly don't know."

"Could we refocus please?" Ico clapped his hands together. "You—" He pointed at Celestia, who scowled at his rudeness. "You said Lindon's looking for Kjari in the Seraphine. You really think he might help us?"

"Of course," Celestia said, shocked that Ico even asked. "He's my *husband*."

"Lindon will have to be convinced not to kill Kjari," Izara said slowly. "I'm afraid that if Kjari dies, we won't have fulfilled the bargain."

"I can ensure that," Celestia said, lifting her chin. "I'm his wife. He'll listen to me."

Ico scoffed, rolled his eyes. Celestia did not deign to respond.

Izara looked down at her plate. Pushed at her plantains. It was always a bad habit of hers, playing with uneaten food. "I suppose it's the best idea we have."

"Unless you want to reach out to do some more of that

magic of yours and call on the big guns," Ico said. "The Exalted Twins. Get their help."

Izara's eyes went wide. "Are you insane?"

"You called on the Lady of the Seraphine."

"And look where we're at now," Izara snapped.

Ico shrugged.

"Besides, I don't have their true names."

"Going to Lindon is the best idea we have," Celestia said. Her heart beat more quickly—it would be so easy, wouldn't it, to hand this task over to Lindon? It would be painful to confess that he was the prize for which she is now paying her debt, of course, but it benefited him, too, with his newly claimed title. Plus, he would want her to be home before the baby started showing.

"We don't even know where the hell he is!" Ico said, throwing up his hands.

"Izara can find him," Celestia said. "Can't you? With alchemy?"

Ico whipped his head over to Izara, his eyes glittering. She looked up at Celestia.

"Yes," she said. "I should be able to find him."

Celestia was swallowed whole by relief.

———

After dinner, Ico slipped up to the engine room. He wanted to get away from the sisters. Wanted, too, to get to know the boat. It was an old seaman's superstition that you shouldn't captain an unfamiliar boat—not that he was really captaining this one. The fires stoked themselves and the wheel jerked itself, moving as if under some invisible spirit's control. Ico could hear the wood turning over in the engine as he stood in front of the big glass pane that looked out over the river.

It was uncomfortably hot in there. Ico had gotten used to

the sailboat that Xima had given him up north, gotten used to the chill wind blowing across his face as he cut across the sea. Here, the air was so thick with steam it was like trying to breathe in the river itself.

Still, he didn't leave. It reminded him of the days when he was going straight. The labor had been hard but rewarding, in its way, and the danger inherent in steam always brought a crew together. As he stood watching the river, his thoughts drifted even further back, to his years of piracy. Now, *that* had been camaraderie.

But Ico shook his head. Whenever he thought of the past, he inevitably thought of the Kozas. Of what they'd done.

He turned away from the window and scanned the engine room. There was a trunk shoved up in the corner, across from the engine. *More magic,* he thought, but he crossed the room to look at it anyway.

When he flipped open the lid, he found a bin of dusty old river maps, the paper yellowed and brittle, and an ancient, crumbling ship's log book. He pulled out the maps and spread the largest out on the table by the wheel. It was old, and some of the labels he didn't recognize, but the shape of the river hadn't changed. He traced the boat's current path: they were moving upriver, toward the mountains. But depending on the whereabouts of Celestia's husband, they might be turning around before morning anyway.

He rolled the maps back up and shoved them into the trunk and then grabbed the log book. It felt like it would fall apart in his hands, but when he opened it on the table, it stayed together, although the pages felt like dried leaves. The first handful of pages were filled with scribblings about some voyage—entries about weather conditions and sail repairs, about squabbles among the crew and lists of food rations. Boring stuff, really. But then Ico looked more closely at the date of the entry, and his breath caught in his throat.

The log book was nearly a hundred and fifty years old.

Ico flipped through the pages, but most of them were empty, waiting to be filled. He turned back to the front. *Log Book, the Coloma.* But this book couldn't possibly belong to this boat. They were still using sails and rowers a hundred years ago.

Ico shoved the log book away, his skin crawling on his bones. Riding on a ghost ship felt more like the domain of Decay, not the Lady of the Seraphine, and he didn't want to dwell on that more than he had to.

He turned back to the window. The boat churned through the water, and the sun was sinking low into the trees, letting off streaks of orange in the sky. Izara would be going into her trance soon, if she hadn't already. Said she had to wait till nightfall.

Ico didn't want to be in this steaming, stuffy room anymore, so he slipped out on deck. The sisters weren't up at the bow of the ship, thank the ancestors. He did not want to deal with them and their alchemy or their enchantment or whatever it was they were doing right now. Dealing with them was what got him into this whole sordid affair in the first place.

The air was balmy and lit with the greenish streaks of fireflies, and Ico stood at the bow and watched the sun vanish. The wind pushed his hair away from his forehead. The horizon was slowly disappearing into darkness, and occasionally lights glimmered in the forest. Firelight, mostly, but a few magic-lanterns, the glow steady and unnerving. Nothing on the river. That was something.

He wondered, not for the first time, if the Koza clan had gotten word of him yet. The port of Istai-Seraphine had never been one of their stomping grounds—too far inland—and that shithole had been too broken-down to be benefitting from any other pirate money. Pirate towns didn't have abandoned streets and dirty children staring at you from the doors of dilapidated hovels. But the Koza's alchemists didn't need to have people in a town to find an enemy. Their eyes were the forest itself, the rumors went, that prickle up your skin you felt as you walked an empty path alone. Maybe you dismissed it as some animal of prey, a jaguar or a caiman or an anaconda. And maybe you'd be wrong.

A voice drifted from the stern of the boat, rough and throaty. Goosebumps rippled over Ico's skin. He'd heard that voice before. He'd heard it the night he got trapped into this mess.

Izara's ritual was starting.

She wasn't singing tonight, but chanting. The wind caught her voice and he couldn't make out what she was saying. But he could *feel* it, a deep rumbling in the marrow of his bones, as if his body was pulling apart.

And then she fell silent, and the world seemed to go silent, too. He couldn't hear the lapping of water, couldn't hear the insects in the forest. His skin crawled. He edged along the side of the boat, moving toward the stern. The stars were coming out, and so were the fireflies, and he couldn't tell one from the other. His head felt full of cotton.

Izara sat on deck, a notebook open in front of her. She scribbled on it, her hand moving too fast. Ico's stomach flopped around. He crept closer. Her eyes were open, he saw, open and full of light.

"You shouldn't get too close." It was Celestia, whispering into his ear. Where had she come from? But she was pulling him away, until Izara was out of view. He could still hear her pen scratching across the paper.

"What the hell is she doing?" he said.

"Traversing the Aetheric Realm," Celestia said. "She learned it at the Academy."

Ico looked up at the sky. The moon was a narrow crescent,

hanging sideways, and the sight of it grounded him. He took a deep breath.

"The magic's bothering you?" Celestia asked.

"I guess." Ico looked at her. "You can't feel it?"

She shrugged. "A little, I suppose."

"You aren't worried about that baby of yours?"

Celestia's hands floated near her stomach, then curled into fists. "It shouldn't take her long."

As if on cue, Izara let out a loud, choking gasp. Celestia bustled away from Ico. He followed. His head was starting to clear, thank the ancestors.

Izara was stretched out on her back, staring up at the stars. She wore an expression of dazed ecstasy, and it reminded Ico of the first time he'd ever fucked a woman, how he'd laid on the bed too stunned by the revelation of desire to move.

"Izzie! Are you all right?" Celestia knelt at her sister's side, slipped a hand under her back, and moved her up to sitting. A wind picked up, stirring the pages of the notebook, and Izara slammed her hand down on them.

"I found him," she said, her voice hoarse. "He's in the forest somewhere. I just need to derive the location." She flipped through the pages of the notebook. Ico just watched her. He was shaking a little. He wondered if that was how the Koza alchemists did it. If they'd felt his presence somehow, if they'd slipped into some dizzying trance and scrawled rows of numbers and symbols in a notebook.

Izara flipped to a clean page and began writing furiously, turning back to the marked pages, her cramped handwriting turning them black. Ico glanced over at Celestia, who was frowning, worry lines carved deep into her forehead.

"I got it," Izara said. She looked up at her sister, her expression still dazed and far away.

"So where are we going?" Ico asked.

Izara handed him the paper. Underneath the scrawl of her

calculations was a name Ico recognized immediately—the statues there had been a landmark when he served as a riverboat guide. He'd ridden past them dozens of times.

"The ruins of Aikha," he said.

Izara nodded and slumped back down on the deck.

Right on cue, the boat belched a cloud of white steam, and the paddle churned more quickly, forcing the boat upriver.

They were on their way.

FIVE

Celestia heard the bell clanging out on deck, a tinny sound that seemed rough with disuse. She set aside the dress she'd been mending—it was her traveling linen, her sole reminder of Cross Winds, although the needle and thread had come from the boat's mysterious stores—and darted out of the cabin. The sun flashed in her eyes, nearly blinding her. She'd spent so much time in the captain's quarters, sewing by the light of the lanterns.

Izara bustled past her, a tattered knapsack clutched in one hand. Another gift of the boat, no doubt.

"Why's that bell ringing?" Celestia called out. "Have we arrived?"

Izara looked over her shoulder. "I hope so. The timing seems right, don't you think?" She'd taken to wearing trousers after they set out on the river, loose baggy things with wide suspenders, like rough boys in Jaila-Seraphine. She said the pants let her move more easily. But Celestia wasn't willing to give up her skirts.

Celestia followed Izara up to the bow of the boat, where Ico was waiting, one hand yanking on the bell. It fell silent when he spotted them.

"Good," Ico said. "Hoped that would call you."

Celestia blinked, her eyes still adjusting to the sun. Izara scurried over to Ico's side and leaned out over the railing.

"We're here!" she called out. "Celestia, come look! It's the statue!"

Celestia walked across the deck. Izara bounced excitedly up on her toes. "Look!" she cried again. Her face shone with excitement, the way it had when they were children, and their family had visited the Hall of Alchemy at the Museum of Natural History in Jaila-Seraphine. Always a scholar, even before she was old enough for a tutor.

Celestia looked. She had seen the statue in paintings, of course; it was a popular subject. But those paintings never captured the enormity of it, rising up among the trees, nor the sheer *antiquity* of it. As the boat glided toward the turnoff, Celestia felt herself shrinking down into a speck of dust. The Statue of Loryn had been ancient when the Eirenese marched on Lord Kjari's army here in the jungle, and now even that battle had faded away into history.

The statue's dark, carved eyes followed the boat as it made its slow arc toward the turnoff. Ico was still on deck, the wind ruffling his hair, although he didn't seem quite as taken by the statue as Izara. Celestia did not let herself think about what *was* captaining the boat.

"It's beautiful, isn't it?" she asked, glancing over at Ico.

He grunted. "Seen it before." Then he walked over to Celestia's side. Izara was still gazing up at the statue like it might speak to her. "You see a lot of things, when you don't have to serve as wife to a husband."

There was a sharpness to his words. *Give me a husband,* Celestia had wished five years ago. The wish Ico was now paying for.

"I imagine that's true," she said, and smoothed down the side of her hair. The turnoff to the tributary appeared amid the tangle of trees and vines, the water sluicing and rippling toward it. The forest surrounding the tributary seemed to soak up the sunlight. Celestia shivered despite the damp heat of the air.

"So how do we know where this husband of yours is?" Ico eyed the land. He almost looked nervous. And his eyes were sunken down in his skull, like he hadn't been sleeping.

"I don't know," Celestia said. "Izara? Did your magic tell us *where*, exactly?"

"It's not that specific." Izara gazed out at the tangle of woods. "We'll have to search the ruins themselves."

"And go ashore?" Ico said.

Celestia frowned at him. "Of course. What did you expect us to do?"

"Figured we'd spot him from the river." Ico turned away from her. "Make a rendezvous on the water. Don't we lose the Lady's protection if we leave the river?"

"He's my husband," Celestia said, crossing her arms over her chest. "We don't need the Lady's protection from him." She burned with indignation—Lindon was their way out of this.

Ico ignored her.

"Stop the boat when we arrive at the ruins," Izara said from her place at the railing. "We can disembark and investigate along the shore. It shouldn't take us too long to find him."

Ico grunted in response.

The Aikha tributary was wide enough for two large riverboats to pass one another without trouble, but the jungle grew so tall and thick around it that the trees formed a tunnel to block out the sun. Celestia tipped her head back and looked at the branches crisscrossing overhead. Patches of sunlight shone through, flicking like a candle flame. The air was thicker here, as thick as the river itself. Celestia moved closer to her sister, her breath tight in her chest. She was used to the tamed forest of Cross Winds, forest that had been cultivated and shaped by human hands. This forest was wild, untouched for five hundred years.

"We're almost there," Izara said in a flat, disaffected voice. Celestia looked over at her. Her face was ashy beneath her brown skin, her eyes glittering in the dark.

"What's wrong?" Celestia asked, and wrapped one hand around the railing. "Izara? Are you okay?"

"There's magic here," Izara said. She stared straight ahead. Her hair curled in the humidity. "I can feel it on me."

Celestia's heart thumped. "Magic?" she said. "What kind of magic?"

Izara shook her head, once, a quick movement like she was waking up from a bad dream. "I don't—" she stopped. "It feels old. Stale. It can't harm us, but it's out there."

"Is it—*him*?" Celestia whispered, her chest tight.

Izara shook her head. "I don't know. It's not like—the strangeness I saw in the Aetheric Realm, if that's what you mean."

The strangeness in the Aetheric Realm. That was what she meant. She didn't want to see dead men in those ruins.

Celestia looked out in front of the boat, as if she would be able to see the magic herself. The water was the color of ink in the shadows, although something pale emerged out of it up ahead. A figure, a woman, her shape sinuous and beautiful even as the elements had worn down her features over the decades. Some sculptor's depiction of the Laniana of this tributary, its protector spirit.

Her heart fluttered. When Lindon left Cross Winds, she never thought she'd get to see him again so soon, even if it was under unfortunate circumstances.

She turned around to look at Ico, but he was already moving toward the engine room, one hand lifted in acknowledgement. "I see it," he called out. "Don't need to tell me what to do."

He disappeared into the engine room. Celestia sighed.

"He's in a mood," said Izara. Her voice had returned to normal again, but she still looked washed out. She rubbed at her forehead. "I hope this works."

"It will," Celestia said, straightening her spine. "He'll help us."

The boat shuddered and tilted toward the shore. The jungle grew right up to the river's edge, tree roots jutting out into the open, and those roots slapped against the boat as it moved in closer to land. Celestia kept squeezing at the railing. Her fingers turned white and numb.

"This magic is so *strange*," whispered Izara. "Like—walking into a spiderweb."

The boat's engine cut off. The deck stilled beneath Celestia's feet.

"Can it help us?" Celestia asked. The forest loomed in front of her, the rich black soil, the thick moss-covered tree trunks.

Izara shook her head. "It doesn't have any power to it anymore. It's just the shell of it, like when a snake sheds its skin. But still so *strange*."

Footsteps on the deck. Ico, moving toward the river side. A few moments passed. The air buzzed with insects. Then a splash. The anchor. Ico reappeared at the fore deck, his forehead gleaming in sweat.

For a moment, the three of them stared at each other. The jungle shrieked around them.

"Now what?" Ico said.

"We go ashore," Celestia said, although she made no move to do so.

Ico sighed. "I wish this boat would see fit to conjure me a pistol." He looked over at Izara. "At least we have your magic, eh?"

"I'm hesitant to use magic in this place," Izara said.

"Well, that makes me feel better," Ico muttered as he let down the ramp.

"What's there to be frightened of in the ruins?" Izara said, making her way to the ramp. "Half of the students at the Academy had made sojourns here before they climbed the mountain. It's wild, but not terribly dangerous, as long as you don't get lost." She pulled out a piece of parchment, yellowed with age and rolled into a tube. Her eyes twinkled mischievously. "And we have a map."

"I guess I do have my knife," Ico said, patting his belt with a roguish grin.

"Truly, we're all much safer with you in our party," Celestia said.

"Don't make fun of me, my lady."

"I wasn't!"

Izara tapped her foot impatiently against the ramp, and Celestia scurried down to meet her. Ico ambled along behind them.

They walked through the underbrush. The forest floor was soft and spongy beneath Celestia's feet. Soft dark dirt streaked along the sides of her boots. She sighed. Well, they weren't *her* boots, at least.

Izara unrolled the map. It had been hand-painted, although the paint was fading in patches, and the ink had smeared in the lower corner, obscuring the compass rose. But the map was still readable.

"Let me guess," Ico said. "From the boat?"

Izara nodded. "Here, take this." She shoved one end of the map at Celestia, who took hold of it while Izara traced a path of the splotches of green paint. "We'll need to go west, away from the tributary. That'll take us into the heart of the ruins. We can start looking there, then work our way out."

Celestia looked up from the map and squinted into the dark, overgrown forest. "How will we know which way we're going?" Celestia realized with a start how unprepared she was for this sort of thing. What would she have done if Izara or Ico weren't here? Stalked off into the forest without the boat's knapsack or even a knife for self-defense, not even thinking about a map or how she would follow the sun when it was blocked by the forest canopy or *anything* related to her survival out here. She would probably have screamed Lindon's name until she was hoarse and never once spotted him.

"Track the sun's movements," Ico said, squinted up at the trees. "Though it'll be tough in this much growth."

"No need. There should be a compass in here." Izara rolled up the map and then dug around in the knapsack again. Celestia peeked over her shoulder. The knapsack also contained skeins of water, bandages, a vial of some kind of glowing, alchemical potion—probably protection against snakebites. Gods, she was grateful for Izara. Getting lost would have been the least of her worries, had she undertaken this adventure alone. She hadn't even thought about *water*.

For the first time since she had stepped off her personal river boat at the port of Istai-Seraphine, Celestia missed Cross Winds. *Really* missed it, its big airy rooms, the servants moving quietly in the background, bringing her tea and sweets when she asked for them. The surrounding forest suddenly seemed suffocating. These plants grew where they wished, undisturbed by human touch.

"There we are!" Izara pulled out a tarnished silver compass. Celestia sighed.

"You lead the way," she said, and she felt like a child again.

They set off. Izara watched the compass as they walked, picking their way around the fallen, decaying logs that marred the forest floor. Ico, playing as much of a gentleman as he could, hacked at the dangling vines, clearing a path for Celestia. Gnats and mosquitos buzzed thick around all of them, and Celestia pulled the mesh netting scarf of her dress up around her nose and mouth. Izara didn't seem to notice the insects, or care. She marched on, weaving them off at an angle. Ico at least swatted and cursed at them.

Sweat dripped down Celestia's back. Wisps of hair pulled out of her braid and clung to her damp cheeks. They walked for long enough that the sparkle of the river disappeared behind the trees. Celestia tried not to think about the remoteness of the forest. She tried not to think about Cross Winds, or Jaila-Seraphine, or civilization. Instead, she focused her attention on Lindon, all her memories of him. The way he smiled at her across a room when they had company, the way the rough calluses of his hands felt against her smooth brown skin.

Lindon would save them.

Soon, they passed a tumble of white stones, vines curling around them like long greedy fingers. Not stones, though, not exactly—one of the stones had half a face, an eye and shattered nose.

"The ruins," Celestia said happily.

Izara glanced back at her and smiled. "Looks like that old map was accurate."

"Now we just have to find this husband of yours," Ico grumbled.

They marched onward. The forest had grown around the ruins. Thick flowering vines pulled the statues apart, and the forest floor crept up around them, lodging them into place. However, a few paces past the first of the statues, it became clear to Celestia that they were walking on an ancient stone path. The dirt and dead leaves of the forest floor were thinner here, and swept away in patches.

Izara stopped in front of a pair of crumbling columns and turned to Celestia and Ico. She rolled up the map and stuck it back in her bag along with her compass.

"That him?" Ico said. "Because you didn't tell me he'd been turned to stone."

Izara shot him an annoyed look before turning back to Celestia.

"So what's going to be the best way to find Lindon?" she said.

Celestia took a deep breath and glanced around, taking in those huge, broken-down fragments of the past. It made sense that Lindon would be here, if he were searching for Lord Kjari. This was the place where Kjari died. The stories said that his fallen blood had turned to anene flowers, brilliant crimson blossoms that grew in the rot and decay of the forest floor. There were no anene flowers here.

If he was coming back, or if he was falling into darkness— either way, it made sense to look for Lord Kjari in this place.

"I don't know," Celestia finally said. She looked to Ico. "What would be your suggestion?"

Ico shrugged. "I was a pirate, not an adventurer. I stayed out of the forest."

Izara frowned, then nodded back toward the path. "We'll have to walk, I guess. Let's see what we can find."

They set off again, winding more deeply into the ruins. The damp heat of the forest pressed in on Celestia, as if it were trying to collapse her lungs.

Up ahead on the path, Ico stopped abruptly. Izara did, too, and they looked at each other. Izara held out one hand to stop Celestia.

"What's the—" Celestia said.

"Shhh!" Ico whirled around and put a finger to his mouth. "Do you hear that?"

At first Celestia didn't hear anything but the forest. Then, distantly—raised voices. Splintering wood. The clang of metal.

Of swords?

Fear gripped her heart. She pressed her hand to her stomach. "Lindon," she said, whirling to find the source of the sound. Why was he fighting out here? Who was he fighting?

Gods and monsters, were they too late? Was Lord Kjari *here*?

"We have to find hi—"

A gunshot rang out, splintering the calm of the forest. Birds bolted out of the trees in a shower of leaves. Celestia screamed and grabbed at Izara's hand.

"We have to get back to the boat," Ico said. He'd gone white, his eyes wide. "Ladies, run."

Before Celestia could respond, Ico had bounded back in the direction they came, disappearing into the forest.

"Did he just *leave* us here?" Celestia squeaked.

Another gunshot. More voices. Male voices, angry and hard. They were coming closer, the forest breaking around them.

"Yes," Izara said grimly. "He just threw us to the wolves to get a head start."

Celestia clung to her sister's arm. She knew she was right; the river was hidden behind a curtain of trees. They'd never make it.

"We lose them?" came a voice inflected with a lilting, unfamiliar accent.

"Doubt it."

And with those two words, all of Celestia's fears vanished. "Lindon! We found him!" Tears brimmed on the edges of her eyes. A thatch of vines rustled a few paces in front of her. Celestia moved forward, but Izara grabbed her arm, pulled her back.

"We don't know for sure," she whispered.

"I *know*," Celestia said.

A sword sliced through the vines, and a man stepped out of the forest.

It was not Lindon. He was shorter, and his skin was Eirenese-pale. He swung his sword once through the clear air, as if testing for invisible strengths. One of the other adventurers. "Excuse me!" Celestia called out. "We're looking for Lindon De Malena."

The man turned to her and his eyes widened and his face went even paler. He shouted something in Eirenese. Movement erupted amid the vines. Shouts of confusion echoed out into the jungle. Three more men spilled out into the path. For a moment all Celestia could see was a flurry of limbs and ratty old clothes and weapons—the glint of a sword, the cruel metal muzzle of a gun.

A gun that was pointed at her, its owner's face obscured behind its scope.

"No!" she screamed, just as the gun hit the ground.

"Celestia?"

Lindon stood on the path before her. He was nearly unrecognizable in his muddy, torn clothes, his unwashed hair pulled away from his face in a tight queue. He gaped at her, mouth moving up and down. Lindon at a loss for words.

"You know these women?" one of the other men said, speaking with that same lilting accent.

"You see them, too?" Lindon rubbed at his eyes. He stepped closer to Celestia. "Is that really you?" he asked softly. "What are you doing here?"

Celestia's throat had dried up. She licked her lips, glanced over at Izara, who still had her hands in the air.

"We're on business for the Lady of the Seraphine," Izara said. "I went into an alchemical trance to find you. We're in desperate need of your aid—"

Izara's plea faded into the sounds of the jungle. Celestia kept her eyes on Lindon's face. He barely looked like himself. Barely looked like her Lindon. She tried to recreate what he'd looked like before he left, without the strikes of grime and— blood? Was that blood?

"Please tell me you're not some Kjari trick," Lindon whispered, gazing down at Celestia. "Please—"

"Of course it's a Kjari trick. They're illusions. Both of them."

Lindon jerked his gaze away from her. One of the Eirenese men had his gun pointed at Izara.

"Stop," Lindon said. "Put your weapon down. What the hell is going on here?"

"I was trying to explain," Izara said. "The Lady of the Seraphine requires us to find Lord Kjari and bring her to him."

Lindon whipped his head around to Celestia. *"What?"*

"It wasn't my choice!" Celestia said, her voice wavering. "I made a deal with her years ago, and this is the favor she wants from us!"

"She asked you to do *what*?" he sputtered, his eyes bright with confusion. He seemed on the verge of laughter. "Bring her Lord Kjari? How did she expect you to do that?"

"What is this bullshit?" one of the Eirenese men said. "Who is this woman?"

"Who cares!" shouted the other. He turned back from the forest. "The kajani are coming."

Celestia blinked. Kajani?

But Lindon's eyes widened, and he straightened up, shook out his hair. "Fucking hell! Celestia, you can't be here. Especially not in your state." He bent over and picked up his gun

186

and whirled around to look at the forest. "You see any sign of them?" He propped his gun up on his shoulder, and with that one action he transformed. The glimmers of her husband that Celestia had seen vanished, replaced with this hard, wild-man facade.

"Did you say kajani?" Izara asked.

"I sure as hell did," said Lindon, still peering down the barrel of his gun.

"Kajani aren't real," Celestia said. She glanced over at Izara. "They're a children's story, just some myth from the Last War. There's no evidence—"

The three pale men laughed at that, grim, cold laughs that made Celestia's skin crawl.

"Celestia, I don't know what you're actually trying to do here, but you are in very real danger." Lindon crouched in a fighting stance with his three Eirenese partners, weapons drawn, shirts soaked through with sweat. "Both of you need to run. *Now.*"

"They're coming," one of the Eirenese said. "I can smell them on the wind."

"Get into the fucking woods!" Lindon roared.

Izara's hand clamped down on Celestia's arm. "Gods and monsters," she said breathlessly. "I can feel them. I can—"

The forest came alive.

Figures erupted out of the trees, moving in fast dark blurs. Lindon let out a harrowing, animalistic scream and fired his gun into the attackers. A thick liquid, too dark to be blood, sprayed across his face and he immediately knelt down and fumbled with his gun as the Eirenese men swung their swords in wide glinting arcs.

Celestia stood frozen in place. Even Izara looked frightened. Lindon looked over at them as he rose to his feet, his features twisted with a violent rage that made Celestia's chest hurt. "Run!" he shouted, and then he pointed his gun at

Celestia and fired and hot liquid splattered across her back and shoulders and she thought he had *shot* her but when she grasped around for the wound her hands came away smeared with a dark purplish-black liquid and she realized it was blood.

Just not human blood.

She screamed and leapt off the path, landing hard on her hands and knees in the soft mulchy earth. Izara chanted behind her, soft and melodic, and the air rippled with an unearthly charge. She scrambled forward, her head bent down. The creatures stomped past her, grunting and shrieking, their heavy black boots caked in mud. She slid into the overgrowth of the forest just as a burst of heat exploded out on the path. Someone shouted in Eirenese; many voices shouted in a harsh guttural language she'd never heard before. Celestia twisted herself around, trying to catch sight of Lindon and Izara between the bars of woody vines. All she saw were the creatures converging on one point like ants crawling over a piece of fallen food. Celestia leaned up against a tree trunk and sucked in deep gasps of air. She couldn't get enough.

She'd thought, for one wild moment, that the creatures were human, that Lindon and the others had been mistaken. But as she crouched in her hiding spot, surrounded by the heavy growth of the forest, Celestia saw that she was wrong. The creatures' skin was the gray of riverclay, and most of them had horns growing in spirals out of their forehead—she'd thought them helmets at first, but these creatures didn't wear helmets, only rudimentary leather armor. They moved with the fearsome grace of jungle cats, loping and powerful, and when they shrieked at each other in their dreadful, gravelly voices, their teeth were sharp as knives.

Tears streamed down Celestia's face. She dug her fingers into the soil, trying to squeeze out her panic. One of the creatures fell backward, roaring, into the vines she was using to hide, and Celestia kicked him away and lunged deeper into the forest. There was another burst of heat, another burst of screams. Izara and her magic, Celestia told herself, even though she didn't know for sure, and anyway she was a lady who could not fight and so she crawled over the forest floor, branches snapping in her face, insects biting at the bare skin of her legs. Her skirt was hiked up to her waist, but what did she care about propriety out here? Nightmare monsters from her childhood were trying to kill her sister and her husband.

Celestia crawled deeper into the forest. The sound of fighting receded. Soon all she could hear was the soft panting of her breath and the reverberating hum of the forest. She slumped down in the dirt and lay for a moment, listening. No more gunshots. She wondered if that meant Lindon was dead.

The thought struck her like a slap across the face. *Dead before his heir could be born.* Tears welled in her eyes, but she forced them back. She would not give in to despair.

The forest buzzed. Celestia nestled into a thick thatch of ferns, the fronds feather-soft against her skin. Her dress was ruined, streaked with black dirt and black kajan's blood. It was dizzying to see kajani in real life, childhood figments made real.

The stories all said that the kajani had been created by Lord Kjari to serve as warriors during the Last War—but those stories had been dismissed as myths by historians. *Eirenese propaganda,* she remembered reading in a book as a little girl. *One of many flights of fancy to grow in that country after the very real side effects of Kjari's fearsome magic wracked through the landscape. But in truth the only Sera lives lost in the Last War belonged to human men.*

Celestia drew her knees up to her chest. She had to protect her baby. She had to hide herself, until the battle was over. There had been so many of them, so many against four ordinary humans and a mage acolyte, and Celestia's future suddenly seemed much shorter than it had that morning.

Tears beaded along her eyelashes. Celestia let them fall. She clamped her hand over her mouth to keep her sobs silent. Her shoulders trembled and shook. Her vision blurred, and she blinked, and then wiped at the tears with her free hand, smearing dirt across her face. She had to be able to see, if the kajani came. She had to know when to run.

Something snapped in the distance. Celestia bit down on her palm to keep from screaming in terror. But the sound wasn't repeated. She didn't hear any footsteps, any words in that strange guttural language. The burst of fear had evaporated her tears, though, and she eventually let her hand fall to her side. She sat very still, straining to hear anything that did not belong to the forest proper. But there were only insects, birdcalls, monkeys shrieking from the branches.

Her leg had fallen asleep. Celestia shifted carefully, holding her breath the entire time. Each rustle of the ferns sent a charge running down her spine. She twisted her body around, glancing through the dense greenery of the forest, looking for a glint of a sword.

Something flashed.

Celestia froze mid-twist, her body contorted in an unnatural, uncomfortable position, arm crossed over leg. She stared ahead, straining her vision.

Another flash. Not a sword, though. Too small.

Celestia's heart thudded. She dropped back down to sitting, then leaned forward, squinting, her breath in her throat.

Something lay half-buried in the dirt. Something straight-edged and sharp-cornered. Something that flashed in the dappled sunlight.

Celestia took a deep breath and crawled forward, pressing her body low to the ground. Every few seconds, she stopped and listened. Nothing. She inched forward. Her entire sight was focused on that object. When the kajani came, at least she would have a weapon.

She ducked under a low-hanging net of vines and then crouched next to a log. She could smell the sweet rotting scent of it. Fungus grew in pale rings over the log, devouring it. A beetle crawled through her line of sight, its abdomen glistening dark blue. She reached out for the object. Brushed her fingers against it. Stone, it was made of stone. And set with tiny glittering jewels.

Celestia's heart quickened. She scraped the dirt away. The object grew larger. Through the haze of her sweat, she could see carvings, twisty and beautiful and utterly foreign. She kept digging. She wasn't even listening for kajani anymore. The silence had lulled her into a sense of placidity. She cleared the dirt away. It looked like a jewelry box, she thought, and she grabbed it and tugged on it, and the thing came free with a shower of black soil.

It *was* a box, stone-carved, with a rusted metal latch. It was only about the size of her palm and so not heavy enough to be a weapon. Still, there was something entrancing about it. Celestia sat down beside the log. She assumed the box would be locked, but she touched the latch with her thumb and the metal fell away. The elements had eaten it clean through.

Celestia pushed back the lid. The box was empty, but it was carved on the inside, although not with the runes that decorated its exterior. Celestia frowned. She could see long, swerving lines, and writing, neat labels in— She peered closer and gasped. The writing was in Old Sera. Difficult to read, but not impossible, and Celestia had been trained in Old Sera as a child, like all of the aristocracy.

She spelled out the syllables under her breath, trying to latch onto the Modern Sera lurking beneath the surface. *Essir,* she read. Then *Tanez*. Tributary. The Old Sera word for Tributary.

Celestia's cheeks flushed with heat. This wasn't just a box.

It was a *map*. Written in the Sera that had been spoken during Lord Kjari's time.

Without thinking, she shoved the box into the pocket of her dress.

And then a wave of heat and light exploded through the forest, turning everything into shadows. Celestia tasted magic on the back of her throat, a sharp burning tang.

Then darkness.

———

A sword swung above Izara's head, close enough that the breeze it generated lifted up a few loose strands of hair. She screamed and reacted with the elemental magic that came so easily in the forest, hurling a wave of soil-power, invisible and burning with heat, toward her attacker. It slammed into his chest and flung him backwards into another pair of kajani. The three kajani crashed into the splayed tangle of a walking palm.

"There's more coming!" shouted one of the Eirenese men as he linked swords with a huge-shouldered kajan wearing his hair in a long black queue. The kajan howled in his own language, the sound grating against Izara's ears. There was a rough magic in the kajan's language, the way there was a rough magic about all of the kajani, despite the fact that none of them were using magic to fight.

A story, Izara thought. They were just supposed to be stories.

But then, Lord Kjari was supposed to be have been dead for the last five hundred years.

Izara drew more power up from the decaying soil and sent another blast of magic out toward the forest. Kajani screamed among the trees. Izara stumbled backward, her energy seeping out with the magical attacks. A lull in the fighting for her, if not for the others: The Eirenese whirled their swords with fierce deftness, and Lindon had abandoned his pistol for a pair of daggers, which flashed and glinted as he sliced back against his opponents. Up ahead, the trees trembled. *No,* she thought numbly, just as another wave of kajani poured out, swords upraised, horns smeared with black war paint. Or kajani blood.

Izara dove behind a nearby statue and pressed her back against the cold stone and breathed in deep. She was running out of strength. Elemental magic wasn't her forte, and anyway, she had gone to the Academy to become a scholar, an alchemist, not a warrior.

The Eirenese shouted in their language, words as sharp and rough as the kajani's. The earth thundered from the fight. She closed her eyes and felt down deep inside herself. Iomim's Treasure was a part of her body, she had learned at the Academy, a candle burning perpetually inside her heart. And in the middle of this fight it was guttering, trembling, fading. She had to reignite it. Had to keep fighting, to keep Lindon alive, at the very least—not just because he could help them, but because he was the entire reason they were here. The gift from the Lady they were trying to repay.

A howl of pain erupted on the other side of the statue; an arc of thick black blood came sailing overhead and then splattered over her like rain. *Blood.* Like the blood magic Grand Mage Papazian had shown her. It had been too powerful for that small cramped office. But they were out in the open here, and she was desperate.

Izara smeared the hot, sticky blood along her arm. The strange magic of the kajani's existence prickled against her skin, and she knew this was dangerous, what she was about to do, and stupid, but she did not want to die here, run through on the sword of a creature from a children's bedtime story.

She rubbed the blood along her other arm, moving steadily, without thinking. Then she rubbed a few streaks of blood along her face, following the lines of her cheekbones. She couldn't remember the sign Papazian had shown her, but if she used her body as a conduit, it would probably still work. Assuming she didn't kill herself first.

Screams rebounded through the forest. Izara prayed that none of them belonged to Celestia, that Celestia had somehow caught up with that coward Ico and the two of them had made it to the boat and were moving safely down the river, away from the horror Izara was about to do.

Slowly, Izara turned around. She was shielded from view, but she could hear kajani grunting and the tinny clink of swords. She didn't dare go into a trance in the middle of a battle and was grateful that elemental magic didn't require it.

The blood seeped into her skin and interacted with Iomim's Treasure, the mixture sparking and burning inside of her. The forest glowed. All that life here. All those living things: plants and insects and lizards and monkeys and hunting cats and fungi and spiders. The blood let her see it, showed her how to draw on its power.

This wasn't exactly elemental magic. She didn't know what it was. But it seemed to be working.

Iomim's Treasure burned hotly in her chest. She could barely breathe. Everything was too close. A kajani howled in pain, and the sound echoed in her ears.

She scrambled up the side of the statue, the power from the blood magic propelling her forward. Four knots of kajani, a tangle of arms and swords and knives. At the center of each, Izara knew, was a member of Lindon's party.

The magic swelled inside of her.

She began to sing the hymn she'd sung that day in Papazian's office. The words rolled off her tongue. They tasted like blood.

The magic swelled—

And swelled—

And then it exploded, so strong she could *see* it, a ring of light erupting out of her chest and flowing over the forest. It was bright enough that her eyes watered. The trees bent. The kajani collapsed at once in a jangle of swords and chainmail, revealing Lindon and his three Eirenese men. They froze, their weapons poised, as the magic shimmered away.

"Izara?" Lindon gasped.

Izara nodded, then slumped down on the top of the statue. Her head was heavy, and her eyelids drooped. Her stomach roared for food, as if she hadn't eaten in weeks.

"What did you do?" demanded one of the Eirenese men. Lindon held up one hand and he fell silent, although he glowered at Izara from beneath a brow covered in sweat and kajan's blood.

"Magic," Izara said weakly. She could feel herself sliding off the statue. The world tilted. Lindon darted forward and caught her at the waist just as her feet touched the ground. The Eirenese men gaped at her.

"You have magic in Eiren, don't you?" snapped Lindon.

"What's that on your skin?" hissed another Eirenese man, the short one.

Izara laughed. It turned to a dry a cough. "The same thing that's on your skin." She stumbled away from Lindon and knelt down beside a pile of kajani. They were still alive; she could hear their raspy, throaty breathing.

"We have to leave," she said. "Before they wake up."

"You didn't even kill them?" demanded the shorter Eirenese man.

"Shut up, Njáll," snapped Lindon. "We don't use magic for killing in the Seraphine."

Njáll glared at him.

"Where's Celestia?" Izara asked, gazing around the path. Nothing but kajani.

"She ran," said Lindon. "Like the smart girl she is. We need to find her, fast." He glanced over at one of the other Eirenese men. "Our boat's not nearby, is it? Didn't we leave it at the Tahin Turn?"

"Aye," the man answered. "A good half day's hike from here."

"Shit," muttered Lindon.

Izara lifted her head, blinking through her daze. "Our boat is close by," she said, her words slurring together. "It didn't take us long to walk here. We can take you upriver." Her head dropped down and she swayed side to side, unsure of her footing. That would be the last of her contributions, she thought. *Gods*, magic had never exhausted her so thoroughly before.

"Your boat?" Lindon said. "So that's how you brought my pregnant wife out into the ruins."

"She was pregnant?" squawked Njáll.

"I told you, we are under the Lady of the Seraphine's command. We owed her a favor."

"A favor for *what*?" asked Lindon, his voice burning with a kind of desperate sorrow.

She shook her head. "That's for Celestia to say."

Lindon glared at her, his eyes full of fury. Then he turned to the Eirenese men and starting barking orders: "Into the forest! Find my gods-damned wife before these monsters wake up."

Izara picked at the drying kajan's blood. She should have told him—*The favor was for you.* But Celestia had begged her not to, and even now she wasn't going to break her promise.

"Come with me," Lindon said. "I'm not leaving you here."

"I'll only slow you down," Izara protested.

"And Celestia will never forgive me if I let you get eaten by a kajan. Come on."

Did kajani eat humans? Izara did not remember that detail from the stories. She glanced at the collapsed bodies. Spiral horns, sharp teeth. Monsters created by magic. She felt that much.

She shuffled behind Lindon, following him into the woods.

⁓

They found Celestia lying in a bed of ferns, her hair rippling out around her like an aura. Lindon rushed over to her and gathered her up in his arms. She hung limply, one hand trailing along the ground. Izara hung back, her breath frozen in her lungs. *I did that,* she thought, her head buzzing. *I killed her.*

I killed her baby.

The thought appeared unbidden. But no—that magic was not intended to kill. It hadn't killed the kajani. But she'd used kajani blood, and perhaps it was stronger than she expected. Celestia was a lady and not suited to adventuring in the forest. And if she was pregnant—

Izara's head spun, dizzy with fear. But then Celestia's fingers fluttered, tapping arrhythmically against the ferns.

Izara gasped with relief. She slumped up against a nearby tree and pressed her hand against her head, her heart hammering inside her chest. Lindon smoothed Celestia's hair away from her face and kissed her forehead with a gentleness that didn't suit his ripped, bloody clothes, his sweat-tangled hair.

"We need to get away from this place," Njáll said. "We don't know when those kajani will be waking again."

Lindon nodded. He glanced over at Izara and she stiffened, pressing the heel of her palm against the tree's rough bark.

"Will she recover?" Lindon asked.

Izara's head buzzed again. "Yes," she said, even though she didn't know for certain. "If she rests."

"You should never have brought her out here." He gathered Celestia up in his arms and stood, Celestia draped like a rag doll over his forearms. "She's not like you. She's a true noblewoman. She doesn't have your strength. If she dies before the baby—"

One of the Eirenese men lay a hand on Lindon's shoulder, and Lindon closed his eyes, took a deep breath. Izara trembled and fought back tears. As if she wouldn't suffer if Celestia died. As if she wouldn't have to live with the weight of her mistake for the rest of her life.

Lindon looked up. Didn't meet her eyes. "Take us back to your boat." He jerked his head at Celestia. "We need to get her to safety."

Izara nodded. She turned and picked her way through the forest, her chest tight. She walked numbly to the path. The kajani still lay in their bloodied piles. A few limbs twitched against the dirt. Izara took a deep breath and stared past them, down the line of the path. She could feel Lindon and his Eirenese partners staring at her back. Waiting.

"Get a move on, girl," one of the Eirenese men said. "This curse of yours doesn't seem that long-lasting."

Izara swallowed her anger. "This way," she muttered. As she followed the path, she dug around in her pack—her pack, miraculously untouched in that battle—and dug out the map and the compass. The needle spun and danced. Get Celestia back to the boat. That was her primary goal.

The walk back to the river did not seem to take as long as it had before. The men talked softly among themselves, mostly in Eirenese, and Izara was able to pick out a handful of innocuous words—*river* and *longer* and *why*. Izara followed the compass until she saw the river glittering between the trees.

Her chest tightened for a moment as she picked her way down to the shore—the boat should be protected by the Lady, but if something had happened to it, she would have to face the fury of Lindon and his men, and she would have to tend to Celestia in the woods. But when she stepped out of the shadow of the trees, the boat still bobbed in the water, the engines silent, the smoke stack empty. The ramp had been brought up, and Izara felt a breath of relief: Ico had made it back.

"This isn't the Cross Winds boat," Lindon said, stepping to Izara's side. Celestia's hair fell in a long dark waterfall from his arms, and it tickled against Izara's skin when the wind blew.

"I told you," Izara said, "We are here on behalf of the Lady of the Seraphine. This is her boat."

"Why's the ramp up?" he asked.

Izara swallowed. "There's a third with us. He ran before you arrived and must have made it back."

Lindon looked at her with eyes like burning coals. Izara tensed, readying herself for his questions. But instead, Lindon only stomped up to the boat and pounded his fist on the side. Izara startled at the sound of each *thump*. They reminded her of the gunshots from the battle. "Let the ramp down!" he hollered.

For a moment, the only sound was the rustling of the forest. Then Ico stuck his head out of the engine room doorway. "Oh, thank the ancestors, you made it back."

No thanks to you, Izara thought.

His gaze flashed over to Lindon. "Is this him? The husband? And I take it these are his Eirenese companions?"

"Who the hell is this?" snarled Lindon.

"Our third," Izara said weakly.

Ico leaned against the railing, the breeze stirring at his hair. "Is that the lady? What happened—" He jerked back, fear streaking across his face. "Oh, no. Don't tell me—"

"Let us aboard the gods-damned boat!" Lindon shouted. "She's got a curse on her, and there are kajani waiting in the forest!"

Ico's froze. His fear turned to confusion. "Kjani?" he said. "Those boogeymen from the stories? *That's* what we heard?"

"Yes, that's what you ran from!" Izara shouted. "Let the ramp down, you fucking pirate!"

Izara's own vehemence frightened her. Ico stepped out onto the deck and loosed the rope to drop the ramp. Lindon fixed her with an angry gaze. "A pirate?" he snapped. "What have you gotten my wife into?"

"His name is Ico," Izara said, and she didn't say anything more, only walked up the ramp. She could hear the footsteps of the others behind her, those heavy, warrior thuds. Ico watched them warily, his eyes narrowed.

"We need to sail them to their own boat, upriver," she said softly to him. "I promised."

"Was it really kajani?" he asked. "And not just men in masks?" He glanced over at Lindon and his party.

Izara felt suddenly very tired. "Yes, I'm sure," she said flatly. "You abandoned us. Left us to die."

"I told you to run with me!"

Izara shook her head. She didn't have the strength to argue with him.

"Where's the captain's quarters?" Lindon asked. "I assume that's where Celestia's sleeping."

Izara turned toward him. Celestia's eyes moved beneath her closed eyelids. The tallest and strongest-looking of the three Eirenese men kept his fingers rested lightly on the hilt of his sword. He wasn't looking at Ico, though, but out at the forest.

Izara wished she were back in her bed at the Academy, curled up beneath a down blanket as the mountain rain pattered softly against the roof. Anywhere but the hot, sweltering jungle, kajani blood staining her skin, her sister half-dead from magic.

"This way," she said to Lindon. Then, to Ico: "Get us moving. Now."

Both men did as she said.

———

Celestia opened her eyes and stared up at the ceiling and jolted with panic: that was not her ceiling. Her ceiling was painted with scenes from the jungle, orchids and passion flowers and the tented base of a lupuna tree. This ceiling was wooden, and dull, and dark.

And this room was moving.

She sat up, her head spinning. She could not remember the last thing that had happened to her—Lindon, she thought. Telling him about the baby. *The baby.* Her hand dropped down her stomach, still smooth and flat, still hiding her secret. She lifted her head, blinking. A lantern swung from that unfamiliar ceiling, casting eerie shadows across the floor.

And then the last few days flickered back to her, in bits and pieces. The Lady collecting her favor. The Aikha ruins. The kajani—

Kajani?

Celestia shoved her legs off the side of the bed. The room seemed to tilt, and she gave out a shout of surprise and fell backwards onto the blankets. Feet pounded somewhere outside. She could not tell how far away they were. It was as if she were lying in a tunnel.

The door swung open, and a man moved into the doorway.

"Lindon!" cried Celestia, and her heart thumped, because she was certain he was a waking dream. She had been going to find him, hadn't she—no, she *had* found him. In the Aikha ruins. And then the kajani had come.

"Celestia," Lindon said, and it sounded like him, his lovely mellifluous voice. He rushed across the cabin and threw his arms around her shoulders and buried his face into her hair. She sank into him. He smelled like the forest, thickly organic, the way he did when he came back in from a day's work at Cross Winds.

"You're alive," he murmured. "You're alive." He pulled away and pressed a hand to her stomach. His clothes were spotted with dark stains. Dirt? Blood? She felt dizzy. "And the baby—please tell me the baby is all right."

Celestia nodded, even though she had no way of knowing, not really. Her sheets weren't stained with blood, and she told herself that had to be a good sign.

Lindon stepped away from the bed, away from her. She stared at him, hopeless, trying to remember. She caught flashes of things: The trees shaking as the kajani spilled through. A glint of swords. The sweltering heat of magic.

"Why are you here?" Lindon said, his voice coarse.

"What?" she said, hazy.

"Putting aside this nonsense about finding Lord Kjari—Izara said you were on business for the Lady of the Seraphine." Lindon dropped his hands to side, clenched them into fists. "She said you owed her a favor." He met her gaze. His eyes gleamed. Not tears. She couldn't imagine Lindon crying. "What does that even mean? What favor?"

It was you, she thought, but when she opened her mouth she couldn't say the words. She had never told him about that night in the jungle, about the boon that had been granted the first time he'd seen her. She wanted him to stay blind to the role magic had played in their marriage. Some secrets a woman should keep.

"You're too frail for this." His voice trembled, and Celestia pulled the blanket up around her shoulders, hiding herself from him. "You should have refused. You should have—you almost *died*, Celestia. Our baby almost *died*."

He spat the last word like it was poison. His eyes bore into her, burning with a frightened anger.

"I couldn't refuse!" she cried. "I owe the Lady a favor. It was from a long time ago. I couldn't say no. But I was hoping—"

"How could the Lady send you out here like this?" Lindon's voice was pleading. "Why couldn't she find some other task for you?" He stroked her hair. "You'll shatter if you stay in the woods too long."

"I don't know," Celestia murmured.

Lindon stood up, his hands shaking. "This was Izara's doing, wasn't it? Her and her magic. That's just like an acolyte, to go asking favors from fucking gods."

"Don't blame Izara," Celestia snapped. "I asked her to do it."

Lindon whipped his eyes up to hers just as someone knocked at the door. "Go away!" Lindon shouted, but the door opened anyway. Izara.

Celestia felt a surge of frustration. This conversation had just gotten more complicated.

"Why the hell are you yelling?" she demanded.

"Because my wife and child almost died," he shot back. "Because of you and your gods-damned alchemy."

"I saved your gods-damned life," Izara said.

"Stop it." Celestia dug the heel of her hand against her temple. "Stop fighting. I can't—"

Izara and Lindon were both suddenly at her side, Izara leaning an ear to her chest, Lindon squeezing her hand so hard the bones in her fingers ground together.

"Heartbeat's normal," Izara said.

"I just wanted you to stop fighting!" Celestia yanked her hand away from Lindon, and he stared at her with big sorrowful eyes. "Why are you blaming Izara for what happened?"

Silence. Lindon glared at Izara.

"Because it was my fault," Izara said softly, looking down at her hands. "I had to stop the kajani. It knocked you out, too. I'm so sorry." Izara wrapped her arms around Celestia's shoulders and squeezed her tight. Celestia blinked past her. Lindon had started pacing back and forth across the room, his head tilted down, his matted, tangled hair falling in his eyes.

"You see?" Lindon said. He scowled. For a moment he looked like some cutthroat on the Jaila-Seraphine docks, and not like her husband at all. "This is what I mean. This—this *favor*—it's a death sentence for a lady like you. And that's not even getting into the fact that you're contradicting the wishes of the Emperor."

"The Emperor is contradicting the wishes of the Airiana," Izara said.

Lindon's eyes narrowed. "I have no way of knowing if that's true. But I do know what the Emperor does to traitors."

Celestia felt Izara's hand tighten around her own.

Lindon shook his head. "She can't be out here. She belongs back at Cross Winds, in the parlor, drinking her sparkling mango. And you know it."

Izara said nothing. Celestia couldn't blame her: after all, what was there to say? In so many ways, Lindon was right. She had been lucky to crawl away from the battle when she had, lucky that none of those dreadful, vicious monsters had tracked her through the woods. Luck. She was only alive, her baby was only alive, because of luck.

And he was right about the Emperor. If only the Lady would appear to him and explain their mission. But she remained scarce.

"We don't have a choice," Izara said.

"There's always a choice!" Lindon shouted.

"Lindon, don't," Celestia said, and she struggled to sit up. The room tilted. Was the boat going under? No, no, she was just swooning. The air felt hot and glittering the way it had when the magic swept through the jungle.

"You're upsetting her!" Izara shouted. She pressed her hand against Celestia's forehead and pushed her back against the pillows. Celestia blinked up at the ceiling.

"She's weak," Izara went on. "She needs to rest."

"Of course she does." Lindon's voice was sharp-edged. It made Celestia feel cold. "You blasted that fucking spell all over her, all over my *child*."

"We were trying to find you," Izara snapped. "To end this madness as quickly as we could. But you're refusing to help us—"

"I'm refusing to see my wife cut down by kajani—or pirates, for that matter," Lindon said. "Take her back to Cross Winds before the Emperor drags you all to the gallows."

"Wait," Celestia said, trying to push herself up to sitting. The effort exhausted her and she slumped back against the far wall. Lindon turned to her, his eyes glittering. "Lindon, we have to deliver Lord Kjari to the Lady of the Seraphine. But it doesn't matter how we fetch him. You could find him, bring him to her—"

Another wave of dizziness swept over Celestia. For a moment the world seemed to fall away.

Lindon darted over to her, so quick she startled at his movement, and knelt beside her bed. Stroked one hand against her hair. It always calmed her, the gentleness of her husband. "You need to go home to Cross Winds," he said. "Where it's safe."

"She's right, though." Izara stepped forward. "You could find Kjari for us."

Lindon stood, his touch slipping away. "This is the real world, not that academy in the mountains." The anger was back in his voice again, burning away the edges. "I'm not about to commit treason against the Emperor because you went dabbling in something you didn't understand. What the Emperor does to traitors is far worse than the Airiana." He flung one finger at Celestia. "Take her home. Now."

Celestia blinked and tears fell over her cheeks, marring the sheets with dark spots.

"Lindon, *please*," Izara said. "You can't kill him."

Lindon threw up his hands. "Listen to yourself! Of course we have to kill him! Gods and monsters, we can't go against the wishes of the Emperor!"

"Lindon," Celestia whispered. "It's the *Airiana*."

"The Airiana don't rule this Empire," Lindon snapped. "The Emperor does. And I've been assigned to kill Lord Kjari once and for all. If I do as you ask, we'll both end up tortured by a gang of Starless Mages."

"We *have* to," Izara said. "The Emperor has misread the situation."

Lindon sighed. "That might be the case. It's not for me to say."

"No, it's for the Airiana to say!" Izara cried. "Help us!"

Lindon's expression softened then, and he braced himself against the wall and rubbed at his forehead. "I spent years working for the Emperor," he said. "Trying to earn my way into his good graces."

Trying to earn a title, Celestia knew. One that was never granted to him.

"I've been the man to drag traitors from their homes," he said in a rough voice. "I've marched through the forest with Starless Mages at my side. I know what they would do to you, to all of us, if I went along with this."

"But the Lady—"

"The Lady did not give me my assignment," Lindon said. "Please, Izara, I'm begging you. Take Celestia back to Cross Winds. You have a strength she does not. You and that pirate can complete this mission."

The room filled with silence. Izara slumped, and Celestia knew they would never be able to convince him. She felt a flare of anger then, not at Lindon, but at the Lady of the Seraphine. How could she trap Lindon in such an impossible situation? Celestia was certain she could convince him to help if she wasn't also asking him to defy the Emperor in the same breath.

It had been such a strong plan. Ask him to be her husband, and do this for her. But it *was* treason. And now she knew that any hope she had of returning to Cross Winds quickly was shattered.

"Lindon," she said softly, and he turned toward her, his eyes bright with fear.

"I understand why you can't bring Kjari back to the Lady," she whispered. "It was wrong of me to ask you to go against the Emperor's commands."

"Celestia," Lindon said, his features softening.

"But I cannot go back to Cross Winds. The Lady would torture and kill me far worse than the Starless Mages."

His face twisted with fear, and Celestia's heart almost stopped. But he said nothing. He only stood, his eyes wet with tears.

And then he turned and stomped out of the room.

Celestia wept.

~

They arrived at Lindon's boat at sunset that same day. Celestia saw it through the narrow window beside her bed, the water stained orange. She was too weak to crawl out of bed, too weak to say goodbye. But Lindon came into the room, knocking and then pushing the door open, not waiting for an answer. The sunset poured around him.

"Please, Celestia, I'm begging you," he said. "Just go home. I can't bear to think of you in the grips of the Starless Mages."

"If I go home," she said, "I'll have to face the Lady's wrath instead."

Lindon rubbed his forehead and gave a deep, aggrieved sigh. "What you're doing is still treason," he murmured.

"I was actually considering that," she said carefully. "The Emperor hasn't asked anything of me."

Lindon dropped his hand and looked up at her. "Celestia."

"It wouldn't be treason if I do it," she continued, her voice shaky. "If you didn't help."

"You're *pregnant*. As soon as you start to show you need to be in bed." His eyes shone. Tears, she thought. "The pregnancy could kill you otherwise."

"Please," she said, "I don't want us to part on a fight."

"Then please go back to Cross Winds."

She sighed. She was too tired for this, and even the thought of answering was too much. She slumped back into her pillows, one hand on her belly, protecting her baby.

And then, like the sun disappearing behind a cloud, he was gone. For a moment Celestia lay unmoving, listening to Lindon tell his Eirenese partners that it was nothing, he didn't want to talk about it, let's get the hell out of here. Then she pushed herself up, pain shooting through her legs, so she could watch as they boarded their boat from the shore. Tears stung her eyes. It didn't feel real, him leaving like that. But she knew it was.

A cloud of white smoke puffed out of the smokestack; the ship's wheel began churning the water. Celestia sank back down into the pillows and stared at the ceiling so she wouldn't have to watch him leave. And she wondered about the cruel irony of the Lady, to pit her in competition against her husband.

A few moments later, a knock sounded against the cabin door. "Come in," Celestia called out weakly. She half-expected to see Lindon on the other side, announcing that he'd changed his mind, that he would help fetch Lord Kjari after all. But it was Izara, looking mournful in the bronzed sunlight pouring in around her.

"Are you all right?" she asked, not looking Celestia in the eye. Izara had never been good with emotions.

"I suppose I have to be."

Izara fell silent. The boat's engine kicked on suddenly, a roaring that Celestia felt from within the walls.

"That's Ico," Izara said. "I came to ask you—"

"Could you shut the door?" Celestia interrupted. "The light's hurting my eyes."

Izara blinked once, then nodded and pulled the door shut. The room's dimness was a balm against the pain in Celestia's bones.

"I came to ask you," Izara started again, and Celestia wanted to tell her to leave, that she was in no mind to make decisions right now. "Ico was talking to one of Lindon's men, and he found out they're heading south, to Konmar."

Konmar. The southernlands, the frozen desert at the bottom of the world. She dropped her head to the side, stared at the wall. "Do they really think they'll find Lord Kjari there?"

"It's from an Eirenese legend." Izara sat down on the edge of Celestia's bed. "I read it at the Academy. Something about kajani coming from the frozen wastes of the south." She paused, and Celestia tried to imagine Lindon in the Konmar desert, crawling his way through the ice and snow. Then Izara said, "I suppose following him wouldn't be the worst idea."

Celestia fiddled the hem of her nightgown, rubbing the fabric back and forth between her thumb and forefinger. Her whole body ached; so did her heart. Follow Lindon. It made sense, if she thought of it intellectually. But he would be furious to see her again, and she didn't think she could stand another round of his terror of what would happen to her and the baby at the hands of the Starless Mages.

"So what do you think we should do?" Izara said.

Celestia jumped and her muscles cried out in protest. "I don't think we should follow him."

Silence again. Izara slipped off the bed and stood with her arms crossed over her chest. "Then where do you think we should go?"

Celestia closed her eyes. Everything before waking up in the captain's quarters was still a haze, coming to her in fragments.

"We could try Eiren," she said. "The places where this—this darkness is occurring."

Izara frowned, and Celestia could see the hesitation all over her face. "I spoke to Ico about that," she said. "He says he saw the, um, the dead man—" Her voice wavered. "In Sra Slarin."

Celestia gaped at her. "That's in the far north!"

Izara nodded.

"It would take months for us to get there!"

"I know," Izara said. "And the Lady did say Kjari is in the Seraphine. "I think we should focus our search here. Not Eiren and not Konmar. *Here.*"

Celestia nodded. It made sense. But the Seraphine was an enormous swath of land, comprising forest and riverbed and mountains and even the cold desert in the west. She had no idea where to start—

And then something sparked in her memory.

"I found something," she said.

Izara looked up at her. "What?"

"I found something. While I was hiding. I—brought it back with me—it was so *strange*, such a coincidence—"

Izara knelt down beside the bed and grabbed Celestia's hand. "A coincidence? Oh gods, what was it? What did you find?"

"A box," Celestia said. "With a map. It was in my pocket, the pocket of my dress. If it didn't fall out—" She settled down into her pillows. Even talking was exhausting her. "It was sticking out of the dirt. Just before the light hit me—"

"It's the magic fallout," Izara said. She jumped to her feet and paced around the room. Just watching made Celestia's legs hurt. "Of course, all that magic I used—there had to be something—"

"What are you talking about?"

"I tossed your dress down below after I changed you," Izara said. "Wait here."

"Izara—"

"Magic creates coincidences, Celestia!" Izara flung open the cabin door. "I don't have time to explain. Just—it could be something!"

And then she slammed out of the cabin. Celestia settled back into her bed. The conversation had left her drained and weakened. Lindon was right: she shouldn't be here. The Lady should have required a payment more suitable to Celestia's skills.

Footsteps bounded across the boat. Each echoing thump made Celestia's head hurt. Ico's soft accented voice. Izara's response. Both were too muffled for Celestia to hear what they had said.

And then the door opened. Izara had Celestia's dress balled up in her arms, the fabric streaked with those awful dark stains.

"Let's hope this can tell us something," Izara said. She fumbled in the tangle of fabric. Celestia's chest felt tight— what if the box was a trap, a danger? But then Izara extracted her hand and in her palm was the box. Izara turned it around in her hands, frowning.

"Can you read the runes?" Celestia asked.

Izara shook her head. She flipped back the lid of the box. Her brow furrowed. Then she looked up at Celestia. "Essir?"

"I think that's what I read, yes." When she tried to think of finding the box she only saw the green light of the jungle.

"Where is Essir?" Izara began pacing again, although she didn't take her eyes off the inside of the box. "I mean, it must be some Old Sera name, but this map is—" Her voice trailed off and she turned the box upside down and squinted down at it.

Celestia hadn't recognized the name, either, and she couldn't recall it from any of the history lessons she'd been given as a child.

"It's a map," Izara said triumphantly. "We could follow it. Oh, gods, this is exactly what we needed!"

Celestia thought of Lindon sailing south to Konmar on the whim of an Eirenese story. That really wasn't any less reasonable than following a map carved into a box that had been lying half-buried in the Aikha ruins.

They were both chasing dust and shadows.

Izara hunched over the box, one finger tracing a path through its interior. "This map is leading us deep into the western forest," she said. "Near Relira." She frowned. "Sort of near Alriel."

Celestia listened. The western forest had been a staple of their childhood stories. The kajani lived in the western forest, the stories said, moving there after the war and carving out homes in the Alriel Mountains.

The kajani, created by Lord Kjari during the Last War, with a dark magic so powerful it had been forced out of existence by the Airiana. Only women had the right to create life. It was a gift from Growth. Kjari's actions had been an abomination, completed as part of a pact with Decay.

But they'd also been fictional, a story told to teach children a lesson. And yet Celestia had seen them fighting in the sunlight, gray skin and black hair like the feathers of carrion birds.

Celestia lifted her gaze and found Izara staring at her. She wondered if Izara had made the same connections, plotted the same points in history and myth.

"I think we should follow the map," Izara said.

And Celestia was too tired to do anything but nod.

SIX

The sky was turning purple with twilight when Ico learned they would be traveling into the western forest. Izara handed him a crumbling jewelry box and said, "Take us there," flipping back the lid to reveal a map carved into the stone.

"Where the hell is that?" Ico said, annoyed "Essir Tanez? The fuck's that supposed to mean?"

"It's old Seran," Izara said, and then turned and stomped back to the captain's quarters, where Her Ladyness Celestia was laid up with a magical hangover. Ico stared down at the map in the box, then looked up at the river, gloomy with moonlight. The Eirenese adventurers were long gone. He sighed. "Just do what they tell me," he muttered. "Easier way to get out of this alive."

He ambled into the engine room, having resigned himself to the whims of the two sisters. Personally, he would have preferred to follow Celestia's husband and his Eirenese pals; at least they seemed to know what they were doing. But sure. He'd follow a piece of trash Celestia picked up in the woods.

He kicked open the engine door and shoved the coals around, heat wafting off them in waves. Not that it mattered; the boat ran on magic. "You heard the ladies," he said to the engine. "We're going to the Essir Tanez." He closed the engine and tossed the box on the table. It clinked up against something. A pipe, carved in the Seran style, and a little silk pouch lying beside it. Ico laughed.

"Is this like the food?" he said. "A gift to keep us happy?" He wasn't sure if he was talking to the boat or the Lady of the Seraphine. He never was.

At any rate, neither one answered.

Ico opened the pouch and sniffed at it cautiously. He was greeted by the pungent scent of sweetflower. Well. That was a delicacy he hadn't had in a while—not since his piracy days. Sweetflower was expensive stuff, the sort of thing Celestia's husband probably smoked as he sat reading the evening paper, servants scuttling around him.

"What's the occasion?" Ico muttered. The fires in the engine crackled. He decided to take this as a sign that Izara and her rotting box were leading them in the right direction. Not that he was going to tell her that. Let her sweat it out a bit.

Ico pinched some of the sweetflower between his thumb and forefinger, relishing the sticky feel of it against his skin. Quality stuff. He packed the sweetflower into the pipe, then rolled up a piece of blank parchment from the logbook and ignited it with the engine fire. He puffed on the pipe, clouds of pinkish-gray smoke drifting up through the room. Ico stamped out the lit parchment beneath his feet and then settled back in his chair, kicking his feet up on the table. An evening rain shower had started up, pattering softly against the roof of the cabin.

The sweetflower made Ico's limbs loose and wobbly—another mark of quality—and it left the taste of scorched honey on his tongue. Smoke gathered up along the ceiling like rain clouds.

"I could get used to this," he said. "Guess I did the right thing running out of there when I did? Izara can handle a couple of kajani, at least. Let's just be glad it wasn't the Kozas, like I thought."

The boat didn't answer, and Ico was too languid from the sweetflower to care that he was talking to himself like a madman. Maybe Xima could hear him somehow anyway, watching him through some strain of Airiana magic. He liked the idea. It made him feel protected. Safe.

He smoked down the sweetflower he'd packed into the pipe, then set the pipe down on the table, next to the pouch. His head swum around with a delicious kind of wooziness. The rain had slackened, and Ico had a desire to be outside in the steamy night air, away from the engine fires and the smoke still gathering near the ceiling. So he lurched his way over to the door. The air was as thick as molasses. By his ancestors, it'd been too long since he'd smoked sweetflower. That was a young man's drug.

"Maybe it wasn't a gift at all," he muttered, pushing the door open. Humid, rain-scented air slammed into him. The sky was starless, all the light blocked by rainclouds. Ico shuffled out onto the deck. Neither of the sisters was around, thank the ancestors for that, and he leaned up against the railing and breathed the soupy air in deep. The rain had brought a breeze down from the mountain that was laced with threads of coolness. Ico's skin prickled with goosebumps and a distant memory of Xima's touch. It was so much easier to feel the world when you were buzzing from a pipeful of sweetflower.

He opened his eyes and stared out into the woods. In the

filtered moonlight the plants seemed to glow. He pressed himself against the railing for balance and watched, transfixed, as the trees shook their long leafy branches, lines of darkness against the lighter sky. The river water was the color of ink. Just like the ocean was, when you sailed far away from the shore, when you'd been exiled by the Koza clan.

Out in the forest, something flickered.

Ico froze. The languor from the sweetflower fought against his instinct for alertness.

There it was again. A flash of metal moving through the trees. Ico's heart started thumping. He gripped the railing tight and leaned forward off the side of the boat. The trees swayed. He didn't see anything else.

The Kozas.

Ico stumbled backward. He'd loosened his guard after they never showed up to torture him in Istai-Seraphine, and when the sisters came back from the forest ranting about kajani, he'd let it slip further. He'd convinced himself they weren't coming.

But something was clearly out there. And this stretch of forest was isolated, rural. There weren't any acreages out here, no towns, no settlements.

An animal wouldn't be carting metal around.

Ico pressed himself up against the outside wall of the engine room. He stared out at the woods and saw it again: another blink of metal, a glimmer like a star. Whoever it was must have a torch as well.

Ico eyes watered. He wiped at them, then turned back to the forest.

The metal and the firelight vanished, swallowed up by trees.

The Lady had said he would be protected on the water, not hidden. Did that meant this scout could watch him from the shore, lurking through the trees, waiting for him to step on dry land?

Waiting for the *sisters* to step on dry land?

Ico squeezed his eyes shut, willing himself not to think of his slaughtered crew, with Izara and Celestia's face's superimposed on the corpses. They dragged him into this nonsense, but they didn't deserve to die like that.

No one did.

Ico shuffled along the wall, moving toward the engine room door. The forest glided by, a curtain of endless shadows. He swore he saw eyes glowing in the leafy darkness—that old Koza trick to scare merchants out of their boats.

"Fuck," he muttered as his hands found the handle to the engine room. He pushed the door open and tumbled inside and slammed the door closed. He sucked down deep drafts of air, trying to calm his heartbeat. Didn't work. The pipe and the pouch of sweetflower were still lying on the table, though, and Ico slumped down on the chair and picked the pipe up with trembling hands.

"This why you gave this to me?" he said to the boat. "Because you knew I'm being hunted?"

The coals collapsed into the pit, the only answer Ico was getting.

He should have known better than to trust the Airiana. Xima was the only one of them worth a damn. The Lady had given him protection on a gods-damned technicality. When they got to Essir Tanez or Tanzer or whatever the fuck, he'd have to convince the two sisters they needed to stay aboard the boat. For their protection. Not just his.

Ico puffed on the pipe, the smoke crawling like twisting serpents through his lungs. He leaned back and breathed out. The haze settled over him again. His anxiety peeled away, turning to smoke with each exhale.

He'd fucked himself over five years ago, agreeing to take those two girls on a trek through the wood. That was what he got for trying to go straight.

───

It took two days to get to the Essir Tributary—Izara had explained to him over dinner the first night that *tanez* was just the Old Seran word for *tributary*. "Already learned one type of Seran," Ico muttered, speaking around a trout bone. "Ain't learning another." But his thoughts had really been on the flicker of metal in the forest. He'd spotted it at least five more times as the boat wove deeper into the unpopulated parts of the forest. Adventurer's territory, that was the pirate's term for it. Pirate's territory was down at the mouth of the river, in the brackish waters of the Seraphine Bay. That was where the money was.

There was nothing out here but trees and rain and heat and strange shrieking animal cries.

Celestia and Izara were feeling it, too. Ico could tell, even though he only saw them at mealtimes. The first post-ruins, post-kajani-fight dinner it had just been Ico and Izara, and aside from the etymology lesson she had just picked at her food, not saying much. By the next morning, though, Celestia was shuffling around the boat again, trailing swatches of gauzy white fabric like an ancestors-damned ghost. Ico knew to blame the boat. It conjured up whatever clothing it felt like. Hell, he'd been wearing the same forest-workers' shirt and trousers for the last few days since the boat kept coughing up a nobleman's suit. Too hot for that shit.

Nobody spoke much, though, not even when Celestia was up again. She spent most of her time up on deck, sitting on the bench, watching the forest go by. He wondered if she saw the same glints of metal and flashes of torchlight he did when he went out there. Never asked her, though. Didn't want to deal with her worrying on top of everything else.

It was late afternoon when the boat finally puttered up to the Essir Tributary. Ico'd been in the engine room, flipping through the old ledgers—he'd read through them once already, but there wasn't much else to do aside from staring at the forest hoping to get a glimpse of whoever was following them—when he heard one of the sisters shouting out on the deck. He didn't recognize which one it was, but he tossed the book aside and crept out there, his fingers resting on the hilt of his knife. Could be the Koza clan found their way through the Lady's protection. He wasn't taking the risk.

The light was liquid, a thick golden-purple that seeped into all the crevices of the boat. Both of the sisters were out at the bow. Celestia dangled a lamp over the edge, its yellow fire-light swinging back and forth over the water. Ico's chest tightened. He didn't like the look of this.

"What the hell's going on?" he called out.

They both ignored him. Typical with those two. He pulled out his knife.

"Well?" he said. "You got an answer for me?"

"We're here." Celestia glanced over her shoulder. The lantern light brightened half her face and cast the other half into darkness. "The Essir Tanez. We're here."

Ico looked out into the lengthening shadows. The forest was a dark mass in the gloaming, but he could make out a carved stone sign reading *Essir Tanez*. The river split off into a path shimmering through the woods. Lights gleamed somewhere among the trees; he could see them reflecting on the water.

"What exactly is this place?" he asked.

"We don't know," said Izara. "We were just following the map."

"Let's hope that was a good idea," Ico muttered.

The boat tilted, turning toward the tributary. The river up ahead was definitely illuminated; light streaked like paint across the surface of the water. Celestia drew in her lantern and set it on the deck. Ico knelt down and extinguished it.

"I don't like this," he said. He thought of the glint of metal that had been following them the last two days. "There shouldn't be lights in this part of the forest. No one lives out here."

"Someone does," said Celestia. She was staring ahead. The breeze blew her hair away from her face.

"It could be a trap," Ico said. *The Kozas. Trying to get us to shore. They must know they can't attack us on the river, somehow.* "The kajani, maybe."

Celestia and Izara glanced at each other. Neither spoke. The boat drifted forward, moving slowly. It ought to be picking up speed by now. Ico pulled his knife out of his belt. Izara looked over at him, frowned. Ico grinned at her.

"One of us has to protect the boat." He tossed the knife up in the air and caught it by the blade. Showing off. Trying not to let them know he was scared as hell.

Izara pulled that stone box out of her dress pocket and flipped it open. The lights up ahead were bright enough that even though Ico couldn't see their source yet, they cast a wide-net glow over the entire river. Izara squinted down at the map.

"There's another turnoff," she said. "But that doesn't make sense, does it? This close to the first?"

"May I see?" Celestia took the map from her and leaned over it. Ico tensed. He didn't give a damn about the map. But they had to be drawing close to that light source.

"Maybe you two girls should go down below," he said.

They ignored him.

"I don't think this is a river path," Izara said. "I think we'll have to go the rest of the way on foot."

Ico tightened his grip on his knife, angled his body. They weren't going any damn place on foot. Not if there was a chance that the Kozas were waiting for them.

The boat drifted around a turn, revealing the light source.

The knife slipped out of Ico's hand and clattered to the deck. He scooped down to pick it back up, his gaze fixed firmly on the fucking *impossibility* up ahead.

It was a house.

A great house, in fact, one of those sprawling, stately acreage homes you found on the eastern part of the river, closer to civilization. It was lit up with alchemical lanterns, the light creamy and unwavering. A dock jutted out into the river, a lantern swinging at the end of it, dots of green dancing across the water.

"What the hell?" Ico said. He looked over at the two sisters, who were both gaping at the house in rather unladylike fashion. Normally he'd find it funny. Not tonight. "Did you know this was going to be here?"

"No," said Izara, gazing up at the house.

"This can't—I mean—who *lives* here?" sputtered Celestia.

Izara shook her head.

"No one lives in the west," said Celestia. She counted on her fingers. "The De Mizells live at Shadowplains, near Malill-Seraphine. They're the farthest out. Right? Is there a family we don't know?"

"I never kept track of the families," Izara said. "You know that."

The boat slowed to a crawl. They were approaching the dock, Ico realized. They were *turning*.

"The boat's putting us up here," he said.

The sisters ignored him. Celestia kept murmuring the names of nobles' houses to herself. Izara just stared ahead, as if the house would give her the answers she wanted. Ico cursed and picked his knife off the deck and peered out at the dock.

It was empty. No dockmaster, no guards. If it weren't for the lights, Ico would have assumed the place was abandoned.

"Girls," he said. "We're stopping."

No answer.

"Will you two fucking pay attention?" he roared. "We're pulling into the dock."

Celestia fell silent and looked over at him. The lights hollowed out the bones of her face.

"What?" she said.

"The boat is taking us to that damn dock."

As he spoke, the boat turned lazily and drifted up toward the shore. Izara looked down at the map again.

"This is it," she said. "This is the turnoff. We're going to have to go the rest of the way by foot."

Like hell I am, thought Ico. He pushed past the two sisters and scanned over the house gardens, looking for some sign of their tracker. Nothing. The place was bathed in light, and he didn't see anyone.

"I don't like this," Ico said.

"Me, neither," said Izara. Ico breathed with relief. One of them was being reasonable. "But I don't think we have much choice."

Ico looked over at her sharply. He realized he was hoisting up his knife without thinking. "What the hell do you mean?"

"Don't point your knife at me." Izara's eyes glittered in the alchemical light. "I mean, we have a map. We have to follow the map. That means going into the woods."

"No," said Celestia.

Ico turned to her. She was standing very still, looking out at the house.

"No?" said Izara. "What do you think we should do?"

"We won't be going into the woods, not exactly," said Celestia. "We'll be going into the house's forest-farm. Their property." She turned to Izara and she looked like she was carved of stone in the lantern light, as hard and cold as a soldier. "We'll have to ask permission first."

Silence.

"Maybe not," said Izara. "I studied a bit of defensive magic at school. I could easily hide us from view, at least until we're far enough in—"

Celestia glowered at her. "Do you really think a house like this won't have wards against alchemists?"

Izara sank back into the shadows, her gaze cast down. "You're right," she murmured.

The idea of wards and magic didn't make Ico feel any safer.

"We should introduce ourselves as travelers," Celestia said to Izara. "Tell them we were visiting a nearby house and found this charming box and we decided to take a detour on our way home. Shadowplains, perhaps. This house is so isolated I doubt they'll check with Lady De Mizell. And anyway, hospitality says they have to take us in and at least show us the path."

Ico toyed with his knife. If they were being tracked by the Kozas, he'd have even more blood on his hands: the sisters and whatever aristocrat was locked away in this house.

He wondered if he ought to say something. Warn them. But then they'd want to know why the hell he hadn't said anything earlier. He could just hear Celestia shrieking about it. Could just see Izara rolling her eyes. No. Not worth it.

Especially since he didn't *know* it was the Kozas. Not for certain.

"Ico, go put on one of those merchant's jackets the boat is always creating for you," said Celestia.

"What?" Ico jerked out of his thoughts and frowned at her. "Why?"

"Because you have to look respectable if we're going to do this properly. We'll try to pass you off as an eccentric cousin. Do you think that will work, Izara?" Celestia's eyes brightened. "Oh! I wonder if that's why the boat was giving you the jackets in the first place? Because it knew we would be arriving here? That we'd have to pass through this house?"

Izara frowned thoughtfully, but Ico just thought of that sweetflower that had materialized in the engine room.

He still wasn't going to risk stepping foot off this boat, though.

"Really?" he said. "An Akuranian cousin? Better I just stay on the boat. Keep guard."

The two sisters stared at him. The deepening twilight was as thick as smoke, and the insects chirped and shrieked up in the trees, a whining symphony that bore into Ico's head.

"Are you afraid of the land, Captain Ishi Kui?" said Celestia with a mocking smile. You almost wouldn't know her husband had ditched her not two days ago. "Forest is protecting us from Kjari's watchful eye."

Ico glared at her. "But not his kjani, apparently."

"Those kjani were chasing Lindon, not us," Izara said primly.

"Well, I just ain't comfortable leaving the boat unattended."

"We left it unattended at the ruins," Izara shot back. "This is the dock of a great house. It won't be unattended here."

"Are you kidding me?" Ico strolled over to the railing and gestured out at the shore. "Do you see anyone around here? 'Cause I sure as hell don't."

"We're on their property," Celestia said. "There are spells and enchantments in place for protection."

A cold bead of sweat dropped down Ico's spine. "Yeah, but you really think they'll buy me as some cousin of yours? Isn't it better for me to pass as a servant? Stay here?"

"And are you going to stay here when we follow the rest of the map?" Izara waved the box around. Ico glared at it. He hated that fucking box, taking them off the river. "We're not going into the woods unaccompanied again. We were lucky to find Lindon at the ruins."

"It was the Lady's doing," said Celestia softly, and she bowed her head reverently.

Ico sighed. "You don't need me. You got your magic."

Celestia lifted her gaze and glared at him. Izara just looked bored.

"Go get the jacket," she said.

"I told you, it's better if I stay here—"

Izara sighed then, and mumbled something under breath, a string of syllables that were foreign to Ico's ears. His head buzzed. The air smelled as if something was burning. And then, for a half a heartbeat, he was drifting through mist and storm clouds.

"What the fuck?" he shouted, just as he realized he was no longer standing on the deck of the boat, but on the soft, mulchy soil of the house's lawn.

Panic seized him at the throat. He yanked out his knife and crouched into a fighting stance. "What did you do?" he snarled. "What did you do?"

Izara and Celestia stood a few paces away, both of them luminous in the pearly light from the house. Both of them looking at him like he'd lost his mind.

"What's gotten into you?" Celestia said.

Ico whipped his head around. It was nearly full dark now, the sun having vanished beneath the treeline. The wind blew across the top of the forest, carrying with it miles and miles of jungle sounds. Goosebumps prickled along his skin. The insects and the cries of animals were too loud. He couldn't hear anyone coming up on him—

Out of the corner of his eye, glinting metal swooped into shadow.

"You won't take us!" he screamed, and he hurled his knife

into the darkness. He heard the thump of the knife as it landed, but no screams of surprise or pain.

"Shit," he muttered. Stupid. He panicked. Now he was without a weapon completely.

The sisters gaped at him.

"What?" he snapped. "Do you have any idea the risk you might have put us in?"

"What are you talking about?" asked Celestia.

He glanced in the direction he'd thrown his knife. Nothing but darkness. But then he heard a scraping, wood on stone. His blood spiked. The house, it was coming from the house.

This is it, he thought, and he told himself he would die like a man, like a pirate, without screaming or tears.

A figure stepped through the grand archway. It was a small figure, clad in a dark, simple suit. Celestia let out a sharp hissing through her teeth in Ico's direction.

"Fool," she spat out, before raising her hand in greeting.

"No—" Ico started, but Celestia was already speaking, already striding across the lawn, her dress streaking out behind her like a beam of moonlight.

"Good evening," she called out, and her voice was like sugar cane, sweet and cloying. "I do hope we haven't disturbed you. My name is Celestia De Malena, of the De Malena family. We had expected to arrive earlier."

Ico held his breath and told himself the tracker wasn't here. That for now, they were safe.

The figure on the porch bowed deeply, his hand sweeping out in front of him. "My Lady," he said. "Welcome to Essir Manor. I am certain Lady De Lisista will be absolutely delighted to meet a member of the De Malena line. Please, do come in."

Celestia suppressed a long breath of relief as the butler led her into the foyer. It was designed in an antekjarin style, with a high arched ceiling that stretched up all the floors of the house. The D'Nale family had a foyer like this, although they had decorated the space in a more modern fashion, with delicate Imardi paintings lined up in gilded frames on the walls. Here, the decorations themselves were trapped in the antekjarin period, with carved frescos on the wall, and ivy growing around the banisters.

"I'm afraid Lady De Lisista isn't used to visitors," the butler said. He stopped next to a carved wooden statue of one of the Airiana, the lines twisted and stylized and gruesome. Decay. Celestia took an inadvertant step backward, shocked at the appearance of Decay in a great house. Only the desperate worshipped him.

"I hope we aren't too much of a bother," Celestia said quickly. She was aware of Ico and Izara lurking behind her. Izara had never been good at these types of social niceties, although she tried—gods only knew what the butler thought of Ico, in his shabby forest worker's clothing. *Why* had he put up such a fuss about leaving the boat? She would need to draw it out of him later, find out what he was so frightened of.

"Oh, no bother," the butler said quickly. "I apologize if I misled you. Lady De Lisista is always happy to greet visitors, of course." He smiled wanly. Celestia returned it. She couldn't tell if he was lying. A skillful butler, this one.

"We won't keep her too terribly late," Celestia said.

The butler nodded, then gestured toward an open door at the end of the foyer. Celestia swept into it. She was aware that she wasn't exactly fit for visiting; she was still sticky from travel, and her hair had no doubt come unraveled. Her clothing was stiff with old sweat. Still, their late arrival time gave her an excuse.

The door led into a sitting room, also decorated in the antekjarin style—this Lady De Lisista must be a traditionalist, then. The chairs were high backed and carved with images from the forest, birds and insects and trees, and there was a large mosaic of a panther on the far wall, its eyes two gleaming opals. Celestia noticing Ico staring at those opals, a grin toying at the edges of his mouth. Her cheeks flushed with anger; she hoped he wouldn't forget that he wasn't a pirate anymore.

"Who shall I say is accompanying you, Lady De Malena?"

Celestia whirled around. The butler stood in the doorway, hands folded behind his back. His posture was utterly polite, but had she heard a mocking timbre in his voice? Even with her short time on the river, she'd forgotten what civilization was like.

"My sister, Izara De Malena," she said. Izara was admiring another wood-carved sculpture, although this one was of a Laniana, some flower spirit, her eyes like blossoms. Celestia coughed politely in her hand—their old signal. Izara whipped around and curtsied by rote. The butler did not react.

"And this gentleman is—is our cousin." Celestia smiled as dazzlingly as she could. "Ico De Malena."

"Very good, Lady De Malena." The butler bowed. "I shall alert Lady De Lisista to your arrival. Feel free to contact the kitchen if you'd like anything to drink." He stepped backward out of the room and pulled the door shut behind him. Celestia's shoulders sagged with relief.

"You really think it's going to be that easy?" said Ico.

Celestia looked at him over her shoulder. He seemed to have calmed himself somewhat. And at least he didn't have that knife anymore.

"That wasn't the hard part," she said.

"She's right." Izara looked up from the statue. "No servant could turn us away. But the lady of the house can."

Ico frowned. He looked as if he wanted to speak, and

Celestia watched him, waiting. But he only turned back to the mosaic.

"Don't you dare steal those opals," she said.

"Didn't even occur to me."

Celestia scoffed. She glanced at Izara, who looked as unhappy as she usually did in these kinds of situations. Her arms were crossed over her chest and her hair hung in tatters around her face. Celestia sighed. Most of the noble families along the south river knew Izara and had long since learned to accept her peculiarities. "The scholar," they called her, whenever Celestia would meet with them. "And how *is* the scholar doing?" But Lady De Lisista was a stranger, and if she was as old-fashioned as her decorating tastes, that could prove a problem.

"Oh, sweetie, your hair," Celestia said, and she bustled over to Izara and pushed the loose strands away. Izara stood compliantly. They'd done this a thousand times.

"Do you really think this is going to work?" Izara asked in a low voice as Celestia combed her fingers through Izara's hair. For a moment Celestia was transported back to their childhoods, all those times Celestia had rebraided Izara's hair before they walked downstairs to meet their parents' guests. Two days ago Celestia had been bedridden from the side effects of Izara's magic, and yet standing in the drawing room of a great house was enough to cast them back in their usual roles.

"I hope so," Celestia said. "Because I'm not sure what to do next."

"Go to Konmar, I suppose." Izara frowned. "Or Sra Slarin."

Gods, this really *had* to work, then.

Izara pushed Celestia's hands away, just like she had when she was a little girl. "I'm sure my hair is fine now."

"You look better than Ico."

"Heard that," said Ico.

Celestia ignored him. "Who do you think that is?" she asked, gesturing at the statue behind Izara.

"I don't know," Izara said. "Perhaps a Laniana sacred to the land around here. Whoever it is, the depiction is old-fashioned."

"Yes, well, old-fashioned seems to be a theme in this house."

The knob on the door turned. Celestia's chest tightened, and all thoughts of the statue flew out of her head. If only they'd had more time, she could have done something to make Ico more presentable. And of course there was the matter of his heritage—but that could be explained away by an errant uncle who'd gone traveling in Akuran in his youth.

The door swung open. The butler stepped in. Celestia stood very still.

"May I present Lady Antonia De Lisista, mistress of Essir Manor." He bowed again. Celestia and Izara exchanged glances, and Celestia knew that even Izara was thinking it—*such formality.*

The butler vanished into the hallway. Celestia didn't dare turn around to see what Ico was up to; she could only hope he was making himself look respectable.

Soft, shuffling footsteps. And then a woman materialized in the doorway, as grand and old-fashioned as her house.

Her white hair was piled in a series of loops and braids on the top of her head, and she wore a silky draped gown of the sort that had last been fashionable nearly forty years ago. Jewels glittered at her throat and her wrists. Celestia hoped Ico wasn't staring at them with his pirate's gaze.

"The De Malena sisters," Lady De Lisista said, spreading her hands wide in greeting. "What a charming surprise."

Celestia didn't let her smile falter, even though she could feel Izara glancing furtively at her. "You've heard of us?"

"Oh, I know all the great families. Please, sit." Lady De Lisista glided across the room, the hem of her gown swishing against the floor. She offered a thin smile at Ico, who stood awkwardly next to the painting of the jaguar. "And you're the cousin, I hear, from Akuran."

Celestia held her breath. Her ears buzzed. Ico grinned rakishly. It made him look like a pirate.

"I'm the eccentric one," he said, and winked.

Lady De Lisista giggled, covering her mouth with her hand. Celestia breathed out in relief.

"I could use some eccentricity in this old house." Lady De Lisista slid into the high-backed velvet chair next to the window and made a vague gesture toward the love seat. "Please, my dears, sit! I'd hate for you to take stories back to Jaila-Seraphine about what a dreadful hostess I am."

"We'd never do any such thing," Celestia said. She sank down into the love seat across from Lady De Lisista, and Izara did the same. Izara was falling into her old trick of imitating everything Celestia did. Celestia knew it meant she was nervous.

Ico didn't sit, but instead lounged up against the wall, one foot crossed over the other, one shoulder hitched higher, like he was some lesser nobleman posing for a painting. Perhaps she'd underestimated his ability to play at the aristocracy.

"Tell me, dears, would you like something to eat? I'm afraid dinner has already been served, but I can ask the kitchen to fix something simple for you." Lady De Lisista reached over and tugged the servant's cord before waiting for an answer. "You must be famished. I know I'm a bit up the ways from Shadowplains. How is Lady De Mizell doing? I haven't seen her since she was a little girl."

"Oh, she's doing quite lovely." Lady De Mizell was older than Celestia—well past thirty, with a trio of little girls of her own. If Celestia was lucky, her lies wouldn't get back to the great houses in the east.

"I don't travel much," said Lady De Lisista. "Not since my husband died. He left me with the dreadful task of running this place." She sighed.

"Oh, I don't think this place seems so dreadful," said Celestia. "Your home is lovely."

"Yes," chirped Izara. "Lovely."

Lady De Lisista gave a sad smile. "Why, thank you, darlings. I do what I can."

The door to the drawing room opened; it was a serving girl, her uniform as out of date as Lady De Lisista's gown.

"Dulce," Lady De Lisista said airily. "Bring up a light dinner for my visitors. They've traveled here all the way from Cross Winds."

The girl bobbed in acquiescence and vanished into the hallway. For a moment Celestia was gripped with a cold, damp fear: was this Lady De Lisista being *too* hospitable? Was such a thing even possible? A woman of her age would have learned the lineages of the great houses as part of her schooling, and it wasn't terribly strange for her to keep up with things. Celestia had been too lax in that regard since marrying Lindon; his wealth brought a prestige she didn't have to fake. But in those lean years before, she had pored over birth announcements and obituaries, scribbling names in her record book. A noblewoman as unknown as Lady De Lisista would likely do the same.

And yet Celestia couldn't shake that sense of eeriness from her skin, as if the house itself were watching her.

"So tell me," Lady De Lisista said, turning her gaze between each of them in turn. "What compelled you to give an old woman like me a visit? Especially someone as renowned as you, Lady de Malena. Surely you have a full social calendar in the east?"

Celestia smiled politely. "My sister and I wanted to show Ico the Seraphine. He's been living in Akuran these last few years, with his mother."

"Akuran's such a charming place."

"You've been there?" said Ico, blinking in surprise.

"Oh, yes, a long time ago." She tittered. "It was part of my honeymoon. We toured the islands. Such a lovely trip. Just lovely." And then she smiled in a way that suited the white in her hair and lines in her dark skin, a smile that spoke of a lifetime's worth of small sadness, accumulated over the years. Then, in a heartbeat, it was gone, and her expression brightened again. "Tell me—Ico, is it?—what do you think of the Seraphine?"

"A veritable paradise," said Ico, swooping down in a surprisingly graceful bow. "The women and the flowers are the most beautiful I've ever seen."

Celestia resisted the urge to roll her eyes.

"Oh, stop," said Lady De Lisista. "I'm too old for that sort of thing."

"I beg to differ," said Ico, and he gave that rakish pirate's grin again.

Celestia slipped her hand into the pocket of her dress and ran her fingers over the box from the ruins, her fingertips brushing against the carved runes. Her heart fluttered. The visit with Lady De Lisista was running more smoothly than she could have expected—who could have guessed that Ico would prove so charming? But she still knew that the box and its map could raise questions, that she could be introducing an impropriety into the situation, which could turn it all sour.

She took a deep breath. Told herself to act clueless, like a silly girl who wanted to stumble across an adventure. She slipped her hand out of her pocket and laid it across her stomach. *The sooner we leave,* she thought, *the sooner I can get home.*

"I hope you won't find this forward—" she started, just as the door opened, and a trio of kitchen girls marched in with silver trays. The scent of spices and savory cooking oils filled the room, and Celestia's mouth watered. She hadn't eaten since lunchtime.

"We hope you won't mind coconut soup," the girl said as she set the tray on the table in front of the sofa. It was the same girl from before, and on closer examination Celestia could see she really wasn't a girl at all, but a woman her age or older, fine lines already etching out from the corners of her eyes. She kept her gaze downturned, in the old-fashioned style. Everything about this house was a recreation of the past.

"Coconut soup will be perfect," Celestia said, as the girl pulled away the serving lid, revealing a bowl filled with steaming white broth.

"My cook makes the best coconut soup," said Lady De Lisista. "Please, eat up! We'll be quite informal this evening. Now, please, dear, what were you going to say?"

Celestia's stomach lurched. Suddenly the soup seemed too rich.

"We were trying to show Ico a proper Seraphine adventure," she said, smiling. "And while we were at Shadowplains we stumbled across a funny little box." She wished she could shove the soup across the room. Her stomach churned. "It had a map in it."

"A map?" Lady De Lisista smiled mischievously. "My, that is a funny thing."

Celestia couldn't decide if Lady De Lisista was mocking her or not. Beside her, Izara stirred her soup around, keeping her eyes downcast. Ico was still lounging next to the painting. She was the only one who could do this. She plunged forward, on the assumption that Lady De Lisista was too well-bred for mockery.

"Yes," she said. "I'd never seen anything like it. We decided to follow the map, on a whim—and it brought us here."

The room fell silent save for the clinking of Izara's spoon against the side of her soup bowl. Celestia reached into her pocket and pulled out the box and set it on the table beside her untouched soup. Lady De Lisista reached forward and picked it up. Her eyes glittered.

"My, my," she said. "I haven't seen one of these in years."

Celestia plastered on a smile. Lady De Lisista didn't seem angry, at least, or upset. She held the box in front of her and turned it around slowly in her hands, like she was drinking in the letters along the side. Celestia wondered if she could read them.

"Do you know what it is?" Ico asked. Celestia jolted at his voice. The muscles in her shoulders tensed up. But Lady De Lisista didn't seem to mind the question.

"I do indeed," she said. "It's a Yinel's Box. They used to be manufactured here at Essir Manor. Centuries ago." She laughed and set the box down on the table. "I never thought I'd get to send someone to Bloodvine!"

"Bloodvine?" said Izara, looking up from her soup. She looked over at Celestia questioningly, but Celestia had never heard the name, either.

"Is that one of the great houses?" Celestia asked politely.

Lady De Lisista laughed. "Oh, no, dear! But don't worry if you haven't heard of it. It's a hidden city, and the wards are strong. In fact, you may have heard its name before. But the magic makes it so easy to forget."

Celestia wasn't sure how to proceed.

"Bloodvine is a flower, isn't it?" Izara said suddenly. "And the statue there, of the Laniana—"

"Very good!" Lady De Lisista's eyes flashed with delight. "Yes, the Laniana of the bloodvine flower is a bit of a protectress for us here at Essir. Although not so much these days."

"That's fascinating," Celestia said politely. "We don't have a Laniana protector at Cross Winds."

"Most of the great houses don't anymore," Lady De Lisista said. "But my ancestor by marriage, Yinel De Lisista, was a great mage, and he had a special bond with her. That was many centuries ago, during the Last War."

Celestia tensed. "The Last War?" she said, her heart fluttering.

"Yes. Yinel actually founded Bloodvine, along with Essir's guardian Laniana. It was a sanctuary during the Last War."

Celestia snuck a glance at Izara, whose eyes were wide.

"Would you like to know the story?" Lady De Lisista asked slyly

"We'd love to," Celestia said.

The lady's laughed with delight. "Oh, wonderful, wonderful. It's been so long since I've had the opportunity to share it." She straightened her shoulders. "My late husband's family was the only aristocratic family to stand in opposition to Lord Kjari. With the help of a trio of Laniana, they founded Bloodvine, a place where they could work against him. Compatriots were only allowed entry through Essir Manor, in order to be properly vetted."

Celestia's heart pounded. She shook her head and glanced over at Izara, who still looked skeptical.

"Of course that's not the situation anymore. There are other points of entry, and there's no need to confirm visitors are of the correct ideology. It's just an ordinary city now, albeit one that still exists behind a complex web of magic meant to keep it hidden. But they have rituals to get around it these days, and they do trade with the Seraphine, and with Eiren, of course." Lady De Lisista beamed. "For my husband's entire life, not a single person came asking about Bloodvine. And here you are!"

Celestia smiled politely. As a landed lady, she'd never had

any dealings with the business aspect of Cross Winds—the estate manager had always taken care of it. She wondered if Cross Winds had ever traded with this hidden sanctuary in the forest.

Lady De Lisista lifted the box and cupped it gently in her hands. "Yandel kept one of these in his bedroom," she said softly. "Next to his bed. I had him buried with it when he passed. So strange to see another one. His father had been the one to convert the factory where they were produced, when Yandel was a little boy. It's a guest house now. Not that I have many guests." She looked up at Celestia. "Oh, I've been terribly rude, haven't I? Of course the three of you are welcome to stay there for the night. There's no need for you to go sailing back up the river after dark. And if you want to give your cousin that true Seraphine adventure, I would be simply *delighted* to make the arrangements for you. There's quite a bit of magic involved, I'm afraid."

Ico stepped forward and said, "I for one would love to see a hidden city of the Seraphine. My mother would be so happy to hear the stories."

"Then I will have to ensure you remember your visit!" Lady De Lisista cried. "That's the trick of Bloodvine, you know—a visitor without the proper spells will forget the city as soon as they leave."

Lady De Lisista reached over and tugged on the servant's cord. "This is so exciting! I'll have to start the arrangements right away—the blood tea takes hours to brew."

"Blood tea?" Izara said. "You mean blood magic? Are you saying that Yinel De Lisista was a *blood mage*? Because that's not what I learned."

Celestia stiffened and coughed into her hand—another signal, one that told Izara she was being untoward. Izara glanced at her and then settled back in the chair.

"No, no, no," Lady De Lisista said, "The name is a bit of a

joke, you see. It's alchemy that was taught to Yinel by the Laniana. Blood magic was Lord Kjari's purview, and the De Lisistas wanted nothing to do with him, you understand."

The door to the parlor opened, and in stepped the butler from earlier, bowing deeply.

"I have wonderful news!" Lady De Lisista cried, struggling to her feet. "Our visitors will be traveling to Bloodvine."

The butler, for his part, only nodded and said, "Very good, my lady."

———

"I can't believe you fell for that," Izara said.

They had been settled into a guest house that was nestled in the edge of the forest, a squat square building with large windows covered in layers of silky curtains to keep the insects out. The air smelled musty and disused, although everything was clean. No dust, no grime. But still Celestia could tell that no one had visited this estate for a long, long time.

"We are tracking down a five-hundred-year-old wizard for the Airiana," Celestia said. "You fought kajani. You really can't accept the idea of a hidden city?"

Izara scowled and dropped down in the sofa, her arms crossed over chest. "She wants to use magic on us," she said. "Magic tied to the Laniana. They aren't as powerful as the Airiana, but it could still be dangerous."

"It was a little too easy." Ico paced around the perimeter of the guest house's sitting room, pulling back the curtains and peering out into the forest. "I can't disagree there."

"Will you stop pulling back the curtains?" Izara said. "The mosquitos will eat us alive tonight."

Celestia sighed and sank down in the soft cushions of a chaise lounge. Not Ico, too. "Well, then what do you two suggest? We have no other options, and this Bloodvine place ties *directly* to Lord Kjari—"

"This Bloodvine place doesn't exist," said Izara. "I studied Yinel de Lisista. There's no mention of Bloodvine anywhere in his histories."

Ico said nothing, only crossed his arms over his chest, although he stayed next to the window, like he didn't want to turn his back on the forest. He'd been like that all evening, as they'd gotten themselves settled, as they had walked across the gardens to get to the guest house. And of course there had been that nonsense with the knife earlier.

"If there's something you're worried about," Celestia said, "you need to tell us. We have a right to know."

Ico hesitated. "It's nothing."

Celestia rubbed at her forehead. She didn't want to deal with Ico right now. She didn't even really want to deal with Izara and her sudden bout of skepticism. In truth, she was grateful that the box had brought them to a great house, to a landed lady who knew the rules of hospitality, to an actual *home*, with furniture and food and, she assumed, washing basins. She had not realized until she passed through the doorway that she had been coming unraveled, that seeing Lindon covered in kajan's blood—*kajan's blood*—had stripped her sense of reality away from her. And if there was a chance that their journey could take them into a city, into another civilized place, so much the better. For her baby if nothing else.

She closed her eyes and fell back against the chaise lounge and stared up at the ceiling. The lights glowed with that unwavering intensity. She'd assume they were alchemical, but part of her wondered if they were actually electric, like the lights Aurelia had told her about.

A knock came at the door. Celestia pushed herself up. Izara was already walking across the room to answer, but Ico darted in front of her. "Let me do it," he said in a low voice.

Izara frowned at him. Looked over at Celestia questioningly.

Celestia shook her head, defeated.

Of course it was only the butler, bringing them their chest from the boat. He dragged it inside with a strength Celestia wouldn't have expected of him. "Where shall I place this, my lady?" Looking at her.

"In the corner there is fine," Celestia said, and she gestured with one hand, an easy, familiar movement, as if she were back at Cross Winds. For a moment she was struck with an unbearable longing for the world to be normal again.

The butler did as she asked. "We have begun preparing the blood tea," he said. "It should be ready by tomorrow at midmorning."

"What exactly is this blood tea?" Izara said.

"Bloodvine flowers," the butler said stiffly. "Surely you are aware of their magical properties."

Izara slouched down, scowled. She was being rude, but perhaps this information would be enough to sway her. Celestia smiled at the butler and told him they didn't need anything else, and thanked him, and he gave a bow and then disappeared out into the night.

"See?" Celestia said to Izara. "Flowers. Elemental magic—"

"Fine, so it's not blood magic." Izara scowled. "But that doesn't mean we're going to find anything after we drink it. This is a waste of our time."

"This is our only option," Celestia said.

"We could go to Konmar, like Lindon."

Celestia stiffened. "No," she said. "I don't want to do that."

Ico gave no opinion, having taken up his post by the window again. Gods and monsters, what did he think was out there? Had their account of the kajani terrified him so much?

The three of them sat in silence. Celestia listened to the insects chirping on the other side of the curtains. Her stomach roiled with pregnancy sickness—it had gotten better in the last week, but perhaps she should not have eaten that coconut soup. She stretched on the divan, one hand pressed against her stomach, trying to relieve the pressure.

"I'm pregnant," she said, "in case you've forgotten."

She tilted her head toward Izara. She shouldn't have this conversation in front of Ico but right now she realized she didn't care about propriety.

Izara looked up, her expression unreadable.

"I want this trip to be over," Celestia said. "You said magic creates coincidences. I found the box that brought us here because of a coincidence. Please, Izara. Just trust it."

Izara sighed. Looked away. "I don't know enough about it."

"I won't travel to Konmar. Not when I'm pregnant. A journey like that, it would shape the baby irrevocably—"

"That's a superstition," Izara muttered. "The type of pregnancy you have doesn't affect the baby's personality."

"How would you even know?" Celestia sat up. She was aware of Ico watching them, whatever terror of his that lurked in the woods forgotten. "Even if you're right—" She took a deep breath and glanced over at Ico. He looked away, trying to pretend he wasn't listening. She lowered her voice. "Lindon would be furious. He would—" She closed her eyes. "He would try to stop us. We have to find Lord Kjari through some other path."

Insects screamed in the forest. No one spoke. Celestia looked at her sister, who paused for a moment, then stood up and sat down on the chaise lounge beside Celestia. She leaned her head on her shoulder. "I'm sorry," she said. "I just—I don't know what I'm going to do when we're done. They won't let me back in the Academy."

Celestia felt a pang of guilt. Of course, she should have known. She had a life to return to, but Izara didn't. Not the life she wanted.

The Airiana could be so cruel.

"I just want the life we asked for," she said, barely a whisper.

Izara nodded, the movement brushing against Celestia's arm. Ico guarded the windows against his unknown threat. And they stayed like this as the night wound down.

———

The next morning, Izara found herself sitting in the parlor in Essir Manor against her better judgement. She still didn't think they were going to find anything in Bloodvine but ruins and bloodvine flowers, but after Celestia's plea last night she had kept her mouth shut.

Lady De Lisista was positively glowing, however, her eyes lit up like a little girl's. "Oh, you'll have to come back and tell me about it," she said. "I'm too old to make the journey, you understand, but I would like to hear what's become of the city."

Celestia gave a thin-lipped smile, probably worrying more about the effect that traveling was having on her baby than drinking magic-infused tea would. But that notion that pregnancy shaped a child was embedded deep in the aristocracy, a snobbery that Izara had unlearned a long time ago. There were benefits, sometimes, to not fitting in.

A knock at the door, and then the butler entered with a tea tray, the teapot transparent so that it revealed the red blossom billowing inside the hot water. Izara felt a sudden lightness: so it really was made with bloodvine flowers.

"My lady," he murmured as he set down the tea tray. Then he disappeared into the shadows.

"Blood tea, a specialty of Essir Manor." Lady De Lisista poured a glass and handed it to Celestia, who took it and held it in her palm, waiting as Lady De Lisista poured one for Ico and one for Izara. "And the original method of remembering travel to Bloodvine, developed five hundred years ago by Yinel De Lisista."

Ico peered down at his tea suspiciously. When Lady De Lisista handed the tea to Izara, Izara's hands trembled as she took it—she remembered a time as a little girl, drinking guayusa tea at a party at some great house or another before she was supposed to. Her mother had yelled at her afterwards, and even now Izara didn't understand *why* she had done something wrong, only that it had been wrong.

She didn't drink the tea too early today. Neither did Ico. Perhaps he knew more of the aristocracy than they expected.

"I do hope you'll forgive the formality," Lady De Lisista said suddenly, smiling a little. "But this is how I learned the ceremony. It's all so exciting to have a chance to do it!"

Perhaps this should have made Izara feel more comfortable, but really it just made her more self-conscious.

Lady De Lisista set her tea cup on the table. Celestia and Ico did the same. *Just do what Celestia does,* Izara told herself, her mantra at all the parties of her childhood, before the money had gone away. She set her own cup down.

Lady De Lisista plucked a slim silver vial off the tray and uncorked it. She added a dash of the powder inside to her cup of tea, and the tea shimmered and bubbled. She passed the vial to Celestia, her eyes gleaming, and Celestia added the powder to her own tea. When Izara received the vial, she had to stop herself from sniffing it, from dumping a bit of powder onto her palm. She glanced up at Lady De Lisista, who was watching her with her hands folded neatly in her lap, her expression bright with excitement.

"You don't have to go into the Aetheric Realm to do this?" Izara asked.

Lady De Lisista laughed. "No, of course not. The spell was

a gift from the Essir Laniana, designed so that anyone can complete. Even those without Iomim's Treasure." She pressed her hand to her chest. "Such as myself."

Izara frowned. The tea and the powder did remind her of the folk magic she'd studied when she was younger. Simple magic, barely recognized by the Academy as magic at all. But it came from the Laniana?

"Go on, dear," Lady De Lisista said. "It's perfectly safe."

Celestia coughed and gave Izara a dark look.

Without thinking on it, Izara added the powder to her tea and passed the vial on to Ico. She watched her tea bubble up and hoped she hadn't made a mistake.

"Now we shall wait," Lady De Lisista said, spreading her hands over the tea. She closed her eyes and hummed a flat note. In the teacups, pink froth billowed up like cloud and let off a scent like rotting flowers.

The magic rattled around inside Izara's head. She didn't recognize it. "This isn't alchemy," she said.

Celestia shot her angry look.

Lady De Lisista's eyes flew open. "I told you, it's alchemy that was taught to Yinel by the Laniana. It's not the alchemy you would learn in the Academy. Now, please, we must be quiet so that the magic can work."

Izara scowled, annoyed that she had been corrected. Granted, the magic did not feel chaotic. Unfamiliar, yes, but there was an orderliness to it—

Still. *Not* alchemy.

Izara could feel Celestia glaring at her, but she didn't acknowledge it.

Lady De Lisista hummed again, a different note, sweeter this time. The tea's froth died down, and the tea itself had deepened into a brilliant red that truly did look like blood. The magic faded from the air, leaving a tingle on Izara's skin. It didn't feel *wrong*, but it wasn't alchemy, either.

Could the Laniana have their own brand of alchemy? It would mean the Airiana would be able to work alchemy, too. What knowledge could a mage like Izara uncover if she was able to learn the formulas of Airiana alchemy?

Lady De Lisista picked up her teacup and swirled the tea around. It gleamed with streaks of light. Then she began to speak—at first it sounded like gibberish, but then Izara caught fragments of words she recognized and she realized it was Old Seran. An incantation! This did feel like folk magic.

Meanwhile, Celestia had picked up her own tea cup, and was swirling it around as well. Ico glanced at her, then did the same, tentatively. Lady De Lisista's Old Seran filled the room, and Izara sighed and swirled her own tea around. The four of them swirled and swirled, their teas throwing shards of light against the wall. Izara felt stupid and self-conscious; there was no magic in this. Only ceremony.

And then Lady De Lisista stopped swirling. She closed her eyes and held the teacup up to her noise and breathed in deeply. Light was still clinging to the walls.

She began to hum, a low, throaty song in a language Izara half-recognized—she could not remember its name, only that it was very old and nearly dead. Not Old Seran.

A language of magic. A language of the Airiana.

Lady De Lisista's eyes flew open. "Drink," she said. "It's ready now." And she took a sip, leaning back in her chair, and smiling contentedly. "It's been too long since I've had blood tea. I used to make it for Yandel—he enjoyed drinking it without needing its magical properties."

Celestia was the first to sample the tea. Izara watched her with a tightness in her chest. She refused to go to Konmar because of the baby but she would still drink a folk potion from a stranger.

"Oh," said Celestia, her eyes widening. "I've never tasted tea so sweet."

"It's the poison in the bloodvine flowers," Lady De Lisista said. "The powder neutralizes it and gives it that sweetness." She smiled at Izara. "The powder is derived from bloodvine roots," she said. "They manufacture it in Bloodvine."

Izara felt a flicker of curiosity—they were manufacturing folk magic powders in Bloodvine? What other sorts of magic might be in the world that the Academy ignored?

"All of you, have a drink! That's the only way you'll remember Bloodvine after leaving."

Izara picked up her tea and held it under nose.

"It's quite good," Celestia said to Izara. "You ought to try some."

Drink or you'll ruin everything, that was what Celestia was really saying. And so Izara drank, carefully and tentatively, thinking not of propriety but of the promise of a city filled with magic with no ties to the Academy. The tea had cooled during the ceremony, and she barely felt the temperature of it, neither hot nor cold. It was the sweetness of it that struck her first, as if she were drinking the nectar of honeysuckle. The tea seemed to sparkle on her tongue.

"This is something," Ico said, holding his cup aloft. Lady De Lisista beamed at him.

"Drink it all down, my three little imps! As soon as you're finished, you'll depart."

As Izara drank, the magic in the tea began whispering to Iomim's Treasure, a strange sensation, although not an unpleasant one. They spoke like old friends.

And so she drank until there was nothing but a crimson residue in the bottom of her cup.

~

They rode in a carriage through the forest, dapples of sunlight falling through the gaps in the curtains. The carriage rattled and jostled over the uneven, overgrown path, and Izara had to brace herself against the wall. She felt woozy and indistinct from the tea—Lady De Lisista had warned them that could happen, but Izara did not care for the way her thoughts were becoming loosened, especially knowing the tea's magic came from the Laniana—which was only a step away from the Airiana.

No one spoke on the carriage trip. The wheels clacked too loudly for anyone to be heard. It was a torturous sound, running over and over in Izara's head. When the carriage finally slowed to a stop, the silence overwhelmed her.

"Ah," said Lady De Lisista, peering out through the curtain. "Here we are."

The footman pulled the door open, and green sunlight flooded in. A clearing? The woods had seemed too thick for such a thing. But perhaps it wasn't naturally occurring.

Lady De Lisista stepped out first. Ico gestured toward the door. "Ladies," he said. "Allow me to be a gentleman."

"Oh, don't act like this is about politeness," Izara snapped. Celestia put a warning hand on her wrist, then moved toward the door. She stopped, though, before stepping outside.

"What is it? What do you see?" Izara's heart thumped. The tea made her thoughts as gauzy as a spiderweb.

"I don't know."

Celestia gathered up her skirts and pushed out, offering her hand to the footman, as if she were just stepping out for a night at the opera. Celestia had always been the braver of the two. Always the better at adapting.

"Oh!" cried Celestia. "Oh, Izara, you *have* to see this."

Izara glanced at Ico, who hung back, his expression dark. "Go on, then," he said, and she did, shoving her way through the door, forgetting to offer her hand to the footman the way Celestia had. The sun splashed hot across her face. For a moment her vision blurred and her eyes watered. And then shapes came into view: mechanical shapes, not natural to the forest.

"It's a *train*," Izara said stupidly.

She had heard about trains. Seen illustrations of them in books. They were not feasible here in the Seraphine, that was what she had learned—the forest was too thick, the land too mountainous. Trains were a marvel of Eiren and the grassland countries of the East, where they could cut easily across great swathes of golden wheat.

And yet—a *train*. Here. In the forest.

Each car was the size of a riverboat, and there were four cars total, each one decorated with stone carvings, delicate and elaborate, of runes that Izara couldn't recognize. The train sat huffing on the tracks, white steam billowing up into the patch of blue sky overhead. Sky! They were in a clearing, the trees a dark wall surrounding them. Here the only thing that grew was soft feathery grass.

"This is incredible," Izara said, stepping over beside Celestia. The runes nagged at her—they struck a familiar chord in her thoughts and she was certain she should be able to recognize them, even if it was only from looking at them in a book at the Academy. And yet her thoughts were so diaphanous from that blood tea, and she couldn't grasp on to anything too long to study it properly. Even the train cars themselves seemed to glint and shine in such a way that it forced her eye to look beyond them, at the dark oasis of the trees.

"What the hell?" It was Ico, finally joining them. He stood beside Izara with his arms crossed over his chest. "A *train*?"

"Yes," said Lady De Lisista. "Although it is not the same sort that you'd be used to in Akuran. This train is—unusual. A gift from the Laniana to aid us in our fight against Lord Kjari."

Unusual. The light flicked across Izara's vision. The runes crawled over one another. Iomim's Treasure trembled. *Magic.*

The trains of the East ran on fire and steam. This was something else. She could barely sense it, a thin, weak thrumming on the air. But it was ancient, and it was powerful.

"How does it run?" Izara asked, turning to Lady De Lisista. "I know you said magic, but—"

Lady De Lisista's smile was sharp and stern and cut Izara off mid-sentence. "I'm afraid that's not my question to answer." She paused, and then added, "I don't quite understand it myself, you see. As I said, it was gifted to us by the Laniana. My ancestors built it. Now I'm merely the guardian."

A piercing *clang* rang out then, rippling through the forest. Izara jumped, Iomim's Treasure murmuring inside her.

"It's about to leave," Lady De Lisista said. "On board, all of you! Your belongings have already been brought aboard."

None of them moved. Izara stared at the train, trying to piece together its history, its construction. The runes wavered in front of her. The steam belching from the train's smoke stack was thicker riverboat smoke, and it smelled sweet, like burning flowers.

"Oh, don't tell me you've changed your mind!" Lady De Lisista cried. "I was so looking forward to sending you to Bloodvine."

Izara and Celestia looked at each other. Celestia dropped her hand to her belly. Her eyes glittered with fear. "It's the best way," she whispered. "Better than going south, like Lindon did."

Izara nodded. Ico said nothing, only stared at the train warily.

"This thing secure?" he asked.

"Of course it's secure," Lady De Lisista said. "It carried political refugees to safety during Lord Kjari's reign, and that magic is as powerful as it ever was. You won't be waylaid by bandits today." She chuckled. "Anyone who sees this train will forget it without the bloodvine extract."

Izara moved closer to the train, curiosity dragging her forward. She gripped the railing and felt the train rumbling against her palm. Then she pulled herself inside. She expected to see the interior of a riverboat, sparse and damp from the steam. Instead she found herself inside a great house's sitting room. Silk-covered sofas lined the walls. An ornate table was laid out with miniature cakes from Lady De Lisista's kitchen. Murky portraits watched over the room. Izara glided forward, breathing in deeply. The magic hummed beneath her feet with the engines. Airiana magic blended with Eirenese technology—and all of it *ancient*. Izara wondered if she would be able to talk her way aboard the engine room, to see how things ran. She was curious not just about the magic, but the mechanics of the train as well.

They did not know about this sort of magic at the Academy, this blending of sorcery with technology. Izara felt a thrill of excitement—here was her chance to learn something the Academy couldn't teach her. Surely no one in the Seraphine would care about her lack of credentials if she could weave magic and technology together.

Ico and Celestia climbed aboard. Ico glanced around, gave an impressed little nod, and then flopped down on one of the sofas. Celestia only stood by the door, her hand touching her stomach. Behind her Izara could see the forest, and Lady De Lisista, and the carriage that had brought them here—it felt like peering into another world.

And then the door sprang shut with a loud, ominous clank. Celestia let out a shout and tottered sideways; Izara darted over to her and caught her before she could fall. Celestia's eyes fluttered.

"I feel so woozy," she murmured.

"It's the tea. Here, sit." Izara guided her over to a fainting couch and helped her down. The magic was humming more powerfully now. The engines rumbled.

There was another blaring *clang*, a loud hiss of steam, a shudder of unknowable magic. And then the train was moving, chugging into the forest.

~

Two of the train cars were sleeping rooms, with luxurious beds and thick curtains covering the windows. Celestia made her way to the first of the sleeping cars, even though she did not want to step out into the walkway between cars, where the wind whistled and spat at her. But she also wanted to lie down—the tea was affecting her, just as Lady De Lisista had warned them. The vagaries of magic.

Compared to the rush of air outside, the sleeping room seemed lifeless. Celestia collapsed onto the bed and gazed up at the light fixture hanging from the ceiling, its glow bright and steady, the same as the glow at Lady De Lisista's house. More magic, she was certain, even though she couldn't feel it like Izara. She closed her eyes and breathed in deeply. The wind roared outside, a constant rumbling that she knew would drive her mad.

Something thumped on the roof.

Celestia sat straight up, her heart pounding. *Bandits,* she thought stupidly. This train wasn't nearly as hidden as Lady De Lisista claimed.

She listened, her heart in her throat, but she only heard the wind on the other side of the walls.

Or was that a shuffling on the roof? Pattering footsteps? Celestia stood up—too quickly, and for a moment she swooned, leaning up against the bedpost for support. No, it was only the wind, she told herself. The clacking of the train's wheels. But then she remembered Ico peering out the window of the guest house, looking for a threat he wouldn't name.

Celestia whipped her gaze around the room. Surely there had to be some means of communication through the different cars—she was certain she'd read about such wonders on northern trains. All she saw, though, were gilded sculptures and bas-reliefs hanging on the walls alongside paintings of the forest. Pillows and little figurines. Vases of flowers. Worthless clutter.

Another thump on the roof. Celestia froze. Another. She didn't dare scream. She had to get out of this car, back to the others.

She moved toward the door, feet tangling in her skirts. A shadow darkened the curtain covering the door's window, and Celestia let out a sharp, short scream, slapping her hand over her mouth to strangle it.

The door's handle turned. Oh, why hadn't she thought to *lock* it?

Celestia skittered backwards through the car, knocking up against a writing table. The vase jostled, spilled a few drops of water. Celestia grabbed the vase without thinking and hoisted it up.

The door slammed open. Hot, damp wind rushed in.

A kajan filled the doorframe.

Celestia screamed and hurled the vase with all her strength. It missed the kajan and shattered against the wall, water and flowers exploding in a shimmer of light. The kajan stepped inside and slammed the door shut behind him. Celestia ducked behind the table and pushed it up to serve as a shield. "Help!" she screamed. "Help! Ico! Izara!" She prayed they would hear her over the train's rattle.

Lady De Lisista had lied after all, then. If this train was designed to take refugees from Kjari's reign into some hidden city, how could a *kajan* come aboard?

The kajan stepped forward. His boots thumped heavily against the carpet. He was armed, swords crossed over his back, knives glinting at his waist, but he did not brandish a weapon at her.

"What do you want with Lord Kjari?" the kajan asked.

The kajan's voice was more musical than Celestia expected, rich and melodious like temple bells. He moved closer, scowling, and Celestia leaned down behind the table.

"Nothing!" she cried, aware of the waver in her voice.

"Lies." *Stomp stomp stomp* and the kajan was towering over her, the table-shield a worthless defense. Celestia lifted her gaze and realized with a start that the kajan was not built like a man—there was a curve at the hips, and a swell of breasts beneath the leather armor.

"You're a woman," Celestia blurted.

The kajan stared down at her for a long moment. Then she threw back her head and laughed, the laugh as musical as her speaking voice.

"Humans," the kajan said. "Yes, I'm a woman. Now tell me why you are hunting Lord Kjari."

Was a woman kajan safer than a male kajan? Celestia didn't know—in the stories all kajani were men, and yet she wondered if that was just an inaccuracy of history. How many of the kajani at the Aikha ruins had been women, as willing to kill her as the men were?

"We're not hunting him," Celestia said.

"Don't lie to me!" The kajan's eyes flashed with an angry red light, and Celestia choked down her fear and stood up, shaking. She came to the kajan's shoulder, and she could see the tattoos crawling over her gray skin, swirling and complex and half-hidden in the armor.

"You misunderstand," Celestia said, and she forced herself to make eye contact. The kajan's eyes were no longer burning, but Celestia wouldn't say that her expression had softened. "We are looking for him, yes, but we're not *hunting* him."

The kajan frowned.

"I'm afraid I can't tell you more than that." This came out in a string of fearful syllables, and Celestia stepped back, tugging at the fabric of her dress. The kajan's brow creased.

"Do you know where he is?"

Celestia stopped. The kajan had asked the question with a softness, a sadness, that didn't befit her armor and her weapons. Celestia's fear wobbled inside her, a top about to fall.

"No," Celestia said. "We're trying to find him. To—to bring him to one of the Airiana."

The kajan's eyes widened. "You? Why would you do such a thing?"

Celestia hesitated. She wasn't about to let her guard down, even though the stories had never presented kajani as tricksters—only warriors, enflamed with bloodlust. She didn't know how to gauge this situation anymore.

"We were tasked with it," she finally said. "Please, there's no need to kill us."

The kajan studied her. Celestia's skin prickled under her gaze.

"Can I offer you something to drink?" Celestia said, because politeness had gotten her out of so many scrapes before. "Some tea, perhaps?"

"There's no tea here," the kajan growled. Her eyes flitted around the room. "Don't think you can trick me, human."

"No!" Celestia held up her hands. "I would never—I was only trying to be hospitable. Even if you *did* break into my sleeping room."

"The door was unlocked." The kajan turned away from Celestia and seemed to take in the room for the first time. "What is this machine? Is it taking you to him? To Lord Kjari?"

"I—I don't know." Celestia paused. "I hope so."

"Then why did its magic try to keep me out?" The kajan looked over at her, eyes cold and appraising. "This machine is shrouded in alchemy. I had to chew bloodvine root to break through it."

A chill shot down Celestia's spine. How did this kajan recognize the magic protecting the train—and know how to break through it?

Could kajan *do* magic?

"The train is taking us to a place that will help us find Lord Kjari," Celestia finally said.

The kajan sniffed. "I knew this machine wasn't going to him. What did you call it? A train?"

Celestia nodded numbly. The kajan still hadn't threatened her, not really. And yet Celestia didn't want to be in a room with this creature, away from the water and the Lady's protection. Perhaps she could convince the kajan they were allies—perhaps they *were* allies, a thought which made her shiver. They were both seeking Lord Kjari, after all.

"I will accompany you to this place," the kajan said. "I've sworn an oath to protect his Lordship and I do not take that duty lightly." She stomped over to the bed and sat down, her bulky frame sinking deep into the cushions. Celestia shivered—had the kajan claimed this room for her own? It seemed that way, as the kajan leaned back on her elbows, settling down into the soft plumes of the bed. Her weapons clanked against each other, but right now, she didn't seem like a warrior at all. If anything she reminded Celestia of the girls who sold trinkets from carts in the cities—too young to be worn down by the world. And then Celestia wondered when she'd begun to think of the kajan as *young*. But she did seem young, her gray skin smooth and unblemished, her long hair shining in the car's light. How did kajani age? It wasn't a question Celestia had ever considered until now.

"I've been following you since the battle at Aikha," the kajan said, sitting up suddenly. Her sword caught the light and gleamed. "The others would not—" She stopped. "It does not matter. I preferred to follow you."

Her black eyes glittered. Celestia felt she should respond and so she said, "Oh?" so softly it was almost a sigh.

"You had magic," the kajan said, voice gruff. "His Lordship adores magic. He made my kind with it."

She stood up and marched across the room, straight toward Celestia, who resisted the urge to cower. Instead, she stood straight and tall and looked the kajan in the eye. The kajan stopped a few paces away.

"I'm going where you're going," she said. "You aren't getting me off this machine." Her fingers hovered over the hilt of her sword, and Celestia's heart started pounding again.

"Of—of course not," she stammered, forcing her gaze back up to the kajan's face. "You can have this room, if you like."

The kajan didn't say anything.

"We're not warriors," Celestia offered, leaving the rest unspoken: *Not like Lindon. Not like the Eiren men at Aikha.*

The kajan stared at her. Cold sweat dripped down Celestia's spine. Had she misspoken? She did not understand the rules of propriety for dealing with kajani. If such rules even *existed*.

But the kajan laughed, her eyes lighting up with mirth. "Oh, that I knew. You aren't in danger from me, human. Not unless you attempt to harm Lord Kjari."

Celestia shook her head quickly. Blood thudded in her ears. The kajan was still staring at her, her monstrous face unreadable. And so once again Celestia reverted to politeness.

She curtsied.

A shallow curtsy, nothing more than an acknowledgement of the other person's presence. The kajan stiffened, though, and for a moment looked baffled.

"My name is Celestia. You're welcome to travel with us to Bloodvine." Celestia hoped her words at least sounded sincere.

What she really wanted was for the kajan to crawl out of the train and back into the stories of Celestia's youth.

"I'm Omaira," the kajan said, and she gave a stiff bow, one hand pressed into her stomach. "As long as you do not aim to harm his Lordship, I will not bother you. You have my word."

Celestia smiled, thrown off by the kajan's formality. She edged over to the door, and the kajan—Omaira—did nothing to stop her. Although she did watch, her gaze steady. Her expression was unreadable again. It was once again too inhuman.

"I'm going to speak to the others," Celestia said.

Omaira flipped one hand dismissively and turned toward the bed. Celestia shoved the door open and stepped backward into the rushing wind. The forest zoomed by in a blur; the train's engines roared around her. And she still felt safer out here, with a door shut tight between her and Omaira. She inched along the walkway, her hair whipping into her face, her skirt tangling around her legs. She gripped the walkway so tightly her knuckles turned white. And she still felt safer.

Finally she grabbed the doorknob and shoved the door open and tumbled into the first car. Ico and Izara were sitting at the dining table, eating from a plate of cheese and pickled vegetables.

"Celestia?" Izara stood up as Celestia tumbled into the car. The door slammed shut behind her.

"Kajan," she gasped.

"What?" Ico paused, a slice of cheese halfway to his mouth. "Did you say *kajan*?"

Celestia nodded.

"Gods and monsters!" Izara rushed forward, gathering Celestia up in her arms. "Are you all right? How did you get away?"

"I thought this ancestors-damned train was supposed to be protected!" Ico yelled, throwing his cheese back onto the platter.

Now that Celestia was back in the front car and was no longer alone the encounter with Omaira seemed absurd, almost hallucinatory. But she trusted her senses enough to know it had all been real.

"The kajan didn't attack me," she said.

Shocked silence from Ico and Izara, dull rhythmic roaring from the train.

"Really?" Izara said.

Celestia nodded. "And she recognized the protection spells somehow. She took bloodvine root, just as we did." Celestia stumbled over to a nearby chair and collapsed into it.

"A fucking kajan," said Ico. "How come it's just the two of you who've seen these things?"

"If you want to see one," Celestia said, "then go over to the next car. She's laid claim to it."

Ico glared at her. But he also made no move to check the car himself.

"So you spoke to her," Izara said. "In Seran? *Really?*"

Celestia nodded and then explained what had happened, explained that she'd let Omaira stay in the sleeping car.

"There's another one," Celestia said. "Another place where we can sleep." Of course, they would have to go through the car with Omaira, but she didn't mention that.

"Do you really think that army of kajan don't know where Lord Kjari is?" Izara said. "How do you know this isn't some kind of trick? Some of way of—entrapping us? She could be a scout sent to sabotage the train."

"It's a kajan," Ico said. "They're not that smart."

"She's clearly smart enough to learn Seran and figure out her way past the protective spells," Izara shot back. "All we know about kajani comes from Eirenese propaganda."

Sabotage. Celestia hadn't even considered that possibility. But the kajan in the car had seemed devoted to Lord Kjari above all else.

"Well, regardless, we don't have many options now," Celestia finally said. "I certainly can't think of any way to remove her from the train."

The three of them looked at each other.

"I'm not interested in fighting a kajan," Ico finally said.

"Fine," said Izara. "But I'm reinforcing the locks on the door with alchemy. Unless she's a mage, she won't get through. We're sleeping in here until we get to Bloodvine." She didn't say *If we get there,* and Celestia was grateful for it.

The train rumbled on.

───

Celestia woke with a sore neck and a clear head. For a moment she was disoriented: was she on the boat? Back in Lady De Lisista's guest house? Or back home at Cross Winds, Lindon sleeping peacefully in the room next door?

But then she remembered.

She was curled up on a fainting couch inside a train taking her to a hidden city. She sat up and blinked the sleep from her eyes. Ico and Izara were still asleep; Izara was stretched out on the floor and Ico was sprawled across one of the dining room chairs, his head leaning against the wall of the train.

At least Celestia's thoughts were no longer cobwebbed like they'd been yesterday. The blood tea must have finally, mercifully, worn off.

Celestia pushed herself off the fainting couch and rubbed at her neck. She'd slept with her head jammed into the corner of the couch, but her sleep had been surprisingly refreshing. The yellow sunlight shining through the windows enlivened her, and she felt a relief at seeing the car suffused with brightness. She wondered how close they were to Bloodvine. *Two days' trip by train,* Lady De Lisista had said, and here was the start of the second day.

But then Celestia's good mood dampened. If they were close to Bloodvine, then they were closer to having to deal with the problem of the kajan.

In the bright light of morning, without the haze of the blood tea, the possibility of the kajan being some desperate figment of her imagination seemed more likely. Why would such a creature jump onto the train? *Omaira,* Celestia thought, turning the name around inside her head, examining it. In the stories kajani never had names. They were just the faceless mass that comprised nearly two-thirds of Lord Kjari's armies. When Eiren invaded during the Last War, the Seraphine had tried to fight with strength of numbers, and it was said that was where the story of the kajan had come from. They certainly weren't created by a mage, regardless of how powerful. Magic didn't work that way. It could not suffuse dead materials with life, with souls.

Or at least, that was what Celestia had been taught. But if the dead were rising in Eiren, if Kjari had brought himself back—then Kjari was more powerful, more dangerous, than anything she had been taught.

Celestia combed her fingers through her hair, smoothed down her dress. The trunk of clean, old-fashioned clothing from Lady De Lisita had been placed in the sleeping room, of course, and the dining room table only offered a breakfast of fried plantains and bread pudding. Celestia stared at the dining car's exit. It was absurd, cowering in here. Omaira had made no attempt at hurting her yesterday and indeed had seemed more intent on finding Lord Kjari than anything else. Perhaps she wasn't even on the train at all anymore. Izara had cast those protection spells—maybe they'd been enough to drive Omaira away.

Celestia took a deep breath and pulled the door open. Wind blasted across her face. It smelled of machinery, of burning coal and hot metal, although there was an underlying sweetness from the surrounding jungle. As Celestia picked her way across the walkway, the jungle rose up as a wall of green on either side of her. Her heart hammered. *She won't be there. She'll have leapt from the train in the night to get away from Izara's magic.*

Celestia made it to the sleeping car. She opened the door and stepped inside.

It was dark, the curtains drawn tight over the windows, and Celestia's eyes took a moment to adjust. Shapes bloomed into focus. There was a large, shuddering lump lying on the bed.

Celestia felt the air go out of her. So the kajan was still here. She realized it had been wishful thinking for her *not* to be, a desire born in the shimmering yellow sunlight of the dining car.

The kajan—Omaira, she had given Celestia her name and it was only polite to use it—was snoring a little, her breathing heavy and rhythmic. The trunk was tucked away neatly in the far corner, and the washing basin was set up on the table beside it. If Celestia moved quietly enough, perhaps she could pull out a change of clothes and gather the basin without Omaira waking.

So Celestia crept along the side of the car, her skirts gathered up in two fists. The train rocked back and forth with the force of the wind, and the engine's roar masked the sound of her footsteps. Her stomach knotted up, and she kept her eyes focused on the trunk.

A dagger slammed into the wall a handswidth from her head, the blade thrumming.

Celestia screamed and threw up her hands. Omaira sat up in the bed, eyes glowing golden in the sleeping car's dim light. She was naked, Celestia realized with a start, and Celestia jerked her gaze away, her cheeks warming.

"You," said Omaira. "What are you trying to do?"

"Nothing," Celestia said, staring at the floor. "I only wanted to get a change of clothes."

The bedsprings creaked. Celestia peered up as Omaira slid off the bed. Her body was bulky and broad, and the black tattoos that Celestia had seen peeking out from her armor wrapped around her form, accentuating the curves of her muscles. She walked, brazen, across the room, with no shame in her posture. She yanked the knife out of the wall. It was easier when she was close; Celestia could look her in the eye, away from her nudity.

Omaira grinned. "It's nothing you haven't seen before."

Celestia's cheeks grew hotter. Except Omaira *was* like nothing she'd ever seen before. She couldn't imagine a woman so strongly muscled as her—not even the female adventurers who stopped at Cross Winds were as imposing. And the tattoos! Celestia had never seen such tattoos, twisting elaborately over Omaira's body.

"Humans cover themselves," Celestia finally said.

"I'm not human." Omaira turned away from her and Celestia's gaze dropped down in spite of herself. She took a deep breath, jerked her eyes back up to the glossy dark waterfall of Omaira's hair.

Omaira grabbed the trunk and dragged it out into the middle of the floor. "Take it," she said, before picking up the washing pitcher and tilting it toward the basin. Water flowed, sparking a little with the magic of the train. It took Celestia a moment to realize that Omaira planned to *bathe* in front of her.

"This city where you say you're going, it has layers of

protection spells." Omaira set the pitcher on the table and picked up the washing rag. "I can already feel them pounding at me, here. We must be close." She tapped at her temple and Celestia immediately busied herself with the trunk, kneeling down and carefully pulling out the folded outfits that Lady De Lisista's butler had seen fit to pack.

"Does the bloodroot not protect you?" Celestia asked politely.

"The bloodroot let me see this train. The magic surrounding this city is designed to keep my kind out."

"I see." Celestia found a green silk day dress, thirty years out of style but still in good condition, the sleeves and hemmed edged in antique lace. A pair of matching green shoes was nestled beside it. But she still needed a change of underthings.

Omaira grunted. Water splashed in the basin; *I will not look,* Celestia told herself. She pulled out a set of neatly folded undergarments and tucked them under the green dress, out of sight. Then, she moved toward the door leading to the other sleeping car, her eyes fixed down on the lush, carpeted floor. She was aware of Omaira moving beside her.

"Wait," Omaira said, just as Celestia reached out to open the door. Forgetting herself, Celestia glanced up, and Omaira was standing naked beside the bed, gray skin gleaming.

"Are you really looking for His Lordship?" she asked, a dangerous roughness at the edge of her words. "Or did you just say that last night to keep me from killing you?"

Celestia trembled, clutching her change of clothes to her chest. Omaira stared at her, rubbing the washing rag over the back of her neck.

"I wouldn't lie," Celestia finally said, choking back a tremor in her voice.

Omaira tossed the washrag into the basin. "Then why are you going to a place that uses magic against his creations?"

"I—it's complicated." Celestia's clutched her clothes so tightly her knuckles turned white. "Bloodvine is very old," she finally said. "It was founded during the Last War as a refuge against Lord Kjari. It seemed the best place to search for him. Perhaps we can find a record of his palace—"

Omaira laughed. "A record of his palace! You think humans can find his palace? It moves from place to place, beyond your reach." She reached for the clothes that lay piled up on the floor beside the bed.

"We didn't know—we weren't sure—" Celestia took a deep breath, steadying herself. "We didn't know what else to do."

Omaira pulled a tunic over her head, strapped it in place with a belt. Then she flinched. "This cursed magic is getting stronger. Do you know how to counteract it?"

Celestia shook her head, eyes wide.

Omaira glanced at the car window, frowning. "No, I suppose you wouldn't."

Celestia edged toward the door. She should never have come back into the car.

"You won't find His Lordship in that city," Omaira said, stalking across the car, gathering up pieces of her armor and tossing them onto the bed.

"Then where would we find him?" The question spilled out of Celestia with a rush of bravery. Omaira stopped and turned to her, eyes blazing.

"I told you," Omaira snarled. "I don't know." She pulled on her chest plate, moving with quick efficiency, and Celestia felt a dizzying wave of confusion.

"Why not?" Celestia found herself blurting out.

"Because I'm not in his army." Omaira yanked on her armor. It clanked and rattled like the train. "Not yet. When I prove myself, when I find him, I'll become one of his defenders." She finished dressing and walked over to Celestia, rising before her, fully armored, fully armed.

"You aren't in his army now?" Celestia shook her head in confusion.

"No," said Omaira.

And then she flung open the door and jumped out into the jungle.

SEVEN

I zara was lying down on the fainting couch when she felt the train slowing. She had been attempting to fall into a trance during the length of their trip, with a mind to uncover the formulas that made the train run, buried in the Aetheric Realm. But she couldn't concentrate. Her mind had kept wandering over to that kajan Celestia had seen in the sleeping car—and to worry that they were once again the early days of the Last War. And so despite her best efforts, she stayed firmly pressed in this realm, the train's engines roaring around her head.

The slowing of the train was followed a heartbeat later by a surge of more unfamiliar magic, as all the magic had been the last few days. Izara gave up on her trance, stood up, and trotted over to the window and peered out. The forest was no longer a green blur, and amidst the tangled undergrowth she caught signs of civilization, actual, real civilization—little round brick buildings tucked away behind the trees, gleaming metal signs written in a language she didn't recognize. She could hardly believe it.

"What do you see?" Ico pressed beside her, the faint reflection of his features materializing in the glass of the window.

"A few little buildings. There's definitely something here."

"Ico, could you go into the sleeper car and fetch the trunk for us?" Izara asked.

No answer. Izara glanced over her shoulder, where Ico was staring out the window, sunlight illuminating his face.

"Ico!"

"Look," he said.

So Izara looked. And then her breath caught in her throat, and she had to press one hand against the wall to steady herself. The forest was gone, replaced by glass buildings that shimmered and shone in the sunlight. She hadn't thought such buildings were possible. Even at the Academy they didn't have buildings like this.

How could such a place stay hidden for five hundred years?

The door leading out to the walkway slammed open, bringing a rush of hot wind. Celestia darted in, dressed in an old-fashioned green dress. "The kajan's gone," she announced. "We must be getting close—she said she could feel the city's wards."

"You're still the only one who's seen this kajan," Ico muttered.

If Celestia heard him, she chose to ignore it. She slipped up behind Izara and Ico and peered through the glass. "Oh my," she said softly. Then: "You and Ico should change. You two have been wearing the same clothes for two days."

Izara rolled her eyes. "You see a city like this and all you can think about are clothes?" She laughed. "Look how advanced they are! I doubt they'll care about whether we're wearing the latest fashions."

Celestia frowned, and then, without speaking, slipped out into the walkway between cars.

"She's probably not wrong," Ico said suddenly. "It's always better to be overdressed if you don't know the situation."

"And you would know, pirate?" Izara rankled with irritation. Even Ico was giving her lessons on manners now.

"I would, actually." Ico turned away from the window. "You've got to look respectable if you want to do some real thieving. Just the way the world is."

The train continued to slow. Ico left the car, too, and so Izara was alone, standing by the window and watching the city flicker by. She caught glimpses of people now, ladies walking arm in arm down the narrow pathways alongside the train tracks. They stopped and looked over at the train, but the train was still moving too quickly for her to catch their expressions. She thought she might have seen glimpses of surprise.

The car door opened and in swept Celestia, having added gloves, a handbag, and a veiled hat to her ensemble. "We won't be wearing the latest fashions regardless," she said. "But we have to at least try. And at least Ico is taking my advice."

Izara said nothing.

The train rumbled to a stop. For the first time in two days the engines died away, and the car was met with a sudden, deafening silence.

"We should wait for Ico," Celestia said. "I think it's important we all disembark together. We don't know exactly what we're going to find out there."

Izara nodded, although this city did not seem like a treacherous place. The magic felt safer now. Cleaner. More precise.

Ico came back into the car, dressed in a dark suit. Izara scowled at him. Traitor.

Ico swept his hat off his head and gave a theatrical bow. "Shall we?" he asked, one hand on the door handle.

Izara glanced over at Celestia. She looked scared. But Izara only felt the thrill of excitement.

He pushed the door open, and they went out. Ico. Then Celestia. Then Izara.

In the open air, the magic was even stronger, a sharpness that twinkled over Izara's skin. She gazed up at the buildings growing up among the trees. Metal and glass twisted together in a strange, beautiful dance. The earth was paved over with smooth gray stones, but unlike the stones in Jaila-Seraphine, these were not cracked or battered, and they shone in the sunlight. Horseless carts rumbled between the buildings, puffing clouds of white steam that twinkled a little—magic! They were magic-fueled carts!

Izara never wanted to leave this place.

Even Celestia was gazing out at the city, her mouth hanging open. The three of them were the only ones on the train platform, and no attendant waited behind the ticket counter. This platform, indeed, looked older than the city surrounding it.

"Now what?" Ico said, his gaze tracking one of those puffing carts. "How is that thing moving?"

Izara stepped off the platform, heading toward the street. The city's magic flowed through her, lighting up Iomim's Treasure inside her heart. She had felt like this only once before: when she first arrived at the mountain where the Academy was housed. But the magic there had been a comfort. It had been familiar, a wild tangle like the jungle around Cross Winds. Here the magic was ordered and neat and quite alchemical, but at the same time it was completely foreign and completely, Izara was coming to realize, wonderful.

"Izara!" Celestia's voice dragged her back into the physical realm. "We shouldn't split up."

Izara turned around. Celestia and Ico huddled close to

each other on the train platform, as if they didn't trust this place.

"Well, then, come over here," Izara said. She turned back to the city. It looked like a diamond jutting out of the jungle. Was there an academy here, that taught this strange, ordered magic? If only she had asked Lady De Lisista! But of course, back at Essir Manor, she had refused to trust any of this.

She knew they needed to focus on finding Lord Kjari, but surely the other two would understand if she made one little digression to find out how this place had been built, and how those carts rumbled, and what it was like to live in a place so soaked in magic that she could feel it like the humidity in Sera Harbor.

"We don't know about this place." Celestia's voice was close to Izara's ear, and Izara jumped at the sound of it. "We must be careful. We're strangers here, and we don't know how this city treats strangers."

Izara laughed. "Look at this place! Look at the progress of it! We aren't in some rural backwater."

Ico snorted. "That's exactly where we are, in case you forgot the two-day train ride we just took."

Izara glared at him.

"Stop squabbling," Celestia said. "We need to decide what we're going to do here." She sighed, looking out over the road. "We can't assume it's safe to just go up and ask someone about Lord Kjari. This city was built in opposition to him, remember."

"Five hundred years ago," Ico muttered. Celestia ignored him.

"So we just find an archives, or a library," Izara said. "Tell them we're scholars."

Ico rolled his eyes. "All this way for a library."

Celestia nodded at Izara. "Yes, I think you're right. A hidden city will likely have hidden information."

Celestia turned toward the street, and Izara and Ico followed her, Ico carrying the trunk, its corners banging against the stone. Celestia had insisted they bring it, claiming they didn't yet know how long they were staying. The people of the city, who even to Izara's untrained eye seemed glamorous and well-dressed, largely ignored them, their heads bent together in conversation, or their eyes staring ahead at some point in the distance. They darted quickly around the trunk, leaving trails of magic in their wake. Izara tried to grasp at that magic, tried to learn its secrets. But she wasn't successful.

They had not been walking long when one of the horseless carts jangled to a stop beside them. A man stuck his face out the window and shouted, "Oy! Why drag that trunk behind you like that? I can give you a ride, ten *rov*."

Rov. The people of Bloodvine used the same currency as the Seraphine. And spoke the same language. But then Lady De Lisista said they did trade with the Seraphine.

Ico stopped and looked over at Izara and Celestia. "Sounds good to me. Not like we even know where we're going."

"Ah!" the man cried, and his face vanished inside his cart momentarily before a door sprang open, and he leapt out, arms outstretched. "Visitors! We love visitors here in Bloodvine. Just don't forget to take some bloodvine root so you can remember us and come back! Please, allow me."

He grabbed the trunk away from Ico and dragged it over to the cart. Celestia gave him a wary look, and he just shrugged and said, "The damn thing was heavy."

"We'd like to go to an archives," Izara called out to the man, using her request as an excuse to get closer to the cart. He was sliding the trunk into a panel in the back, and Izara reached out one hand and pressed it against the cart's smooth, warm side. Magic bolted through her and she jerked her hand back and then stared down at it in wonder. Usually she couldn't feel magic like that unless she was in the Aetheric Realm.

"The public archives is on 31st Street." The man stepped away from the cart and studied them. "I'd be happy to take you there. But surely you'd like a place to stay? We have one of the finest hotels in all of the Seraphine, the Grand Isangi. The restaurant there is," he kissed his fingers, "sublime." He grinned at Celestia. "Surely a lady such as yourself, with such refined taste, would appreciate the glamor the Grand Isangi provides."

Celestia gave an aristocratic smile. "Perhaps later. We'd like to go to the archives first."

The man nodded and pulled open a door on the side of the cart, then gestured for the three of them to enter. Izara clambered in first. Magic thrummed in the marrow of her bones. She settled into the soft, thick cushion and peered around. It could have been a cart in Jaila-Seraphine. It was lined with the same ruby-colored velvet, at once luxurious and going to tatters, and an icon of Growth was painted along the side of one wall, her body wound up with flowers and curling leaves.

"The Grand Isangi," Ico muttered. "Not a soul in any Seraphine city has ever offered me a chance to stay at any hotel with the word Grand in the name."

"They consider themselves part of the Seraphine," Celestia said. "Isn't that curious? 'The finest hotel in the Seraphine,' he said." She clasped her hands in her lap and gazed out the cart window. "I wonder if the Emperor knows of this place."

Izara didn't answer; it was curious, but she was more interested in the magic here, the way it pulsed through the air. She peered out her window and watched the city rattle by. Perhaps the strangest thing was that nothing about Bloodvine seemed *old*. It certainly didn't seem as if it had been built five hundred years ago. Everything in the city gleamed, and there was hardly any wood in the building, just metal and glass, shining like diamonds in the sun. A secret city in the jungle that had somehow advanced further than any other in the Seraphine? Perhaps it was the city's strange magic—magic could renew, if that was what the mage desired. It didn't *have* to speak to the past, even though it so often did. The icon of Growth suggested renewal as well. That was her domain, after all.

The cart slowed. Izara scanned across the signs of the buildings but saw only shops for clothing and food. She leaned across Celestia's lap to look out the opposite window, and Celestia gave a squawk of displeasure. "You're acting like a little girl!" she cried.

"I don't care." There it was, the archive, rising up like a grand palace. *Bloodvine Archives* was etched in big block letters above the revolving glass doors. Revolving doors! Izara had heard of such a thing, a new-fangled fad in Jaila-Seraphine, but she'd never seen them for herself.

A thump came down from the roof of the cart. "Here we are! The Archives on 31st Street."

Izara didn't hesitate. She flung the cart's door open and spilled out onto the busy, bright street. The driver hopped down, put his hands on his hips. "Shall I take your things on to the Grand Isangi?" he asked. "That way you don't have to lug that trunk all the way through the archives."

"That would be perfect, thank you." Celestia emerged out of the carriage, blinking in the sun. Ico slunk out behind her. She reached into her purse and extracted the driver's payment, her movements easy and relaxed—even in a city like this she knew the rules of propriety. Izara turned back to the archives and made her way toward that novel spinning door. A man breezed out as she approached, dressed in the bright linen robes of an alchemical scholar. Izara tried not to gape at him. He'd clearly graduated from the Academy, given his robes, but the Academy knew nothing about this place as far as she was aware.

"Wait up!" Ico shouted. Izara sighed and glanced over her

shoulder at him and Celestia. They made their way toward her slowly, and she stamped her foot like she really was a little girl again.

"We don't want to get separated," Celestia said when she and Ico finally arrived at Izara's side. "We don't know this place, and you don't have any money."

Izara didn't say anything; she knew her sister was right. The three of them walked into the archives, one after another with Izara leading the way. The revolving door swished against the carpet as it circled around them, a glass cylinder like an aquarium.

Izara stepped into the lobby of the archives.

It was cavernous, the ceiling soaring up overhead. Windows were cut into it so the room filled with light, and there were statues of the Airiana set up in alcoves along the far wall: Forest and the Lady of the Seraphine, of course. Ocean. Sky. And Growth, set into the largest of the alcoves, her expression benevolent as she held out a palm overflowing with flowers.

A single desk was set up on the far end of the room, where a woman sat flipping through sheets of paper, a pair of spectacles perched on the end of her nose.

"Now what," muttered Ico.

The woman looked up at the sound of his voice. Her gaze was piercing even across the vast empty space of the lobby. She said nothing, only stared at them, and for the first time since arriving Izara's excitement and curiosity was tempered with a little thrill of fear.

"May I help you?" The woman's voice was as crisp as her gaze, and it echoed against the walls.

Celestia and Ico both turned to Izara expectantly, and Izara's fear shivered and she choked it down—an archives like this was *her* world, just as the bizarre labyrinths of the great houses was Celestia's.

"We're interested in researching the history of the Seraphine." She walked across the lobby, her shoes sinking into the plush carpet. The woman watched her, face unreadable. "Specifically, the period of the Last War, and of Lord Kjari's rule."

"Ah." The woman slid her papers aside and stood up. She was dressed like a governess, a drab gray dress that cinched in tight at the waist and fell in thick folds to her ankles. "Yes. I'll show you to the Kjarin Room."

Izara's fear evaporated. She glanced over at Celestia and flashed her a triumphant smile, which Celestia returned, politely. No one called out for their arrest; it wasn't some crime to say Lord Kjari's name.

They followed the woman through the lobby and over to a spiral staircase that twisted up for at least four floors. The air smelled of paper and ink, a scent that Izara had always found relaxing.

"As you're probably aware," the woman said, "most of our collection focuses on the history of Bloodvine, not the larger Seraphine. What information we do have about the Last War and about Kjari is largely related to accounts from early settlers." They stepped off the staircase on the third floor. The air up here was hushed and still, save for the occasional rustle of turning pages. They walked through shelves and shelves of books, the spines fat and old-looking. Izara gazed up at those shelves, wondering what subjects their books explored. If the archives focused on the history of Bloodvine, perhaps she could find out more about the magic that infused everything here, that seemed to have pushed the city into the Seraphine's future.

"Here we are." The woman stopped at a simple wooden door and pushed it open. She turned the knob on the lamp sitting on a table beside the door, and it was bright enough to reveal a small cube of a room, low shelves running along the walls. Tables were set up in the center of the room, each with their own lamp. She held the door as Ico, Izara, and Celestia stepped inside. "There is an index cabinet along the far wall there." She gestured to a wooden cabinet, as familiar to Izara in its design and purpose as Cross Winds itself. All index cabinets looked the same. "I'll be happy to answer any questions you may have." She paused, looked them over, and when none of them offered a question, said, "I'll leave you to it, then."

She swished out of the room, letting the door swing shut behind her.

Izara was the first to move, and she swept over to the cabinet. "I'll tell you which books I think might be useful," she said, "and then you can pull them off the shelf and start looking for something."

"Great," Ico said, and he slumped down at one of the tables and switched on his lamp.

"You do know how to read, don't you?" Celestia said sweetly. When Ico glared at her, she just laughed. Then, to Izara, she said, "I think that sounds like a perfect plan. We want to get through these as quickly as possible." She took a deep breath. "And hope the answers we need are here."

Izara pulled out the P drawer of the index cabinet and flipped through the cards until she came to *palace*. Everything in the room was related to Kjari in some way, but there were only five books with information about Kjari's palace. At least it was a start.

She called out the titles as Celestia and Ico searched for them, stacking them up on the tables. And then they all began flipping through the pages. But there was nothing in those books that couldn't be found in a hundred histories of the Last War anywhere in the Seraphine, Kjari's palace only warranting a passing mention in all of them. Otherwise, it was the same information that Izara had learned as a child—

that Lord Kjari had brainwashed the people of the Seraphine and marched against Eiren, that the Last War was a dark time in their history, that it should be studied so no mage would ever wield such terrible power again. She looked up books about the Last War in general, and they found discussions of the battle strategies, and an ancient, dusty tome on the economic trade between Eiren and the Seraphine at the time. There were a few books that focused on the magic of the Last War, and those Izara found interesting, even if they weren't particularly useful. They didn't even acknowledge that kajani were real creatures, just laughed them off as myths and tall tales passed around by the Eirenese.

"This is pointless bullshit," said Ico when she read this last passage aloud.

"Not totally pointless," Izara sighed, "but I agree, it's not taking us anywhere." She looked over at Celestia. "What do you think?"

"Hmm?" Celestia lifted her gaze from her book, a collection of accounts from the first political refugees to settle in Bloodvine. "Oh, yes, I agree. It's disappointing. I did find something interesting, here, but I don't think it's useful, either."

"You're as bad as your sister," Ico said. "We don't give a shit about interesting. We give a shit about finding Lord Kjari so we can get home."

Celestia pointed to a place in her book. "In the accounts, the refugees keep bringing up the Founders."

"The what?" Izara frowned. Ico sighed with irritation.

"The Founders. Of Bloodvine." Celestia's eyes glimmered in the yellow lamplight. "I think they're the Laniana that Lady De Lisista mentioned. The ones who helped build Bloodvine." And then she began to read:

"Founder Moich—"

"That can't be a real name," Izara said. Celestia waved her off.

"Founder Moich was still living in his palace in the city at the time, although he did not debase himself with matters of war. His focus, as was the focus of all the Founders throughout the centuries, was on the city itself, on its development and protection. Despite limited resources and the constant threat from the south, he was able to oversee the construction of Vesom Road, which extended the boundaries of Bloodvine deeper into the surrounding forest. Vesom Road eventually developed into the neighborhood of Vesom, now a cultural epicenter. In those days, however—"

"What is this?" Ico interrupted. Celestia peered up at him. "How does this help us?"

"These Founders interacted with the people of Bloodvine. They didn't hide themselves away. If they *are* the Laniana who helped build the city, they might know how to find out to Kjari." Celestia closed the book.

Izara shook her head. "The Laniana are the children of the Airiana. They have no reason to help us."

"Children rebel against their parents," Celestia said lightly.

Izara resisted the urge to roll her eyes.

"They aren't written about as spirits here." Celestia tapped the book. "They're written about as people. They might still be here, in the city. It's worth trying, at least." She sighed and leaned back in her seat. "Or maybe it was hopeless, coming here. Perhaps that map was just a dead end."

They sat in silence for a moment. Izara fiddled with the cover of her book. The fabric was starting to fade at the corners. They'd been here for nearly two hours, reading and lugging books to and from the shelves. Izara lived for this sort of work, and yet even she was feeling tired and discouraged.

"We should go to the hotel," she said. "And rest. We can come back tomorrow."

Ico snorted. She glared at him.

"I agree," said Celestia. "We can consider what we learned today—"

"Nothing," Ico grumbled.

"—And use that as our starting point tomorrow. What do you think, Izara? You're the scholar among us."

"I think that sounds perfect," Izara, hoping it would lead them somewhere.

Celestia would never admit it aloud, but the Grand Isangi Hotel was the sort of place she'd been dreaming of for the last few weeks. When they breezed into the lush, opulent lobby, with its glittering chandelier and the bellhops milling around in their crisp uniforms, she felt the tension ease out of her shoulders for the first time since she'd left Cross Winds. She was in her element again. She was *home*.

They were given a suite on the eleventh floor, with big, luxurious beds and a balcony that looked out over the city. Izara was up there now—she said she wanted to visit the Aetheric Realm and study the magic of Bloodvine. Ico and Celestia left her to it, and come down to the lobby. Ico wanted to drink, which was why they were now sitting at the gleaming bar, a bottle of rum sitting beside them. Ico had drunk most of it.

"We're never going to solve this," he said, knocking back his glass. Celestia sipped at hers—a lady such as herself should never get drunk, even in the face of certain failure.

"Don't say that," she said half-heartedly.

"It's true. We're not." Another swig. He was drinking like a pirate. Celestia reached over and guided his hand down.

"You shouldn't drink so much," she said.

"Why not?" He laughed sharply. "We're chasing down a five-hundred-year-old mage. Drinking is the best option here."

Celestia frowned and dropped her hand down to her belly, felt the faint hint of a curve there. She'd be showing soon. When she had set out from Cross Winds, she assumed she'd be back home before that happened, that she would be able to wait out the rest of her pregnancy the way a lady of her standing was supposed to, draped across a bed while servants brought her mango drinks and slices of sugar-dusted lemon.

"Drinking is rarely the best option," Celestia said.

"Shows what you know," Ico slurred.

Celestia wrinkled her nose, disgusted by his drunkenness. He was going to make a scene. None of the people in this lobby, with their expensive-looking, well-tailored clothing, would tolerate his loutish behavior.

"Now," he said, brandishing the bottle, "if you'll excuse me, I see some ladies of the night that need tending to."

Ladies of the night? Celestia gazed around the room, studying the women who milled around the little candle-lit tables. None of them looked like prostitutes to her.

But Ico was already making his way to a pair of women sitting side by side on one of the sofas. They sparkled like the chandelier, jewels glimmering in the hair and at their throat. If they were prostitutes, they were adept at blending in, but Celestia suspected Ico had an uncanny sense about these things.

She watched as he slid onto the sofa beside them and offered the rum bottle before turning back to her own drink.

"I see you've been abandoned."

The voice was as smooth and thick as oil. Celestia turned toward its owner, a man in an elegant gray suit, the lines cleaner and, in Celestia's opinion, more sophisticated than those of the suits worn by men in Jaila-Seraphine.

"I wouldn't call it abandonment," Celestia said. She folded her hands on top of the bar so that the mark of marriage on her right wrist was clear, even in the dim light.

The man took no notice of it, however, and gestured for the barkeeper. "Can we have two midnight blood teas?" he said, before turning back to Celestia and saying, with a flourish, "I hate to see a woman sitting alone."

Perhaps she wants to be alone, Celestia thought, but the truth was, she didn't, not tonight, not after they had traveled all this way into a city of magic and found nothing to help them.

The barkeeper brought the drinks over. They were blood-red shot through with a shimmery swirl, and Celestia had never seen a cocktail like them.

"It's a way of taking blood root," the man said. "I assume you're a visitor. The blood root makes sure you don't forget our fair city when you leave."

"Oh." Celestia smiled. "I've already taken precautions against that."

The man grinned back at her. "Well, you should try the midnight blood tea. It's a bit of a speciality here, even if you've no need of its magical properties."

He handed Celestia one of the glasses, then picked up his own and held it up for a toast. Celestia smiled a little, then did the same. If she had been in any other hotel bar in the Seraphine, she would never have done this, allowed herself to be seen drinking with a stranger. But these people had no ties back to Seraphine high society. They were a galaxy unto themselves.

"Before we drink," he said, "we say, *'Chal ajil etzlawaj,'* which is a charm for a prosperous future in the language of the Founders."

The Founders. Celestia pricked up with interest.

"So, *Chal ajil etzlawaj.*"

"Shall ajeel eslawaj," Celestia said, stumbling over the words.

The man laughed. "Close enough." He clinked his glass against hers and took a sip. At least he was a better drinking companion than Ico.

Celestia sipped at her drink, too, and it was as sweet as Lady De Lisista's blood tea had been. Like sugar cane. The cocktail, though, also had an undercurrent of bitterness that melded together on her tongue.

"It's delicious," she said. "Thank you." She took another sip. "It tastes rather like the blood tea I drank before coming here. That had no liquor, though. It was simply a brewed tea."

"Blood tea?" the man arched his eyebrows. "Well, that's an old-fashioned preparation. This drink was inspired by it, of course. The liquor comes from the nectar of the bloodvine flower. Then it's mixed with rum and melted sugar." He smiled, offered a hand. "My name's Ganon, by the way."

"Celestia." She sipped her drink again.

"So you've had blood tea?"

She nodded.

"You must have come through one of the old great house entrances, then?"

Celestia nodded. "Essir Manor, actually."

Ganon looked impressed. "Essir Manor! I don't think we've had anyone come in that way in a long time. No need for subterfuge, you understand. Still, we like to keep to ourselves. Don't want to be overrun with tourists."

Celestia smiled politely. "I wondered why I'd never heard of this place before."

"It's a secret city." Ganon laughed. "And we're a secretive people. Plus, the mages who run this place don't want Academy interference. Some kind of agreement with the Founders. But that's all above my head." He laughed again.

The Founders. Perhaps those Laniana were still in the city. But Celestia didn't want to be too forthright.

"So you live here?" she said, an innocuous question.

Ganon nodded. "You'll find that most of the bar's patrons do. It's rare to find a visitor from outside of the city. I only recognized you because you're dressed like a northern aristocratic woman who used to visit my home as a boy. She was a friend of my parents."

Celestia's cheeks warmed. "Yes, my clothes are a bit out of date. It's—well, it's a long story—"

"Oh, I didn't mean it like that!" He smiled. "I've always admired the styles from the north. Such classic lines. And your accent has a touch of Jaila in it." He paused. "Oh, I do hope I haven't offended you."

"No, of course not." Celestia glanced around the room in new interest. The coach driver had said visitors were rare, but she hadn't really thought about what that meant until now. And it was true that the people in the lobby did not look like the society she was used to back home. Even their movements were different—more languid, as if the world moved more slowly for them.

She caught sight of Ico. He was in the process of telling a story to the two women he'd befriended, his gestures big and extravagant. The women laughed and it twinkled across the room.

"So what brings you to Bloodvine?" Ganon asked.

Celestia turned back to him. "I'm here doing research."

Ganon's eyebrow raised. "Oh? You don't seem like the scholarly type."

Celestia laughed. "I'm not. But my sister is. She has an interest in—in your history." She paused. "Particularly the Founders."

"We do have a fascinating history," Ganon said. "If it's not too gauche of me to say so." He ran his finger around the lip of his glass. "I'm afraid I'm also not a scholar, so I don't imagine I'll be much help to you—I'm a businessman, you see, with exports going out to the north. Family business." He raised his glass.

Celestia smiled politely. "You probably know more about the Founders than we can find in books. Which hasn't been much, I'm afraid."

Ganon laughed. "Books! Your sister's scholarly ways seem to be rubbing off on you."

"How else are we to learn about the Founders?"

"Well, you could talk to one of them," Ganon said.

Celestia felt her mask of polite interest slip. Her mouth dropped open, her eyes widened. This was exactly what she'd hoped for.

Ganon laughed. "It's true almost all of them are gone. Whisked away to the mages' realm, that's what we learn as kids. But one of them stayed behind. He's a bit of a recluse, you see, but," and here Ganon leaned forward, his eyes glittering, "I've got the connections, through my business, to speak with him on occasion. He's a fascinating fellow. Not like anyone else you've ever met."

Celestia wondered about that, having met the Lady of the Seraphine.

Ganon leaned back. Sipped from his cocktail. Celestia sat very still, even as her mind whirred, trying to find the best way to approach this situation. Were the social rules different here? She couldn't tell.

"My sister had no idea," she finally said, "that the Founders were still in the city."

"Well, just one Founder, like I said." He took another drink and peered at her. "I might be able to arrange it. A meeting, I mean."

Celestia did not move. She watched Ganon, studying him, trying to decide what price she might have to pay to do such a thing.

"Oh?" she said. "That would make my sister very happy, but if he's a recluse—"

Ganon swiped one hand dismissively through the air. "Nonsense. I can make it happen. Especially," and here his eyes glittered again, "especially if a lady like yourself might see fit to speak to your husband about my export business."

A sigh of relief rushed through her. So he had seen the marriage mark. He was angling for money, not less savory proposals.

"I would be delighted," she said, trying not to think about Lindon's frustration as he left for the south.

Ganon clapped his hands together. "Excellent! I'll make the necessary arrangements. Meet me here tomorrow morning and I'll tell you where to go. I'll also bring some of my papers, for you to pass along to your husband."

"Of course." Celestia smiled, before taking another long drink of her cocktail.

———

Ico left with the two girls. Probably it was stupid, but he'd drunk too much of the rum and he was feeling impulsive. Whoever had been following them along the river did not seem to have followed them along the train, nor did they seem to be in Bloodvine.

So he let himself relax and staggered out of the hotel without fear, the two girls giggling at his side. They told him their names were Aviana and Oriana, but he figured that was bullshit, and he didn't bother remembering which was which, and just used the names interchangeably. The girls responded to either one, and he thought maybe they didn't remember who they were supposed to be, either.

"So where you taking me?" he slurred, leaning up against the girl on his right—Aviana, he'd just stick with Aviana for now. She wore her hair in her long thick ringlets that fell loose down her spine, gems glittering in them like stars. She put a finger to his lips.

"It's a surprise," she said.

"A surprise," said Oriana, who was dressed exactly like some old-fashioned Seraphine aristocrat, down to the pointy-toed boots and the swirling complicated pile of braided hair lying on top of her head. They both looked like aristocrats, actually, Aviana the new and Oriana the old, which meant they were going to be expensive as hell. Ico would worry about it later.

"That doesn't bode well for me," Ico said.

The girls dissolved into giggles. "Do we look like that sort?" Aviana asked.

"Never can tell," Ico said.

More giggles. Oriana slipped her arm into his, like he was a suitor taking her out for a stroll. Really, he wasn't that worried. People were out on the streets despite the late hour, and lanterns drifted through the air, casting their soft magic glow into the darkness. Oriana darted out into the street, her skirts lifted up around her ankles so they wouldn't get muddy. Ico and Aviana followed. Aviana leaned into him. "We're here," she whispered into his ear, and Ico gazed up at the big, stately building waiting on the other side of the street. Vines grew over the bricks—actual bricks, not the shining metal this city seemed to favor—but the windows glowed with a dreamy blue light. Ico knew what that meant.

"You kept your word," he said.

Aviana laughed. "Told you."

They went inside, and even though so much about Blood-vine was different from the Seraphine, this place smelled like any other high-class whorehouse Ico'd been in, that sweet sulky scent of incense. No madam waited in the foyer; the girls must be self-employed. They led him up the stairs, any pretense of aristocracy thrown away. Aviana slid her hand into his jacket and then into the waistband of his pants, inching lower and lower; Oriana was already undoing the ribbons and ties of her dress, revealing flashes of brown skin beneath the shimmering fabric.

Ico sighed with contentment.

The girls took him into a room with a big four-poster bed.

Oriana slid the curtain closed and shimmied out of her dress, her skin stained blue from the lanterns hovering near the ceiling. Ico fell backward onto the bed and let the girls get to work: first on each other, then on him. It was a good night. He might have drunk too much to worry about being lulled into some trap, but he wasn't so drunk he couldn't enjoy himself.

Afterwards, they let him fall asleep, sprawled out naked beside their two entwined bodies.

In his dreams he was back on the train that brought them to Bloodvine, the car rocking back and forth. A coldness crept in. He watched as ice crawled over the windows, obscuring the view of the trees of the Seraphine.

"Xima?" He stood up, looked across the car. She stood several paces away, her white gown shimmering in the light. Weirdly, the four-poster bed from the whorehouse was in the car, too, and the two girls were sleeping on it.

"Having fun without me?" Xima asked, lips teasing into a smile.

Ico blushed. "I got drunk."

"Oh, you know I don't care." She glided toward him, bringing wisps of ice and snowflakes. "You humans are always such transitory delights."

Ico frowned. But he also knew *transitory* meant something different to Xima. He could spend the rest of his life in her palace and she would see him as brief affair that burned white hot and then dissipated into steam.

"You found the coldest room in that place," Xima continued. "They have an ice-fan, you know. In the attic. Blowing straight down above where I stand." She put a hand on his arm and pulled him down onto a plush velvet sofa that had sat in Xima's palace, not the train car. She was orchestrating all of this. Figures a whorehouse would be the only place cold enough that she could appear to him.

"I've missed you," she said, and she kissed him once on the neck. Ico closed his eyes.

"We're trying," he said. "But everything just leads to dead ends." He turned toward her, cupped her perfect face in one hand. "You sure you can't help?"

"I told you, I don't know where he is, my north wind." She sighed, and her breath chilled his skin. Gods, he'd missed that. "But you must hurry. That's why I found you."

"We're going as fast as we can."

Xima's eyes glittered. "But it's spreading," she said. "What you saw in Sra Slarin."

Ico froze, his skin clammy. "Celestia said she'd heard of it happening somewhere else in Eiren—"

"It is moving south," Xima said. "Following the path that Lord Kjari took during the war, from the north where he—" She stopped.

"Where he what?"

"Was born," she said flatly. "Now it has arrived in the Eirenese islands, where the kajani were born."

"Ah, so you knew about them," Ico said.

"Of course," Xima said. "They were the abomination that shattered the Eirenese peninsula into an archipelago of uninhabitable islands."

Ico fell silent.

"And now death has fled those islands too," she said. "Just as it had in Sra Slarin and the other villages of the north."

Death had fled the islands. Ico stared up at her, his thoughts numb. He had not fully understood what he'd seen that day in Sra Slarin, the priest with this seeping wounds. Suddenly, he did. Suddenly, he was thinking of the Kozas, of the night they attacked his boat. His crewmates' death had been the only end to their torture.

"Wait," he said. "If this—illness, whatever it is—if it's following the path Kjari took in the war—"

South. Kjari moved south. He fought his final battle in the Seraphine. Even Ico knew that much.

"Yes," Xima said softly. "The landscape of these places is changing. Soon, death will flee the Seraphine."

Ico's throat went dry.

"Hurry, my king killer," she said. "You must find him. You must bring him to the Lady before his withdrawal destroys the world. You must tell him—he's wanted."

And then a cold wind rushed through the train car, and Xima vanished in a swirl of snow.

Ico sat up, shivering beneath the thin blanket. He was back in the whorehouse. Lights from the city spilled in through the window, turning the air murky. He glanced down at the two girls. They were still asleep. One of them—Aviana, maybe—snored softly.

Ico scrambled out of the bed. He pulled his clothes back on and fumbled around in his coat for a stack of bills, which he set on the bedside table. Then he rushed out of the house, Xima's voice echoing inside his head.

It was coming to the Seraphine.

Ico spent the rest of the night in the lobby of the hotel, smoking cigars he purchased from the concierge, and thinking. He watched the sun rise over the city, the light turning gray then pink then a brilliant lemony yellow that hurt his eyes. They should leave this place, he thought, go south like Celestia's husband and his troop of adventurers did. Lord Kjari wasn't in this city.

He was about to snub out his cigar and march up to the room to inform Celestia and Izara of his decision when he heard, "Ico? Were you down here all night?" in the soft twinkle of Celestia's voice.

He craned his neck around to find her and Izara staring at

him. Both of them were dressed as if they were about to go visiting. Jewels glimmered at Celestia's throat, and her dress was a dark blue silk confection that struck him as absurdly frivolous. Even Izara was dressed more nicely than she usually did, her hair pinned up with a jeweled clip instead of hanging loose and improper around her shoulders.

"Where the hell are you two going, dressed up like that?" Ico jabbed his cigar into the ash tray and leapt to his feet. "We don't have time for tea parties."

The two sisters looked at each other, then looked back at him.

"What's gotten into you?" Celestia asked. "You didn't seem terribly interested in our progress last night."

Izara stifled a giggle.

Ico scowled at them both. "Listen, I learned something last night. We don't have time to fuck around with whatever this is—" He gestured at their clothes in frustration.

Celestia's gaze turned brittle and angry. "While you were drinking yourself into a stupor, I was speaking with a man who has promised us access to one of the Founders."

"And you trust him?" Ico blurted out.

Celestia glared. "More than I trust you right now, yes. Go change. You smell like incense and rum. Not the sort of impression we wish to make."

"You don't know how desperate this is." He stepped up close to the sisters and said in a low, urgent voice: "It's spreading. The darkness in Eiren. It's coming to the Seraphine."

The sisters stared at him.

"How do you know that?" Celestia asked.

Ico hesitated. "The whore had heard about it," he finally said. "It's popped up in in the Eirenese islands."

Izara gasped. "It's moving south."

He nodded. "It's going to be in the Seraphine soon. We have to—"

"Mr. Tsal!" Celestia cried out. Her expression changed abruptly, turned as bright and glittering as a diamond, and she rushed past Ico, her skirts rustling.

"Please," a silky voice said, "I told you to call me Ganon."

"I believe you," Izara said in a fierce whisper. "And I'll check the status of its spread in the Aetheric Realm as best I can. But this is a chance to meet with a Founder. It might give us direction to find Kjari."

Ico scowled. "And it might not do anything."

"We have no other leads, Ico."

"Ganon, I'd like to introduce you to my traveling companions." Celestia breezed back over to them, her hand on this Ganon's arm. "My sister, Izara."

Izara gave a lopsided, awkward curtsy, her face still ashen.

"And our Akuran cousin, Ishi Kui Ico."

Ico leaned backward on the couch to get a better look at Ganon. He was dressed respectably enough, but Ico'd been around enough to know that didn't mean anything.

It might give us direction to find Kjari, Izara had said, and Ico knew, unfortunately, that they had no other leads.

"Hey," Ico said.

"He's a bit of a dilettante," Celestia said in a stage whisper. Ganon chuckled, but she still fixed Ico with a vicious glare.

Ico jumped to his feet. "I hear you can take us to a Founder."

"That I can," Ganon said. "Anything to help a lovely lady of the Seraphine." He patted Celestia's arm, and she smiled indulgently at him. "Our appointment is in an hour. I've arranged for a carriage to take us, but the Founder's home is on the outskirts of the city, and if we don't leave now, we run the risk of being late. The Founder *hates* tardiness."

Ico repressed the urge to roll his eyes. He desperately hoped this wasn't a waste of time.

Celestia was already letting Ganon lead her to the front

door, and Izara followed. She glanced over her shoulder at Ico. She still looked shaken.

"I will confirm as soon as we're done," she said, her voice stretched with urgency. "Perhaps I can determine how long we have."

That didn't do much to make Ico feel better. For a moment he considered staying behind, mapping out the best way to make their way south in case this Founder proved fruitless. But at the same time, if this was a trap—

Sure, Izara had her magic, but he'd feel like shit if he'd let them walk into it. Even if they had brought in on themselves.

Gods and monsters, what was happening to him?

He stood up, straightened his belt, double-checked that his knife was still strapped to his hip, and accompanied Izara out to the street.

They arrived at a shining glass building nearly an hour after they left the hotel. The carriage was a luxurious one, and under ordinary circumstances, Celestia might not have even noticed the time passing. But she spent this trip in a tight bundle of anxiety, worried that it was a trap—she wasn't stupid, no matter what Ico might think—or that the Founder would be worthless. And if this failed, what would they do next? Try to track down the kajan Omaira and follow her to Lord Kjari? But she claimed she didn't know where he was, either.

And if Ico was right, if that dreadfulness in Eiren was moving south—

She touched her hand to her belly and tried not to picture her baby growing and growing until it destroyed her from within.

"My Lady," Ganon said, offering his hand to help her climb out of the carriage. She accepted, blinking up at the glass structure rising out of the woods. She didn't think she would ever get used to these buildings.

Ganon helped Izara out after her, and then Ico clambered out on his own. He looked like a drunkard, with his greasy, unkempt hair and his mussed clothes. If only they'd had time for him to go change. Perhaps she should have left him at the hotel.

"This way," Ganon said, gesturing toward a stone path lined with flowers that glinted and sparkled like the building. Celestia fell into step alongside Izara, who was gazing out over the garden.

"What do you think?" Celestia asked in a low voice.

"There's magic everywhere here." Izara tilted her head toward Celestia but kept her eyes on Ganon, walking a few paces ahead. "Weird magic, like the magic in the city—I don't think it's dangerous."

"What are you two whispering about?" Ico asked behind them.

"Assessing the situation." Celestia strolled up the stairs to the front door, which Ganon held open. He gave a little bow as each of them passed. Ico included.

Inside the building everything was filled with light. The entranceway opened up into a cavernous sitting room lined with windows. Furniture was sparse and simple, but plants grew out of the floors, vines and flowers and soft grasses, and, at the center of the room, an enormous banyan tree that stretched all the way to the ceiling. It was too big for an ordinary banyan. Celestia gazed up at it, her skin prickling.

"Is that tree magic?" she asked Izara.

"It's a vessel for a Laniana," Izara whispered back, her eyes wide. "This is where we need to be."

"Have a seat," Ganon said. "Make yourselves comfortable. I'll go fetch the Founder. One of the servants should be in shortly with drinks."

And then Ganon slipped into one of the hallways that branched off of the room. Celestia collapsed onto a divan arranged underneath the spread of the tree's branches. Her clothes felt too tight, too restricting.

Ico clomped around the sitting room, his footsteps echoing off the glass wall.

"Will you please sit down?" she asked him. "It's bad enough that you're dressed like that."

Ico fingered a twist of vine dangling from the ceiling. "We'll see," he said.

Izara sat down in the sofa across from the divan, still gazing up at the banyan tree.

Celestia caught a glimpse of movement out of the corner of her eye. It was a girl, plump and pretty and dressed in pale silks, carrying a tray with a carafe and a trio of ceramic mugs.

"Coffee," she said in a low voice. "From the Eztajos. His Lordship hopes you will enjoy."

She set the coffee on a small table sitting near the walls and then vanished back into darkness.

"I'm not drinking that," Ico said. He looked over his shoulder at Celestia. "I recommend you don't, either. Not until we know what we're dealing with."

"I don't want to seem rude," she told him. "This is too important. Besides, the blood tea didn't do anything to us." She strode across the room and poured herself a cup of coffee. It steamed its rich, velvety scent on the air. At least it didn't smell poisonous.

Still, she glanced at Izara for confirmation.

"It's fine," Izara said. She was clearly distracted, her eyes moving over the lines of the tree's branches.

So Celestia took a small sip. It was like silk on her tongue.

"You're enjoying my Etzajos coffee, I take it?"

The voice startled her. It was quiet and warm, like the strings of a cello. Celestia turned around, her heart pounding—

And saw no one. The room was empty save for her, Ico, and Izara.

"Yes?" Celestia said uncertainly. She found herself looking to Izara for guidance on how to proceed. But Izara was just staring at the banyan tree.

But then the leaves of the banyan tree began to rustle, a soft, susurrating sound. It sounded rather like laughter, and then that rustling laughter became a voice. "The coffee is specialty of the Ixek lands."

New roots emerged from the floor, growing and twining and sprouting leaves that lengthened until they became long and silvery, like fabric.

"In the south," the voice from the tree said. "Please, all of you. Drink."

And then a creature emerged from the newly grown roots— a creature too beautiful to be either human or a banyan. Somehow, it was both.

It took the form of a tall, slim man, his transparent hair long, and his brown skin dusted with flecks of gold. His features were fine, delicate, and his gown was an elaborate twisting of fabric that looked like the roots of the tree he had emerged from.

This had to be the Founder.

Celestia took a deep breath and sipped again from her coffee, savoring the flavor. "It's delicious," she said, and then she set her cup aside so she could pour cups for Ico and Izara. She hoped they would at least pretend to drink.

"I'm glad to hear it." The Founder moved across the room— not walking, exactly, because the twists of his gown seemed to sprout out ahead of him, moving him as the banyan trees moved across the forest. He sank into a high-backed chair near the windows. The dappled light fell across his skin, and for a moment Celestia saw him as the tree he was. "Now, please introduce yourselves. I'm very curious what could bring three

Easterners into Bloodvine." He touched himself lightly on his chest, his movements graceful, like a dance. "My name is Isossa, of the Banyans."

Celestia didn't miss a beat. She set her coffee down and curtsied in the formal style, something she hadn't done in years. "My name is Celestia De Malena. This is my sister Izara De Malena, and our—" Isossa's eyes were boring into her and the lie evaporated on her tongue. "Our traveling companion, Ishi Kui Ico."

Izara managed a polite nod, acceptable enough since she was already seated. Ico jerked up his chin as if he were meeting a chum at an alehouse. Celestia stifled a scowl.

"It's lovely to meet all of you," Isossa said. "What brings you to Bloodvine? I'm afraid Ganon did not give me specifics, only said that a Seraphine lady wished to speak with me." He smiled here, a faint, teasing smile that put Celestia on edge.

Celestia picked up her cup and drank more of the coffee, wanting to delay her answer. Isossa watched her, then flicked his eyes between Izara and Ico, who were sitting quietly. Behaving themselves.

"We're investigating something," Celestia finally said, when she couldn't bear the silence anymore. "Or—someone, really." She glanced over at Izara and wished she could ask Izara how to proceed. This Founder was clearly a Laniana, and while they were not as strong as the Airiana, not as dangerous, they were still spirits of the land, too strong for a human to wrestle with.

Isossa tilted his head, his hair falling in a silky cascade over one shoulder.

"We were tasked with this search by one of the Airiana," Celestia said.

Isossa's expression was unreadable. "Please, my lady, have a seat. There's no need for you to stand while we chat."

Celestia felt suddenly flustered—of course she should have

sat, protocol dictated she should have sat, and yet she stood by the table like a fool. She whisked over to the nearest chair and folded herself into it, balancing her coffee cup on her knee. Ico and Izara were behind her and to her left; she would have to turn her head to look at them. Stupid of her. She should not be having these difficulties. But Isossa put her on edge. He inhabited a space less weighty than that of the Airiana, but he was still too inhuman, too beautiful.

"The Airiana are the creators of my people," he was saying. "Although we rarely interact. My kind prefers to exist in our natural state, in the soil and leaves of the forest, or the waves of the ocean, or the eddies of the river. I'm one of the few who remains in this in-between form." He swept one hand out, encompassing the room. "The Airiana will never fade away into their natural state in the spirit realm. They like to play their games too much. That's why it was a group of my people who built this city all those years ago." Isossa leaned forward, his pale eyes glimmering. "I take it that's what happened with you? You've been ensnared in some Airiana's game?"

Celestia sat with her spine very straight, her fingers curled around the handle of her coffee cup.

Isossa laughed. "Your face gives it away, I'm afraid. Oh, you don't need to worry about me, my lady. I don't deal much with the Airiana if I can help it."

That last line was more of a blow than anything else. "Oh," Celestia said, and she must have looked crestfallen despite her best efforts because Isossa frowned and asked her what was wrong.

"One of the Airiana has asked us to find someone," Izara said.

Celestia was startled by her voice. She glanced over at her. Izara moved forward on her seat. Her coffee cup rattled against its saucer.

"Lord Kjari," Izara said. "The Lady of the Seraphine, she has asked us to find him. She says it's very important, that he's not really dead, and we hoped that you would know his whereabouts, since you helped humans fight against him before." She took a deep breath, looked down at her lap. She must have thought she was rambling, poor thing, but Celestia was grateful for her. Grateful that she didn't have to be the one to ask. "We hoped you could help us," she finished up in a blur.

Celestia turned back to Isossa. He was smiling.

"You don't know, do you?"

A coldness gripped Celestia's spine. "We don't know much," she said. "It's what's made this journey so difficult."

Isossa threw back his head and laughed. His laughter was like the wind rustling through the leaves of trees.

Celestia stared, her cheeks hot with embarrassment.

"Forgive me," Isossa said, calming himself. He ran one hand over his smooth, colorless hair. "I didn't mean to make light of your situation, Lady De Malena, but I can't believe after all these years the Airiana are still snatching up humans to fix their messes."

"What?" blurted Izara. Celestia did not allow herself to shoot her an angry look.

"Lord Kjari is not a human man," Isossa said. "He's not some mage who discovered the secret to immortality."

Celestia felt dizzy.

"A fact I'm certain the Lady of the Seraphine forgot to mention. They feuded a long time ago, you know, Taja and Kjari."

The revelation rattled inside Celestia's head. She couldn't stop herself; she glanced back at Izara and found her looking as confused as herself.

Lord Kjari was an Airiana. And not just any Airiana—he was one of the Exalted Twins. The dark half of Growth.

The Lady of the Seraphine had sent them to find the most feared Airiana in the pantheon.

Celestia turned to Isossa again. He was no longer laughing; in fact, his face had taken on an expression of kindly pity.

"They have elaborate rules for themselves," he went on. "What they can and can't tell humans. Their games are— complex. My people, we never understood such things. But yes, the man you call Lord Kjari is the Airiana named Decay."

The room seemed to spin around. Celestia braced herself against her chair to keep from swooning. How could they possibly find *Decay*, when the Lady could not? How could they call out to him, drag him into the forest, without being beholden a second time—and this time to the most monstrous of Airiana? She wondered with horror if this was the true price of asking for the Lady intercession, if she and Izara and Ico would forever be caught in a series of boons and payment.

"And where can we find him?" Izara again. "I'm not calling on him with magic. I learned my lesson the first time. And I'm sure as hell not doing it with the *Decay*." She strode up to Isossa, her hands curled into fists. Celestia reached out and stopped her from moving forward, then glanced over her shoulder at Ico. He was slumped against the couch, staring ahead, a stunned expression on his face.

"I'm afraid I don't know."

Celestia felt as if the air had been slammed out of her. She peered up at Isossa, trying to decide if she believed him or not. He watched placidly, one hand toying with the ends of his hair.

"I see this comes as a bit of shock."

"She would have told us," Ico said.

Celestia looked back at him. He was still sitting on the sofa, still looking vaguely stunned, vaguely angry.

"She would have," he said. "She wouldn't have played games with me."

"She's playing games with all of us," Izara snapped.

"Not the Lady of the Seraphine." Ico jumped to his feet and began pacing back and forth underneath the banyan tree, glaring down at the floor.

"I'm sorry this information upsets you," Isossa said. Celestia turned back to him—he did look sorry, in his glassy, strange way. "But you asked for my help and I told you what I know."

"It's fine," Celestia said, before the other two could respond. "It's—a surprise, is all, that the Lady would keep such crucial information from us. That she would send us after such a dangerous force—"

"Is it really?" he said softly.

A pause, the silence heavy in the room.

And then Isossa said, "I'm sorry, too, that I don't know where you can find him. He's been in hiding for a long time. He used to make his home in Atharé, on the desert side of the mountains."

"The Atharé desert?" Izara said. "But that's thousands of miles of land. How can you expect us to find him in all that?"

"I don't expect you to find him at all," Isossa said. "River does."

Izara glared at him, and Celestia took her hand to calm her.

"I heard"—she purposely did not say where—"that his palace moves, that it's impossible to find."

Isossa smiled, showing the ends of his teeth. "It does move, yes. But he has always been at home in the Atharé desert. A secret he doesn't like to get out, not even to the kajani he abandoned."

Celestia's chest tightened, and she could feel Isossa's eyes on her, burning her skin.

"But a secret I am giving you. You'll find Decay in the Atharé desert. Somewhere."

Celestia stood up, still clutching Izara's hand. It was still too strange a thought for her to hold onto for too long, this idea that Decay had waged war against humankind. But at the same time, it explained the strength of his magic. She should have known better than to think a human mage could live for five hundred years, could create the kajani—the kajani, who were real!—from the ether of nothingness.

But it meant Decay had created them, didn't it? And that was an abomination, too. Growth created. Decay destroyed. That was the order of things.

"I wish you luck on your search," Isossa said, standing up as well. His gown puddled at his feet. "Any human who gets entangled in the games of the Airiana has my sympathy."

EIGHT

"It wasn't fruitless," Celestia said.

They were sitting in a cafe near the Grand Isangi Hotel, at a metal table in a courtyard draped in orchid vines. The scent of the blossoms hung heavily on the air.

"Are we believing him?" Izara said. "Isossa?"

"What else do we have?" Celestia glanced at Ico. He was pushed away from the table, staring off into space, a glass of rum dangling from one hand. Always with the rum. She doubted he was going to be any help. "It gives us a place to go. And Lindon," she stumbled a little over her husband's name, and her hand went to her stomach, "Lindon was going south."

"To Konmar," Izara said. "On the other side of the Atharé Strait."

"There's still is a logic to it."

"We can't just march into the Atharé Desert," Izara said.

"Not if we don't know exactly where we're going. It's not like the Seraphine. We won't have the Lady's protection—"

Ico snorted at that.

"And more than that," Izara went on, "you can't simply wander the Atharé. We won't have food or water. It's a *desert*, Celestia, and you're pregnant. If we knew where Lord Kjari's fortress had been, maybe . . ."

Her voice trailed off, and for a moment they all sat in silence. A breeze rustled the vines, stirring up that thick scent of the flowers. It was so sweet it almost smelled of rot, of dying things. Celestia had not let herself think of her baby since they had arrived here. It wasn't worth it, to consider the damage she was doing. And now she was considering going into the largest and coldest and driest desert in the entire world outside of Konmar itself. Her child would come out lean and tough like dried meat. Not like the child of a noble-woman at all.

And even if they found Lord Kjari's palace in that sweep of wasteland, what good would it do? The Lady wanted to speak with him, and how could they convince him to come to the water? He was *Decay*.

She still couldn't quite believe it. Perhaps Isossa had been lying, trying to scare them off the search, just as Lindon had tried to do.

"If we don't go into that desert," she said, breaking the silence, "we will never have a normal life again."

The others wouldn't meet her eye.

"We'll have to wander for the rest of our days," she said. "If we're lucky." Heat rushed to her cheeks. She did not want this future to belong to her.

"So we go to the desert?" Ico said. "Then what? You said yourself, the palace moves around." He frowned. "How did you even know that?"

Celestia remembered the dark, rocking train car, the kajan

laughing at the thought of a trio of humans finding Lord Kjari's palace—Decay's palace. An Airiana's palace.

"Omaira," she said softly.

"Who?" asked Izara.

"The kajan." Celestia closed her eyes and wondered, for the first time, where the kajan had gone after she leapt from the train. It had been such a strange experience, finding that monster bathing in a train car. Surely she wouldn't have stayed close to the city, not with the protection magics. And yet she had been following them.

"Celestia?" Izara asked, placing one hand on Celestia's arm.

Izara's eyes flew open. The kajan had said, hadn't she, that she intended to accompany them to the city. But the magic kept her out. If she were somewhere on the outskirts, perhaps—

"Are you all right?" Ico leaned across the table, frowning. He turned to Izara. "Is your sister all right?"

"I'm fine." Celestia sipped from her tea, straightened her spine. Her hand hovered over her stomach, but then she snatched it away. She would do what she must to return to Cross Winds before she did too much damage to her child. "I think we should find the kajan. Omaira. She could lead us into the desert and help us find the palace."

The other two gaped at her. Celestia fixed her gaze on her tea, willing herself not to look Izara in the eye.

"Have you lost your mind?" Izara asked. "You want us to get help from a kajan? You saw what they were like at the Aikha ruins!"

Celestia said nothing.

"Except you didn't," snapped Izara. "You hid. Trust me: they were just like in the stories, Celestia. They aren't *natural*."

"I still haven't seen one," Ico said.

Celestia looked up at her sister, her chest tight. "Omaira could have hurt me, and she didn't. She's trying to find Lord Kjari, too, just like we are."

Izara leaned back in her chair, her mouth thin.

"He's an Airiana," Celestia said. "A god. We need the help. And sometimes the best sort of help comes from those you don't expect."

Izara's expression only hardened. Ico finished off his glass of rum and said, "That sort of thinking hasn't worked out for me."

Celestia glared at him. "Well, it's a good thing we aren't pirates, isn't it?" She softened her gaze, looked back at Izara. "Remember when the acreage first stopped producing, how everything was growing wild with the rot-vines? We would have fallen into poverty so much sooner if it weren't for Lolia D'Neloza. She and Mother *hated* each other, and yet she would bring food for us. Remember? You were so young, but—"

"No," said Izara.

"The honey cakes. They were your favorite."

A shadow flickered across Izara's gaze. She did remember. "That's what this is," Celestia said. "Lady D'Neloza brought us food because Mother arranged for her to get an invitation to one of the grand balls in Jaila-Seraphine—she and her husband were new to the title, they would never have been accepted on her own."

"You're talking about a trade," Ico said. "Tit for tat."

Celestia nodded.

"With a kajan. Some mythical beast."

Celestia sighed. "She's not a beast."

"But she's not human, either," Izara said.

"Well, what suggestions do you have?" Celestia demanded. Thinking about her childhood, the slow decline of her family's acreage, gave her a hard knot in the back of her throat. Better, she thought, to focus on the present. On the future.

Izara crossed her arms and slumped back in her chair.

"Where is this kajan?" Ico asked.

Celestia hesitated. "I'm not sure."

He gave a choking laugh, and Izara rolled her eyes.

"But I think she may be outside the city. I think I could find her. She'd been tracking us, like I told you—"

"Why would she help us?" Izara asked. "What do we have to offer?"

"We can find out." Celestia pushed herself away from the table and stood up. Her legs shook beneath her skirts and she hoped the others didn't notice. "I'll find her and I'll ask."

"By yourself?" Ico said.

"You can come with me if you like."

Ico looked out at the street. "And leave this lovely cafe?" He gestured at the flowers blooming overhead.

"I'll come with you." Izara stood, knocking her chair back. "It's far too dangerous for you to go by yourself. And I've at least fought the kajani before."

Celestia's heart pounded in her throat. She nodded.

"If we're not back by nightfall, send someone after us," Izara said, and they were on their way.

─────

Celestia and Izara went to the woods by the train station. Celestia had said it seemed the best place to start, and Izara agreed. They slipped into the shadow of the trees, and Izara's nice dress slippers grew damp with mud. She was sure Celestia's were as well; neither of them had thought to change before coming out here.

"Omaira?" Celestia called, her voice tremulous in the dense trees. "If you're here, we'd like to speak with you. My sister and I."

Izara shifted her weight, crossed her arms over chest. The forest seemed thicker here than it ever did along the Seraphine. More impenetrable. A strange contrast to that city of light and glass.

"I don't think she's here," Izara said.

Celestia sighed. "I think you're right. But we can't go too far in the woods—I don't want to risk getting lost."

She was right. But like so much on this trip, they didn't have much of a choice.

"There's no sign of her," Izara said. "We have to go further in."

Celestia sighed and nodded. Together, they pushed farther in. Izara shoved aside the underbrush with her hands, the branches leaving thin red scratches on her bare hands. Sweat dripped down her back and soaked through her dress, and her face stung from where she'd been slapped with thin, spiky branches.

"Omaira!" Celestia shouted.

"This isn't going to work," Izara said. "Shouting her name like this. She could be anywhere." She turned to her sister, who gazed back at her, sweaty and desperate.

"I don't know what else to do," Celestia said weakly.

Izara sighed. "I do." She swatted aside branches and leaned up against a thick tree trunk, the bark rough through the thin fabric of her dress. "Let me see if I can find her in the Aetheric Realm."

"Will that work?" Celestia asked, her brow furrowed.

"I don't know." Izara closed her eyes, took a deep breath. She had found Lindon this way, of course, but he was human. Not a creature of myth.

Izara paused for a moment, then let herself sink into the lines of the tree until she was surrounded by the pulse of tree-breath. It rippled the air around her, tracing the lifetimes of the trees through the green, wet air.

To find a human, she simply had to look for the alchemical formula that defined them, an easy thing to do when it was someone close to her, as Lindon was. But a kajani?

Izara pulled herself upwards, scanning for a fuller view of the forest. She didn't dare look north, afraid she would see the sticky mass of the Aetheric disruption in Eiren—or worse, in the Seraphine. So she focused on the forest. From here, Bloodvine was breathtaking, a shard of rainbowed sunlight. She wished she could dive down and read all its formulas.

Concentrate, she told herself. The surrounding forest breathed steadily. Aetheric spirits flitted around, flickering in and out of her vision.

Except for one. It seemed more solid, somehow. More fully formed.

Izara's chest seized. She'd never seen anything like that before. Was it related to Decay and his departure from the world?

The spirit turned in her direction. Izara felt her concentration slipping, replaced by a wave of panic. The spirit loped toward her.

"You," it said, weaving through the tree-breath. "I've been waiting for you."

Izara screamed and jerked herself out of the Realm, her heart racing.

"Izara?" Celestia cried just as a sword sliced through the brush.

"There you are," said a rough voice.

Izara lifted her gaze and saw the kajan. Her black hair gleamed with greenish highlights in the sun. She wore armor, as if going into battle. She had the weapons for it, too.

Her gaze swept over Izara, and for a moment Izara was back at the Aikha Ruins, the horde of kajani slamming through that ancient place, her magic building up to a wild strength inside of her.

"Celestia," the kajan said. "I was hoping you would be here. I only saw your sister in the Aetheric Realm."

Izara gaped at her, all memories of the Aikha Ruins falling away. "That was you?" she gasped. "You were a spirit—"

Omaira looked at her and laughed. "A spirit? Is that what you call it?"

Izara shook her head in confusion. "How did you—"

"I felt you looking for me in the Aetheric Realm," Omaira said simply. "I've avoided passing over, but I knew it wasn't a fellow kajan searching for me."

Izara was wracked with confusion. But before she could ask for an explanation, Omaira stepped forward and wiped the damp strands of hair from her face. "We were looking for you. Both of us."

"And why is that?"

Celestia glanced over at Izara. "I—we wanted to speak with you."

"So speak."

"It's about Lord Kjari."

Did something change in Omaira's features at the mention of his name? A softening, perhaps? It was difficult to tell in the murky light of the forest.

"Surely you didn't find him in that dreadful city."

"No," Izara said. "But we learned something—" She stopped, looked up at Omaira. She stood like a warrior, feet planted hard in the ground, the sword lying across her shoulders, and lost her nerve.

"You didn't tell me that Lord Kjari is the Airiana of Decay!" Celestia blurted out.

Omaira grinned, showing her sharp teeth. "Of course he's Airiana. How else could he create my people? How else could he hide himself from human searchers?"

Izara looked over at Celestia in alarm. But Celestia pushed on. "Our histories told us he was the most powerful mage to ever exist."

Omaira threw back her head and laughed, her voice crawling up and down the trees. "Why would you ever think that? Humans are so arrogant. You assume anyone of strength is like yourself."

"I am not *arrogant*," Celestia snapped. Omaira grinned again—more of a taunt this time, Izara thought, chagrined.

"It's not Celestia's fault," Izara said. "We've been taught our entire lives that Lord Kjari is human."

"Yes!" Celestia cried. "A powerful human, an unnatural one. But not a *god*. And we had to travel to this hidden city in the deepest heart of the forest just to learn something you could have told me on the train." Her voice was pitching into hysteria, and Izara slipped over and put a hand on her sister's arm. "I left behind my home for this, and Izara gave up her *dreams*, and I'm pregnant and I just want to go back to Cross Winds—"

"You're pregnant?"

Izara felt Celestia tense. "Yes," she said after a hesitation.

Omaira said nothing.

Izara took a deep breath. She was starting to suspect that there was more to the kajan—to the kajani themselves—than she'd ever thought. "We were looking for you because we need your help." Her chest constricted; Omaira's face was unreadable. "Celestia said that you told her humans could not find Lord Kjari's palace, that it moves around. But you could find it, yes?"

Omaira lifted her chin, eyes glinting.

"We know it's in the Atharé Desert," Izara said in a rush. "But we can't go there without a guide."

"We won't expect you to help us for free," Celestia added. "We can reach some kind of agreement."

Izara tensed. An agreement? With a kajan?"

"The Atharé Desert," Omaira murmured. "Where is that?"

"You don't *know*?" Izara squeaked.

"I don't live in your realm," Omaira snapped. "My people made their home in the Aetheric Realm after Lord Kjari sent us there for our protection. Only his chosen soldiers accompany him here."

"What!" Izara shrieked. "You live in the Aetheric Realm?"

"Of course," Omaira said. "How else could I see you? We

313

know you human mages creep through there when you have need of magic."

The Aetheric spirits, Izara thought numbly. *The Aetheric spirits are all kajani.*

Her head spun, and she pressed herself up against the tree. Everything she thought she knew about the world was coming unraveled.

Omaira said something in a language like broken glass. "How did you learn this? That his Lordship makes his home in the Atharé Desert?"

Izara recoiled at the force in Omaira's words; the language she had spoken rubbed at the inside of her head. "The F-Founder," she said, stuttering. "He's a Laniana, a banyan tree spirit. But he's the one who told us that Lord Kjari is an Airiana—he said we would find the palace in the Atharé Desert. That Kjari always preferred it."

"Is this Atharé Desert cold?" Omaira asked. "And desolate?"

"Most of it, yes," Izara said.

Omaira spoke in her language again. Izara's eyes trembled. "Follow the stones in the cold desert." She looked at Izara. "That is what all the books say, for those who wish to serve in his Lordship's army."

Izara curled her hands into fists. Sweat fell in fat lines down the center of her back. "I don't know what that means."

"It's a clue to the puzzle," Omaira said. "If I'm to prove myself to Lord Kjari, I must solve it."

"So you can't help us?" Celestia asked weakly.

Omaira smiled, slow and sharp, and turned to Izara. "I was hoping you'd help me, mage. Why do you think I was following you?"

A hot, damp wind blew through the tops of the trees, although none of it reached Izara below, on the forest floor. She wiped the sweat from her brow, feeling pierced by Omaira's gaze. "I don't understand."

"You wielded great power at Aikha. It was the kind of magic I need—" Her eyes glittered. Izara tried very hard not to shrink away. "The sort of magic that will lead me to His Lordship's palace. Lead all of us. He hides it from humans and kajani like myself, who grew up in the Aetheric Realm. But with magic, with the right paths, I will find it and join his army."

"You think I have the necessary magic?" Izara felt breathless.

"I think so, yes." Omaira leaned against her sword, met Izara's eye. "But you don't know the words, you don't know the paths."

"And you do," Izara breathed.

Omaira nodded grimly.

Izara glanced over at Celestia, who had dropped her hand down to her belly. She knew what her sister was thinking: *This is what we came for.*

"I guess we will need to help each other," Izara said.

"It appears we will," said Omaira.

<hr />

"Are you certain?" the cartmaker asked, peering at her over his desk.

Izara bristled, straighted up her shoulder. "Yes, I'm sure. One cart capable of travel over the mountains to the Atharé Desert, please."

The cartmarker sighed, shrugged, then began plucking away on his typing machine. "The soonest I'll have a carriage available is in three days' time. Is that acceptable?"

She nodded, and the cartmarker hit a final stroke of keys, *cuh-chunk*, and then whipped out a sheet of paper lined with figures. "It should be an interesting journey," he said, watching her.

"Yes, it should." Izara took the receipt from him, glanced

over it to make sure nothing was amiss, then tucked it in her bag. Celestia had made some kind of arrangement with Ganon to pay for the carriage—he was giving the money to the cartmaker, with Celestia writing to her staff at Cross Winds to pay him back and broker a trade deal between him and the acreage.

Celestia and her bargains. It was a skill Izara had never learned.

The cartmaker's office was close to the Grand Isangi, and Izara had walked there rather than calling one of the carriages. What money they had—real money, in-person money—needed to be spent on supplies for the trip to the desert. Celestia was already taking care of it, ordering skeins of water and preserved food from the city market. Tomorrow they would all be going to the shops to find travel clothing appropriate for the dramatic drop in temperatures they'd find in the desert. This was all much more difficult without the Lady of the Seraphine's boat, Izara thought, and its wellspring of magic. But they weren't close to the river anymore, and there was no way to contact the Lady, to demand why she had kept the secret of Lord Kjari's identity from them.

And what a devastating secret it was, that the being they sought was Decay. Out of all the Airiana, it had to be Decay. It had been his power Izara had called on that afternoon in Grand Mage Papazian's office. His power she had tasted like rot in the back of her throat.

And now she was riding off to the desert to taste it again. Because she suspected the kajani magic she was going to be learning would be laced with his power.

The Grand Isangi emerged up ahead, glinting in the sun. They had only been here a few days, but already Izara was in love with this shining city, and her memories of Jaila-Seraphine, even the Academy, felt drab and uninteresting in comparison. If only she had come here under different circumstances.

She went inside and cut across the lobby to get to her room. But then she spotted Ico, sitting in his usual spot by the windows and drinking. He was alone. Izara glanced at the stairs: did she really want to go back up to the room, and make more plans about this absurd trip with Celestia? If it was just her and Ico and the kajan, that would perhaps not be so bad—a chance to learn about the kajani and their truth of their creation, a chance to learn new magics. But Celestia was *pregnant*.

And so Izara walked over to the sofa where Ico was sitting. He glanced up at her, took a drink from his glass. Ice clinked against the sides. They used ice like it was river water here.

"You got our carriage?" he asked.

She nodded. He patted the seat beside him. "Sit," he said. "Let me get you a drink."

"I don't want anything—" But he was already gesturing to the barkeeper, some complicated twist of his wrist that the barkeeper recognized immediately. Izara slumped down beside him, pulling her bag into her lap.

"They call it a midnight blood tea," he said, staring at the street outside. "It'll go straight to your head. Supposedly it makes you remember the city, but I think it'll also make you forget about all this other bullshit for a little while."

Izara didn't say anything. The barkeeper brought her drink over, handing it off with a flourish. She sniffed it, the chemicals burning the inside of her nose. Ico saw, gave a sharp barking laugh.

"Too much of a scholar to drink?" he said.

"Scholars don't drink," she told him. "We have to keep our heads clear." But she wasn't a scholar anymore, was she? The Lady of the Seraphine had dragged her away from the Academy weeks ago.

She gulped down the midnight blood tea and immediately regretted it. The back of her throat felt as if it were on fire. Ico laughed again, and when she started to cough and sputter, he hit her half-heartedly on the back a few times until she slumped against the sofa, slightly recovered.

"I don't see how you can do this to yourself," she muttered.

Ico lifted his glass. "Cheers," he said, and took a drink. "I don't see how you can't."

Izara sighed and looked down at the blood-colored liquid, at the broken chunks of ice.

"So you're really going to be teaming up with the kajan," Ico said, after a time. "Think it'll work? We'll actually find the bastard?"

Izara swirled the drink around in its glass, watching the ice catch the light. "I don't know."

"It's fucking Decay. Who saw that coming?" Ico drained his glass, then gestured at the barkeeper for another. Izara bit her tongue—there was no use nagging him about it.

"It makes sense," Izara murmured, not sharing the rest of her thoughts: How at the Academy, all the professors had spoken of Lord Kjari as a human man, as a warning to the students. If you did not follow the acceptable forms of magic, they said, you would wind up tipping the whole world into chaos.

Izara wondered if they knew the truth, if they perpetuated the myth of Lord Kjari in order to keep students from uncovering magic the Academy didn't want them learning. Magic like the sort employed by the emperor and his Starless Mage army, which had allegedly been taught to them by Lord Kjari himself. Magic strong enough to defeat even the Airiana. Magic that was supposed to turn you into a madman.

"You want to know where I was when the Lady of the Seraphine dragged me back here?" Ico said.

Izara looked at him. He was watching the barkeeper make his drink.

"Okay," she said.

He smiled bitterly. "I was up north. North of Eiren, even." He peered at her sideways. "Living with one of the Airiana. The Lady of the Cold."

Izara blinked in surprise.

"It was nice." The barkeeper made his way over to where they sat; Ico held out one hand to pluck the glass away. "I ran errands for her. Acted as an intermediary between her and some of the Eirenese priests who worshipped her." He took a drink. Izara listened to all of this with a tremulous fascination. She could hardly imagine this rough, brutish pirate serving one of the Airiana.

"Even told me her true name," Ico said.

"What!"

He looked over at Izara and grinned. "She did. Not that I'm sharing that with you—ancestors know you've already gotten us into enough trouble thanks to some Airiana's name."

Izara scowled at him, angry because there was truth in what he said.

Ico took a long drink, fixed his gaze back on the window. "She knew what I was doing out here, the Lady of the Cold. In fact, she was the one who told me about the darkness spreading south."

"Really? The Lady of the Cold appeared here?" Izara blinked in shock.

"Not *here*. In a whorehouse. They had an ice fan."

Izara was not sure how to respond to that.

"So she's willing to tell me what she wants. But she never told me Lord Kjari was an Airiana. Told me her name, wouldn't tell me that." He shook his head, greasy hair falling into his eyes.

Izara thought about what Isossa had said, about how the

Airiana loved their games. She had learned something similar at the Academy—part of the lesson as to why it was so dangerous to do what she had done when she didn't know any better. "The Airiana aren't human," Grand Mage Papazian had said, talking to a group of students, a different lesson from the ones she gave Izara one on one. "They don't think like humans. Their magic doesn't work like human magic, which can make it safer—there's less fallout—but also much more dangerous."

And yet whatever Decay was doing that required the Lady to send a trio of humans after him was clearly generating fallout. Leaving the world, as the Lady has said Kjari was doing? But that made no sense. The world needed Decay.

Izara felt a twist of discomfort in her stomach. What would a world without decay look like? Without death? A world of endless growth?

She thought of the dense formulas in the Aetheric Realm, twining around her fingers.

Izara took a long drink of her midnight blood tea. This time, it didn't burn her throat so badly.

"The carriage will be ready in three days," she said. "Do you know of anything else we can do?"

But Ico only stared at the window, and drank.

～

Izara spent most of the next three days in the library, reading books about the desert. The disquieting thought of Decay, one of the Exalted Twins, leaving the world made her stomach twist up with a thick, nameless anxiety. The library at Cross Winds had brought her solace when the family ran out of money, and then later too when her parents died. She suspected the archives here could do the same. And so she settled down at table in the back of the building, flipping through the silky pages of the books, drinking in the words.

She started with book about Decay, reminding herself of the old myths about him. He was one-half of the creators, although he was the half everyone feared. It was said that he had destroyed the world that existed before this one, rotting it into nothingness, and Growth, weeping at the destruction, had conjured life out of the blackness. Izara was not one to take such stories literally, but she knew Decay was focused on undoing Growth's creations.

In one account, written in a thick old book with words printed on onionskin-thin paper, she read that some northmen believed Decay was envious of Growth's ability to create life, and so he destroyed all she made. They did not see Decay and Growth as twins, but as enemies, eternally at war.

The Eirenese five hundred years ago couldn't have known who Kjari really was, Izara thought. They would never have marched on him otherwise. But she wondered where the truth lay. Why had he created the kajani? Was there jealousy there? A desire to experience creation instead of destruction?

Eventually, she gave up reading about Decay—it only created more questions. She turned her attention to their trip and read an adventurer's account of a journey through the Atharé, the details no doubt embellished, like all adventurer's tales—he spoke of slaying a sand monster and encountering an evil enchantress who could control the dust with a sweep of her hand. The evil enchantress was also uncommonly beautiful, and offered herself to the adventurer once he defeated her—Izara rolled her eyes at that. Typical adventurer nonsense. And yet there were details she could glean from her readings—how to extract water from the sparse plants that grew in the expanse, how to build cover when the winds blew cold and dry from the frozen lands of the south. Izara wrote notes to herself in a notebook she purchased from a shop near the archives. She hoped they would be useful.

She also read about pregnancy. Celestia was just starting to show beneath her fine clothes, a bit of an unfashionable curve where her waist should be pinching in. If things were normal, this would be the time for her to retire to home-rest, where she would be pampered until the birth of her child. There was, of course, no advice in the medical texts for a pregnant woman planning on traveling the Atharé. Izara imagined that the doctors who wrote such books—probably all staid and serious, the lot of them—would have roared with derisive laughter over the very suggestion. But she made do with what she could, sketching diagrams of how to give birth outside of the home, writing lists of symptoms of trouble with the baby. By studying and learning, she was able to stave off the worry. It was what she had always done.

And then the day of departure finally came.

They walked to the cartmaker's—Celestia had arranged for the supplies to be sent ahead. She wore a look of grim determination and an expensive traveling outfit, boots and lightweight fabric that could serve, she'd told Izara, as underthings for when they reached the desert. Izara had an identical frock, but it was packed away with the supplies.

Izara and Ico walked side by side, a few paces behind Celestia. He was pale, his hair lank and unwashed, and he smelled of liquor. He'd probably been up all night, drinking and dreaming of his Airiana mistress.

It was hot out, even for the early morning, and Izara was sweating by the time they made it to the cartmaker's, where their carriage was waiting, a big dark thing with reinforced wheels for traveling over the mountains. No horses, like all of the carriages in Bloodvine.

"Say goodbye to this heat," Ico said, wiping his brow. "You're going to miss it soon enough."

Izara didn't say anything; she had known the cold of the mountaintops, windy and damp, and had always preferred it to the wet swelter of the Seraphine. Of course, she suspected the Atharé was nothing like the Academy.

Celestia took a payment note up to the cartmaker, who was waiting in the shade of an overhang. She spoke with him for a few moments, their voices low. She flashed a smile at him, and Izara watched him soften around the edges. Then they shook hands, and Celestia gave a little curtsy and walked back toward the others.

"The carriage is ours," she said. "It's already been loaded with our things. We just need to pick up Omaira."

Izara and Ico exchanged glances. Izara wasn't sure what he thought of the kajan, not really; he was a pirate, who knew what he really disapproved of? She shivered, thinking of the battle at the ruins, the terror that had swept over her before she'd unleashed her magic. At least Omaira seemed more reasonable than *those* kajani had.

Celestia pretended she didn't see the look that had passed between Ico and Izara, however, and instead walked toward the carriage, waiting for them next to the trees. Ico sighed. "Might as well get this over with," he said, and followed. Izara glanced over her shoulder, to catch one last glimpse of Blood-vine, city of glass and magic. She wondered if she'd ever see it again.

"You coming or not?" Ico called out. He had already climbed on top of the carriage. He claimed he could steer the thing, even without horses. Celestia was peering into the door, frowning.

Izara tore her gaze away from the city and joined her sister. Magic radiated off the carriage, heady and thrilling. She stood for a moment, letting the magic wash over her. Then she climbed inside.

The carriage was larger on the inside than it was on the

out. Izara's head thrummed with dizziness at the unexpected-
ness of it, and she tottered her way over to a sofa in the
corner.

"How is it?" Celestia called.

"It's fine," Izara said. "Just watch your step."

Celestia stepped in, then promptly tilted to the side—but
she braced herself against the far wall, and didn't fall. "Oh,"
she said, "It looks like the train car."

It did, actually—Izara hadn't noticed. She'd been too busy
focusing on the magic, wondering what alchemical formulas
she might find lurking if she dropped into the Aetheric
Realm.

And what kajani spirits she might find, too. When she
worked up the nerve, she would have to ask Omaira to
explain it in more detail.

Celestia closed the door and then eased herself down into a
chair, her eyes closed. Ico thumped on the roof. "You ready?"
he shouted.

"Yes," Celestia said, not loud enough for him to hear.
Celestia never shouted.

"Yes!" Izara called out, her thoughts still tied up with the
magic.

And then they were moving. Izara closed her eyes and
slipped halfway into a trance state, just enough that she could
see the line of alchemy moving beneath the surface of things,
glowing pale white like lightning. She studied them, trying to
make sense of Bloodvine's strange, baroque formulas. They
were as dense as poetry, the magic layered on top of itself.
Beautiful.

The carriage stopped.

Izara jerked out of her trance, blinking. They'd barely
moved. But when Celestia pushed open the door, she only
saw the thick tangle of the jungle.

Of course. They had to pick up Omaira.

Izara walked over to the door, but didn't leave the carriage. Celestia was picking her way into the trees, one hand up to shield her eyes from the glare of the sun. They were stopped in a narrow path, Izara noticed, stretching all the way to the horizon.

"What's it like," she called out to Ico, who was still sitting in the driver's seat, "driving this?"

"I'm not doing shit," Ico said. "It's like driving the damn boat."

They sat in silence, the forest humming with sound all around them. Izara wiped the sweat from her brow. Celestia was taking an awfully long time, wasn't she? Her stomach twisted. Maybe this was a trap. Omaira had seemed reasonable in the forest, but perhaps that had been a ruse.

But then there was a rustle among the trees, and Celestia and Omaira stepped out of the woods.

"My mage," Omaira said, eyes burning into Izara. Her mouth quirked up into something like a smile.

She stalked forward, and Izara slipped back into the carriage, her heart pounding. This was really happening. They were really going to ride to the Atharé Desert and work kajani magic to find the eldest and most fearsome of the Airiana.

She slumped down on the sofa, suddenly very tired.

~

No one spoke on the journey away from Bloodvine. Celestia could see everyone withdrawing into themselves. Izara curled up on the sofa and fell asleep; Ico kept lookout up on the driver's seat. Omaira sat stiffly, her spine pressed against the back of the chair, her hands resting on her knees. She stared at the empty wall as if it held some treasure or work of art.

After awhile, Celestia studied her, wondering if kajani simply slept like this, with their eyes open, their spines straight.

But then Omaira spoke, startling her: "What do you expect to find on my face?"

Celestia jumped, then laughed a little. Izara glanced away from the window at them, frowned, turned back to the view. "I thought you might be asleep. You're so still."

"Stillness is one of the tenets of battle," Omaira said, although a looseness had come into her limbs, and her shoulders slumped and she looked at Celestia sideways. "Much of battle is waiting without being seen."

"I hadn't considered that before," Celestia said.

Omaira looked at her in full then, and smiled, revealing her sharp teeth. "Have you spent much time considering the arts of war?"

A little shiver of fear worked down Celestia's spine—it felt like a threat, the way Omaira was sizing her up, the sharpness of her question. But when she looked closer into Omaira's expression, she saw a glimmer of delight there.

"Are you teasing me?" Celestia asked in surprise.

"I am." Another sharp-toothed smile. "You're too soft to think of war."

Celestia lifted her chin. "In Jaila-Seraphine, for a landed lady such as myself, that would be considered a compliment."

"In my home in the Aetheric Realm, it's considered a compliment, too," Omaira said. "Soft things have their place in our worlds."

A sting of heat rushed through Celestia's cheeks and she looked down at her lap. Lindon used to tease her in the same way, about how she would never survive on his adventures, and didn't he just love her for that? And she'd laughed and kissed him because she'd never had any desire to dress in trousers and boots and travel through the mud and the jungle to seek glory.

The carriage jostled, and Celestia was flung up against Omaira's side, her face slamming into the hard strength of

Omaira's armor—although Omaira reacted quickly, and lifted her arm and caught Celestia and righted her back in her seat.

Izara stirred. "What was that?"

"A disturbance in the road," Celestia murmured. "Nothing." She had caught a whiff of Omaira's scent in the jostle, and it was earthy and sweet, like a thunderstorm. She could still smell it. "Ico!" she called out, although of course he didn't answer.

Omaira reached up and pounded on the roof. "Driver!" she roared. "What was that?"

Izara was staring out the window, one hand pressed against the carriage wall, the other balling up the fabric of her dress.

"Izara?" Celestia said, a sudden dread washing over her. "Tell me what you see."

The carriage jostled again, and then it veered sharply to the left. Celestia screeched and tumbled out of the sofa, landing hard on the floor. The carriage was running too fast. She could feel the beat of its wheels reverberating through the floor. She peered up just as Izara jerked away from the window, her eyes wide with fear.

"We're being attacked!" she screamed.

The carriage veered again, the turn so sharp that the carriage tilted up on its side. Celestia tumbled across the floor, her arms flailing, desperately reaching for the leg of the table. Sunlight poured in—Omaira was hanging out the door, screaming in the rough kajani language.

Celestia pulled herself up to sitting. Omaira vanished out the side of the carriage, still shouting. Celestia kept her eyes fixed on that open door. The forest flashed by. All those dappled shades of green.

And then: a flash of dark shadow.

Celestia gasped and jerked herself back, slamming into Izara.

"I saw something," Celestia whispered.

There came a shout from above: Ico, cursing in protest. A thump against the roof. Celestia jumped and Izara grabbed her hand and squeezed.

"I saw them too," Izara said in a low voice, "and they have magic." Her voice quavered. "Dark magic."

The carriage veered again, whipping around in a circle, stirring up a cloud of mud and fallen leaves. Celestia braced herself against the wall and screamed, terrified that she was going to topple out of that still-open door. And then the carriage tipped, and rolled, and Celestia crashed up against the roof, against the wall, her thoughts coming to her in fragments. Impressions. A flash of dark cloak. A glint of sword. Ico shouting pirate's curses. The screams of dying men.

The carriage rolled to a stop.

For half a heartbeat, Celestia thought it was over. She didn't even have time to register the battered pains in her limbs. But then the carriage door was flung open again—this time it was above her, like a hatchway—and blinding sunlight flooded in.

"Get them," said an unfamiliar voice.

"Get your hands off of me!" shouted Ico, although he sounded distant, far away. There was a loud *crack*, like an axe splitting wood. Celestia propped herself up on one arm, dazed. She caught a glimpse of Ico through the open door, a black gloved hand gripping his arm.

Terror struck her then, sharp and painful. She screamed, scrabbling across the floor. Her head spun. Izara—where was Izara? Celestia spotted her, lying in a pile on the other end of the carriage, moaning.

"Izara," Celestia sputtered, and she crawled forward, her arms shaking. She didn't let herself think about the baby. She focused all her attention on Izara.

A shadow came over the door.

"Come with us, my lady," the shadow said. "There's no need to make this difficult."

Celestia crawled faster, her arms getting tangled up in her dress. Izara stirred, lifted her head.

"Cele—" she cried, just as strong hands grasped Celestia by the waist and yanked her up. Celestia screamed and kicked at her attacker, but he held true. As he pulled her through the doorway, she grabbed the frame, digging her fingers into the hot metal of the carriage.

"I'm pregnant!" she shouted. "You wouldn't dare bring harm to the heir of Lord and Lady De Malena." It was an act of desperation: did these men even care about her title?

"Believe me, I'm trying not to hurt you." Her attacker yanked on her with a sharp burst of force and dragged her free from the carriage. He whirled her around, his arms still tight around her waist.

They were in a mangled patch of forest, the vines and undergrowth crushed, the trees marked with black scorch marks. Ico knelt in the middle of that tangle, his hands behind his back, his head tilted down. He wasn't alone. There were three men out there with him—men who covered their faces with black masks, men who held the swords drawn.

"Is this what you were so terrified of at Essir Manor?" Celestia asked Ico.

Ico looked up at her through the matted clump of his hair. "No," he said.

"I told you, we're not interested in hurting you." Celestia's attacker jumped off the carriage, bringing her with him. They landed hard, and he shoved her toward the other three men.

"Careful with her," her attacker said. He was masked like all the others. "Says she's pregnant."

Their eyes were impossible to read behind their black masks. "Then she should come easily, yeah?" one of them said.

"What did you do with Omaira?" she demanded.

"Get the other one," one of the men said.

Celestia's attacker nodded and then jumped back onto the top of the carriage, in one huge, graceful leap. Celestia whirled around. Was that a body, over on the edge of the path? But it wasn't Omaira's. It was dressed in the same black cloaks as the rest of the men.

"You stay right where you are," one of the men said, "or we're going to tie you up like your companion here."

"Fuck off," said Ico

The man kicked Ico in the back, knocking him forward into the ground. Celestia gasped and dropped down at Ico's side; the man made no move to stop her. She helped him up to sitting. His hands were bound with silken rope, and his lip was split, a drop of blood trickling over his chin.

"Who are these men?" Celestia asked.

Ico laughed bitterly, shook his head. "I have no fucking idea."

"Watch how you speak in front of the lady," one of the men said.

Celestia glared at the three of them, not knowing which had spoken. "You dragged me out of my carriage, you bound up my friend, and you murdered my traveling companion—"

"We didn't murder anyone," the man said. "It was your *traveling companion* who murdered our partner before it turned tail into the woods." His eyes glittered. "Tell me, what sort of lady travels with a monster?"

Celestia jerked her gaze away from them, her face hot. Omaira had fled. She had killed one of the bandits and vanished into the woods. It had been stupid to trust her. Celestia should have seen that.

Over at the carriage, one of the men dragged a struggling Izara through the doorway. A shimmer haloed around them, like a heat mirage—magic, Celestia realized. She was trying to fight back with magic.

A crack of light sliced through the forest, and when it cleared Izara was lying curled on the ground beside Ico. Celestia screamed and knelt beside her, fury rising up through her veins. "Izara, wake up, wake up," she whispered, pressing her fingers against Izara's neck until she felt the faint flutter of a heartbeat.

"You were told not to do that," one of the men said to Izara's captor.

"She fought back," the captor responded with a shrug.

A hand clamped down on Celestia's shoulder and pulled her away from Izara. Celestia didn't fight it. She gazed down at her sister, the sight of the soft rise and fall of her chest the most beautiful thing she'd ever seen. Ico looked up at her, his hair hanging into his eyes. Then he looked away.

"Who are you?" Celestia said, still watching Izara.

One of the men—the leader? She couldn't tell, they were all dressed the same—stepped into her line of vision. His face was still covered. She could only see the two dark burning coals of his eyes.

"We are here on behalf of His Radiance, the Emperor Osmin del'la Ashutia—"

Celestia let out a strangled gasp, and covered her mouth with one hand. Her knees buckled.

"He has urgent business with you and your party." The man nodded. "We must make our way to the mountaintop. Come."

And then he clapped his hands twice, and a carriage emerged from the woods, two alpacas lashed to its yoke.

"I was told to ask you first," the man said, staring at Celestia with his smoldering eyes, "But I will force you if I must."

The Emperor. The Emperor had sent these black-cloaked men to capture her, to drag her to the Palace in the Sky.

And she knew then who they were. The Starless Mages.

Those Eirenese men must have sent word to the Emperor about her argument with Lindon. Now the Mages had come to arrest her for treason.

Celestia's knees buckled again, and then she lost the sense of herself completely.

NINE

The carriage had no windows, and the door was barred
from the outside—of course Ico had tried it as soon as the
Mages set out, underbrush swatting at the carriage walls.

"Shit," he said, kicking at the door. He turned to Izara.
She could barely make him out in the uncomfortable darkness. Only a few slivers of light made it through the cracks in
the construction. "Do something with your magic and get us
the hell out of here."

Izara glowered at him. "We've been captured by the
Emperor's Starless Mages," she snapped. "This magic—it's not
something I can fight against."

Not that she hadn't been frantically considering what
Aetheric formulas she had memorized that could break
through the protections layered like perfume over the carriage.
She didn't dare risk going into a trance—she didn't want to
see which of the rumors about the Starless Mages she'd heard

at school were true. Human sacrifice, deep blood magic. Something worse that no one could quite work up the nerve to describe.

"How do you know until you try?" demanded Ico.

"Because I can feel it!" Her voice pitched high. "You think I don't know how magic works?" Still, she closed her eyes, envisioning the simple formulas that hung around them. She picked one loose like a thread and flung a surge of magical power at the door, too angry to think about what she was doing. The power absorbed into the wood of the carriage, and for a moment everything glowed and she could see the large, frightened eyes of her sister before the carriage sank back into darkness.

"Told you," she hissed.

One of the men thumped on the roof. "Knock it off," he shouted. "You keep that up and we'll put you in chains."

Izara slumped down beside Celestia, who sat with her legs curled up against her chest. Ico kicked at the door again. It was hopeless, of course.

"He heard what we were doing," Celestia whispered. "The Emperor. Those Eirenese adventurers must have told him. Do you think he'll have us executed?"

"Or Lindon did," Ico muttered.

Izara glared at him. Then she put her hand on Celestia's shoulder, trying to comfort her.

"The Emperor commanded Lindon to find Kjari, not you. What we've done is not exactly treason."

"Not exactly," Celestia murmured.

So much for offering comfort. The darkness swam around, made it hard to concentrate on anything. Izara toyed with the alchemical formulas again, but this time she only formed a pale yellow flame that cast a warm light on the inside of the carriage. She paused for a moment, but the man on the carriage roof didn't protest.

"So this is our prison," Izara said, lifting her gaze. There was nothing to look at. Just plan wooden walls, the rickety wooden bench across the way where Ico was glowering at them.

"How far are we from the mountains?" he asked.

"I don't know." Izara watched the flame flicker and jump.

They fell into silence after that. The carriage kept pushing its way through the forest, and Izara leaned up against Celestia and closed her eyes. Maybe she could sleep the nightmare away. But of course she couldn't. The scraping and grinding of the forest was too much. If only they had been captured on the river. Then the Lady could have come in and set them free. But they were on land, away from her protection.

Or maybe the Lady wouldn't have set them free. Maybe this was all part of her games. Certainly the kajan hadn't proved useful.

Eventually, the carriage slowed to a stop. Ico jolted up from his sleep, hands curled into fists, and turned toward the door. The men were chattering outside, voices low and indistinct.

"Why have we stopped?" Celestia roused herself. "We can't be at the mountains yet."

From outside came the metallic clank of a key in a lock. Izara immediately extinguished the yellow flame, plunging them into complete darkness. It must be nighttime.

The door swung open, revealing one of their attackers, still dressed in his dark robes, his face still covered. "We're stopping here for the night," he said. "You," he pointed at Ico, "hold out your hands."

"Fuck off," said Ico.

Above his mask, the man rolled his eyes. Then he lifted one hand, twisting his fingers into peculiar shapes. Izara sucked in her breath and pushed herself in front of Celestia. She'd heard stories of those hand gestures at the Academy.

Magic rushed in like a blast of wind. Ico was thrown back against the far wall; the carriage tilted backwards, and for a moment Izara was sure they were going to roll again. But then strong hands dragged Ico out of the carriage and the carriage righted itself. Ico slammed into the ground, groaning.

His attacker had lashed his hands behind his back, the chains still glowing from the magic.

The man peered into the carriage. "My ladies," he said, "you may step out freely. We are not to chain you, unless you attempt to escape or attack us. Acolyte magic, I should mention, is worthless against our skills. Do you understand?"

Izara's mouth was too dry to answer, but Celestia said, "Yes, thank you," and then slid out from behind Izara, toward the door. Izara hesitated, taking in the scene outside the carriage: the night-draped forest, the man in his black mask, Ico struggling to sit up. Celestia slipped out of the carriage and helped him to his feet, although he just glared at the man in response.

"This isn't fair," he said.

The man ignored him. Celestia turned back and looked at Izara with big, imploring eyes, and Izara caught a scent of fire on the air, and, beyond that, the sizzle of fat and the char of smoked flesh. Her mouth watered. She hadn't realized how hungry she was until this moment.

She crawled out of the carriage, casting an apologetic look at Ico. They were only treating her and Celestia so well because they were of noble birth; Ico was right, it wasn't fair. But Izara was also too tired and too scared to protest. She was only grateful that her hands were free.

The men had set up a fire in a clearing a few paces away from the carriage. A boar roasted over it, one of the men turning the spit in slow, steady increments. Sleeping packs had been laid out over the ground; Izara counted six. Well. At least they wouldn't make Ico sleep on the damp, mulchy ground.

"If you need to relieve yourselves," one of the men said from his place beside the fire, "you may do so now. If you do not return, we will track you and put you in chains. Do you understand?"

"Yes," Celestia said in a small voice.

"How the hell can I take a piss chained up like this?" Ico asked.

"You will be accompanied to the woods after the ladies." The man gestured toward the dark mass of trees. "Go. But remember my warning."

Izara and Celestia looked at each other, and Izara saw the expression of terror on Celestia's face and knew she had no desire to attempt to escape.

"Let's go," Izara whispered, and she grabbed Celestia's hand and led her into the woods. They walked several paces from the campsite and then stood in the darkness.

"Omaira," Celestia whispered. "Do you think she'll come back for us?"

Izara gazed out at the shadows. She considered lying. But she didn't think it was worth it.

"No," she said.

～

The journey up the mountains continued, unchanging from that first day. During daylight they rode in the carriage, and Izara burned an eternal flame so they would not have to sit in the dark. They sat in silence, the threat of what awaited them at the Emperor's palace hanging thick in the stuffy air. Izara worked up their defense in her head and wished she had access to the Cross Winds library—or the Bloodvine archives, for that matter. Surely there had been similar cases in the past, when the will of the Airiana conflicted with that of the

Emperor. Surely there was an argument to be made in their favor.

"I don't understand why the Emperor saw fit to send Lindon," Celestia whispered. Something in her voice seemed to crack. "Not when he has those—*creatures* to do as he wishes. Perhaps then our involvement wouldn't have gotten back to him."

Izara said nothing. She found it strange as well, but there was nothing in the mages' actions, or their magic, to offer an easy answer. Nor any reason to think whispers of their journey wouldn't have found their way to the Emperor's ear regardless.

When night fell, the carriage stopped, Ico would be chained, and they would eat—always grilled boar glistening on large flat banana leaves. The men pushed their masks up just enough to reveal their mouths, but never their entire faces. They would talk and laugh with each other, like ordinary men. Wouldn't this be a story to tell at the Academy, Izara thought. That the fearsome Starless Mages acted more like adventurers than murderous demons.

They slept during those stops as well. The Starless Mages took turns keeping guard, not that Izara had any inclination to escape. They were already halfway up the mountains, in the mountains' wild, unforgiving terrain. She could not survive alone out here, certainly, and neither could Celestia.

Izara worried about Celestia on that endless, wracking journey. She worried about the baby. Whenever Celestia fell asleep in the carriage, Izara would feel Celestia's forehead, her breath caught in her throat, afraid she would be hot with fever. She never was, but it didn't alleviate Izara's concern. This was not the right environment for an expectant mother. She needed more food, more water.

One evening, Izara approached one of the Starless Mages as they were preparing for sleep. She had been watching them the last few days, hoping to gain insight into their magic, and suspected he was the leader, inasmuch as they seemed to have leaders; he was the one to call out when they were leaving for the day, at any rate. He sat by the fire, sharpening the blade of his sword. He looked up at her before she spoke.

"Iomim's Treasure," he said. "You have quite the gift burning inside of you."

Izara's breath caught in her chest. It was the first time he had spoken to her directly. "As do you, I'm sure." He must be strong, if he could sense Iomim's Treasure. It was a method she hadn't yet studied at the Academy.

He laughed, then swiped the stone down the length of his sword. "You want to know about our magic? Is that why you're bothering me?"

Izara trembled, thinking of the rumors of blood sacrifice. "No," she said, although her curiosity flared inside her. The Starless Mage magic was so strange, so unfamiliar—

"Good. I wasn't going to tell you anything. What do you want, then?"

Izara fumbled for words. She'd been distracted by the talk of magic. "My sister, Cel—Lady De Malena." The Starless Mages seemed to put a lot of stock in titles. "She's pregnant."

"Yes," the man said, "we know."

Izara took a deep breath. "Then you should let her have water during the day. It's not good for the baby, for her to go without."

The man paused, midway down the sword. He looked up at her. His eyes glittered above his mask.

"Please," Izara said.

"I'll see what I can do, Lady Izara." He jerked his head over to the bedrolls. "Now sleep."

Izara assumed her request had gone unheard—certainly Ico's pleas to be unchained during the breaks had fallen on deaf ears, and the men gave no mind that the clothing of their prisoners was filthy and tattered and, on top of that, no longer appropriate for the cooler air of the upper mountains. "Make do with the fire," they'd snapped once when Celestia had complained politely of the cold, and during the day, Izara infused the eternal flame with a touch of heat. But the next morning, as they were clambering back into the carriage, one of the men tossed in a skein of water after them.

"For the Lady Celestia," he said to Ico. "For her baby."

Then he slammed the door shut, clicked the lock into place. Izara illuminated the eternal flame. The skein of water lay in the middle of the carriage, incongruous.

"We can split it," Celestia said quickly. "It's not fair for the water to just go to me—"

"You get the bigger split." Ico shoved the skein over to her with his foot, rubbed at his free wrists. "You're pregnant."

Celestia tilted her head down, nodded once.

The magic of the carriage burned in the walls. It had changed since they'd been taken over by the Starless Mages. There was a coldness in it now. A touch, Izara thought, of Lord Kjari.

Of Decay.

Izara wondered what punishment waited for them at the top of the mountain.

~

Ico's wrists ached from the manacles. Every night they slapped those things on his hands and shoved him around like a prisoner. Sometimes he watched the two sisters through the orange glow of the fire, resentment simmering inside of him. They were allowed to walk freely into the dark of the forest. He always had an audience.

At least he wasn't chained in the cart. Small fucking favors, sure, but it was better than nothing. One day, as they bumped along inside that dark, stuffy box, he asked Celestia why she and Izara hadn't tried to flee at night. He'd been wondering about it the last few days, a little seed of an idea that he kept turning around inside his head. They weren't chained. They could run if they wanted.

She just looked at him, her face carved up by her sister's strange light.

"We couldn't survive out there," she said. "Not alone."

Maybe she was right. They weren't in the Seraphine basin anymore, that was damn sure. They'd left the forest behind, the landscape transformed into walls of jagged mountain faces, covered with a soft fur of green grass. And it was cold, their sad little caravan having traveled high enough up into the mountains for it. The air was changing, too—Ico could feel the thinness of it, the way it had become diaphanous and insubstantial. He missed the humid thickness of the air of the river, the way you could taste it sliding down the back of your throat.

Ico kept track of the days in his head, the way he did when he was at sea. It helped keep him sane. Izara scratched notches on the inside of the carriage. The two numbers lined up. Eight days. Eight days spent in that cramped carriage. Eight nights sleeping out in the open with chains wound around his arms. His head ached most of the time, too, although whether that was from the thin air or from the meager scraps the guardsmen tossed him each night, he couldn't say. The sisters, of course, got a full meal, and the guardsmen would "my lady" them like a trio of sniveling servants. Maybe that was the real reason they didn't take off. They knew they had it better with the guardsmen than they did out on the mountains.

Nine days went by.

Ten.

Eleven.

"How much longer until we reach the palace?" Celestia

asked on the eleventh night, her arms wrapped around herself, her whole body shaking despite the heat of the fire. They were surrounded by a rocky expanse scattered with dry pale grasses. The wind buffeted them, whipping Celestia's hair into her face.

None of the mages answered.

"Well?" she demanded. "How much longer?"

Ico rattled his chains. "I've been wondering the same thing myself."

The biggest of the mages, the one who never bothered to chain Ico himself and as such was probably their leader, glanced away from the meat he was roasting over the fire. "A few more days," he said.

"Can we get cloaks?" Izara asked. "Especially for my sister. She's pregnant." Izara was always reminding them of that fact.

"Don't have cloaks," the mage said. "Sit closer to the fire. You'll be fine."

Ico wasn't sure about that. It wasn't as cold here as it had been at Xima's palace, and he hadn't yet seen snow drifting on the air. But the surrounding peaks were white as clouds, and it wouldn't be long before their thin Seraphine clothes wouldn't be enough to protect them from the elements.

"You kidnap three people and don't think to throw some furs into the bag?" he asked.

The mage, predictably, ignored him.

That night, like all nights, Ico was shunted out to the edge of the camp, although at least he got one of the bedrolls that were always laid out waiting when they disembarked from the carriage. He figured that roll must have belonged to the man that Omaira killed. He'd seen her fighting when they were attacked, brutal and furious. And he'd seen her race into the woods just as soon as she got the chance. Maybe it was a good thing they hadn't gotten to the desert after all.

Ico curled himself up tight into a ball, looping the chain

around himself like it could lock in his body heat. He was used to sleeping in bad conditions, but this was the kind of cold that shocked you awake, even with the bedroll. He stared at the fire, watching the flames dance and pop in the darkness. Sometimes the heat reached him. Most of the time, though, it was just that cold, blustery wind.

Icoooooo, the wind said.

Ico sat up, his heart pounding. His mouth was dry; had he fallen asleep, after all? The rest of the camp was silent and still.

Icoooooo, whispered the wind.

"Xima?" he hissed, whipping his head around. "Is that you? Get me out of these damned chains."

The wind blustered; the fire guttered. Bits of snow and ice swirled on the air, glinting like stars, until they settled into a form that had been burned into the deepest parts of Ico's memory. She didn't solidify completely, but strode toward him in her ice-and-wind formation. He could barely make out her face.

"My north wind," she said, kneeling beside him. A glimmering hand reached out and cupped his face. Cold shivered through his skin.

"What the hell is happening? Are these assholes really with the Emperor?" He tilted his head toward the mages, sleeping peacefully beside the fire.

"I'm afraid so," Xima said. "And I'm afraid their magic is too powerful for me to free you."

Ico felt as if he'd been punched hard in the chest. He stared at Xima, at the silvery outline of her.

"What?" he said. "How's that even possible?"

She sighed, a puff of wind accompanying her breath. "The Emperors of the Seraphine have found ways to keep the Airiana away from the palace for centuries. Ever since—" She looked away.

"Ever since Lord Kjari went to war with Eiren?" Ico said.

"Yeah, I heard about that. Nice of you to tell us he was Decay, by the way."

"I couldn't tell you," Xima said. "The Lady of the Seraphine forbade it."

"Really."

"Really." She turned back to him, and her eyes shone like the moon on a snowy night. "We have rules that we must abide by. They're too complicated for a human—"

"Yeah, yeah." Ico flicked his wrist. "You love your games, right?"

Xima just looked at him sadly. Or maybe not sadly. It was hard to tell, when she was nothing but powdery snowflakes and cold wind.

"Why are you even here?" Ico asked. "If you can't free me and you can't help me?" He shrugged. "What's the point?"

"I wanted to see you, my north wind." She reached for him, but Ico pulled away, glaring at her. For a moment her hand hung suspended in the air, glimmering. And then she withdrew it. Ico expected her to explode in snow flurries and blow away, but she didn't.

"I've been trying to reach you since you passed into the cold," she said. "But it seems the Starless Mages have found a way to carry the palace wards with them. I can get close, but not close enough" She pressed toward him, and Ico felt the cold of her, and shivered. "The Emperor doesn't want any of us interfering," she said.

"And what does he want?" Ico turned toward her. The snow flurries were stronger now, and he could see the familiar lines of her face. Part of him wanted to lean forward and kiss her, even though he knew it would be a kiss that would only leave him colder. "It's about Lord Kjari? Decay, I mean?" He spat it out, still angry she had kept that from him.

"Almost certainly," Xima said, "but I don't know why he would try to stop you. Not with the slow loss of death."

Ico's stomach knotted up. "It's come to the Seraphine, hasn't it?"

Xima closed her eyes, two lanterns blinking out. She nodded. "My sister Mixa, the warmth—she told me. The forest is starting to choke itself. Men pull nets of fish that never stop wiggling. And the dead—"

The dead never die. She didn't have to say it, and Ico thought of the priest holding out his arms, telling him they had to test it.

Ico clenched his hands into fists. "This is a waste of time. The Emperor—" He shook his head in disgust. "We could be looking for Lord Kjari. We had a lead, or an idea, at least—a way to find his fortress in the Atharé desert."

Xima tilted her head. "Ah," she said. "Of course he would retreat to the dust."

Ico sighed and lay back to the ground and looked up at the starry sky.

"This is bullshit," he said. "I'm getting carted off for treason and I'm not even in my own country."

Xima stretched out beside him, her diaphanous form sinking into the ground. She lay one hand over his, and this time he let her.

"If I could help you, my north wind," she said, "I would. But my presence would only make things harder."

It didn't offer him any solace.

———

Ico kept Xima's message about the spread of darkness into the Seraphine to himself. The sisters had enough to worry about as it was, and he didn't want Izara doing anything desperate against the Starless Mages. So he just mulled it over in his thoughts as the carriage rattled farther up the mountains. She didn't come back to him, despite the colder air. He also wondered what sort of magic the mages had cooked up that were warding off the Airiana. He tried asking Izara, but she wouldn't talk about it, just said the Starless Mages' magic was beyond her, even as she spent the day with her hand pressed to the wall of the carriage, her eyes closed, like she was feeling something inside the structure.

So there was something to the magic. But Xima could still be lying. Maybe she just didn't care enough to rescue him.

No, he didn't really believe that. The Emperor was the most powerful man in the human realm; it made sense for him to have the most powerful men in the magical realm as well.

Although clearly they weren't powerful enough to dig up Decay.

Four days went by, the same as all the others. But on the fifth day, the carriage stopped after only a few hours of travel, and voices spilled in from outside.

Celestia sat up from the little ball she had curled into on the carriage floor. "Have we arrived?"

"I don't know," Izara said.

"None of us will know until they let us out of here," Ico said, although he felt a flicker of hope in the pit of his stomach. Stupid.

The voices grew louder, and there were more of them, too, shouts of instruction—*Move to the left gate, await orders.*

"We're here," Izara said miserably.

The carriage jerked forward. It moved more slowly now, and Ico could hear metal clanging, men shouting outside. He leaned against the wall of the carriage and took a deep breath. The sisters didn't say anything.

Eventually, the carriage rolled to a stop. The driver thumped on the roof. "Ready yourselves!" he shouted, and Ico, not for the first time, wished he still had his knife. One last chance to make a run for it before he was dragged in front of an Emperor he'd never even sworn loyalty to.

The carriage door swung open. The mages gestured at the

sisters. "My ladies, please step out. One of the Empress's ladies-in-waiting will tend to you."

"Are you shitting me?" Ico asked. "You keep us locked in here and now you're handing them over to some ladies-in-waiting?"

The mage fixed him with a cold, hard stare. "Shut your mouth, Akuranian scum."

"At least I know I'm scum," Ico muttered.

"I'm sorry," Celestia said as she crawled past Ico. "We'll get this sorted out."

He rolled his eyes. If he couldn't count on them to flee when they were in the woods, he sure as hell couldn't count on them now that they were going to play at being courtiers for the Emperor.

The mage held out a hand to help Celestia step out of the carriage. Izara, too. Ico craned his neck, trying to look out the door. All he could see was a woman dressed in silks and furs, her face painted into a colorful mask. She smiled at Celestia, gave a little curtsy.

Ico slumped back against the wall, looked up at the ceiling of the carriage. There were scratch marks there, as if someone had tried to escape.

"Now, Akuranian," the mage said. "Hold out your hands."

"Why do they get treated so much better than me?" Ico demanded. The painted woman was leading Celestia and Izara over to the palace majordomo.

"Because they are landed aristocracy. We've been through this. Hold out your hands."

Ico glared at the mages.

"We have orders to keep you alive," the mage said. "But I'll slice your head off if you think about attacking me. Now. *Hold out your hands.*"

Celestia and Izara had vanished out of his line of sight. Damn it. None of them could afford to stay in this palace. But they'd also die on the side of the mountain if they didn't plan their escape properly.

Ico held out his hands, and the guard slapped on the manacle and chains and then yanked him out of the carriage. Ico was expecting it, though, and although he stumbled he landed upright, on his feet. The wind slammed into him, a sharp blast of icy air. His eyes watered, his teeth chattered.

The mage pulled on the chain, dragging Ico away from the cart. Ico followed. He peered up at his surroundings. All he could see was an endless stone wall stretching up to the sky.

They went inside through a narrow door lodged into the stone. It was warmer in here, the walls lined with burning sticks that let off a golden heat. They stood in a hallway that split in two directions. The mage went left, and Ico, of course, had to follow.

"You'll be registered and bathed," the mage said. "And given clean clothes."

Ico snorted. "I'll believe it when I see it."

The mage pulled hard on the chains, yanking at Ico's arms. "Don't question the hospitality of His Radiance."

The hallway tilted down, and the stone walls had a cold dampness to them despite the burning torches. It was exactly no surprise to Ico when the mage led him into a dungeon, the cells divided with gleaming metal bars. At least each cell had a cot in it, and a little stone table and chair. Ico'd been in worse dungeons.

A guard was waiting for them—fortunately, he was not dressed in the clothing of the Starless Mages. He was also young, bright-eyed. He looked over at Ico and wrinkled his nose.

"He can't be expected to go before His Radiance like that."

"What?" said Ico.

"Shut up," said the first mage, and he yanked on the

chains. "Of course not. We've been traveling for over ten days. He needs to be bathed and given clean clothes."

"What the hell is going on?" Ico said, hoping one of them would let slip some salient detail.

He didn't get an answer. The dungeon guard just nodded and made a note in his book, then reached to his belt and extracted a long, slim key, which he handed to the first mage.

"You'll wait in here," the mage said, dragging Ico to the closest cell. He unlocked the door and then tossed Ico inside. Slammed the bars shut.

"You're not even going to take off my shackles?" Ico shook his chains. They clanked loudly against the stone floor.

"They'll come off when you get your bath," the mage said. He tossed the key at the guard, who looked alarmed as he caught it.

"He needs to be ready by tomorrow morning," the mage said, and then he stomped out of the dungeon, his footsteps heavy.

The dungeon guard peered at Ico through the darkness, and for the first time, Ico felt a glimmer of actual, genuine fear.

"You're not really going to bathe me, are you?" he said. "That's just code for torture, isn't it?"

The dungeon guard closed his book and stepped around from behind his podium.

"His Radiance wishes to speak with you," the guard said. "It's my duty to ready you for that meeting."

"The Emperor makes a habit of visiting with criminals?" Ico rattled his chains again for good measure.

The guard coughed. "His *Radiance* does not visit with criminals, no, but he's apparently making an exception for one Akuranian pirate."

Hope rose up in Ico. Maybe they could actually reason with the Emperor, instead of sneaking around against him.

Explain the situation. Surely he didn't actually want to rule over a kingdom of walking corpses.

"It's not my place to question His Radiance's decisions," the guard said primly. "Only to ensure that they are carried out. And he wishes to see you in his chambers." The guard moved toward Ico's cell. "Now, let's see about getting you clean."

Celestia sank into the warm, satiny bath water, her skin tingling. She had been so cold for the last few days that she had forgotten what it was to be warm. And it had been longer still since she had been truly clean.

She dropped her head under the water and stared up at the distorted lights shimmering overhead: magic lanterns that drifted languorously through her room. The tub was cut out of the stone of the mountain, and servants had dropped sweet-scented oil into the water and left a bar of soap with flowers pressed into the surface. Izara had been taken to her room, with her own bath. And Ico . . .

Celestia pushed herself out of the water. Ico was the reminder that neither she nor Izara were here as guests, no matter how well they may be treated. It was improper for a landed lady such as Celestia or her sister to be imprisoned as the lower classes would be—Celestia would have to commit a crime grave enough to have her title stripped away before she ever saw the inside of a dungeon cell.

Like treason.

She had not forgotten the possibility that her flowery baths and the dress she was certain had been laid out for her on the sumptuous bed one room over were the last luxuries she would ever experience. At least in the Seraphine a pregnant woman couldn't be executed. The Emperor would allow her baby to be born before she was killed.

She couldn't let herself linger on those thoughts. She picked up the bar of soap and scrubbed at her skin, ready to rub the grime away. She wondered where Ico was now. It had upset her, the way the Starless Mages had treated him on the journey into the mountains, but she knew she was in no place to speak out against his treatment. Because they couldn't take it out on her, they would have taken it out on him. Celestia knew how these things went.

When Celestia finished cleaning herself, she stepped out of the bath, water dripping across the stone tiles, and wrapped herself in the fluffy towels that hung from the walls. There was a chill in the castle, but she was still warm from the bath, and for the first time in days a chill was welcome again. She went into the bedroom, and, just as she had expected, a change of clothes had been laid out on her bed. For a moment she stood in the doorway, staring at that pile of silks and furs and Eirenese lace, a confection of a dress like the dresses hanging in her wardrobe back at Cross Winds. She knew she might never see those dresses again. She knew she might never see Cross Winds again.

You don't know that yet, she told herself, before she dropped the towel to the floor and strode naked across the room, her wet hair still dripping water down her spine. Her belly was starting to swell; when she looked down she could see it curving out beneath her breasts. Her heart fluttered. *Please don't let the baby be punished for my mistakes,* she thought, a prayer to all the gods she knew.

Celestia dressed, fumbling with the unfamiliar undergarments, which were voluminous and, she assumed, designed for warmth. The dress itself was cut in the Alrea style, very modern—she pulled it on herself and wound the sashes around her body, tying them off at the side as she had seen the more daring women in Jaila-Seraphine do. The gray fur at the collar was soft against her neck, and she braided her damp hair and pinned it on top of her head to dry. She had to admit that the snowy white fabric of the dress was striking against her dark skin.

A knock came at the door.

"Celestia?" Izara's voice was thin and wavery. "Are you in there?"

"Yes, the door's not locked." And it never would be, either. She could come and go as she pleased, assuming she didn't leave the palace itself. But there was also no way for her to bar herself inside.

Izara spilled into the room. She wore another Alrea-style dress, the white fabric just as striking—but her dress hung crooked, her sashes knotted at her hips. She collapsed onto the bed, her wet hair splaying across the blankets. "Are we imprisoned or not?" she wailed. "The servants won't tell me anything."

"I don't imagine they know anything." Celestia closed the door—she could at least allow them that little bit of privacy. "Stand up, let me fix your dress. I imagine we'll be going down to dinner soon."

"Dinner?" Izara cried. "If the Emperor's going to kill us, why send us down to *dinner*? Why give us these damned dresses? Why not just get it over with?"

Panic spiked in Celestia's system, but she shoved it down. "Most of the aristocracy never learned to be as forthright as you." Celestia swept over to the bed and sat down beside Izara. Her sister's presence was a comfort.

Izara sighed. "I tried going into a trance—the magic here is intense. Almost choking. But I'm blocked from the Aetheric Realm." She threw up her hands. "I should have known. The Emperor can keep even the Airiana out of his palace. He and his mages are the only ones allowed to use such restrictive magic." Izara sat up and slid off the bed before Celestia had a chance to adjust her dress. She paced back and

forth across the room. "I'm sure no one unauthorized can get
into the Aetheric Realm within the palace walls. Otherwise,
someone unauthorized could come in through it."

"Do you think that would help us, going into one of your
trances?" Celestia put a hand on Izara's shoulder to stop her
pacing. "Please, Izzie, let me fix your dress before we have to
go down to dinner."

Izara glared at her. "Stop playing into their stupid charade!
We might need the Lady to convince the Emperor not to kill
us. Or did you forget there's a chance we're about to be
condemned for treason?"

Celestia undid the knots in Izara's sashes. "I most certainly
did not. But if we are to plead our case to the Emperor, then
playing into their charade, as you put it, is exactly what we
should be doing."

Izara's shoulders slumped.

"We haven't been stripped of our titles yet." Celestia
straightened Izara's dress, making sure the fabric folded over
itself in the proper way. "That means we still have the opportunity to plead our case as aristocracy. We cannot jeopardize
that." She tied off the dress sashes in the back—a more modest
approach, one more appropriate for an unmarried girl.
"There," she said. "Much better."

"I just hate it." Izara turned around. "I could be dead
tomorrow and you're fixing my dress. At least you'll have
another six months before they execute you."

Celestia's cheeks burned as if Izara had physically slapped
her. "You think I'm not worried?" she hissed. "You think I'm
not devising our defense every moment I can spare? You
should know by now that these are the games we play." She
gestured at the dresses, at the opulent room. "Even if the
Emperor is toying with us, we can use our *current* station to
our advantage. So you would do well to practice your
etiquette and dinner decorum."

For a moment they stared at each other. Celestia drew herself up imperiously, daring Izara to protest.

But Izara just sighed and ran her hand over her hair. "I've been devising a defense as well," she said.

Celestia's anger metabolized back into that creeping dread. She drew her Izara into an embrace. "I know," she whispered. "And this dinner tells us that you will have the chance to use it."

Someone knocked on the door.

Celestia and Izara fell out of their embrace, and Celestia squeezed Izara's hand, trying to act braver than she felt. Then she called out, "Yes! You may come in."

It was the palace majordomo, the same tall, stern man who had fetched Celestia and Izara away from the guards when they first arrived at the palace. He bowed deeply, but eyed them as if they were a dirty spot on the palace silver. *We still have the title,* she told herself.

"The Lady D'Ilora requests your presence at dinner," he said. "You'll be joined by Lord and Lady De Iso, Lady del'la Aduni, and Lords Akele and Thren, from Eiren." His eyes glittered, daring Celestia to refuse the invitation. "I will be happy to show you the way to the dining hall."

"Thank you very much," Celestia said, gazing at him as if she really were a guest in the palace. "My sister and I would be delighted to join Lady D'Ilora."

"She'll be very pleased to hear it." The majordomo didn't sound pleased at all, but he bowed again, then stepped out of the room. Celestia knew he was waiting for them in the hallway.

"Here we go," Celestia said softly to Izara.

"Just like old times," Izara said. She did not sound happy.

Celestia took hold of Izara's arm and together they walked out to join the majordomo. He closed the door behind them and then led them through the wide, dim hallway. The stone walls were carved with images of the courts of the past, all the lords and ladies of the Seraphine who had fallen into favor with their respective emperors. Flame torches—not magical and not electric—burned in their sconces, and the flicker of the flames made the carvings seem to move and dance along the wall, as if they were imbued with the spirit of the people they represented. The Emperor was a traditionalist, and those new electric lights were an unknown novelty.

"This way," the majordomo said testily, and they veered off down another hallway, narrower and dimmer, which ended in a grand staircase that Celestia suspected would take them down to the main wing of the castle.

They wound through the twisting, serpentine hallways of the palace, gowns rustling. The dining hall where they would be meeting Lady D'Ilora and her guests was clearly not the royal hall; there was a simplicity to its design that would not fit an emperor. Still, it was warmly lit and elegant, with candles shimmering on the table and magic lanterns drifting overhead. The other courtiers were already seated, and were drinking aperitifs of what looked to Celestia like pear wine from the east. They were all chattering and laughing, and a panic seized at Celestia's heart. She had to resist the urge to grab her sister's hand and squeeze. What news would they have for her? She could imagine them telling her over those aperitifs that Lindon had already been imprisoned, that her title would be stripped away come morning, that she and Izara were both about to die.

One of the lords, a plump, baby-faced man, was the first to acknowledge them. He stood up and gave an elegant bow.

"May I present Lady Celestia De Malena and her sister, Lady Izara De Malena," the majordomo said in a voice like spoiled honey. Celestia grit her teeth together and curtsied, and Izara, blessedly, did the same.

With their formal announcement, the other lords were

obligated to stand, and so they did, although their bows were shorter, lazier, less respectful.

"Welcome," said the woman at the head of the table, who must then be Lady D'Ilora. She was not required to stand, and so only lifted her wine glass in greeting. "We're so delighted you could join us tonight. Please, sit."

Two places had been set, one on either side of the table. The pear wine in the waiting glasses bubbled and glowed.

"We're very grateful for your hospitality." Celestia swept over to the spot beside the baby-faced lord—he seemed the type to make conversation, and she didn't want to put Izara through that. It also meant he was more likely to know gossip.

"But of course," said Lady D'Ilora, twisting her face into a child's pout.

"Yes," said one of the other ladies, the most beautiful in the room, with sharp-angled features and roses twisted into her hair. "I imagine your journey must have been *very* difficult."

The lord sitting beside her laughed. Celestia's face burned.

"Don't mind Lady De Iso," said Lady D'Ilora. "She's in a poor mood because Lady del'la Aduni started wearing flowers in her hair too." Lady D'Ilora was a bold one, Celestia thought, hosting palace dinners and mocking Lady De Iso.

This was clearly a delicate subject, as Lady De Iso shot Lady del'la Aduni a vicious look and then tossed back the last of her pear wine in a manner more suited to an adventurer than a lady. Brazen of her, since Lady del'la Aduni's name indicated she was part of the imperial family and was doing Lady D'Ilora an honor by even dining at her invitation.

Celestia glanced over at Izara, who had sunk into her seat and was recoiling into herself as if she could vanish from sight. If such a trick were possible, Celestia wouldn't stop her. It was clear to her now they had been invited here as curiosities: the traitors called to the palace, the aristocrats about to be stripped of their title and their lives.

She took a long drink of her pear wine.

Lady D'Ilora rang a bell beside her plate, and the servants bustled in with the meal's first course, an onion soup that was a specialty of the mountains. Despite the dread coiling inside of her, Celestia's mouth began to water as soon as she smelled the savory golden scent of the soup, and when the bowl was set down in front of her and then uncovered, it took all her willpower not to pick it up by both hands and drink. She hadn't realized how much she'd missed these kinds of fine things until they were set down in front of her.

But she—and Izara, to her relief—waited until Lady D'Ilora began to eat before she picked up her spoon.

The meal proceeded like most meals of its sort, the conversation light and inconsequential. Celestia tossed out a few seeds of inquiry, but none of them had any news of Lindon— a relief, as it meant he hadn't been arrested. However, the baby-faced lord, who turned out to be Lord De Iso, Lady De Iso's brother, did turn to her and say, "I believe I may have some dealings with your acreage. Cross Winds?"

Celestia straightened up, but tried her best to keep her tone conversational. No matter what the Emperor intended to do with her here, at this dinner, she had to act as if things were normal. "Oh?"

"Yes. I'm courting Lady D'Kinan, and her father does trade with Cross Winds."

The D'Kinan family. Yes. Their title had only been given to them a generation ago. The De Iso family must be losing their money as well.

"I hear things are robust in your absence." He smiled. "I knew Lindon had been called away, but when I heard you were here—a bit of surprise, I tell you!" He spoke earnestly, no hint of malice or gossip in his voice. "Because I just spoke with Lord D'Kinan and he just helped broker a crop of— mangos, I believe?"

It was all so ordinary, Celestia thought, picking at her plate of buttered greens. Talk of mango sales. It made her chest hurt. "I put my utmost trust in Master Gregori."

"I can see that! And Cross Winds had always had rich land. I'm from the Liyone tributary myself. Dreadful place. Have you ever been?"

Celestia shook her head and took a bite of her greens.

"The ground there is so soft that the first De Iso actually built his estate up in the trees," he said. Out of the corner of her eye, Celestia could see Izara listening in; she was seated next to one of the Eirenese lords, Lord Thren, who had been steadfastly ignoring her all evening. "So it's not really a house so much as a collection of rooms, really, linked by walkways."

"It sounds fascinating," Celestia said. "I'd never heard about the Liyone great house. It sounds like your ancestor had an eye for ingenuity."

Lord De Iso shrugged. "It's what got our family the title."

The meal continued like this, each dish delivered steaming and delicious, and the conversation sparse, a bit dull. But then Lord Thren pulled his attention away from Lady D'Ilora and Lady del'la Aduni and turned to Izara. She froze, her banana leaf halfway to her mouth. Lord De Iso was chattering on about his lessons in swordplay, but Celestia tuned him out, afraid of what was about to transpire.

"I hear you're meeting with the Emperor tomorrow," Lord Thren said.

Izara's eyes widened, and she looked over to Celestia for help. But Lord De Iso was still talking, on and on, about parries and thrusts and blocks.

"I hadn't heard," squeaked Izara.

"Oh?" Lord Thren arched one of his eyebrows. "Well, I suppose he hasn't officially invited you yet. I'm on the Emperor's advisory board. You were a matter of some interest in our meeting this afternoon."

Celestia had been lulled into a sense of normalcy after all that bland conversation, but now her heart began to pound against her chest. She put a hand on Lord De Iso's arm to quiet him. Fortunately, he took the hint. Why would a member of the advisory board be so loose with information? Unless this was a trap of some sort, a way of retrieving damning information from the less socially adept of the two De Malena sisters—

"That seems like private information, Lord Thren," Celestia said sweetly.

Lord Thren turned to her. Grinned. "Information flows more freely at dinner. Isn't that always the case?" He tilted his pear wine at her and then took a drink. He must be drunk, Celestia decided. "Besides, I'd assumed you'd already received word. His Radiance is very interested in speaking with you." He smiled, slow and wide. "*All* of you."

Ico. Celestia took a deep breath.

"And why is that?" she asked, keeping her voice light. She was aware of the other conversations having fallen away; finally, the confrontation all the guests had been waiting for. She and Lord Thren were the centerpieces of the meal tonight.

"Oh, I'm sure you know." Another sly smile. "And you'll find out tomorrow, at any rate."

"Who's the third, Lady Celestia?" asked Lord De Iso. He turned to Lady D'Ilora. "And why weren't they invited as well?"

"Because Lady Celestia's traveling companion was an Akuranian thief," said his sister. "A pirate, if the rumors are to be believed. The very pirate who commanded an extremely high asking price in Eiren twenty years ago."

"A pirate!" Lord De Iso's face lit up. "Now, there are some stories there, I imagine."

Lady De Iso sniffed her disapproval. Izara was no doubt

coiling up inside herself again, but Celestia kept her gaze fixed on Lady De Iso's face. She would not let it drop away. She would not let herself lose this stupid, petty game.

"He was a pirate," Celestia said. "In the past. Those days are behind him."

"And how do landed ladies such as yourself and your sister come to travel with a pirate?" asked Lord Akele, who had been quiet almost all evening.

"A *former* pirate," Lady De Iso added, eyes gleaming.

Celestia could feel herself being hemmed in. They wanted dirt; they wanted blood. But their focus on Ico was a balm, in its way. No mention of treason, only the Akuranian pirate.

"We needed a guide," she said flatly. Then she took a drink of pear wine, and smiled.

The courier was waiting for Celestia and Izara when they returned from dinner. He bowed when he saw them, and Celestia caught a glimpse of the rolled parchment in one hand. Her breath caught.

"Lady De Malena," he said. "Lady Izara." A smaller bow inclined in each of their directions. "I have a message from His Radiance."

The courier offered the scroll in the formal style, both palms up, the scroll resting on them like a curio on a shelf. The parchment was wrapped in a long red-and-gold scarf: the mark of the Emperor.

"Thank you," Celestia said, and she plucked the parchment from his hands and flicked her wrist to dismiss him. He bowed again, much more deeply this time, then scurried off down the hall.

"Open it!" Izara cried.

"Shh. Wait until we're in my room." Celestia pushed her door open and stepped inside. The room had been prepared for her while she was down at dinner: night clothes were laid out on the bed, the blankets were turned down, a fire burned hotly in the brazier. Once Izara was inside, Celestia closed the door and slipped the scarf off the parchment. Izara watched her with wide eyes.

"What does it say?" she said. "Are we being charged with treason?"

Celestia skimmed over the writing. The penmanship was very formal and very stylized, swoops and swirls piling on top of each other. She hadn't read something of this nature in a long time. She sighed and collapsed on the sofa, still trying to decipher the letter.

"Well?" Izara prompted.

"No." Celestia's voice wavered a little. Her heart pounded. "It's an invitation to meet with him tomorrow. First thing in the morning."

Izara played with the ribbons tying her dress closed, twisting them around her wrist. "Is that a good thing? Will he charge us then?"

Celestia shook her head. "I doubt it." The letter was filled with all the usual flourishes: *It would be a great honor and privilege to speak with the daughters of the house of De Malena* and *Shall we meet post-breakfast on the morrow, in the northern room?* The Emperor—or his scribe—said very little in a great amount of words.

"He wants to meet with us. That's all it says." Celestia handed the letter to Izara, who scanned over it like it was one of her arcane texts, her eyes flicking back and forth across the paper. Celestia leaned back on the sofa. "The phrasing is polite enough," she said. "But bland. I don't think you'll find any clues there."

Izara looked up from the letter. "You're right," she said. "It's nothing."

Celestia shrugged. "That's how formal letters are always

written. They're meant to flatter, not to reveal." She sighed and pressed one hand against her forehead. She was exhausted from the rigors of socialization, and the rich food unsettled her stomach after all that time traveling with the Starless Mages.

"Everything keeps piling up," Izara murmured. "It wasn't enough for us to return the boon with a single favor." She peered over at Celestia. "Maybe he's not going to charge us formally. Maybe—" She trembled, and the letter slipped out of her hands and floated down to the stone floor. "At the Academy," she whispered, "they said the Starless Mages would use human sacrifice to conjure up their power."

Celestia closed her eyes. Was such a horror possible? "We shouldn't jump to conclusions." Celestia wrapped one arm around Izara's shoulder and pulled her in close. "There was no mention of treason at dinner this evening. There's a chance everything will turn out all right." This was what she had said when their parents died, when they had realized they were slipping inexorably into poverty. She had hugged Izara then, too, given her that small measure of comfort.

For years she had thought she hadn't lied in that moment, that everything had become all right. Now, she realized how wrong she'd been.

———

Celestia sat at the vanity while a palace girl twisted her hair into a complex, married-woman's braid. Her breath felt tight in her chest, as if it were caught there, unable to exhale. She found herself thinking constantly about Lindon—had done so, in fact, all morning, as she picked at her breakfast and stood limp as a doll while the girl dressed her. Thinking about him in the luxury of Cross Winds, his hair tousled from working in the forest, his grin easy. Thinking about his touch, the soft feathery kisses he'd given her the last time they'd lain together.

"Does this meet your approval, my lady?" the girl asked.

Celestia blinked, jerking herself away from the shining warmth of Cross Winds and back into the dark shadows of the Emperor's palace. She stared at her reflection, watery in the candlelight. "Yes," she said. "That will do nicely."

"His Radiance is expecting you in the throne room," the girl said. "A porter is waiting for you at the base of the main stairs, and he will accompany you there." She curtsied and backed up next to the wall, eyes lowered.

"Yes, thank you." Celestia stood up from the vanity, her skirts rustling. She left the room in a haze. Izara's door was closed, but Celestia did not hear voices coming from inside, and she assumed Izara had already made her way to the throne room.

When Celestia descended the great spiraling staircase, the porter was waiting for her, just as the girl had said, and he bowed as she approached, then offered one hand to aid her down the last few of the stairs. "My lady," he murmured.

Celestia curtsied, one side of her dress lifted to reveal the colorful silk beneath the brocade, and smiled sweetly. "I thank you for your assistance in helping me navigate the palace."

"But of course." They left the stairs and wound more deeply into the hallways. Celestia had learned as a child that the throne was located at the very center of the Imperial palace, in the middle of a quite literal labyrinth of hallways designed to confuse would-be assassins. Only a select few were allowed to learn the way. The porter walked with the quick assurance of someone who had followed this path many times, who had no fear of getting lost. And he didn't, because a few too-short minutes later they were standing in front of a pair of towering stone doors, images of Growth and Decay carved into either side.

Celestia stared at that carving of Decay, his features twisted so grotesquely that he barely looked human, and wondered why she had been chosen to bring a monster back to the Lady.

And where is Growth in all this?

Celestia dropped her hands down to her belly, thinking of the prayers she had said to Growth, begging for life to quicken inside of her. After four years, it had felt as if she'd been screaming into a void.

Perhaps she had been.

The guards at the door nodded at the porter, and then the guard on the left pushed the door open. The porter went through first, clearing his throat and then announcing, in a voice as loud and clear as a bell: "May I present Lady Celestia De Malena, current head of the House of De Malena, daughter of Aiyana and Junious De Malena, and wife to Lindon De Malena."

Suddenly Celestia's beautiful dress was too constricting. There was a pause after the porter finished, a pause when she should be sliding through the door and she wasn't: she was only standing fixed in place, afraid to step farther.

"My lady," one of the guards said in a low voice, his gaze still fixed firmly ahead.

That was enough to break the spell. She had not been condemned yet.

Celestia glided into the throne room.

For a moment she did not know where to look. The room was cavernous, the stone walls soaring high overhead. The hugeness of the space only highlighted its enormous emptiness; the Emperor sat on his throne at the far end of the room, perched atop the spring that fed the Seraphine River. The river itself—nothing but a thin, snaky trickle here, at the top of the mountain—ran through the throne room, disappearing through a cutout in one of the walls, where it would flow through the palace and out of a spout carved into the palace's side. The soft babble of the stream was the only sound in the room, even as Celestia began the long walk toward the Emperor. He sat stiffly on the throne, his hands folded neatly in his lap. Guards stood like statues at his side. Izara was already here—finally Celestia could pick her out of the emptiness, kneeling before the Emperor. And Ico, too, dressed in simple peasants' clothes.

Celestia walked, careful of each step, aware of the soft thud of her slippered feet against the thick carpet. The Emperor watched her. He looked younger than she had always imagined him, his hair still black and his dark brown skin unlined, his body frail and thin beneath his ceremonial clothes. He sat as still as his guards as he watched, and the weight of his gaze burned into her. When she reached the end of the carpet, she prostrated herself, another detail she had learned in childhood, and waited.

"You may kneel," the Emperor said. His voice had a nasally whine to it that didn't fit the grandeur of their surroundings. Celestia did as he asked, rising to her knees. She peered over at Izara, who was staring hard at the ground.

"I imagine you're curious as to why I brought you here," the Emperor said.

No one spoke. Even Ico kept his mouth shut—another tiny relief.

"I do feel that I must apologize for the nature of your journey here—I asked my Starless Mages to be kind to you, and if that was not the case, then you may speak freely of it, Lady De Malena, without fear of recrimination."

Celestia took a deep breath and looked up at the Emperor. He watched her, his face unreadable.

"We were treated very well," she said, knowing he only asked about the care of her and Izara. "We were fed and given pallets to sleep on."

The Emperor nodded. "My Starless Mages can be coarse

men, and I was afraid they might not heed my commands in that matter. But I am glad to hear that was not the case."

Celestia forced herself not to look over at Ico, to see what his expression told her about this exchange.

"I do not want this to be a formal audience," the Emperor said. "All of you may stand, Lady De Malena, Lady Izara, and Ishi Kui Ico."

A held breath, and then a rustle of clothing, of silk and brocade. Celestia glided up to standing as gracefully as she was able, due to her condition and the constant tremor of fear in her limbs.

"Much better," the Emperor said, and then he smiled, an easy smile, a human smile. He might claim Airiana blood, but no one had truly believed that about the Emperor for centuries. Still, it was a lovely story, born of the Last War. All Seraphine schoolchildren knew it: one chosen family, to unite the tribes of the Seraphine.

"Let us talk freely," the Emperor said. "It's been brought to my attention that the three of you have been given a rather unusual task. That task is why I called you to the palace. You understand, of course, that we are currently allied with Eiren—a partnership that has taken many centuries to develop, and one I do not hold lightly."

Celestia tilted her head in acknowledgement of his words despite the panic surging up inside her. He'd said he wished to speak freely, but she didn't dare.

"And Lady De Malena, you understand the importance of this partnership well, given that your husband, the adventurer Lindon De Malena, is currently tracking an old nemesis of Eiren with three Eirenese men."

The panic tightened. Celestia tried to take a deep breath but her dress was too binding, squeezing all her insides together into a knot.

"Yes, Your Radiance," she whispered.

The Emperor watched her with his dark, burning eyes, although he smiled a little when she made eye contact. "There's no need to be so formal, Lady De Malena, as I said. All three of you—you are guests in my chamber." He swept his arm out, encompassing the entire room. The Seraphine babbled gently in the background. His kindness did not fit with the stories of the paranoid madman hiding himself away in the mountains she had been hearing all her life.

"Of course, Your Radiance." She risked glancing up. "I am grateful to hear that my husband is still well."

"Alive and presumably well, yes. Perhaps we could find a way for you to send a message to him during your stay? So that he knows your condition as well."

He did not sound like a man about to accuse a pregnant woman of treason, but still the terror swirled inside her. When she spoke, her mouth was dry, her tongue thick. "I would like that very much, Your Radiance."

The Emperor smiled and turned to the others. "What of the rest of you? Shall we be less formal this morning?"

Izara murmured her agreement, stuttering her words a little. Ico said nothing. Celestia tensed.

"Ishi Kui Ico," the Emperor said, "Do you not agree?"

Celestia knotted her fingers together, hiding them in the folds of her skirts. She looked sideways at Ico, wishing she could catch his eye, give him a warning. But she couldn't, of course, and Ico lifted his head toward the Emperor and said, in a silky aristocratic voice, "Your Radiance, if I am your guest, why must I stay in the dungeon?"

The Emperor laughed. "Because you're from Akuran, Ishi Kui Ico, and I didn't know if you could be trusted. After this talk, I'll see about finding you rooms with the servants."

Ico, may the gods bless him, only nodded in response.

The Emperor smiled at the three of them again, looking at each of them in turn. "Now that the matter of your welcome is settled," he said, "I'm afraid we must talk of more distasteful things. Your task at the behest of the Lady of the Seraphine—you must cease immediately."

Celestia was dizzy. Was the Emperor toying with them, showing sympathy, calling for informality? She didn't think so.

"I understand that this is an unfortunate situation. But the Lady of the Seraphine wishes to find Lord Kjari so that she may protect him, and that, I'm afraid, can't happen."

"Your Radiance," Celestia said, keeping her gaze lowered to show humility. If he wasn't going to execute them, then perhaps she could convince him to protect Kjari after all. "With the utmost of respect, the situation is more than unfortunate. I'm sure my sister can explain better than I—"

"More than unfortunate." The Emperor's voice was suffused with pity. "Yes, perhaps I understated the truth. But when Isossa came to me with news of your journey—"

"The Founder?" blurted Izara. Celestia whipped her head around to glare at her, and Izara immediately covered her mouth, and bowed, and said, "Forgive me, Your Radiance." Ico looked like he wanted to laugh.

"Yes." The Emperor's tone and expression didn't change. "Isossa is a very old friend of my family's. It was in his city, Bloodvine, that my ancestor, the First Emperor, was selected by the Laniana to unite the nations of the Seraphine. An act of desperation in the final days of war."

Celestia blinked back her surprise—the official story, of course, was that the Imperial family had been chosen by the Airiana. But political machinations in a hidden city made more sense.

"But he understands the conflict here, which is why he came to me. The Lady of the Seraphine wants to save Lord Kjari. Isossa told me that he told you that Kjari is Decay, not some overly powerful human mage."

Celestia sucked in her breath. How could he know that,

and still try to kill him? She glanced at Izara, who looked as stricken as Celestia felt.

The Emperor smiled wryly. "Kjari's true identity is an Imperial secret we've kept since the days of the Last War. One of many reasons I forbid the Airiana from entering my palace."

"Your Radiance," Celestia whispered. "Then why—"

But the Emperor interrupted her. "Eirenese scholars are claiming they've seen signs of Lord Kjari's return. They do not understand the Airiana, and they know Decay, even in his Airiana form, as a monster like the human monster he became. What does this really mean, you ask, if Lord Kjari and Decay are one and the same? My own mages have also noticed strange stirrings in the world. Perhaps Decay is manifesting himself as Lord Kjari again. Who knows? But with the threat of Aesri in the West, I am forced to make a decision. Eirenese loyalty is crucial to the survival of our people. Of our lands. We must let them destroy this monster of their past once again."

But Decay was leaving the world, not coming into it. Frustration bubbled inside Celestia, and she opened her mouth to speak, still unsure of the protocol. The Emperor smiled at her.

"You disagree, Lady De Malena?"

Celestia went still. She could feel Izara staring at her.

"Your Radiance," she said, her mouth dry. "The Lady of the Seraphine has told us that Decay is not manifesting as Lord Kjari—he's hiding himself."

The Emperor's expression did not change. Celestia swallowed and glanced at Izara, who nodded at her encouragingly.

"The strange stirrings you mentioned," she said. "I assume you mean the dead walking among the living?"

The Emperor's eyes narrowed. "You know of that?"

"Yes!" Izara snapped. Celestia jumped and squeezed the fabric of her dress in her fists. But the Emperor did not seem upset. He only tilted his head, listening. Izara took a deep breath. "This is what we're trying to tell you. Decay is retreating from the world and taking his realm with him."

But the Emperor only shook his head. "I'm afraid you've been tricked, Lady De Malena. River, the Lady of the Seraphine, does the work of her older sister Growth. She seeks to protect Decay as he manifests. That's why she told you he was hiding, not returning. That's why she sent you to find him." The Emperor smiled sadly. "I know all the various allegiances of the Airiana because they have been unchanging for thousands of years. As Decay manifests in the world once again, bringing his destruction with him, Growth will do all she can to protect him. She'll pull back, let him run rampant. She'll coddle him. She no longer interacts with mortals, you see, after we fought her precious twin brother. And so she sends the Lady. But her loyalties never change." The smile faltered. "Unlike ours, here in the Seraphine. We must remain loyal to Eiren. We must work together to destroy him, as we did five hundred years ago."

"Listen to yourself!" Izara blurted. Celestia shot her a horrified glare, and Izara faltered backwards, her expression still furious. "Your Radiance," she mumbled. "Forgive me."

The Emperor gestured lazily with one hand.

Izara took a deep breath. "But I feel, Your Radiance, that you are refusing to see what's in front of you. Why would Decay return as Lord Kjari? The Seraphine is not as it was five centuries ago. Your rule is so much stronger, and he would never be able to rise to power."

Celestia's heart thudded. It was an excellent touch, complimenting the Emperor like that, even if Izara had probably only been telling the truth, not hoping to flatter him.

"Let's say you are right." The Emperor shrugged, the jewels on his elaborate cape glinting in the light. "Let's say my own mages have made similar suggestions. I will tell you what I told them: It doesn't matter."

"Your Radiance?" Celestia said weakly.

"It doesn't matter because Eiren is not going to accept that explanation. They expect us to show a unified front against Kjari. They are amassing their troops, which I refused to do; the assignment for Lindon De Malena was my compromise. You must understand our alliance with Eiren is of supreme importance given Aesri's stirrings in the West."

Celestia shivered. This much was true, at least. The Seraphine needed Eiren. Their two nations together might be enough to face the threat in the West, but alone, they would be destroyed.

Ico stepped forward. "Your Radiance," he said.

Celestia tensed—this was improper, as her years of training had taught her. But the Emperor seemed uninterested in propriety, didn't he?

The Emperor lifted his head. "Yes, Ishi Kui Ico?"

"You don't seem to understand the gravity of the situation."

Celestia gaped at him in horror. He ignored her.

"Do I?" the Emperor's lips curved into a teasing smile. "I would think Akuran would have no worries about Aesri, being so difficult to reach. But Eiren and the Seraphine are much closer."

"I don't give a damn about Akuran," Ico said. "I haven't had a country since I was a boy. This is about what's happening out in the world. What's being caused by Decay hiding himself, not coming back into the world. Just like Izara there said."

The Emperor sighed.

"I spent some time in Eiren before the Lady of the Seraphine whisked me back to the jungle." Ico curled his hands into fists, lifted his head high. "And I might be some peasant, but that made it easier for me to see what's happening." He stepped forward.

Celestia trembled. But perhaps this would make the Emperor understand.

"Tell me, Ishi Kui Ico," the Emperor said, composing himself, smoothing down his voice, "What did you see?"

"I saw a pirate clan torture a crew of good men." Ico's eyes gleamed. "This clan, they're known for their torture. They make it slow. But they eventually let death come."

Celestia looked over at Izara and was relieved to see the confusion on her face, too. What in the name of the ancestors was Ico even talking about?

"What are you saying, Ishi Kui Ico?" the priest said.

"Death never came, Your Radiance." Ico drew himself up. "Those poor souls were never released from their suffering. Now they'll live forever as hunks of flesh, incapable of rotting away into nothingness."

Celestia pressed her hand to her mouth, feeling dizzy. She knew Ico was exaggerating. But it was an effective exaggeration.

"Don't you understand?" Ico said. "You're condemning us to a world without death. We'll all be corpses. These ladies, they run an acreage—" He gestured over at Celestia, and she stiffened when the Emperor's gaze flicked over to her. "Decay is necessary for their crops to grow properly. Without the right kind of rot in the soil, our food will turn out *wrong*. I'm certain of it—"

"What you describe is an awful thing for Eiren," the Emperor said. "And they believe that destroying Kjari will end it. We must maintain our alliance, and so we will aid them in their endeavor. These—*issues* won't affect us this far south. Lord Kjari's magic only ever altered Eiren."

"But you're wrong!" Ico shouted, his voice echoing off the walls of the throne room.

The Emperor's expression darkened. "I will not tolerate a peasant raising his voice in my presence."

"But this madness will affect us!" Ico said. "Your *Radiance*. It's already reached the Seraphine."

The Emperor's face went ashy. "How could you possibly know that?"

"Maybe you shouldn't keep the Airiana out of this palace of yours," Ico snarled. "Because Xi—" He stopped himself.

Izara blinked, looking surprised. Celestia looked at her questioningly, but Izara stared at Ico, transfixed.

"The Lady of the Snow," he said. "She told me that the disease is here, in the Seraphine. I'm sure if you came down from the mountains you'd see it yourself."

Terror gripped at Celestia's heart. She looked over at Izara, whose eyes were bright with the same shivering fear. The silence in the throne room was as thick and dark as molasses.

"You almost said her true name," the Emperor said softly. "Xima."

Ico lowered his head, and nodded.

"I can't say why the Airiana would choose someone of your stature as her . . . consort."

Ico scowled, and Celestia stiffened, hoping Ico would not lash back further against the insult. Instead, he said, "I washed ashore her island. She took me in. Why she chose me is irrelevant. What is important is that you need to stop basing our alliance with Eiren on their ridiculous fucking superstitions."

Celestia froze, terror pounding at the side of her skull. The Emperor lifted his chin, expression darkening. He pretended not to care of propriety, surely but Ico's anger was a step too far.

"You need to listen to us," Ico said. "You—"

"I *need* to do no such thing. I have made my decision. If what you claim is true—and I don't necessarily believe it is, although I will investigate—then we will find a way to contain the fallout. And until Eiren is satisfied that Lord Kjari has once again been vanquished from the world, regardless of what may or may not be the truth, you will remain as guests in this palace."

Ico wore an expression of desperation that Celestia had never seen on him before. He opened his mouth to speak, but the Emperor lifted one hand, and his guards stepped forward. Ico wavered.

"Ladies De Malena, you will be accompanied back to your chambers. Ishi Kui Ico, I shall ask the majordomo to find room for you in the servants' quarters." The Emperor touched two fingers to his forehead. "So it has been decreed. Enjoy your stay in the Imperial Palace."

TEN

T he palace mages worked from a laboratory in one of the upper levels of the palace, in a cavernous room that swelled out like a bubble from the side of the mountain. Izara stood beneath the glass ceiling, warm sunlight streaming in despite the usual palace chill. Equipment lined the far wall: glass beakers and jars of elements lined up in neat classifications. Now that she knew they weren't going to be killed for treason, merely imprisoned in order to stop them from committing it, Izara had decided she ought to make the most of her situation.

She had to find a way for them to escape.

Ico's revealing that the darkness had come to the Seraphine had struck a knife through her chest. He must have learned from Xima while they were on the mountain; why he had not seen fit to tell her was another matter. She would concern herself with it later. Now, she could only hope that she could find out *something* to help them continue on their journey.

Izara drifted over to the elements and read through the labels, barely registering what she saw. Chunks of silver from the base of the mountains, black sand from the Atharé Desert, a jar painted red that seemed empty but which, Izara knew, contained iljan, a toxic gas known for its aid in traversing the Aetheric Realm.

"Do you see anything that intrigues you, my lady?"

Izara turned away from the supplies. The mage drifting toward her was very tall and very thin, as if he had been stretched out. He smiled kindly at her, and Izara, after a moment's pause, remembered to hold out her hand.

The mage laughed, took it, pressed his fingers to his brow. "It's been a long time since I've had the chance to speak with a lady of the aristocracy," he said. "It's so rare that a female mage finds her way to the palace."

"I'm afraid I'm not a mage yet," Izara said, and the words dissolved on her tongue. *I never will be, either.* "I—I hadn't yet finished my work at the Academy, when—"

The mage waved his hand. "Yes, we all know the story here. Is it true you called the Lady of the Seraphine before you'd ever attended the Academy?"

Izara nodded, wary.

"Impressive." The mage looked at her sadly. "A shame you won't be able to finish, of course. But I'm happy to share a bit of what I know." He leaned close to her, his eyes closed, his breathing deep. "Iomim's Treasure is strong inside you," he murmured. "I could teach you well, I think."

Izara trembled. This was her chance. If he thought her just an interested scholar, perhaps he would tell her something useful.

"I haven't been able to go into the Aetheric Realm since I've been here," Izara said, studying the items on the shelf. "I miss it, honestly."

The mage chuckled. "You aren't the first Iomim-blessed aristocrat to lodge that complaint, my lady."

"I assume you can go into the Realm," Izara said, knowing she wasn't being nearly as subtle as she wanted to be.

The mage laughed. "Not within the palace walls, I'm afraid."

Izara blinked. "Then how do you—" She stared at him. "Do you have it all memorized? All the magic you do for the Emperor?"

"My lady, you'll find I'm much older than I look." The mage's eyes twinkled. "Yes, I have most of the formulas I need memorized. When I don't, I leave the walls of the palace. It's the same when I need to call upon the Airiana—I practiced Airiana magic when I was younger, your age. I studied it at the Academy."

"So you've been Beholden," Izara said.

"Once or twice. Lifetimes ago." The mage swept over to the shelves and pulled down a sleek notebook bound up in leather. "I'm afraid there's only so much I can share with you. But if you're curious about the magic of the place, this provides an overview."

He handed her the notebook, and Izara flipped it open. *On the Practices of Imperial Wards and Reassurances.* The entries were hand-written, the language simplified.

She looked up at the mage.

"Sir, with all due respect, I was at the *Academy.*"

The mage burst into laughter. "I should have known that wouldn't have worked on you. But I'm afraid there's not much I can share."

Izara decided to change tactics. "What about the Starless Mages?" she asked.

The mage's face immediately darkened. "I'm afraid I'm not part of that particular order."

"I know," Izara said quickly. "But so little is known about

them. And I just wondered—do they pull magic from Decay? I had the opportunity at the Academy to begin studying ways of reaching out to Decay, and I—"

"Oh no no no." The mage shook his head wildly. "Oh, no. Not Decay."

Not Decay? That was unexpected. Izara tried to keep her face blank. "Really?" she asked, as innocently as she could.

The mage smiled indulgently at her. "I told you, I'm not part of that order."

"But it's so fascinating," Izara said, knowing she was pushing her luck—and also not caring. She needed *something*.

"Now, that I agree with." The mage hesitated, then leaned forward, lowered his voice. "There's something I have heard," he murmured softly. "But you mustn't share this with *anyone*—even I don't know if it's true."

Izara leaned into him, her head tilted, her heart pounding.

"There is a rumor. My mentor here told me when I first came on as a palace mage. He let it slip while he was drinking one night." The mage's eyes glittered. "He said that the Starless Mages have struck a pact with Growth."

Izara stared at him. She had felt nothing of Growth in the magic of the Starless Mages. Not fertility, no renewal.

"I know, it sounds strange," the mage said. "And they're so secretive, it's hard to know for sure. But they all pray to Growth every morning. They have a shrine in the garden that no one is allowed to see—" He held up one hand. "And don't take this an excuse to go looking for it. You will be killed if you get too close."

Izara nodded, her eyes wide.

"But my mentor told me that Growth is not as simple as the commonfolk make her out to be. She is not all healthy crops and healthy babies." He smiled weakly. "After all, she's still Decay's twin. So perhaps there is some truth to it."

Izara nodded, feeling dizzy. She felt like she had just seen a piece of something bigger—but she didn't know what it could be.

~

Izara ambled through the rocky, snowy garden on the western side of the palace. It was a narrow thing, carved into the side of the mountain, and the edge of it dropped off into a dizzying ravine. It was also the only place where Izara and Celestia were allowed to go outside.

Celestia sat on one of the carved stone benches, her court finery shimmering in the light of the sun. She flipped through the pages of a book that one of the courtiers had loaned her, the spine resting on the soft curve of her belly. But her expression was unfocused, and Izara knew she wasn't really reading. For all her dallying around with the courtiers, she really was terrified. Izara also knew Celestia had already sent a message via the Emperor's couriers, letting Lindon know that she was at the palace, that she was safe—and that Kjari was Decay. But Izara suspected *that* piece of information would be burned away, censored like the letters Izara had sent her at the Academy.

Izara kicked at a few loose stones, sending them flying toward the edge of the garden, although they skittered to a stop before they fell over the ledge. How could they possibly escape? They didn't have time to come up with some elaborate scheme. Celestia was already showing her pregnancy, and soon she would be far enough along that travel through the desert would be dangerous and impossible.

Izara trudged along, moving closer to the garden's edge. Being out here reminded her of the Academy, the treacherous paths she had to take every day to go to her classes.

Izara picked her way around the large, moss-covered stones. She glanced up at Celestia, and then at the guard standing behind her, tucked away in the shadow of the wall of the palace. Even this floating garden was too much of a risk of escape.

Izara made her way around to Celestia's bench. Celestia looked up from her book, squinting a little in the sun. "How was your walk?"

"There was hardly any walk to speak of." Just endless pacing around the garden, running her hands over the mossy stones. "How's your book? Did you read any of it at all?"

"A little. Mostly I studied the pictures." She laughed, although it sounded forced. "Lady del'la Aduni said I might find it useful, as I've not had the opportunity yet to prepare for the baby." She smiled sadly and placed one hand on her belly, and Izara was strung with a pang of sorrow. She might not care about the silly custom of keeping an expectant mother on bedrest, but Celestia did.

We can't possibly escape. We can't.

A muffled grunt echoed through the garden.

"What was that?" Celestia's eyes went wide. Izara's whole body tensed, and she pulled up the alchemical formulas she had memorized.

Izara swept her gaze over the garden. Nothing looked unusual. Except—

Except the guard was gone.

"Celestia," Izara hissed, and gestured to the place where the guard been standing. Celestia twisted around. One hand went to her mouth.

"Where did—!" she cried. "The guards never leave us alone!"

"I noticed."

Celestia said, "Omaira!" and Izara blinked in surprise.

The kajan stepped out of the mountain's shadow, her gray skin blending into the gray landscape of the garden. The guard lay in a crumpled heap at her feet, and she stepped over him as if he were a boulder.

"What are you doing here?" Celestia asked.

"You weren't in the dungeons," Omaira said. She stood with her arms crossed over her chest. Her armor gleamed. "I assumed you had been taken prisoner, but it seems you weren't." Her eyes glittered like the night sky. "I was wrong to trust you."

Izara's heart pounded, and she kept her gaze on Omaira's sword, still tucked away in its scabbard.

"Trust *us*?" Celestia said. "You're the one who abandoned us when we were captured by the Starless Mages!"

Omaira scowled and kicked at the stones on the ground. "They used magic to drive me off. I've been watching the deliveries to the dungeons for days, waiting for the moment I could rescue you." Her eyes glittered. "But I see now that wasn't necessary."

Celestia drew up her spine in that aristocratic bearing she had learned from their mother. "Just because we aren't in the dungeons does not mean we aren't prisoners."

"You're dressed awfully well for a prisoner."

"She's right," Izara said, her voice coming out thin and frail. "It's Seraphine custom that the aristocracy only ever be bound by house arrest, never placed in dungeons."

Omaira glowered at this.

"We aren't free to leave. You saw the guard. He's not here for our protection." Celestia stood up and drifted over to Omaira, her movements cautious. "Did you really come to rescue us?"

Omaira stared down at her and Izara thought she saw a softening in the kajan's features. But then a heartbeat passed and it vanished.

"Yes," Omaira said. "I rode in on a delivery cart. There's a particular guard who's less thorough than the others. I waited until his shift."

"The wards didn't keep you out?" Izara said.

"These wards are for Airiana," Omaira said. "I am not Airiana." She clapped her hands together. "Now that I have risked myself coming into the palace proper, it is time for us to leave. We have to find his Lordship, and I cannot do so without your magical ability." She jerked her head at Izara.

"I'm not leaving my sister," Izara said.

"I would not ask you to," growled Omaira. "We need to go quickly, before more guards arrive."

Celestia made no move to leave. Izara sighed and looked at Omaira.

"Were you visited by the Airiana, too?" she asked, curious.

Omaira frowned. "I don't worship human gods."

"You worship Decay," Izara snapped.

"He is the creator of my people. I don't worship him."

Izara rolled her eyes. "It doesn't matter. All of the Airiana could still speak with you. You know that Decay is trying to leave the world completely."

Omaira blinked and jerked back as if she had been slapped. "You lie," she whispered.

"Why would Izara lie about this?" demanded Celestia, and Omaira just glared at her.

"He's corrupting the world by withdrawing," Izara said. "He's taking death with him, and that will be devastating for all of us."

Omaira stared at her. Celestia took Izara's hand in her own and squeezed, and the three of them stood like that, the cold wind whipping off the mountains and blasting through the garden.

"If what you say is true," Omaira said, "then it's even more important that we leave the palace and find His Lordship."

"Now?" Celestia looked up at her. "But we're not dressed for travel." She gestured down at her elegant gown, the layers of silk and furs. Omaira scowled.

"You're never dressed appropriately for travel," she said. "Do you know where the third one is?"

Izara knew their escape hinged on trusting Omaira, which she was not keen to do. But what choices did they have?

"I do," Izara said. "He's up in the servants' quarters."

Omaira's scowl deepened. "So we'll have to go back into the palace."

"We would anyway," Izara said, "unless you planned on scaling the side of the mountain."

Omaira looked over at the garden's edge and frowned thoughtfully.

"No," said Celestia, "Absolutely not."

"We don't have the equipment," Omaira said. She turned to Izara and Celestia and fixed them with that cold gray stare of hers. "In my reconnaissance, I found a way out of the palace through an underground entrance—looked abandoned. I can lead you two out that way, but we'll need a way to get back to the third one."

Izara stood up and paced around the bench. The wind bit at the skin of her face, and she felt dizzy with the possibility of escape. She looked over at her sister, who smiled grimly back at her.

Izara took a deep breath.

"Show me the entrance of the tunnel," Izara said. "You take Celestia out to safety. I'll gather some supplies and fetch Ico. Then I can take him down to the tunnel."

Omaira rubbed her chin, nodding. But Celestia leapt to her feet and grabbed Izara's shoulders. "What if you get caught? If the Emperor sees you're trying to escape, he'll execute you immediately. He's already been too lenient with us as it is."

"It'll be easy. No one notices me anyway. There are benefits to being a little mouse at court." Izara's heart hammered against her chest, but she tried to look calm. "This is the best way," she said. "You know we can't stay here."

Celestia stared out at the peaks of the mountains shrouded in clouds and mist. "I know," she finally said.

Izara felt a rush of relief, only to immediately be stricken with twin rushes of fear, of terror—it seemed Omaira would see Celestia to safety, but now she had the more dangerous job.

"Good," Omaira said. "It's decided. We've already wasted too much time debating this." And then she pulled out a short, vicious-looking dagger, the blade rippling like the waves of the ocean. She held it near her hip as she strode toward the palace.

Celestia just stared after her, the wind rustling her skirts.

"We have to go," Izara said softly. "We have to finish this before the baby is supposed to come. Otherwise, he might not come at all."

Izara grabbed Celestia's hand and together they walked through the garden. Omaira didn't even glance at the guard lying in a jumbled heap as she pushed the palace door open and leaned inside. "It's clear," she said in a low voice, and then she slipped through the threshold.

Izara and Celestia followed. Celestia's hand trembled in Izara's, and Izara wished she could show weakness in this moment, too. But she had always thought of herself as the brave one. The one who didn't need to follow the rules of propriety, the one who didn't care about marriage and producing heirs, the one who was willing to sell her life to the Airiana in exchange for a chance to study the dangers of magic. And now she was the one who would protect her sister and her sister's unborn baby from the wrath of the Emperor and the madness of the Airiana of Decay.

Omaira led them into a narrow servants' corridor. The flames of the torches had been extinguished, and the air was cold and dark. Izara could barely see.

"Keep your hand on my back," Omaira said softly. "Your eyesight is too weak for this."

And so Izara did. She hooked her fingers in the rung of

Omaira's belt, and Omaira slipped as easily as a cat through the dark corridor. They didn't see anyone, not even servants. Izara wondered for the first time how Omaira had made her way through the palace, how she had known to come to the garden, and shivered.

Omaira turned abruptly, down a corridor Izara hadn't even seen. Beside her, Celestia sucked in her breath and squeezed Izara's hand tightly. It was so dark that Izara was afraid that they had died out in the garden and fallen into the shadow world.

But then a light glimmered up ahead, pale and shadowy. Omaira walked more quickly. Her feet barely made a sound— the constant rustling of Izara's and Celestia's dresses was louder in the darkness, a roar like the wind. Izara took deep breaths and told herself she would be able to do this alone.

The hallway widened into a small storage room, the walls lined with shelves covered in old stone cookware. A tiny square window was cut into the wall and it let in just enough light for Izara to see that everything was covered in a fine layer of dust.

"This is the entrance," Omaira said, turning around to look at Izara and Celestia. Her bulk filled up the storage room but she moved gracefully, without hitting the shelves. "If you turn left out of the door instead of right, it will take you to a lighted path which should lead you back into the palace."

"The entrance?" Izara tried to keep the panic out of her voice. "I don't see anything but shelves."

Omaira glared for a moment. Then she reached down and grabbed at a coil of rope that Izara hadn't noticed in the thin light and the clouds of dust. Omaira tugged hard on it and a portion of the floor lifted up, revealing a few stone steps and then a fathomless blackness.

Celestia let out a little gasp. "There? We're going there?"

Omaira looked up at Izara. "Bring a torch in case your magic won't work down here."

Celestia turned to Izara. "Don't dally," she said. "I don't want you getting caught."

"I won't get caught." Izara's mouth was dry; she knew she couldn't make any promises.

"I'll wait for you at the end of the tunnel," Omaira said. "We need to hurry. There's a chance someone has heard us already, and I don't know how long until someone finds that guard."

Celestia nodded, although she didn't take her eyes off of Izara. "Promise me," she whispered. "I'll see you on the other side."

Izara flung her arms around Celestia's shoulders and squeezed. "We'll be out of here before you know it," she said softly.

"Come," Omaira said. She was already descending the steps. "You will need to hold onto me so we don't get separated."

Celestia squeezed Izara one last time. Then she gathered her skirts in her hands and stepped cautiously onto the first stair. Izara watched her descend into darkness.

———

The tunnel was damp and freezing, and even in her furs Celestia shivered wildly. When Izara shut the doorway to the tunnel, it was as if all the light in the world had blinked out.

"Stay close," Omaira had said, her voice rough and urgent. Her gloved hand enveloped Celestia's as they made their way down the path. Omaira moved with a steady assurance, and every now and then Celestia would catch the silvery gleam of her eyes, finding their way in the dark.

Otherwise there was only the overwhelming darkness.

Celestia stumbled along, her pointy-toed slippers catching on the hem of her gown. The slippers were lined with silky rabbit's fur and had been comfortable for her walks around the palace, but the tunnel's ground was rocky and hard, and it didn't take long before the soles of her feet started to ache. She clutched at Omaira's hand and listened to her steady breathing, a reassurance that she wasn't alone in the tunnel.

The silence pounded at Celestia's head, as heavy and thick as the darkness. It wrapped around her like a snake, squeezing the breath out of her lungs. Sometimes her steps fell on strange sensations on the ground—a sharp point, a patch of dampness. Once she felt something skitter across her ankle and she let out a yelp of fear. Omaira yanked her along.

"Won't bother you," she muttered. "And we'll be out of here soon."

Celestia had no sense of how long they walked. She became convinced that the tunnel stretched all the way to the mouth of the Seraphine, that when they finally emerged from the darkness the sun would be bright and lemony and hot, and she would smell the soil and sweet damp flowers of her home. In the darkness, devoid of sight, her thoughts seemed so vivid they were almost real. When she thought of Izara at the palace, gathering food and coats and more sensible clothes for the trip to the desert, she could almost see her in the darkness up ahead, a ghostly phantom rushing by with her arms full of peasant's trousers. Celestia's breath caught in her throat. She closed her eyes but the image didn't disappear, and there was no difference between her closed eyes and her opened ones.

But then the air in the tunnel changed. It felt cleaner, sweeter, and Celestia caught a whiff of pine needles and ice. A breeze brushed across her face, gentle as a lover's kiss.

"Are we almost out?" she asked.

"Yes," Omaira said. "And keep your voice down." Her grip tightened on Celestia's hand. "We don't know what's going to be waiting for us on the other side."

Fear gripped at Celestia's chest—this hadn't been part of

their discussion. Had Omaira walked her into a trap? What would happen to Izara and Ico when they came this way, looking for escape?

The light shifted; the blackness turned a deep violet gray. Celestia could make out Omaira's outline, her strong, heavy curves apparent in her leather armor. She stopped, pulled Celestia to her side. Celestia pressed close to her—between the darkness and the unknown, all she had left to trust was Omaira.

"I don't hear anything," Omaira said. "But I'm going out first." She pulled away from Celestia and looked at her. Omaira's eyes gleamed and Celestia knew she saw more than Celestia did. "If you hear the sounds of fighting, run back into the dark part of the tunnel and wait for your sister." A pause, and Celestia studied the dark hulk of Omaira in the darkness, wishing she could see her face. "I'll make sure they don't come after you."

Celestia flushed with a sudden warmth. "Thank you," she said.

Omaira turned away from her and pulled her sword. Celestia heard the *shink* of the metal more than she saw the sharp edge of the blade. She pressed herself against the tunnel wall. The coldness of the stone seeped through her gown. Her feet burned and ached. Omaira stalked forward. Celestia took a deep breath, trying to steady herself. She prepared herself to run.

Omaira vanished around a curve in the tunnel, and for a moment Celestia was struck with a dizzying burst of fear—she was alone in the darkness, pain radiating up from her feet into her legs, her hands stiff with cold, her luxurious gown a weight and a danger if the emperor's guards came after her. She pressed herself against the wall and sucked in air. She could run. She could hide. That was all she had to do, if it came to that.

But then Omaira's voice echoed through the tunnel, bouncing off the walls:

"All clear!"

Celestia breathed out a long sigh. She peeled herself away from the wall and hobbled forward, following the dim lines of the path toward the light. Standing still had made her aware of all the pain in her body; now she could barely move. She was so focused on stepping one foot in front of the other that she slammed hard in Omaira's torso.

"Watch out," Omaira said. "Just because it's clear doesn't mean you can't pay attention."

"I know." Celestia's cheeks burned. "My feet hurt, I couldn't see—" She peered up at Omaira. The light from outside radiated around her like a halo. "Thank you."

Omaira frowned in response, looking down at the ground. "You're bleeding," she said.

"What?"

Omaira swept Celestia up, one arm at Celestia's neck, another tucked into the crook of her knees. Celestia was too stunned to say anything. Omaira turned and carted her toward the entrance, which beamed so brightly it hurt Celestia's eyes.

"Is your sister bringing you appropriate shoes?" Omaira asked in her gruff voice.

"I—I hope so."

"Those slippers were too thin for the rocks here. You should have said something."

"I did! And you said none of my clothes would work."

They emerged from the tunnel. Everything was white, and for a moment Celestia had no sense of what she was looking at it. It was as if the world had been drained of color.

"Snow," Omaira said. "Don't imagine you've seen it before. This is the first storm of the season."

"I have," Celestia said defensively, but she didn't add that she'd only seen it in illustrations in books. She tilted her head back, her cheek pressed against Omaira's armor, and looked up at the sky as soft white flakes swirled down from the clouds. The melted when they touched her skin, little pinpricks of cold. The wonder of it struck her dumb, and for a moment she forgot her pain and her fear as Omaira carried her through this strange, beautiful world.

Omaira's boots crunched over the snow. The tree line rose up ahead, green needles not quite covered by white. The air smelled of sap, of pine, an earthy scent that reminded her of the Seraphine. Omaira carried her deep into the shadows of the trees and then lowered to one knee. Celestia slid out of her arms, and she felt colder, more vulnerable. When her feet touched the ground she cried out in pain. Her voice was softer than she expected, muffled by the snow.

"You need to sit," Omaira said. "I can tend to your injuries."

"You don't have to do that." Celestia leaned up against one of the trees.

Omaira just stared with her dark eyes. Celestia slid down into the bed of fallen pine needles, her skirts billowing around her. She wrapped her arms around herself, burrowing into the fur lining the sleeves of her dress. Omaira knelt down and gently pulled Celestia's foot out from the folds of her dress. Celestia sucked in her breath.

"Worthless thing," Omaira muttered, looking at Celestia's slipper. Celestia gasped when she saw how the fur lining had become matted and the intricate designs in the stitching had vanished beneath blood and dirt.

"You didn't give me time to change," Celestia said, defensive.

Omaira looked up at her. "This may hurt. Try not to scream."

"I never scream," Celestia said.

"I've heard you scream." Omaira tugged on the slipper,

working it away from Celestia's foot. Pain shot through Celestia's ankle, and she dug her hands into the pine needles and the snow and the frozen dirt.

And then there was a ripping sound, like fabric tearing, and Celestia's foot burned as if it were on fire and she ground her teeth together and made low little moans under her breath. Omaira tossed the bloody rag that had once been Celestia's slipper off into the trees. "Let's just hope your sister brings you shoes. And that she's not wearing the same slippers."

Celestia took deep breaths; the initial blast of pain was subsiding, but her foot throbbed and ached.

Omaira set her foot back down on the ground and stood up. "We'll need fabric to bind it," she said. "After I clean it out. Your underskirts will do."

"You want me to take off my clothes?" Celestia gasped, the absurdity of it making her want to laugh.

"No. We'll just need a strip." Omaira pulled out the cruel-looking knife from earlier and handed it to Celestia, handle-first. "Use this to cut a piece. I'm going to get fresh snow to clean the wound."

Celestia took the knife with shaking hands. Omaira nodded and then trudged away to the edge of the trees.

Celestia reached down and picked up a handful of her underskirts. They were silk, cool to the touch, and dyed the color of peaches. She stuck the knife into the fabric, yanked down. It tore easily, and the strip of silk fluttered to the ground like a butterfly. The fabric was disconcerting out here in the forest, away from the splendor of the palace.

A snap of breaking branches echoed among the trees; Celestia stiffened, but it was only Omaira, weaving her way back with a ball of snow in one hand. Celestia picked up the fabric she cut, and thrust it in Omaira's direction.

"Good," Omaira said. "Hold on to it for now." She knelt

down and began rubbing the snow against Celestia's foot. The cold burned along with the pain, but Omaira's touch was surprisingly gentle, her brow knitted in concentration. Celestia watched her and found that it calmed her, the way Omaira's hands rubbed the melting snow over the wounds of her foot.

"We'll have to disinfect it when we get a chance," Omaira said, still looking down at her work. "But I don't want to risk building a fire." She looked up, caught Celestia's eye. "You aren't too cold, are you?"

"No," Celestia said, even as the snow fell thicker around her.

"Good. I don't need you getting sick before we find His Lordship." Omaira finished washing her foot and wrapped it in the strip of silk. Then she repeated the procedure with Celestia's other foot. The pain radiated up Celestia's legs, and she ground her teeth together to keep from crying out. Her thoughts were like spots of brightness: worry for Izara and Ico, worry for Lindon, still hunting down Decay in the southern continent.

Celestia closed her eyes against the falling snow and prayed she could have another chance to find Lindon and try to explain that the Emperor was so shortsighted he would let the world fall into corruption rather than risk alienating Eiren.

She thought then of the adventurer who had told her of the boy with the slashed throat—gods, it felt so long ago, sitting at the table at Cross Winds, the shiver of fear nothing like the deep and all-encompassing fear she had felt since leaving home. *The world is coming undone,* she thought, *and we are the ones to stop it.*

She opened her eyes and looked out at the blank canvas of the forest, suddenly numb to everything, even her pain.

Someone pounded hard enough on Ico's door that it shuddered in its frame. He looked up from the journal where he had been drawing, a habit he'd picked up when he was at sea as a way of filling the long gaps of boredom. He'd asked one of the servants for a notebook and a stick of graphite; miraculously, she had dropped them off earlier that day. She'd been a little wisp of a thing, and she smiled at him through stringy hair as she handed the present over. Ico had just grinned at her. If he was going to be stuck up here, he might as well have some fun.

The pounding continued, more urgent than before. Ico doubted it was the servant girl. "Hold on!" he shouted, slamming the book shut and then shoving it under his mattress. He strode across the room, bracing himself for whatever was on the other side of the door—he wasn't going back down to the dungeons.

He yanked the door open.

"Oh," he said. "They let you up here?"

Izara shoved past him and into his room. "Shut the door," she hissed, and then she dumped a knapsack on his bed.

"What the hell's going on?"

"Close the door!"

Ico did, easing it shut. She wasn't dressed in courtier clothes, but in some kind of sporty lady's outfit, a handsome brown jacket and a thick wool skirt. She whirled to face him.

"We need to move quickly," she said. "I don't think I aroused *too* much suspicion but I didn't want to use magic. I was afraid the guards would sense it somehow—" Her gaze flicked around the room, taking in the stone walls, the narrow bed. "Do you even have anything to take?"

Ico's heart pumped. "Fuck me," he said. "We're actually going to escape."

"Keep your voice down!" Izara opened up the knapsack.

"If you have anything you want, put it in there. Omaira found a tunnel out of the palace."

"Omaira?"

"The kajan."

"Shit." Ico blinked in surprise. He'd figured her to be long gone, riding back down to the south with the rest of the kajani army.

"Well?" said Izara. "Is there anything you need?" She gestured at the bag.

"So where is Omaira?" Ico asked. "She just hanging out in the hallway?"

Izara glared at him. "I don't have time to explain. We have to hurry if we're going to get out of here before anyone notices that Celestia is missing."

Where the hell was Celestia, then? But Ico didn't bother to ask. He pulled the notebook out from under the mattress and dropped it in. Might as well.

"That's it," he said. "They bring my clothes to me each morning. I don't get choices like you do, apparently."

Izara bundled up the knapsack and threw it over her shoulder. "Fine. We'll have to find something for you once we get to the Atharé Desert."

"Glad to hear you're finally listening to me."

Izara cracked the door open and peered out. Then she slipped into the hall. Ico followed her. She skittered down the corridor, glancing nervously over her shoulder. Ico grabbed her, pulled her in close to him.

"You look like you've just robbed the throne room," he said softly into her ear. "Walk naturally. Act like you have every right to be here."

Izara softened. She took a deep breath. Nodded.

"You own this fucking place," he said.

He wanted to make her smile; it didn't work. But when she started walking again, her back was a little straighter, and she strode more forcefully. Anytime she started to glance around like she was under surveillance, Ico poked her in the spine.

They took the stairs at the end of the corridor and went down past the courtiers' apartments. When a scullery maid bustled in at one of the stair's landing, Izara tensed, her hand squeezing the strap of the knapsack. Ico wanted to curse at her. But the scullery maid did as she'd been trained, and didn't look directly at Izara—although she snuck a peek at Ico. Ico grinned at her. She grinned back, and winked.

"See?" Ico said the maid was out of earshot. "You've every right to be in this palace."

"That was just a maid," Izara said.

They left the stairwell and went out to a narrow, dingy corridor. The stone was black with soot where torches burned along the walls. It looked like a servant's area—they must be on the lower levels.

"This way," Izara said, although she didn't sound certain.

"You know where we're going, right?"

She walked on without answering. The torches flickered, casting yellow light over their path. Voices echoed through the walls.

"Stop," he said, grabbing Izara's arm. She glared at him over her shoulder.

"You hear that?" he whispered.

Izara's eyes were wide, and she tilted her head to listen. The voices babbled, too low for Ico to make out words. But they didn't belong to the maids. These were men's voices, and they weren't gossiping and giggling, either.

Ico cursed the mages who had stolen his weapons when they were kidnapped in the woods. Even his dinners had been brought to him without a knife. He grabbed one of the torches off the wall. Better than nothing.

"Can your magic work down here?" he asked Izara.

She closed her eyes, twisting up her face in concentration. The flames on the torches guttered in unison, one, two, three. She looked at Ico and nodded.

He jerked his chin—*let's go.*

They moved through the twisting hallways. Ico swallowed questions about whether or not they were lost—it was impossible to know in this maze of a palace. The voices faded in and out, but they were there, on the other side of the wall.

They approached a split in the hallway, and Izara let out a sigh of relief. "Thank the gods," she murmured. "We're almost there." She glanced over at Ico, her smile bright in the torch's light. "Not long now."

"Yeah, I'll celebrate when we're out of the palace." Ico tightened his fingers around the torch. He refused to believe escaping would be this easy.

And when Izara turned left at the split, he was proven right.

A trio of palace guards stood in a clump, talking to one another, their hands on their swords. Izara froze in place, and for one heartbeat of a moment Ico thought they could just turn and walk the other way and they'd be free.

But then the guards saw them.

"What the hell are you doing down here?" the first one said, taking a menacing step toward Izara.

"Um," she said. Not exactly a show of confidence. *Damn it, girl,* Ico thought. *You're a fucking noblewoman, just tell these assholes to screw off.*

The guard walked toward them, his steps heavy and ominous. One hand rested on the hilt of sword.

"Well?" he said.

Izara straightened her spine. "I was . . . exploring the palace?"

Not as convincing as her sister would have done, but it was a start.

"Courtiers don't come down here," the guard said.

"I was under the impression we could go wherever we wanted." Her voice trembled, but she had the right idea.

That's it, Ico thought. *Just lie your way out of this one.*

"There's nothing interesting down here," the guard said. "Get back up to your apartment. And that one"—he pointed at Ico—"doesn't have permission to go wandering."

"Don't talk to me like that," Izara said. Her voice was weak and unconvincing.

The guard rolled his eyes. One of the others laughed and leered at her.

"Go on, then," the guard said. "No one's supposed to come down here. Emperor's orders." He leaned close into Izara, and she took a stumbling step backwards. Ico caught her with one hand. "Unless you're looking for someone down here. Are you, little lamb?" He grinned. His canine teeth had been sharpened into fangs.

Shit, thought Ico.

And then a pulse of white heat blasted through the hallway. Arcs of light bounded off the walls and crackled on the air. The guards slammed down on the ground, but they clambered to their feet just as fast, their swords flying free of their sheaths.

"Shit!" Ico shouted.

"I didn't know what else to do!" Izara shouted.

Ico shoved her behind him and swung the torch at the guards rushing toward him, their swords raised. For a flash he wondered what the fuck he was doing.

Another blast of magic tore through the hallway, blowing the guards back and knocking Ico to the ground. The torch rolled away and burned stupidly next to the wall.

"Will you *stop* that!" Ico shouted.

"They were going to kill us." Izara rushed past him and picked up the torch. "And I think that got them. Come on, before they wake up."

Ico lurched up, bracing himself against the wall. Izara was already rushing down the corridor. The guards didn't move from where they lay sprawled across the floor. When he got close he saw blood running from the guards' noses and heard the labored scratch of their breathing.

"What the fuck did you do to them?" Ico asked.

"I just manipulated the alchemical formulas of the surrounding air. They'll be fine." Izara was jogging now, one hand holding the torch aloft and the other gathering her skirts in a fist. "Gods and monsters, I hope they haven't found Celestia. They knew we were coming down here. They have to know that Celestia escaped—"

"Don't worry about that," Ico said, catching up with her. "Just focus on getting us out of this fucking prison."

They turned a corner, and then another. The torches here had been extinguished, and the only light they had was the bobbing glow of the single hot flame in Izara's hand. In the shadows, Ico made out a doorway up ahead.

"This is it," Izara gasped. She slowed her pace and ducked through the doorway. It was a storage room, shelves covered in old cookware. Izara leaned down and grabbed a rope and pulled open a hatchway. Stairs loomed down into darkness.

"Torch goes first," Ico said, glancing over his shoulder. No guards. No servants. His heart beat fast and he prayed to Xima, the only god he cared about, to see them to safety.

Together, he and Izara descended into the tunnel.

~

Ico felt the temperature drop before he saw any of the light of the outside world. The tunnel itself was cold, but he and Izara moved quickly—an unspoken agreement that they needed to get to Celestia and the kajan before the guards caught up with them. But after they had been running for several minutes, Izara panting and breathless beside him, the temperature suddenly plummeted. Ico stumbled to a stop. Izara turned, her breath steaming the air around her.

"What is it? Did you hear something?"

"No." Ico moved forward, his bare hands stinging from the cold. The torch barely let off any heat. "I don't like this cold."

Ico had hoped the cold was Xima preparing to make an appearance, but the air never iced into her familiar form. And Ico knew the cold was something else, something much more dangerous.

He kept walking, his muscles tight. He could hear Izara huffing behind him. The light changed; it brightened, but there was a gray tint to it that Ico had seen before.

"Fuck," he murmured.

He rounded the corner of the tunnel, head first into a blast of wind. The torch guttered and then extinguished, leaving a trail of smoke in its wake. Izara gasped.

"There's the exit," he said.

The world outside the tunnel was white with snow. The freezing wind blasted over him, stinging his face with a thousand knives. Snow spilled into the tunnel, tumbling up to their feet. Izara just gaped at it, her eyes getting wider and wider.

"What are we going to do!" she cried. "We can't go back!"

Ico tossed the torch stick aside. It clattered and echoed against the stone. "You said the kajan was supposed to meet us?"

Izara wandered toward the exit, her eyes shining. "She'll never find us in this!"

"She's a kajan. She might." Ico took a deep breath. Glanced over his shoulder at the blackness of the tunnel. Couldn't go back. Couldn't stay here, either, and risk getting caught. He'd navigated in snowstorms before, when he did the work of Xima's north wind. She had sworn to him that he'd never be lost in the snow, but that was in her domain, where she held power. The palace's wards would weaken her, assuming she could even get through here.

"Wait here," Ico said, and then he braced himself, a few quick breaths, before plunging out into the storm.

The wind roared, a horrible moaning that pounded inside his head. The snowflakes melted when they touched his skin and then froze immediately, leaving trails of ice running down his face.

"Xima!" he shouted. "Tell me you're out here."

For a moment his answer was only the screeching of the wind, and panic gripped his heart as he whirled around, seeing only white, not even a glimpse of the tunnel.

But then the tenor of the wind shifted, and a hand caressed his cheek. He lifted his gaze and saw her, outlined in the snow. She smiled.

"Am I protected up here in the mountains?" he shouted.

"No," Xima said, her voice rising and falling. "But I can lead you to the others."

Ico nodded. It would have to be enough. "Izara is back at the cave!" he shouted.

Xima dissolved in the wind and then materialized closer to him. She lifted one hand and pointed off into the whiteout. "The cave is that way."

Ico plunged forward. Only when he stepped into the swirling snow did it occur to him this could be some kind of palace magic, designed to deceive. But no. A few steps in the direction Xima had pointed and he stumbled abruptly into the mouth of the tunnel. Izara was huddled near the wall, her arms wrapped around herself, flakes of snow dotting her hair. "Oh, thank the gods!" she cried. "I thought you'd lost your mind."

"We're both about to lose our minds," Ico grumbled. "Xima agreed to lead us to the others. But you need to hold my hand and don't let go. You let go, I lose sight of you, that's it. I can't make any promises."

Izara looked out at the snow. She closed her eyes, lifted her hands, hummed softly beneath her breath. Ico recognized the motions—he'd seen them enough in the guard's carriages on their way to the palace. One of those little lighted globes she made out of magic. He didn't have the heart to tell her it would be worthless in the storm.

The globe formed between her palms and she released into the air. Ico couldn't even feel the heat from it. Izara opened her eyes.

"I'm ready," she said.

Ico grabbed her hand. He wished they had rope or twine, something to lash the two of them together. But this would have to do.

"Don't let go," he said, and then he led her out into the howling winds.

Once again Ico was momentarily blinded. The first thing he saw was the paltry light from Izara's globe. She squeezed his hand so tightly the bones in his fingers crunched together. When he glanced back at her he could barely make out her face in the white of the snow.

"Where's—Xima?" She faltered on the name.

Probably a good thing. Knowing an Airiana's name had gotten her into this mess, hadn't it?

"She's here." Ico moved forward, forcing his gaze up. Nothing but white, nothing but harsh wind slicing at his skin. But then he saw her, a shadow in the distance. She gestured with one hooked finger, and he plowed forward, yanking Izara along behind him. The snow was up to his knees. The cold damp seeped through the fabric of his trousers. Fucking Celestia and her kajan friend better be close. They better have shelter and a fire and hot fucking wine to serve them.

Izara shouted something, but the wind carried her voice away. Ico squeezed her hand to make sure it was still there. Xima's shadow kept moving, shifting in the wind. He passed close enough to a tree that he could make it out in the snow, and then the wind seemed to dampen a little. They had made it to the tree line.

Up ahead, Xima stopped. She turned to Ico and then the wind blasted her toward him, and for a moment she materialized in her true solid form. Then the wind blew and all that was left was her face, her hair streaming in the snow.

"Please tell me we're close."

"The kajani woman is on her way," Xima said. She kissed him, and for a moment Ico was suffused with the eerie warmth of the blue fires of her palace. She pulled away and floated beside him, to Izara, whose body was wracked with violent shivers even as she stared up at Xima in awe.

"A child of the Seraphine," Xima said, smiling a little. "I'm sure you never thought you'd see me." And then she kissed Izara on the mouth, too, longer than she had kissed Ico, long enough for Izara's shivering to stop.

"Find him," Xima said, before the wind blew her away.

Izara stared in the place where Xima had been, her face slack with wonder.

"You act like you've never seen the Airiana before," Ico said. He scanned past her, looking for some sign of Omaira.

"To be kissed by the Airiana is to be blessed," Izara breathed.

"If that's true, I should have had enough blessings to not be in this mess." Nothing but snow. The cold was starting to seep back, too. He put his arm around Izara and pulled her against him. "For warmth," he said, before she could protest.

And then he saw something through the snow. A glint of red light.

"That globe of yours," Ico said. "Can you make it brighter?"

"I can try." The shiver was back in Izara's voice, but the globe's glow strengthened to the color of mead, and the snow

melted around it, leaving little rivers of water dripping down
its sides.

The red light moved closer. Someone shouted.

"Omaira!" Ico yelled. If it were the palace guards, so be it.
But he knew Xima would never lead him into a trap.

Through the curtain of snow, a monster of a woman
emerged. She could have been one of the trees. Ico had
forgotten how enormous Omaira was. Ice fringed her eyes
and hung in daggers off the bottom of her scabbard. The light
came from some kind of torch, an ugly, twisted knot of wood
that glowed with an intense, vibrant magic.

"Praise Kjari," she said. "I thought it was hopeless, finding
you out here."

"Tell me you have shelter," Ico shouted over the wind.

"Of a sort! Come." She thrust the torch between Ico and
Izara, and Ico felt its warmth immediately. "Take it," Omaira
said to Izara. "Your kind does not handle the cold as well as I
do."

Izara reached up with one shaking hand and gripped the
torch. Ico huddled close, the heat warming his cheek. Then
they moved forward, plowing through the snow. Omaira made
her way as if the she could see through the whiteout, leading
them neatly around the jagged branches of dead trees.

"We're lucky this storm came in!" she shouted over her
shoulder.

"I wouldn't go that far," Ico said, huddling closer to Izara.
She looked over at him, her lips already raw from the wind.

"Lucky?" she said.

"The guards knew where we were going." It was hard to
talk, the words coming out in shudders. "They would have
been out here waiting for us if this storm hadn't blown
through."

Finally, the snow thinned, and Ico was able to make out
the trees. The forest was thicker here, the trees blocking out

the sky and the snow. The wind was bitterly cold, but Ico thought he caught the scent of woodsmoke on it, and his heart leapt at the thought of a real fire, none of this magic-induced warmth.

"Almost there!" Omaira called back. "I had to make sure Celestia couldn't be discovered."

"You had to make sure she didn't freeze to death, too," Izara snapped. Ico shot her a dirty look. Omaira glowered in response, but still led them to a place where the ground sloped into a narrow ravine, and there, tucked away in that crack in the earth, was a carriage, a pair of shaggy alpacas, and a leaping fire.

Ico was so relieved at the sight of it that he didn't even register that Celestia wasn't there until Izara shouted, "Where's my sister!"

Omaira fixed Izara with her cold, inhuman gaze. "I imagine she's in the carriage. She injured her feet walking through the tunnel."

Izara shoved the magic torch at Ico and skittered down to the carriage, clutching her bag of supplies to her chest. The carriage door swung open and Celestia stuck her face out, her head wrapped in one of the thick woolen blankets the people of the mountains made. She smiled when she saw her sister.

"Where'd you get the carriage?" Ico asked, sidling up alongside Omaira. She was staring down at the two sisters, her expression almost pleasant.

"How do you think I made it up the mountain?" she said. "I stole it and the alpacas from a settlement near where we were attacked."

Ico grinned at that. "Nice to be around an honest thief again."

"There's no such thing as an honest thief," Omaira snapped. "But your sort is afraid of me, and stealing was the easiest way." She glanced over at him, ice and snow glittering in her hair. "We should leave while we still have the cover of snow."

"I can't disagree."

Omaira nodded and then slid into the ravine, a graceful, balletic movement performed with the ease of someone familiar with harsh terrain. Ico glanced over his shoulder. The storm was beginning to abate.

He only hoped that when they went down the other side of the mountain, they would find Lord Kjari waiting in the desert.

ELEVEN

They traveled out of the snowstorm and through the night, Celestia and Izara and Ico sleeping in the carriage while Omaira ran the alpacas. Celestia fell asleep easily, the stress of their escape having exhausted her, but she was jarred awake by a nightmare that vanished from her memory as soon as she opened her eyes.

For a moment she only lay in the cramped space of the carriage, listening to the others sleep. Her entire body ached, and her feet burned from the cuts she'd sustained in the tunnel. She wore the same clothes from yesterday, and they had dried into a filthy stiffness against her skin.

She pressed her hand against the swell of her belly. *It will all be over soon,* she told herself, a mantra she wasn't sure was worth believing anymore. Then she shifted, extracting herself from her makeshift bed to push open the top hatch of the carriage. She wanted to let in light and to relieve the stale air inside the carriage. She was greeted by a cloudless blue sky.

Omaira leaned over and showed the sharp incisors in the sides of her mouth. Celestia thought it might be a smile.

"You're awake," Omaira said. "How are your feet?"

"They feel a little better."

Omaira nodded in satisfaction and then straightened, disappearing from Celestia's view. Celestia settled back and listened to the clicking of the alpacas' hooves outside. The sound was strange, an echoing *clack-clack-clack* that reminded Celestia of bones.

A shadow fell over the sunlight. It was Omaira, leaning over the hatch again. "Would you like to sit up top?" she asked. "Air's cleaner out here."

Celestia hesitated. "It's considered uncouth for a lady to sit on top of a carriage."

Omaira snorted. "Suit yourself. Not that anyone's going to give a damn out here."

That was certainly true. And Omaira had shown her kindness during the escape. So Celestia stood up, bracing herself against the wall, her movement shaky. She gasped through her teeth when she put her weight on the soles of her feet, still wrapped in the bandages Omaira had prepared.

"Grab my arm," Omaira said, reaching down.

Celestia did, and Omaira hauled her up. Celestia was momentarily blinded by the sun, blinking until her surroundings began to come back into focus. She expected to see trees, a forest, but there was only a wide expanse of gray stones that clattered beneath the alpacas' feet.

"Gods and monsters," Celestia breathed.

"It's a sight, isn't it?" Omaira looked straight ahead. "We must be on the dry side of the mountain. Not enough rain for trees."

Celestia wrapped her arms around herself. Despite the bright sunlight the air was very cold, and she still wore her court gown. She looked out at the horizon. She could just make out the ocean, reaching up to kiss the blue sky.

And then Celestia felt something, a kind of fluttering, like a butterfly. She gasped. Pressed her hand against her belly.

There it was again. A tiny movement inside of her.

"Are you all right?" Omaira glanced at her, frowning.

"I'm fine." Celestia took a deep, shuddery breath. "It's just—it's the baby. I felt him kick." She spread her fingers farther over her stomach but the baby had gone still. This was not how she had imagined this moment, all those weeks ago when the healer mage had told her she was pregnant. She had though she would be lying in silks in her bed at Cross Winds, drinking rosewater and reading books.

"That's good," Omaira said, turning her attention back to the alpacas. Rocks skittered beneath their hooves. "Shows she's strong."

Celestia hoped Omaira was right. It wasn't proper, what she was doing. Would her child prove rough and crude? It was said that the pregnancy dictated the child's nature, and for the last several weeks Celestia had not allowed herself to consider what she was doing to her baby. To Lindon's baby.

Lindon. *Lindon.* At least she knew he was still alive, albeit on a fool's errand. Now that they were out of the palace, on their way to Decay to stop the corruption of the world, Celestia felt a surge of anger at the Emperor. He had sent Lindon into danger for no real reason, only to assuage the superstitions of Eiren.

The reality of the situation made it even worse that she and Lindon had parted in anger. She knew he had only reacted out of fear, but his harshness still burned at her when she let herself think on it. Instead when she thought of him she thought of their life before the Lady's request. It had been a good life. The life she'd always wanted.

"What occupies your mind?" Omaira said.

At first Celestia said nothing. What would a kajan care of her troubles? But Omaira watched Celestia with a furrowed brow. "It's not your feet, is it?" she asked. "We can't have them getting infected."

"No," Celestia said. "It's not my feet." She looked down at the filthy clothes piled in her lap. "It's my husband. He's still out there, hunting down Lord Kjari."

Omaira said nothing, just flicked the reins, guiding the alpacas away from an outcropping of sharp, jagged rocks.

"I sent word to him," Celestia said. "I told him Kjari is Decay, but Izara thinks my message was probably censored by the palace guards."

"*Lord* Kjari," Omaira corrected. "And Decay is the name your people have given him. It's not his true name."

"Neither is Kjari," Celestia said. "He would never broadcast his true name out to the world."

Omaira snorted. "You have such strange beliefs about his Lordship."

Celestia looked out at the endless stretch of gray rocks. She was being rude, and for no reason—Omaira had rescued them. She was the only reason they were on their way to stop Decay's disappearance at all.

"I'm sorry," Celestia said. "I know our ways seem strange to you."

"Very strange," Omaira said. "Your gods and your leaders move you around like pieces on a game board, never seeing the larger picture."

Celestia took a deep breath. The air was thin up here in the mountains. It made it difficult to breathe. "I understand the Emperor's perspective," Celestia said carefully. "He's worried about war with the west. Eiren, who opposed Kjari and the Seraphine during the war—they're our allies now. And he's—" She sighed, heaving her shoulders. "He's arrogant, I suppose, in refusing to allow the Airiana to factor into his decisions. He's risking the the entire world for his schemes."

"As I said," Omaira agreed, "never seeing the larger picture."

Silence fell over them. Rocks clicked and slid beneath the alpaca's feet.

"They said I was mad, to dedicate myself to His Lordship," Omaira said suddenly.

"Who did?" Celestia turned to her. Omaira kept her gaze on the path ahead.

"My family," Omaira said. "We're not warriors, you see. They considered it odd that I would want to leave the Aetheric Realm and come into this world."

"Why did you want to leave, if I may ask?"

Omaira paused. "Only a select few kajani are ever chosen to serve His Lordship in this realm."

"And your family didn't want you to be one?"

Omaira fell silent, squeezing the reins of the alpacas. "I wasn't chosen," she finally said. "But I came anyway."

Celestia stared at her, not sure how to respond. She didn't want to say what she was thinking, which was that she agreed with Omaira's family.

"My family are healers," Omaira continued. "I had studied healing magic my entire life, although I dreamed of becoming a warrior."

"A healer," Celestia said with a smile. "So that's why you treated my feet so well."

Omaira smiled shyly. "I thank you for that." Then her expression turned serious again. "In my studies of magic, I sensed—something was wrong. With His Lordship."

She glanced sideways at Celestia, her dark eyes shy.

"You felt his departure?" Celestia said.

"I don't know. I only felt that something was wrong. And I felt—called. To protect him. I had been training for battle my entire life, without the approval of my family. It seemed it had been for a purpose." Omaira took a deep breath, her big shoulders hitching. "I did not expect to come here and learn that he was trying to vanish entirely."

A pang of sympathy sliced through Celestia's chest.

"I don't know that we can ever understand the actions of the Airiana," she said. "Whether human or kajani."

Omaira snorted a little.

"What we do know is that his death, his true death, it risks all of us. And if you felt it, in the Aetheric Realm—" Celestia dropped her hands to her belly, hoping she could feel the baby kick again. But there was only stillness. "It's like the old stories. That he destroyed existence."

And Growth built it back up again. But Growth was nowhere in all this, was she?

"We're all tied together, it seems," Celestia said.

Omaira stared ahead. "Your people have always seen my Lord as a monster. You do not understand he is necessary."

A strange sting of guilt burst in Celestia's chest. She studied Omaira's strong profile, the sharp cheekbones and the jutting fangs and the gray skin. Of course she wasn't human. But Celestia was starting to understand she wasn't a monster, either.

<hr />

The journey down the mountain went much faster than the journey up the mountain. Omaira rushed the alpacas to escape the Starless Mages. Ico, grumbling about the speed, showed her and Izara how to gather a moss that grew underneath the stones. He mashed it together with the supply of melted snow Omaira had brought along with her.

"What's the point of this?" Omaira asked, watching him work beside the fire.

"It masks our scent," he said. "Confuses their dogs. And lets you slow down before you drive those alpacas to death."

Omaira shook her head, annoyed. But she still helped him and Izara as they trudged back up the mountain, sprinkling the mossy water over the path.

They ate wild game that Omaira hunted and tubers Izara dug up from the thin, rocky soil. She said she'd read about their nutritional value in the books back in Bloodvine. In the mornings they scattered the stones and spread the ashes from the night's fire into the wind. Sometimes in the night Celestia would wake to the sound of rocks tumbling down the mountain, and in the distance she'd catch sight of Omaira's red-flamed torch.

Celestia's feet were slow to heal, even with Omaira's careful treatment of them and Izara chanting over them in a language that made the edges of Celestia's vision go fuzzy. "I'm sorry," she said helplessly, when Omaira swapped out the blood-dotted bandages the next day. "I was studying alchemy. It doesn't offer much in the way of healing."

"Let me focus on the healing," Omaira said. "I have studied it more extensively than you."

"We're on the run," Ico added. "Which means she can't stay off her feet the way she has to. Sometimes, you just got to live with your injuries."

Omaira and Izara shot angry looks at him, which Celestia found amusing.

Down and down they went, winding back and forth along the side of the mountain, and moving farther into the south. The scenery was harsh and unchanging: the gray of the mountain range, the brilliant blue of the sky. Celestia often rode on the top of the carriage alongside Omaira. She liked the solidity of Omaira's presence, and she didn't want her baby breathing in the stale air of the carriage. He would have an outdoorsy life, like his father.

"You're worried about the baby," Omaira said, one bright freezing day when Celestia had joined her on the top of the carriage.

The statement startled Celestia out of her thoughts—about Lindon, about Lord Kjari. "Aren't all mothers?" she said.

"I can fix something for you," Omaira said. "Kajan mothers eat it, to give their babies strength." She nodded down at Celestia's stomach. "The Atharé Desert will be difficult. You want your baby to be as strong as he can be."

"He?" Celestia said. "You seemed to think the baby was a girl before."

Omaira smiled, twisting her mouth and showing her teeth. "That was before the signs started," she said. "You're carrying high. And your right breast is larger than the left."

Celestia gasped, felt her face turning hot. She crossed her arms over her chest.

Omaira laughed. "You humans are too protective of your bodies. But yes, I think you're carrying a boy. And I'll make sure he's a strong boy. A warrior." She nodded.

"I'm not sure I want a warrior for a son," Celestia said. The idea discomfited her—noblemen didn't become warriors. She would have no idea how to care for him, how to make him happy. It occurred to Celestia then, sitting beneath that impossibly wide sky, that before the Lady of the Seraphine, her life had been really quite small.

"A warrior is a blessing," Omaira said. "Strength is a blessing." She sounded as if she were reciting words she had learned a long time ago.

That night, Omaira returned from covering their tracks with a bouquet of small, fragrant flowers. She settled into her place by the fire and began shredding the flowers and dropping them into her pouch. Izara stared at her, frowning.

"What is she doing?" she whispered to Celestia.

"I'm making a tea for Celestia's baby," Omaira said. She looked up at them through the firelight. It cast eerie shadows across the sharp lines of her face. "For strength." She turned back to the flowers.

Celestia felt a tight happiness in the center of her chest. "Yes," she said. "Thank you."

"A tea?" hissed Izara. "What kind of tea?"

"For strength," Celestia repeated. She watched Omaira work. "To keep the baby safe when we get to the desert."

Izara studied her for a long time, but didn't say anything. For that, Celestia was grateful.

Izara woke with a start. Iomim's Treasure was buzzing inside her chest, a constant hum like the drone of a bee. She pressed her hand to her heart and a surge of magic rippled against her palm.

She gasped, jerking her hand away. Only then did she realize the carriage wasn't moving. Celestia and Ico both slept, oblivious to the magic charging the air. It felt as if she had crossed over into the Aetheric Realm, but they were still firmly in this world.

We're here, Izara thought. The books she'd read as she prepared for the trip had barely mentioned the magic. Yet it was everywhere, seething on the air itself.

Izara pushed open the carriage door and peered outside. It was still dark out—Omaira had insisted they travel through the night. The landscape had already been starting to change, the rocks giving away to rough, grainy sand.

A wind kicked up, sudden and fiercely cold. They had moved south from the mountains, into the lower parts of the continent, where winter settled for part of the year. For a moment sand glittered in swirling patterns in the moonlight, and then it washed over Izara, stinging her eyes and coating her clothes.

"Gods and monsters!" she cried, spitting to get the sand off her tongue. She spilled out of the carriage and shoved the door shut. The wind gusted again, bringing up more glittering sand before fading as abruptly as it had begun. The stillness draped over the landscape like a blanket.

"Gales," Omaira said.

Izara jumped, her heart pounding. She whirled around until she spotted Omaira a few paces away, sitting on a rock and sharpening the blade of her knife. Her red torch glowed beside her, but it didn't cast enough light for Izara to see by.

"I know," Izara snapped. "I read about them."

Omaira smiled, swiped her whetstone over the vicious curves of her knife. Its blade glinted red. "So did I."

Izara stepped around to the other side of the carriage, out of sight of Omaira. The magic swirled around her like the sand, as harsh and cold as the desert itself. She wasn't sure she could control it. The magic of the Seraphine was subtler, safer. A pet cat grooming itself on a silk cushion. This magic was like a wild animal.

Or like a kajan.

A chill rippled down Izara's spine. Was this the magic that had created the kajani? This wild chaos spilling through the night?

The thought turned Izara's stomach even as it fascinated her. She crept to the front of the carriage, to where the alpacas were sleeping huddled together beneath a rough-hewn blanket. Omaira's torch glowed in the distance, and there was the *snick snick* as she sharpened her blade.

"What do you want?" Omaira called out.

Izara jumped. The question wavered on the tip of her tongue: *This is the place where your kind were made, wasn't it?* But she lost her nerve.

"Why did we stop?" she asked instead, kneeling beside the alpacas. She stroked the top of one's head, the fur soft against her fingers.

"We're in the desert." Omaira stood up, shoved the knife back in her belt. She was little more than a silhouette against the starry sky. "From what I understand of this place, it's guarded by wards. Ancient ones. My hope is that they'll at least the delay the Starless Mages."

"They didn't keep us out," Izara said.

"But you can feel them, can't you?" Omaira's brow furrowed with concern. "I need your help to understand all this chaos. Otherwise, we'll never find His Lordship."

Izara hesitated. "I can feel—magic," she said. "Intense magic. I would need to go into a trance to even begin to understand what's going on with it." And even then, Izara wasn't sure she could.

"I don't think you'll need to understand it completely." Omaira's voice was much closer. When Izara looked up she was standing on the other side of the alpacas. She moved so quickly, so quietly. It was unnerving. "But just enough that I can show you the signs."

Another gale blasted across the desert, bringing with it not only sand but a surge of that wild magic. It lit up Izara's bloodstream and she gasped, tumbled backward in the sand. The blood rushed through her head; Iomim's Treasure pounded inside her heart. The stars spun overhead, a cosmic dance like gazing upon the faces of the Airiana.

And then, as quickly as it had come on, it vanished again, leaving them in that deafening stillness.

"Lord Kjari's magic," Omaira said. "It has its full strength here."

No one at the Academy had ever talked in terms of magic belonging to one person—even the Airiana's magic came from the world. Because all magic was part of the world, a path of knowledge. It required study and diligence and devotion, assuming one was blessed with Iomim's Treasure. At the Academy they had explained the Treasure as an ability to see beyond the surface of things, to comprehend the hidden truths of the universe.

And yet this magic, out here in the desert, was different. Izara could sense that deep down in her bones.

She stood up, dusting the sand from her clothes. The sky was turning gray, the stars were starting to fade. The others would wake up soon.

"What will you need me to do?" Izara trembled, nervous and excited all at once—a bit like she'd been her first day at the Academy.

"You can understand his magic in ways I can't," Omaira said calmly.

"Iomim's Treasure," Izara murmured.

"Whatever you want to call it." Omaira shrugged. "I've only studied healing magic, and I was terrible at it regardless. If you can unravel the—" She paused, like she was trying to find the words.

"The alchemical fomulas." Izara's heart thudded. "The foundation of reality here."

"Yes!" Omaira smiled. "You'll see the map His Lordship laid out for those who know the way. I can tell you what to look for."

The magic thumped in the back of Izara's head. The curiosity burned inside of her. She lifted one hand. Concentrated on the magic thrumming in the air. A simple formula— a heat globe. Practically a parlor trick, really.

She murmured the words under her breath. A light pulsed in the air above her open palm. She willed it to grow, and the light brightened and expanded. Warmth spread across her face. It felt like ordinary Seraphine magic.

But then power jolted up Izara's spine, and the heat globe

turned white hot and exploded in a flash as bright and furious as lightning. Izara flew backwards. She landed hard in the sand; the air slammed out of her. At first everything was white and hot. Her ears rang. Sweat dripped down her forehead.

And who is this? said a voice like sand scraping against skin.

Izara screamed and flung herself away. The heat globe extinguished into a wisp of smoke, and Izara collapsed on the ground, that terrible voice echoing in her head.

Voices rang out, chiming, fading, swelling. Izara blinked. Sat up. The door to the carriage flew open and Ico leapt out, fists up.

"What the hell was that!" he shouted.

"Izara helping us to find our way," Omaira said.

Their voices sounded fuzzy and far away. Izara pushed up to her knees. Her whole body was shaking. Her palm stung like she'd held it too close to the fire—and she supposed she had.

"What were you doing?" Ico demanded.

"I just—" Izara took a deep breath and pushed herself to standing. "It was an experiment. But I heard—I *heard*—" She trembled uncontrollably, her muscles aching with the strain of holding her upright.

"You heard him." Omaira's voice was close to her ear. "Didn't you?"

"I don't know!"

Celestia had slipped out of the carriage, one of the rough blankets wrapped around her shoulders. She squinted at Izara. "Izzie?" she asked. "What's going on?"

"Nothing!" Izara cried. "It was nothing."

"She's helping us find his Lordship," Omaira said. She turned back to Izara, who shrank away. "As we discussed when we came to our agreement."

"Oh," said Celestia. "Of course."

And who is this?

The voice was an echo inside Izara's head. And yet she could sense its direction, as if it were the wind. It was a southerly voice, like a southerly wind, biting and cold and bringing the chill of death into the marrow of her bones.

"Gods and monsters," Izara whispered.

Omaira smiled.

"He's in the south," she said.

~

The sunrise didn't bring any heat. The sun itself seemed far away, a tiny knot of light in the pale sky. Izara decided to walk alongside the alpacas, now that the ground was flat and smooth with sand. She wanted time out in the thick, magic-choked air. Her scholar's curiosity had gotten the best of her.

Their little caravan was making its way west, toward the sea. Traveling by foot would be difficult, if not impossible, especially with the Starless Mages tracking them across the desert—wards or not, they all agreed they shouldn't take any chances. Omaira had suggested they make their way to one of the seaside villages and procure a ship. She'd peered at Ico as she'd said that, and Celestia had smiled and covered her mouth with her hand.

"You mean steal a ship," Ico had said.

"We don't have much money," Omaira replied. "Or anything to barter."

"Don't act like you've never stolen a ship before," Celestia said. "I remember those stories you told me at that public house in Port Istai."

The mention of Port Istai had sent Izara's thoughts tumbling backwards. A million years ago, she had stepped off the riverboat at the port in Istai. A million years ago, this journey was just beginning.

Ico had grumbled, saying of course he'd stolen a ship before, but with other *pirates*, other *sea men*.

Omaira said the closest village was called Entai, and that they should arrive there by nightfall. But the sun was nearly at its zenith and Izara didn't see any sign of civilization. There was, in fact, no sign of anything alive. Just the sand and the patterns etched into it by the wind. Even the magic on the air had the sharp shock of death about it, a kind of cold emptiness at the core of its chaos. Izara had been meditating on the magic for hours and still couldn't come to an understanding of it. Nor had she heard the voice again. She needed to go into the Aetheric Realm, see the magic from the underside. The thought of doing so out here made her heart hammer inside her chest.

They stopped to rest and ate the last of the tubers and the strips of meat from their trip down the mountain. "Be careful," Omaira said as she passed around a skein of water. "We're running low and won't have more until we get to Entai."

As Izara drank, she realized how thirsty she'd become. She was used to the liquid heat of the Seraphine. Here the air was devoid of moisture, but the cold tricked her into thinking she was comfortable. She had to shove the skein away before she drank all the water herself.

"How much longer are we going to rest?" she asked.

Omaira hesitated. "A bit more," she said. "This place is rough on the alpacas. And on—" She rubbed idly at her temple.

"Are you all right?" Celestia asked, leaning forward, putting her hand on Omaira's arm.

But Omaira swatted her away. "I'm fine," she said. "Just His Lordship's magic moving through me."

She didn't look fine, Izara thought. Her eyes had a glassy sheen, and the dark tattoos on her skin seemed even darker. "It's affecting you," Izara said. "The magic. It makes you sick? I thought it created you. Or, your kind, I mean. Kajani."

Celestia gave Izara a dark look: *You're being rude.* Then she turned back to Omaira. "Is there anything I can do help? You've been so kind to me, it's only fair that I—"

"There's nothing you can do," Omaira snapped. When Celestia blanched, her expression softened a little. "I was not raised in the magic, like those who serve his Lordship. I have not developed my immunity yet." She rubbed her head again. "We'll rest a little longer."

"Perhaps you should lie down," Celestia said. "If only we had honey and green leaf tea! That would fix you right up."

Omaira gave her a sad smile. "Not for this, it wouldn't. But I appreciate your efforts." Then she stood up and hunched across the sand.

Celestia and Izara watched in silence as she moved away from them. Izara was intrigued by this new development. Magic that created and sickened. Or not sickened, she thought—*decayed.*

The magic of Decay was not meant to create life. Izara shivered. She wondered how incapacitated Omaira could get.

"Do you really think it's the magic?" Celestia asked, turning toward Izara. "It's not making you sick."

Izara shook her head. "It won't. It's not a part of me the way it is her."

Celestia sighed. "I'm worried about her. I'm sure there's something we can do. Some kind of herb or something— perhaps Ico would know something?"

"Why would Ico know of anything?" Izara laughed.

"He's a pirate! He knows some herbal remedies. It's worth *asking.*" And then she bustled away, off to the edge of the encampment, where Ico was stretched out on the sand.

Izara sat for a moment. Now that she was alone, she could feel the magic more strongly, stirring the air. She wanted to know more. She only hoped going into the Aetheric Realm wouldn't affect her like the magic was affecting Omaira.

She walked behind the carriage, where she would have privacy, and sank down onto the hard sand. Took a deep breath. All the discomfort of the desert—the harsh winds, the cold, the gritty sand that had made its way into her clothes—helped her to focus her attention. And from there, it was easy to find her way inside.

She felt a quiver of fear, at what she might be plunging into. But she shoved it aside.

At first, she felt the magic pulsing in time with Iomim's Treasure, as she had when they first crossed the border into the desert. She focused on that pulse, counting the beats the way she'd learned, allowing it to drag her more deeply toward the Aetheric Realm. There was a resistance, one she wasn't used to, as if the Realm were separated from her world by a membrane. But she directed her thoughts and she pushed through.

The world fell away.

Izara opened her eyes and she saw the desert from the underside. The carriage was gone; the others were gone, except for a dark shadow where Omaira was standing.

She focused on the Realm. Here, the sands were a dull gray; the sky was a maelstrom of black clouds and white lightning. As Izara watched, the lightning forked down and struck the earth and the sand ignited as if it were coal. The fire burned blue without giving off heat, and Izara felt the crackle of the magic in her bloodstream. *Transformation,* she thought.

And then her mind flooded with images, one after another, blinking by so quickly she could hardly make sense of them. A dead bird squirming with maggots. A man's face decaying into muscle, into bone, into dirt from which flowers blossomed. A fire tearing through the forest, turning the land to ash so rich with nutrients Izara knew the trees that grew there would be taller than before, thicker, greener, that their fruit would be more plentiful. She saw a decadent civilization razed to the ground by an invading army; she saw the survivors finding solace in a cave where they told stories of their defeat and from those stories grew into a new army, stronger than any had seen before. She watched people die. Animals die. Plants die. She watched oceans dry up to become deserts where insects crawled and ate the salt on the sand. She saw a sun burn so brightly that it extinguished itself, plunging the world into a darkness from which new life blinked, slowly, hesitantly—

And then she saw a man shrouded in shadow. *You haven't found me yet,* said a coarse voice inside her thoughts.

A bright light slammed in the back of her head. She gasped in air. For a long time she couldn't see anything, just a buzzing darkness. Then, distantly, she heard her name.

Izara, Izara, wake up! Gods and monsters, what's happened to her?

Celestia.

"I told you," she said, her voice thick. "Not to disturb me."

This wasn't how you were supposed to come out of a trance. Izara forced herself to concentrate on the sound of Celestia's voice as it grew louder and louder. And the world grew brighter, sharper. She felt the sand in her clothes. Felt the gust of cold wind. Her eyes fluttered, and then she could see.

"Oh thank the gods!" Celestia cried, pulling Izara into an embrace. "You're alive."

"Of course I'm alive." Her voice still felt sticky in her mouth. "I was in a trance, trying to connect with Kjari again."

"Did you?" Omaira, standing a few paces away. She seemed steadier, although her face was still ashy, her expression nervous. Ico stood beside her, his arms crossed over his chest.

"You looked like a fucking corpse," he said.

"Hush, Ico, that's not useful." Celestia pulled away from Izara and brushed at her hair. "Are you all right? I was afraid that you had gotten sick, too!"

"I'm fine." Izara stood up and found her limbs were shaking. A corpse? She shouldn't have looked dead. But this was the magic of death. That much was clear from her trance. She might not have learned much else—she hadn't teased out a single formula—but she had learned that. And for the first time since she'd left the Academy, she felt that familiar excitement of learning something new. "I did connect with him again. I have some insight into his magic, I think. But he wouldn't reveal his location. We should just keep going south."

Celestia helped Izara walk to the carriage, which was already hitched to the alpacas. Their resting site was cleared away. Izara felt a burst of dizziness—how long had she been under?

"Get in the carriage," Celestia said. "I'm not letting you walk. I *knew* that would be dangerous."

Izara didn't argue. She clambered inside and settled among the rough blankets, relieved to be able to sit. Just walking a few paces across the sand had exhausted her. She leaned against the back of the carriage as Celestia and Ico climbed in beside her.

"Omaira says we should still make it to Entai by nightfall," Celestia said, not to anyone in particular. Ico gave a snort.

"Let's just hope we can find ourselves a boat," he said. "It's not as easy as the kajan thinks."

"We're not in the Seraphine."

"Are you kidding? It would be easier in the Seraphine. If the village is as small as she's making it out to be, we'll be lucky to find a boat that can even take us that far south. Waters are choppy down there."

425

"Well, it's not as if we have much choice."

They went back and forth, rehashing the same arguments they'd made that morning. Izara closed her eyes and let their voices wash over her. The bickering was soothing, after the anxiety of the trance. Bickering meant they were alive. And all Izara wanted was to be around living things.

The cart jolted forward. They were on their way. Izara kept her eyes closed, but she didn't dare let herself sleep.

~

They did not make it to Entai by nightfall. Omaira's calculations of the distance, it turned out, had been completely wrong.

"I knew it wouldn't be that easy," Ico muttered when she finally relented to let them stop for the night.

Celestia hushed him, not that Omaira could have heard him—she was up ahead, leaning against the carriage, looking weak again. Ico sighed. Of course the desert she was supposed to be guiding them through would turn out to make her sick.

Fortunately, in the morning, Omaira seemed much better. Still, they traveled for the better part of the day, arriving at the edge of the village when the sun was bright and high overhead. Ico was walking alongside the carriage—he didn't think he could spend another second in its stifling confines, the air stale and cold.

He saw the sea before he saw the village. It was a glimmer beneath the brilliant paint strokes of the sky, dots of sparkling light that he took for the lanterns of some encroaching army. But then Omaira pulled on the alpacas, bringing them to a halt, and stood up on the driving seat and peered straight ahead. That was when Ico saw them, too, the little stone huts jutting out of the sand like teeth.

"This is it," he said. "This is the whole village." And despite himself he felt a sinking in his stomach. He'd warned the sisters they weren't likely to find a boat out here but he hadn't quite let himself believe it—easier to hold on to hope when you didn't speak it out loud. But seeing the size of this place he knew he'd been stupid.

Omaira jumped off the carriage and thumped on the door. "We're here!" she shouted, and the door opened and Celestia stuck her head out, the wind whipping her hair into her face.

"That's it?" Celestia said, an edge of disappointment in her voice.

"Told you," Ico said. "A day late for nothing."

They made their way over the sand. Celestia crawled up to the top of the carriage and sat there with her arms wrapped around her chest. Izara didn't show herself.

In the middle of the day, Ico expected to see wives caring for their homes, expected to see smoke from the hearth fires rolling out of the chimneys of the little huts. But the village remained still. He frowned, tugged at his coat.

"I don't like this!" he called out.

Neither Omaira nor Celestia answered him.

"The place looks deserted," he said, shouting a little louder.

"I agree," Celestia said.

The wind picked up. Ico cursed and ducked his head, his eyes stinging from the blowing sand.

They made it to the village's edge—a row of stones marking the boundary between the village and the desert, a rickety stone arch with the name *Entai* carved in big blocky letters jutting out of the sand. And the houses on the other side of that wall were dead empty.

"Stop!" he shouted. "I don't like this!"

"I don't either," Celestia said. She looked at Ico. "Is it—is the aberration?"

"No," Ico said. "There would be—growth. Plants."

"In the desert?"

427

"Trust me," he said.

A loud bang echoed out across the desert. Ico whirled around, his muscles tensing, and found Izara spilling out of the cart, her eyes wild.

"Something's wrong in the magic!" she screamed. "Something's—"

A hot wind swept down out of the village, jarring in the freezing desert. Ico whirled around just as Omaira pushed Celestia back toward her sister, who had fallen to her knees and was clutching her head. He glanced at Omaira. At least she didn't seem sick.

"What's going on?" he said, the wind blustering against him. It didn't smell like the sea, or like the desert. It smelled like wet soil. Like blood.

"I don't know." Omaira pulled her sword as if she could somehow go into battle against the wind.

"Is it the Starless Mages?" he asked, scanning the village. There was no sign of them, though, no fluttering black cloaks or sleek horses.

"It's her!" Izara screamed.

"Who?" Ico twisted around to see Izara gone ashen and shaking, her eyes wide with terror.

Beside him, Omaira gasped.

He whipped back around. The wind was still howling. That was when he saw something move in the village. It was too big to be a human being.

"What is that?" He edged closer to Omaira. "Is that one of yours?"

He knew it wasn't. The shape was too big to be a kajan, too.

"I don't know what that is," she murmured. "Only that it's not part of Kjari. It feels—"

The shape lumbered into the village center, a monstrosity rising nearly ten feet tall. It walked with a strange, loping gait, and the scent of blood rolled off it, and Ico was suddenly certain he was going to die.

"Children of the Seraphine," it said in a voice that sounded like a thousand voices.

With each step it took, the ground shuddered, and as it approached, Ico could see that its form was an amalgamation of muscle and sinew and flowers and vines and fur and feathers. And it was a woman, voluptuous and strong.

He had a flash of a statue in his head. A voluptuous woman, wrapped in flowers.

"Ancestors help me," he breathed.

She stopped, the ground stilling, and gazed down at them. The flowers on her body were constantly blooming, Ico realized, and her heart, nestled between her breasts on the outside of her skin, pumped feverishly fast.

"So you are the ones River has selected," she said in her clamorous voice.

That was when Ico knew for certain. This creature was Growth.

It was Growth, and she was endlessly growing.

She knelt down in the sand, her movements slow and laborious. Plant matter shed from her as she moved and began to grow up in the sand, vines curling and blossoming in spirals. "I had hoped I would find you here."

Her gaze shifted, past Ico and Omaira, and Ico knew she was looking at the two sisters. "A baby," she said. "Growing so healthily. How appropriate."

"Are you here to help us?" Ico asked, the words ashy on his tongue.

Her eyes moved back to him.

"I am becoming what the world will become," she said. "Cancerous and undying. Without my twin. He abandons me."

Ico trembled. Omaira stared open-mouthed.

"I sense him. Near." She lifted her hand and pointed toward the south. "You are the ones. I will help you. He will not let me close but he will let you. A kajani, three humans. He will not know."

She rose up, blood and blossoms pooling around her. "Come close," she said. "All. Come close."

Neither Ico nor Omaira moved. He was struck down in shock, and the kajani looked terrified. But then he heard a shuffling behind him, and the two sisters were stumbling forward, clinging to each other.

Growth smiled. "I need him," she said. "I need the death he brings to the world."

Celestia and Izara came to a stop between Ico and Omaira. All four of them stared up at Growth, who should be beautiful in her fertility, and not horrific.

"I have made you a boat," she said. "Sail it to the south. The mage will know when to stop."

Ico looked over at Izara, who was trembling.

And then Growth reached down and scooped up both sisters, one in each massive, bleeding hand, and set them on her shoulders, nestled on patches of moss. Ico braced himself as she turned toward him and Omaira and then gasped as her fingers curled around his waist, lifting him off the sand.

Ico shrieked and kicked, the desert spinning beneath his feet. The scent of blood and fresh flowers was overwhelming, a steely sweetness that made his stomach lurch.

Growth lumbered through the village, kicking up sprays of dirt. Ico slumped in her hand, clinging to her fingers, and peered down at the little stone houses. Even from up here, he could see that they were abandoned. Entai was a ghost town. A dead place.

Not that it was staying that way. Plants sprouted in Growth's footsteps, thick, glossy green leaves that sprawled through the village. Up ahead, sunlight flashed on the surface of the ocean, and Ico saw the boat—a ship made of living wood, the masts flowering trees, the sails the webs of silk worms.

Growth splashed into the water, surf crashing around her legs. She set Ico down on the deck of the boat, and when she pulled her hand away, his clothes were soaked in a red liquid like blood. She set Omaira down beside him. The poor thing looked stricken.

The cart came next, the alpacas bleating in fear. Then Celestia, her face wet with tears, and then finally Izara, who had the dazed look of a mystic.

Growth straightened up. Somehow she had gotten taller. So tall she cast a shadow on the ship.

"Go south." A thousand voices shouting as one. "Find him. I cannot keep going on like this."

She stepped backward through the water, shedding skin and flower petals, and for a long time none of them could move, only lay there on the deck of the ship that rustled like a forest, their bodies covered in the viscera of Growth.

———

Celestia and Izara stood at the bow of Growth's ship as it drifted into the ink of the ocean. They had both cleaned themselves as best they could with the flat, silky leaves that grew improbably from the ship's railing, using them likes rags wet with saltwater.

"It's so enormous," Celestia said softly. She had grown used to the huge empty sky of the desert, but at sea it seemed to sink into the water, to bleed together into a vast swell of emptiness. She gripped the rough bark of the railing and leaned into the frigid wind blowing off the water.

"The magic feels different," Izara said. "More like what I'm used to."

They were avoiding any talk of Growth. Of the horror she was. Or the horror she had become. It hurt to dwell on.

And so Celestia breathed in the cold salt of the air. She'd spent her entire life aboard boats—but only river boats, small and steam-powered, chugging up and down the Seraphine, with land always in view. She had never sailed on the sea. Neither had Izara.

They stood in silence for a few moments. The baby moved. Celestia was still getting used to it, like an ocean wave rippling inside of her. Ico had told her that it should be a week's time before they arrived at the southern tip of the continent. From there, Izara would go into another trance and find the signs to lead them to Lord Kjari.

All of them, avoiding any talk of Growth.

That night Celestia and Izara slept in spiderwebs as thick and soft and big as hammocks. There was no sign of the spiders that had created them, for which Celestia was grateful. There were only so many horrors she could manage in one day.

A thin layer of seawater sloshed across the floor beneath them, and Celestia woke in the middle of the night and couldn't fall asleep. She lay in her hammock, listening to the soft back-and-forth whisper of the water on the floor, and wondered if Growth's touch had warped the baby.

The baby kicked, as if reassuring her. Celestia moved her hand to her belly. *Shhh,* she thought, and then she pictured Lindon's face. When they reached the southern part of the continent, she would be closer to Lindon than she'd been since the Aikha Ruins. She wondered if he'd received her message. Maybe he wasn't in the south anymore at all. Maybe he had finally come to realize that his mission put the whole world at risk.

The next day was as bright and cold as the previous. Ico did most of the sailing, standing by the ship's flower-covered wheel and squinting at the place where the shore met the horizon. Omaira took over when he needed a break and tended to the sails when he needed them shifted. Celestia spent most of the day wrapped in silkworm webs that Omaira cut down from the masts, sitting along the side of the boat and watching the shore drift by. The enormity of the night before seemed like a dream, and she realized this wasn't a true ocean-going experience, was it? Not with the land always shining in the distance, the golden sand glimmering in the sunlight.

They sailed on. Nothing seemed to change. Not the land, not the sky, not the green-glass water sloshing along the side of the boat.

That evening Omaira cooked some fish she had caught during the day, steaming them in the ship's leaves.

The smoke from the fire drifted up into the darkening sky. Omaira had built it into a little alcove in the deck that she told Celestia was a firepit—"To keep you warm," she said, smiling in that way she did, where she showed her teeth.

"To keep you warm, too," Celestia said.

Omaira snorted. "I don't need it. Kajani have hotter blood than humans." But she sat beside the fire with Celestia anyway, hunched forward, her face intent in the firelight. It reminded Celestia of the carvings that decorated houses built in the Kjarin style. Scowling stone kajan faces that glowered down at the people below. Although they had frightened her as a child, they were supposed to bring good luck. They were supposed to be protectors.

She looked at Omaira now and didn't feel frightened at all.

"Are you feeling better?" she asked.

Omaira nodded. "My immunity is growing."

Celestia nodded. A moment later, Omaira spoke, still looking into the flames. "How's the baby?"

Celestia pressed her hand to belly, thought she felt a flicker of movement. "I haven't noticed anything wrong." But saying that aloud, her voice was thin and unconvincing. How did she know? Just being out here, on the sea, in the desert, meant something was wrong. She was shaping her baby into the wrong form.

"If you feel well, then the baby's well," Omaira said. "Although that won't be the case for much longer." She peered down at Celestia's belly with such intensity that Celestia's cheeks warmed. "You'll be moving into the later stages soon enough, from the looks of it. For kajani women, that's the most difficult time."

Celestia looked down at her hands. "It can be the same for human women. I had hoped to be back home in Cross Winds before then, but—" Her voice trailed away and she gazed at the fire. She could feel Omaira staring at her.

"I can make another tea that will help you."

Celestia looked up. "You have the ingredients on the boat?"

Omaira didn't say anything for a long time, and Celestia was afraid that she had misspoken, had insulted her somehow. But then Omaira said, "I brought them with me. It's brewed from the rhakora flower, and I found some growing in the forest while I was making my plans for your rescue."

Celestia's heart pounded inside her chest. She could barely breathe. "You brought some with you?" she said softly. "For me?"

Omaira shrugged. She stared down at the fire. "I thought I might make your experience more comfortable, if I could. This fish is almost ready." She leaned into the fire, reaching for the folded-up leaves with her bare hand. She picked them up as if it were nothing, as if they hadn't been sitting in the flames all this time. "Are you hungry?"

Celestia nodded, even though Omaira wasn't looking at her. Omaira unwrapped the leaves with a hiss and a billow of smoke, revealing a pile of white, flaky fish.

"It smells delicious," Celestia said, but she was still thinking about the rhakora flower, about all the small kindnesses Omaira had bestowed on her since they'd first laid eyes on each other in the train to Bloodvine, trying to fit them into a pattern she understood.

⁓

They dropped anchor four days later, sometime in the afternoon, when the sun was high and bright in the frozen sky. Ico and Omaira brought the boat in as close to the shore as they could, but there was no dock here, only an empty stretch of sand marked by an outcropping of rocks worn smooth by the elements. As they drifted in to the beach, Izara felt a surge of the desert's magic break through the haze of Growth's magic, like a dark spot growing inside of her.

"Can we be sure this is the place?" Celestia asked. She was kneeling on the deck, tying greens and smoked fish and root vegetables into knapsacks for the trip across the desert.

"Can't go any farther south without heading to Konmar," Omaira said.

"I can feel the desert's magic again," Izara said, drifting towards the railing. "I think we're closer." The sand stretched out from the shore, pristine and pale gold save for a smear of darkness against the beach. At the sight of it, a spark erupted inside Izara's head, and she slumped against the railing.

"Izara, are you all right?" Celestia's voice felt very far away.

"What do you see?" Omaira was closer.

Izara looked up at her. "There's something waiting for us."

Omaira tensed and looked out at the desert. Her eyes narrowed. "That's a rock."

Izara rubbed her head. The sparking felt stronger, and she could taste something like honey, cloying and decadent, in the back of her throat. "It's doing something to me," she muttered.

Omaira leaned over the railing. Then her eyes went wide. "The statue," she whispered.

As soon as Izara heard the word *statue*, an image came to her head. A statue, yes, carved of black stone, towering above the sand.

"A statue?" Celestia asked, moving closer to them.

"Five hundred years ago, during the height of Lord Kjari's empire, His Lordship marked his palace with a statue. It stood ten feet tall and greeted all his ships as they arrived home." Her eyes glittered, and she smiled a little to herself, showing her teeth. "It moved with his palace and would walk across the desert as he traveled, leaving footprints in the sand."

"I imagine that was a sight to see," Celestia said, smiling.

Omaira looked down at her, and her gaze softened.

Something squirmed in Izara's stomach. She still did not understand why Celestia had become friendly with the kajan.

"Omaira, I need your help with the raft," Ico shouted. "Celestia, how are those knapsacks coming?"

Celestia tied off one last knot and then stood up, her skirts swishing around her legs. Four knapsacks were laid out on the deck in a neat row. "There!" she called out over her shoulder. "Finished."

"Well, bring 'em over." Ico yanked on the vines tying a greenery-covered escape raft to the boat. "We want to get ashore and get our bearings before nightfall."

Celestia looked at Izara, then nodded down at the knapsacks. "Would you mind helping me?"

Izara nodded, although her thoughts were still with the image of that statue. Iomim's Treasure throbbed in her chest. Izara shivered with anxiety—and with excitement.

Celestia handed one of the knapsacks to Izara, which jarred her back into reality. She threw the knapsack over her shoulder. It was lighter than it should be. They were going back into the desert without the supplies they needed. But she looked at Celestia, her face set with determination, her belly swollen with child, and bit her tongue.

Ico and Omaira had dropped the raft down into the water. It floated indolently on the green waves, looking small and flimsy.

"Everyone take a bag," Ico said. "Omaira, you go down first, in case the ladies need help with the rope."

Omaira nodded, shouldered her bag, and swung her legs over the railing, moving with that heavy grace that still startled Izara when she saw it in action. It didn't take her long to climb down.

"I'll go next," Celestia said.

Izara nodded, resisting the urge to tell Celestia to be careful. Of course Celestia knew to be careful, for her sake and for the sake of the baby.

Celestia grabbed the thick, woody vine and crawled over the railing, her skirts tangling up in her legs. When Ico offered a hand to help her, she accepted it gracefully, even though Izara saw the tightness in her jaw that meant she was afraid of embarrassing herself.

It took Celestia much longer to inch down the vine. When Omaira grabbed her by the waist and swung her off, Celestia let out a delighted cheer. "I made it!" she cried.

Izara followed next. She didn't let herself look down, but instead fixed her gaze up on the empty sky. The way the boat rocked when she braced her feet against it reminded her of the treacherous mountain paths at the Academy, and she was struck by a sadness, a sense of loss. When she reached the raft, she let go of the vine and jumped, the way she had as a little girl, climbing trees at Cross Winds.

Ocean water sloshed over the edge of the raft and over Izara's boots. Celestia kept her skirts gathered up in two hands.

They waited in silence while Ico descended the vine, and when he was safely aboard, Omaira pushed off with the big rough-hewn stick that she had broken off from one of the tree-like masts. The water was calm, and the waves pushed them toward the shore in lurches and starts. Celestia gripped Izara's arm, and Izara kept her feet firmly planted on the raft, afraid of falling into the water.

When they hit the sand several paces from dry land, Omaira jammed the stick into the water and said, "We're walking from here." She took a deep, shuddering breath, and Izara suspected the magic was affecting her again, that whatever protection Growth's presence had leant was gone. She only hoped Omaira would stay well enough to lead them to the palace.

They splashed toward the shore in single file, unspeaking. Ico and Omaira went last, sharing the raft's weight. The wind whipped Izara's hair out of its braid, and the water was cold enough to sting when the waves splashed up around her calves.

The closer she drew to the shore, the more strongly Izara felt the strange magic of the desert. That statue, in reality lumpen and worn down over the years, loomed in her vision, the one dark spot in a canvas of blue and gold. When she splashed out of the water and onto the sand, the magic surged, and her heart stumbled, as if it had forgotten for a moment to beat. She could hear the others behind her: Ico cursing beneath his breath, Celestia squeezing the water out of her dress. But she didn't look at them. She stared at the statue, an uneasiness settling into the pit of her stomach. Images flashed in the dark parts of her mind: shriveled flowers dropping from a stem, the carcass of a panther sinking into the rich black soil of the desert.

She drifted toward the statue, trying to concentrate her focus. Magic pulsed on the air around her. There was a taste like rotting sugar in the back of her throat. She reached out with one hand and pressed her palm against the stone. It was warm, like a living thing, like a fever.

All around her was the strength of decay.

And she knew they were close.

TWELVE

"There's no way to bring the carriage ashore," Omaira said. "We can bring the alpacas with us, though."

Celestia pressed her hands to her baby and looked down at the sand. The wind howled and the waves rushed in ceaselessly to the shore. Ico sighed, put a hand on his hip. Izara wasn't even participating in the conversation. She stood over by the statue, gazing up at it. Celestia hoped she hadn't gone into another trance.

"So we'll have to walk," Ico said.

Omaira nodded. She didn't look terribly pleased about the arrangement, either.

"And we're bringing the alpacas again—why, exactly?"

Omaira gave a little growl under her breath. "Because we have a pregnant woman in our party." She paused. "And because we are running low on supplies and we may need them for food."

Ico scowled, kicked at the sand. "Fine. Go get the stupid things. Then we can be on our way." He squinted up at Omaira. "How long do you think it'll take?"

"I don't know. It'll depend on what Izara finds in the magic."

Ico sighed. "We're going to die in this desert."

"Ico, stop," Celestia said softly, running her hands over the swell of her baby, not wanting to hear such talk. But Omaira had already stalked off toward the raft. Celestia watched her go, shivering in the dirty rags of her dress. Funny how two weeks ago she had been wearing the finery of the court. It seemed like a dream. Maybe a nightmare.

The baby moved inside her belly, a circular motion she thought must be him turning over. What if she spent the rest of her life searching for the Lord of Decay? And what if she died without ever having found him? Would the obligation pass on to her baby, would this life of hopeless searching be the only life he knew?

She couldn't let herself think like this. It brought the sadness in, and that would affect the baby.

"Bet she kills us and cooks us up in a stew with the alpacas," Ico said.

Anger flushed in Celestia's cheeks. "Don't talk about her like that."

Ico rolled his eyes. Celestia turned away from him and watched Omaira as she rowed the raft back to the boat. Without the rest of them to weigh her down, she moved quickly, although Celestia noticed her pausing and rubbing at her head. That magic sickness again. If only there was something she could give Omaira to treat it.

Still it didn't take long for Omaira to fetch the alpacas and bring them, bleating and shivering, back to shore.

Omaira walked over to where the three of them sat in the sand around their knapsacks. She set the second alpaca down and it joined the other in butting at her side.

"We shouldn't wait," she said.

Ico nodded. Then he stood up and dusted the sand from his clothes.

Izara drifted away from the statue, lost in thought.

Celestia took a deep breath, and Omaira held out a hand to help her. Celestia was grateful—the swell of her belly was becoming more and more cumbersome. Still, she said to Omaira, "I'm fine. I can see you're feeling unwell again."

Omaira shook her head. "It will pass." Then she nodded at Celestia's belly. "The movement will be good for him. You'll see."

The kajani way was not the human way, but Celestia nodded. It wasn't worth the disagreement.

They set off.

The land here was flatter than the land they had sailed from, the sand packed down hard, no gentle slope of dunes rising and falling like ocean waves. The wind blew harder, too, slicing across the bare skin of Celestia's face. She wrapped her shawl around her head, tucking the ends into the collar of her dress, but the chill still vibrated through her body. They moved closer and closer to each other, until they were walking in a tight pack, the heat of their bodies uniting them. No one spoke. If Celestia opened her mouth, sand blew onto her tongue, rough and grainy.

Celestia pressed herself against Omaira and wrapped her arms around her belly. The tip of her nose burned from the cold, and her eyes watered, tears threading through her eyelashes. The landscape was bleak and unchanging save for the sunlight, which deepened in color as the day wore on.

But then they began to see the stones.

The stones were small and polished, and at first Celestia thought they might be a mirage, a trick her mind was playing on her to break up the monotony. The idea spun around inside her head, and she began to count the times she saw the stones. One, two, three—three times her mind betrayed her. The stones shone black against the golden expanse of the sand, and they were arranged in neat piles. Celestia obsessed over them, wondering what message her thoughts could be sending her—why show her these black stones in their little triangular piles? What madness was working its way into her thoughts?

When they passed a sixth pile, the largest Celestia had seen, she blurted, "Do you see those too?"

No one answered, and Celestia was afraid she had only imagined speaking. They had been walking in silence for so long that she had forgotten what any sound was like beyond the constant whine of the wind.

"Yes, I see them," Omaira says. "I believe they are the Xiroh stones. Izara, can you feel them?"

Celestia's relief came on so strong it made her dizzy. She glanced over at Izara, who had her head tilted down.

"So that's what that is," she mumbled.

"So you can?" Omaira's face lit up. "Why didn't you say something?"

"I didn't know what I was feeling," Izara grumbled.

Omaira chattered excitedly. "The Xiroh stones are a marker used by Lord Kjari's army. They're enchanted as well, and provide a circle of protection for the palace, from intruders and from the chaos of the magic of this place." She paused. "It means we're getting close."

Celestia's chest tightened. She was suddenly aware of the pain in her feet, the ache in her lower back. They were close, but what were they going to find when they reached their destination?

They walked on. The sky turned pink with the sunset and then purple with twilight. The stars came out.

"We should stop for the night," Omaira announced when it was almost too dark to see.

Ico let out a loud sigh. "Finally." He broke away from the group and tossed his bag on the sand. The alpacas lowed now that he had broken formation and were exposed to the frigid wind. Celestia reached over and patted the closest one on the head, rubbing her fingers over its soft velvety ears.

"We need a fire," Ico said. "And we'll need to stay close to each other. Best way to keep warm."

"I agree," Omaira said. Then she peered over at Ico. "I told you it wouldn't take long."

"We're not there yet," Ico muttered.

"Oh, will the two of you stop bickering and build the fire?" Celestia demanded. She was already shivering from standing still.

Omaira smiled at that, eyes sparkling, and then built a fire quickly, using wood from the ship that she had carried in her knapsack. It blazed hot and orange in the blue desert, and Celestia huddled close, the heat pressing in against her chest and face but leaving her back exposed to the cold. She picked at the dried meat from her knapsack and sipped from her water skein. Her feet, already swollen from the pregnancy, ached so much that the ache twisted up into her calves, and pain radiated out from the small of her back into her shoulders, around the side of her belly. But it felt good to sit, even on the cold sand.

For a long time the only sounds were the crackle of the fire and the occasional bleat of the alpacas. In the darkness, Celestia could see the others in silhouette—Ico eating, Izara sitting very still. Going into a trance, perhaps, although she didn't look dead as she had when she'd done it before. Maybe it was best that they didn't speak tonight. That they rest for whatever awaited them tomorrow.

Omaira began to move around the fire, the light refracting off her armor as she boiled water in a little metal pot. Steam rolled off it in thick curls. Celestia watched Omaira work. She thought she moved like the dancers Celestia had seen at the theater in Jaila-Seraphine, a million lifetimes ago. Lindon had sat with his arm around her shoulders, but she had been entranced by those dancers, by the musculature of their bodies beneath their flimsy costumes.

Omaira lifted the pot away from the fire and dropped something into the water, then stirred it around once. She walked over to Celestia and sat down beside her.

"It's for you," Omaira said, looking at the fire. "The last of the rhakora. You'll want all the strength you have for tomorrow."

Celestia lifted the pot. It was warm to the touch and the steam billowed around her face. She breathed in the scent of it and took a small, hot sip.

"Thank you," she said, closing her eyes against the steam. Her whole body ached, and she was afraid of what they would find tomorrow. But the baby was moving inside her, and the tea was warm, and she felt safe at Omaira's side.

~

More damn walking. Ico was sick of it. He was sick of the cold, which was empty and harsh without Xima's presence— that magic Omaira and Izara kept talking about was probably keeping her out. He was sick of the sand clinging to his skin and stinging his eyes. He was sick of the pitiful bleating of the alpacas, which trampled alongside him as he and the others made their way across the desert, a sad, miserable little caravan.

Every time Izara reported a new shift in the magic, Omaira swore that the palace was near. But nothing lurked on the horizon except the flat sharp edge of the desert. Even so, Ico walked alongside Izara in the hopes that she'd have some trance or vision, anything, to let him know this damned journey was almost over.

But she just trudged along like the rest of them, eyes down, the wind coating her clothes with a layer of sand.

Ico pulled his scarf around his mouth and glanced at her. "You see anything?" he said.

She didn't answer at first. He thought maybe she hadn't heard him. But then she looked up, squinting. "Something's— changing. There's this charge on the air." She shook her head, wiped at her mouth. Spat. "I think it's him. Decay. It's been strong ever since we started seeing those rocks."

So nothing had changed, then. Wind. Cold. Dust. Rocks. They walked.

The sun rose in the sky, sending out beams of clear white light that didn't do anything to cut through the chill. Ico sipped from his canteen and swallowed mud. He tried not to think about how they were going to die out here, their bodies lying where they fell, unmoving, until they were buried in sand.

At least they would likely *die* out here, he thought grimly. And stay dead. The wasting illness had not reached this place. Yet.

Izara let out a long, choking gasp and stumbled to the ground.

"Izara!" Celestia ran over to her sister and knelt down beside her and pushed her so that she lay on her back. Ico crowded over beside them, his heart pounding.

But Izara wasn't dead. Her chest rose and fell in a frantic rhythm, and her eyes flicked back and forth beneath her closed lids. Ico pressed his hand to her neck—her heartbeat was quick. Too quick, maybe.

"What's happening to her?" Celestia cried, twisting to look over her shoulder. "Do something! Help her!"

Omaira didn't move. She stood with her hands on her hips, her gaze fixed on some point in the distance. Not even looking at them.

"Maybe you shouldn't have trusted her after all," Ico murmured, knowing even as he said it that it was cruel.

"Shut up!" Celestia hissed. She shook Izara, pressed an ear to Izara's chest.

"We're here," Omaira said suddenly, her voice booming out over the desert, her eyes gleaming and bright. "I can sense him. I've never felt anything like this before."

Ico glared at her. "What are you talking about?" he snapped. "There's nothing but fucking desert as far as I can—"

The earth rumbled beneath him.

"What the fuck!" He leapt to his feet, braced his weight against the sand. The rumbling transformed into a low, steady drone. Celestia wrapped her arms around Izara and pulled her to her chest as the sand jumped and vibrated. It moved in rivers, swirling in upon itself like a water snake, twisting and curling and unfurling. Omaira finally—*finally*—strode over to them and knelt down beside Celestia and Izara. She lowered her head as if in prayer. And when she spoke, it was in a language Ico had never heard before, low and guttural and rough.

The sand fell away, revealing shining black stone. The wind howled.

Omaira chanted, calling forth those stone monsters of the earth.

Celestia let out a low, keening sound.

Ico wished he had his knife.

And then Izara screamed. She ripped away from Celestia's arms, jerked to her feet by some unseen force, her back bent and twisted, her face tilted toward the sky. Celestia lunged toward her, but Omaira put out an arm to stop her.

"What's wrong with her?" Ico demanded. "Did you bring us into some kajani trap?"

Omaira glared at him, her eyes sparking like black

flames. "I brought you to the Palace of His Lordship Isidore Kjari," she snarled. "It's not an easy place for humans to venture."

"What's happening to Izara?" Celestia asked in a meek, pitiful voice. Izara's feet had lifted from the ground, and she floated in mid-air, her scream bleeding together with the wind and the roar of the earth as the black mass forced itself skyward.

Omaira's expression seemed to soften. She smiled and said, "Her magic can protect you."

Celestia's eyes shone with tears. A knot twisted in Ico's belly as he watched the mass—the palace, he could see it was a palace now, carved stone towers and gaping dark windows—push out of the earth like new growth. Sand poured over it, kicking up clouds of dust. Izara's scream no longer sounded like a scream, but like a song, high pitched and wailing. The palace grew and grew, shooting up higher and higher into the sky. Ico had never seen a single tower so tall and he didn't understand how it could stand without toppling over.

And then the palace shuddered to a stop. Sand kept pouring off its sharp edges, but where the desert had once been was now a black palace.

Izara collapsed into the sand, her voice abruptly cut short. Celestia scrambled over to her and crouched over her body, brushing the hair away from her face. The palace loomed behind them, so dark it swallowed all the light.

"I made it," Omaira said, in a strange, flat voice. "I finally found him."

And then, a heartbeat later, she pulled her sword.

"I fucking knew it!" Ico said. He raced over to Izara and Celestia and planted his feet into a fighting stance before them. Except for the falling sand, the palace was completely still. It seemed empty. Abandoned.

Omaira strode over to them, sword pressed casually over her shoulder. Ico threw out his arms, his heart pounding.

"Omaira?" whispered Celestia. "What are you doing?"

The last of the sand slipped off the palace, and for a moment everything was as still as death. Not even the wind blew. Ico's muscles tensed, his eyes on Omaira.

The palace doors screeched open, the hinges howling like they hadn't been used in years. Terror rippled down Ico's spine. He wished he could call on Xima, bring her close to him.

Figures emerged, marching two by two. Kajani.

Omaira lifted her sword. Then she shouted something in that guttural language, a sharp, barking word.

The kajani answered in unison. It sounded like an animal's growl to Ico's ears. They kept marching forward, kicking up clouds of sand.

"What's happening?" Celestia asked. She clutched an unconscious Izara to her chest.

"Don't worry," Omaira said. "I will talk for us."

The kajani marched forward. There were ten, and they fanned out into a line as the approached Omaira. One of them wore a sweeping cape of dark purple, and Ico took him for the leader. When he jammed his spear into the sand the others did the same.

Ico's shoulders loosened a little. Maybe there wouldn't be a fight after all. But he knew he shouldn't let his guard down.

Omaira knelt on one knee. She lay her sword across the sand. Then she spoke in the kajani language, growls and barks. The kajan in the purple cape responded. Ico watched him closely, looking for signs of an attack. His hands moved as he spoke, one flicking toward the east, the other curling into a fist. He snarled and then spat once into the sand.

Omaira responded, gesturing at Celestia, who was watching with wide terrified eyes. The kajan leader studied her for a moment. Studied Izara. Then he fixed his night-sky eyes on Ico, and every part of Ico's body froze into place. But the kajan only studied him for a few seconds before turning back to Omaira. He barked what Ico hoped was a word of approval, and then he turned on his heel and led the others back into the open palace doors.

Omaira sighed and turned to the others with that smile that looked like a threat. "They're allowing us to stay in the palace." She paused. "The scryers have seen that a threat is coming, from the east." She tilted her head in the same direction the kajan leader had pointed. "A party of adventurers."

Her voice went flat when she said this, and she looked at the ground, away from Celestia. Celestia's eyes widened, and Ico thought he saw a recoil beneath her noblewoman's facade. But she recovered quickly enough, the way her kind always did.

"Let me talk to him," she said. "Please. I can warn him that the Emperor has misled him. I tried to send a letter from the palace but it probably didn't arrive in time."

"I don't know if they'll let you do that," Omaira said, and then she stood up and walked over to where Celestia still sat cradling Izara close to her chest.

"Why not?" Celestia cried. "He's my husband. I know I can make him understand."

Ico hoped that delusion made her feel better, because it certainly didn't him.

"I will speak to the general," Omaira said. "But I have as much sway here as you do. At least until I prove myself to His Lordship."

Omaira scooped Izara out of Celestia's arms and draped her over her shoulders. Izara moaned a little; her eyes fluttered.

"Is she going to be all right?" Ico asked.

"She needs rest," Omaira said. "Which she can get inside."

With that, she began walking toward the palace, following the track left in the sand by the kajani convoy who had come to greet them. Celestia stayed kneeling, watching them go. Ico knelt beside her.

"Are you sure you want to do this?" he murmured. "With Lindon coming?"

Celestia stared up at the palace. Her eyes were glassy, her lips parted. She had an air of desperation that reminded Ico of that night five years ago, as they rode down the Seraphine by the light of the moon.

"Do I have a choice?" she said.

Then she stood up and dusted the sand from her skirts. She walked toward the palace with her head high, as if she were conjuring up all the strength of her upbringing.

Ico sighed.

He followed. He wondered what was going to happen when Lindon and the rest of his party showed up. If they would listen. It was fantastical, wasn't it, this mad wizard of the past being a god—a feared god, a god spoken about in soft whispers.

Ico didn't want to think about Lindon's response. All men were the same when you got down to it, and if he were Lindon, if he'd spent months looking to kill a man of magic only to find that he had been tasked with killing a god—well, Ico wasn't sure he'd believe it, either. He wouldn't *want* to believe it.

Omaira and the alpacas were almost to the palace doors. Ico shouldered his bag and moved forward. His heart pounded. The palace stone was so black it swallowed the sunlight whole.

And he was about to pass willingly through those doors.

He hoped it would all be worth it.

~

Izara slept among the piles of silky sheets, her hair tousled and gritty with sand, her skin ashy. Celestia sat by the bed, watching her breathe. Omaira had said that Izara needed time, that she needed to sleep off the after-effects of Kjari's magic. "It drained her, finding him for us," she said.

They were in a guest apartment on the third floor of the palace. The rooms were cavernous and stark, the walls gray stone and the furniture simple metalwork lined with luxurious fabrics—silk sheets, brocade cushions. Huge windows looked out over the desert and let in beams of brilliant sunlight. Ico had vanished into the back of the apartment, and Omaira had left them for the palace proper. She said nothing about Lord Kjari, nothing more about the scryers who had seen the approach of Lindon and his adventurers. She didn't even explain how she had known to bring them to this apartment, that it was acceptable to lay Izara in this bed.

When Omaira had pulled her sword out in the desert, Celestia had been struck with a paralyzing terror. And although Omaira hadn't betrayed them then, Celestia did not trust the other kajani. She knew there was still a chance that they were only in this palace so the kajani could use them to lure in Lindon and the others.

A wave of despair wracked violently through Celestia's body; she closed her eyes to stave off the tears, took deep breaths of air. The feeling passed. But it left her numb. Empty.

Izara murmured something unintelligible.

"Izzie?" Celestia leaned over her, smoothing her hair away from her forehead. "Can you hear me?"

Izara mumbled again, tossed her head from side to side. Her lashes fluttered against her cheek. Her mumbling coalesced into a sharp, familiar name. *Kjari, Kjari, Kjari.*

"Yes," Celestia said, slumping back in her chair. "We've almost found him. Lord Kjari."

Izara fell silent. But in the sunlight, it seemed as if the color was returning to her cheeks. Celestia lay a hand on Izara's chest—her breathing was deeper, too.

Someone knocked on the door, a dull heavy pounding that reverberated around the cavernous room. Celestia stiffened, called out a tentative, "Yes."

"It's me."

The door swung open and Omaira stalked inside, a swath of shimmery fabric draped over both arms. "For you," she said. "And another for your sister, when she wakes. I thought you might want to change."

She laid the dresses at the foot of Izara's bed, then stepped back, her hands folded behind her back. There was a formality to Omaira's movements here that Celestia had never seen before. It made her uncertain how to speak to her.

"Thank you," Celestia said. "It will be nice to get out of these rags."

"I asked that the magic of the palace prepare a bath for you as well." Omaira gestured at the narrow hallway that led into the dark parts of the apartment. "It will be waiting for you when you're ready."

Celestia shivered at the thought of a place so infused with magic that it could draw baths of its own volition.

"Thank you," Celestia said, and then, because she was still worried about the possibility of betrayal: "I appreciate it very much. You doing all this for us."

She watched Omaira's expression, hoping to get a sense of her intentions. But Omaira only nodded. For a moment the room was silent save for the soft huff of Izara's breathing. Celestia twisted her fingers together.

"Have you been—allowed into the kajani army?" Celestia asked, unsure if that was the proper way to phrase the question.

"I've yet to prove myself to Lord Kjari." Omaira hesitated. "It seems—seems he does not wish to be seen."

"Oh," said Celestia. "Oh, I see—" Her own disappointment quivered inside her. Some part of her thought she might see Lord Kjari and beg him not to fight Lindon. That she might explain the situation.

"However." Omaira paused. "I will have an opportunity. When Lindon arrives."

Celestia felt as if the air had been let out. She slumped down in her chair. "What—I don't understand—"

But she did. Omaira looked away, her face unreadable.

Celestia closed her eyes to stave off tears. But in the darkness she just saw Lindon's face, golden and handsome as it had been that day she first saw him standing in the river.

Footsteps; a sudden presence beside her. Celestia opened her eyes and looked over at Omaira, who had knelt on the floor next to her chair. She gazed up at Celestia with her black eyes.

"I will not kill your husband," Omaira said. "He travels with two other men—it will be enough to dispatch them."

Celestia wiped at her eyes. The talk was gruesome, but there was something touching in it, too. That Omaira was willing to spare Lindon.

Tentatively, Omaira lay a hand on Celestia's arm. Her hand was bare, the first time Celestia had seen it without gloves. Her skin was softer than Celestia expected. "I've traveled so long for this opportunity to prove myself to His Lordship," Omaira murmured. "But I do not want to hurt you."

Celestia caught Omaira's gaze and felt something tremble inside her chest. "You shouldn't have to kill any of them," she said. "Let me talk to them first. Try to convince them. If I can talk him down, you'll still have protected Lord Kjari from harm. Which is all he wants."

Omaira studied her. "That is true," she said. Her hand was still on Celestia's arm, and Celestia never wanted it to move. "Perhaps I can propose it to the general."

Celestia nodded, something like hope flickering in her chest.

———

A bell clanged violently in Celestia's dreams, shattering the image into a million pieces. She gasped, and with a rush of air she was awake, tangled in the silk sheets of her bed. Moonlight spilled through the window, turning everything a cold hard silver.

The bells rang as if they were rioting.

Celestia shoved the blankets aside and leapt out of the bed. The bells clambered inside her skull. She rushed over to the moon-soaked window and threw open the doors and ran out onto the balcony that looked over the desert. It was an unthinking act; she had no way of knowing which direction Lindon would be coming in. And yet she saw a knot of kajani forming on the sand, preparing to fight.

She went back into her room and pulled on the dark shimmery gown Omaira had left for her yesterday. Her thoughts were in a tumble—had Omaira lied about speaking to the general? Or had he simply refused?

She ducked out of her bedroom and slammed into someone in the dark hallway. They let out a shout of protest. Ico.

"What the hell's going on?" he yelled, his voice still soft over the constant clanging of the bells.

"Lindon's approaching." Celestia rushed past him, into Izara's room. For a moment she just saw an empty bed, crumpled sheeting gleaming in the moonlight. But then a frigid wind brushed across her face, and she realized that Izara had finally woken up, that she was out on the balcony.

Celestia approached the balcony, the wind blowing her skirts. She hadn't buttoned her dress properly and her underdress, pale and creamy and embroidered with strange figures, spilled out into the moonlight. Izara stood at the balcony, staring out at the desert.

"Izara!" Celestia cried.

Izara turned to her. Her eyes were bright and clear, but she looked worn out. And sad.

"It's him," she said hoarsely. "Lindon."

"I know." Celestia felt hopeless. The kajani were stepping into a strange, circular formation. Was Omaira among them? It was too far away to see.

"He's going to die." Izara's voice had an uncanny echo to it, a tremor like she was speaking on the other side of a canyon. "I can feel death in this place."

Celestia went cold all over. Izara turned back to the desert.

"Enough of that." Ico guided her back inside. "She's still half in a trance."

"It's pointless," Celestia whispered. "Pointless for me to try and stop him. He didn't listen before. He's too focused on the Emperor's orders. He doesn't care about magic."

Ico gripped her shoulders and shook her, once, hard. She stared at him, and he regarded her with a sternness that didn't fit his personality.

"You can't listen to what your sister says." He shook her again. "Understand? Who the hell knows what nonsense she saw when she was under. But this is the present, the here and now. Go out and stop whatever Lindon is planning. Save your damn husband. We'll worry about Kjari later."

Celestia nodded dumbly. She need to save Lindon. Her husband, the father of her child. The reason she was trapped in this moment. One simple wish granted five years ago had brought her here.

She turned away from Ico and moved toward the door, smoothing her hair with her hands. Her husband would not be so brash as to ride up on the palace. He and his men were likely planning some kind of infiltration, similar to what Omaira did at the Emperor's palace. She just had to let him know that he was expected. And that he would get caught.

She was certain she remembered the way to the front of the palace—they had not been brought in very deeply, just up some stairs and down a hallway. The bells were louder outside the apartment, and her ears burned with the sound of them. The hallway was empty until she came to the staircase that led down to the main foyer of the palace. It was lined with kajani soldiers, gathering into formation.

She stopped, her heart pounding. It wasn't fair, all these soldiers against three men.

And she had to make her way through them. Without Omaira, without anyone to protect her.

She took a deep breath. Touched her stomach. The baby was still, but she knew he was there, all the actions she had taken in the outside world molding him into someone strange and unfamiliar.

"Protect me," she whispered, a prayer sent up to the Lady of the Seraphine. And then Celestia descended. She did not let herself drop her gaze. She kept it fixed on the carved stone doors gaping open at the base of the stairs. Even so, she could feel the kajani turning their eyes toward her. She could hear the guttural murmur of their voices. She lifted her chin. She took careful, regal steps. She knew that to them she was a pregnant woman, unskilled in battle or weapons or even basic strength, gliding into their midst in a gown the color of the night sky.

The kajani murmured in their rough, guttual language.

She reached the doorway and looked out at the moonlit desert.

"Lady Celestia," said a throaty voice. "You shouldn't be down here."

"How did you know my name?" For the first time, Celestia let herself look at the kajani—at this one kajan. It was a man, his face marked with scars, his black hair twisted with white. He wore gleaming armor, a scarlet cape. She wondered if he was a general.

"Omaira," he said, almost gently. "She shared your request to speak to your husband before his arrival at the palace."

"So why did you not call me?" Celestia drew herself up, trying to conjure all the power of herself. "I can convince him to stand down. Lord Kjari will be protected, so Omaira will have completed her task."

The kajan studied her for a long moment. "She told me," he said finally. "But it's a damned stupid idea. Those men came here for an assassination."

Celestia broke her rule and looked out into the room. All the kajani stared back at her with their blank soldiers' eyes. The room tilted. But she did not fall.

"Where is she?" Celestia asked. "Omaira?"

"Outside," the kajan general said. "Undergoing the rites of her dedication."

Celestia felt dizzy. "All she has to do is protect Lord Kjari. Please. Let me speak to my husband. Let me help her."

She was certain the general was going to have her dragged away, that she would be locked in her room to watch Lindon be slaughtered. But he grinned, and then laughed, a harsh kajani laugh that made her shiver.

"I can see why she likes you," the general said.

Celestia felt her cheeks warm.

"Come," the general said. "I'll give you the chance to speak to your husband first. But if it doesn't work—"

"It will work," Celestia said.

The general smiled grimly. "I'll accompany you to Omaira myself. Come." He held out one hand toward the door, and Celestia stepped outside. The cold wind blasted across Celestia's face, and she had to tilt her head down to stop the cold from burning her eyes. The moonlight bathed the world in silver, but torches burned in a circle up ahead, golden heat spilling across the sand.

The general led Celestia across the sand. Singing lifted up from the kajani, and as they approached, Celestia caught sight of Omaira in the center. She was dressed for battle, her hair covered by a helmet, her face painted with white streaks.

The general shouted something in the kajani language, and the singing stopped abruptly, and the kajani warriors turned toward them. When Omaira saw Celestia, her eyes went wide.

"Omaira Kjarankni!" the general shouted in Seran. "I have decided that you may attempt your original tactic, with the aid of our guest."

Omaira moved forward, her armor clanking. "Sir," she said. "Thank you." And then her eyes fixed on Celestia. They stared at each other, strangers for the first time in weeks.

"I won't let either of you die," Celestia said softly, hoping that none of the other kajani heard.

Omaira only smiled.

A cold wind blasted across them, bringing Celestia back to the present. She squared her shoulders, tried to ignore the weight of the gaze of the other kajani soldiers.

"Where is he?" she asked.

"He and his men have set up an encampment in the north," Omaira answered. "Our scryers tells us they plan to infiltrate the castle in the early dawn. We do not have much time."

"Then we should go now," Celestia said grimly.

They walked. Celestia had walked so much these last few weeks that it was as if she had never stopped walking, as if she had never had a few hours' respite in the palace of the Lord of Decay.

But then they crested a dune, and Omaira halted and pulled out here sword. Celestia stumbled to a stop, tripping over her skirts. "Where is he?" She couldn't see anything but shadows and moonlight and the rolling shapes of sand.

Omaira held up one hand. "Straight ahead. Disguised by rock and shadows. Come. We need to tread carefully. I don't want them attacking us."

Celestia gave a nervous titter. "Lindon won't attack me."

Omaira glanced over at her. "I sincerely hope not." She crept forward, crouched low to the ground, her sword out and hanging at her side. Celestia gathered up her skirts and followed. "Stay behind me," Omaira said.

"No," said Celestia. "He won't attack me. He'll attack you."

Omaira looked at her. "He's human," she said. "He can't see in the shadows like I can. We don't know what he'll take you for."

Celestia faltered at that. After all, she couldn't even see his encampment in the darkness. She fell into step behind Omaira. Her chest grew tight until it was difficult to breathe. Lindon. She wondered how his journey had changed him.

Because her journey had clearly changed her.

Omaira stopped, holding up one hand, and that's when she saw it: a large dark tent the same color as the sand.

"Are they there?" Celestia whispered. "Please tell me they haven't left yet."

"They're there," Omaira said softly. "I can smell them."

Celestia took a deep breath. "Then we should approach."

Omaira nodded, and they clambered down the side of the dune, kicking up dust. They had barely walked at all when a figure pushed out of the tent and lit a blue magic lantern and hoisted it up.

It was not Lindon, but one of the Eirenese men, his snowy hair glowing in the moonlight.

Omaira stopped and jammed her sword into the sand. Then she cupped her hands around her mouth and yelled, "We do not wish to fight!"

Celestia stared at the small circle of blue light and thought of Lindon: his face, the strong lines of his nose and cheekbones, the thatch of black hair that was forever falling in his eyes. She pressed her hands against her belly to feel the baby. His baby.

The lantern extinguished and the Eirenese man disappeared back inside the tent.

Omaira cursed and grabbed her sword out of the sand.

"What are you doing?" Celestia hissed.

But before Omaira could answer, there was the thunder of horse hooves against sand. Clouds of dark shadows swelled up from the dunes, and Celestia whirled around, terrified and confused.

Omaira spat something in the Kjani language. "They were lying in wait!" she said. "In the dunes!"

Three horses with three riders raced toward them. Celestia couldn't tell which was Lindon; they were all swathed in dark fabric.

Omaira gave a little snort, wrapped her fingers around the hilt of her sword.

One of the riders drew back on the horse's reins. He shouted back at the others and although Celestia didn't hear what he said she heard his voice, and her heart swelled.

"Lindon!" she screamed. She ran forward, her skirts twisting out behind her. Lindon leapt off his horse and yanked the fabric away from his face and in the darkness she could see that it was him, it was *her* Lindon.

"Celestia?" He looked wary.

"Yes!" She threw her arms around his neck and buried her face into his chest, breathing in the scent of his sweat, of his days of travel across the desert.

"What are you doing here?" Lindon pulled away from her, his hands gripped tight on her shoulders. "I told you to go back to Cross Winds, and instead you come to this wretched place?" His eyes dropped down to her belly, swollen beneath her gown. "The baby," he said weakly. "What are you doing to my baby?"

Celestia stepped away from him. Her legs were weak. "I told you my reasons at Aikha." She wrapped her arms around her belly protectively. The baby flipped inside of her. "I'm sorry that you didn't listen then, Lindon, but I can't—"

"Where did you get that dress?" Lindon demanded.

The Eirenese man from the tent stepped back out and walked toward them, his hand on the hilt of sword. Celestia felt a quiver of fear.

"Lindon," she said carefully. "I need to speak—"

"Where did you get that dress!" He yanked out his sword and Celestia screamed and stumbled backward. Omaira was at her side instantly, sword lifted.

"You're not my Celestia!" Lindon screamed. "This is some Kjari trick!"

"Agreed." The Eirenese man fell into step alongside him. Their swords glittered in the moonlight. Without thinking, Celestia pressed herself against Omaira.

"This is kajani magic," the Eirenese man said. "That's not your wife. They must have seen us coming and sent this abomination out to trick you."

"I am your wife!" Celestia cried. "I carry our child! I'm here on behalf of the Lady of the Seraphine! I explained all this to you! I'm begging you to stop this fight!"

She saw the hesitation in Lindon's face. She stepped away from Omaira.

"Celestia, no—" Omaira said, but Celestia ignored her and walked toward Lindon. He trembled.

"This is not a trick of Lord Kjari," Celestia said. "It's me."

She spread her arms wide. "Just like it was me at the Aikha Ruins. Yes, I'm dressed in Lord Kjari's clothes. But you have to understand—" One of the Eirenese riders was trotting his horse toward them, and he glared at her from above his desert-wrap. She took a deep breath, and addressed all of them. "The one you call Lord Kjari is not a man."

"Of course he's not a man," Lindon snapped. "No man could bring himself back to life after five hundred years. He's infected with dark magic—"

"No," Celestia spat at him, and she drew herself up, all the strength she had accrued during her years as a landed lady of the Seraphine. "Lord Kjari is the Airiana of Decay. He is not returning to this world, but vanishing from it. The signs—it's him *leaving*. He's taking death with him. Even if you could kill him—and you can't, his kajani are going to slaughter you if you try—it would destroy the world."

Lindon blinked at her. She could not read his expression. But the Eirenese man was scowling. "Lies!" he shouted. "She's trying to befuddle you. To make us put down our swords."

"I want you to put down your swords to save you!" Celestia cried. "I'm trying to make you understand that Kjari's death will bring about the world's ruin!"

"It's true," Omaira said, stepping forward. The Eirenese men snarled, but she ignored them. "He has been in exile for the last five hundred years. But if he leaves the world completely, the balance will fail. A world without death is a world full of suffering."

Anger flashed across the faces of the Eirenese men. "As if we would listen to the ravings of a kajan!" one of them snarled.

Celestia, wishing Omaira hadn't tried to help, dropped

down to her knees and lifted her hands in supplication. "Please, Lindon, if you try to do this, you'll die. And the world our child grows up in will be a nightmare."

Lindon lowered his sword. "Celestia," he said tenderly. He was frowning, though, his eyes full of sorrow. "I understand now."

"Lindon," she whispered.

"You've gone mad."

"No!" She scrambled to her feet.

"This is pregnancy sickness," he said, and he grabbed her arm and yanked her to him. Omaira reacted like lightning, slamming the side of his head with the butt of her sword. Celestia screamed his name as he stumbled backward. A trickle of blood, black from the moonlight, fell down his temple.

"Don't you lay a rough hand on her," Omaira growled.

"Don't defend my wife from me," Lindon said. He turned to Celestia. "Please, darling, I have to get you to safety. You and the baby. We can only hope the sickness hasn't infected him—"

"I'm not sick!" she screamed. "And I'm not mad, either! I'm trying to save our world! And I'm trying to save you!"

"Lord Kjari once wreaked havoc on this world," sneered the Eirenese man. "You would have him do it again?"

"He's wreaking havoc now!" she cried. "As he lets himself disappear!"

The Eirenese man slapped a hand on Lindon's back. "This is not your wife. She's been poisoned by Lord Kjari's magics. If you love her, you'll put her out of her misery."

Celestia choked back a horrified sob. Omaira bounded toward the man, screaming kajani war cries, and then they were fighting, all five of them, a blur of steel and armor. Celestia fell back into the shadows, tears streaming down her face. One of the men—Lindon? No, not Lindon—cried out in agony and then there was a clean wet sound and then his head was rolling across the sand. His glassy eyes stared up at Celestia. She knew Omaira had done it. He had been the one to call for her death.

She leaned over and vomited. Horse hooves pounded against the sand and when she looked up Lindon was galloping toward her, one arm outstretched. He meant to grab her, she realized with a horror, steal her away.

"No!" she screamed as his hand grabbed her arm. Her feet lifted off the sand in a terrifying blur of pain and terror. The socket of her arm burned.

"I'll drop you at the doors of Kjari's palace myself," he snarled, and Celestia heard the wildness in his voice. He wasn't himself. Not anymore. Not with the dreadful magic of this place.

"Let her go!" roared Omaira. "If you approach the palace, you'll be slaughtered, and you cannot take this woman into battle!"

"Stay back, kajan!" Lindon's voice was strained with fury.

Celestia felt hands on her waist, and then a burning searing pain in her arm, and then she was free, rolling across the sand, tangled up in Omaira.

"Lindon!" shouted one of the Eirenese men. "What the hell are you doing?"

Celestia lifted her body shakily, her arm burning. Lindon galloped away from her, toward the palace. He glanced back over his shoulders.

"We've been discovered!" he shouted. "There's only one choice left! We must make a stand!"

"Lindon, you *fool*," roared the Eirenese rider, and he galloped after him, as did the other rider.

Lindon crested over the dune, and Celestia screamed after him, screamed until her throat was hoarse. But then he was gone.

"Why did he do that?" she whispered. "He knows what's waiting for him. At least death still exists in this place."

A weight pressed on her shoulder—Omaira, it was Omaira, her glove stained with blood.

"It was desperation," Omaira said softly.

"Thank you for not killing him," Celestia whispered, even though she knew it was pointless, that he was dead already.

"I'm sorry we could not stop him," Omaira said.

In the distance came the sound of war drums.

THIRTEEN

Izara sat on the balcony, a blanket from her bed wrapped around her shoulders, watching the kajani gather below. They had done something to Omaira, blessing her, preparing her for her trial. And then Celestia had come out, her dress billowing out behind her. Now, Izara's head throbbed and her mouth was dry and if she closed her eyes the palace's magic showed her flashes of the future: Celestia weeping, Lindon lying in a pool of blood, swords clashing against each other. A battle, not an infiltration. Lindon and the others sick with some madness.

"It's not safe out here," Ico said from the doorway.

"Yes, it is." Izara stared out at the kajani. "It will be over soon anyway."

The air tightened around them like a noose; she could feel Ico's trepidation, his concern for her. He was probably right to be concerned. The magic of this place was twisting up with

Iomim's Treasure, interacting with it in strange and volatile ways. And yet if Izara crawled back into bed the visions would be worse. The magic was thicker inside. Out here, with the breeze from the north clearing the air, she could think straight.

Down below, there came the sound of a trumpet, a single, solitary wail. Then the drums began to beat, a steady thump like a heartbeat. The magic stirred. Izara wrapped the blanket more tightly around herself.

"Gods and monsters," Ico said, rushing to the railing. "They're actually going to fucking fight."

The kajani were on the move, marching in their stiff formations. *Thump thump thump* went the war drums. Ico looked over at Izara.

"Don't you care?" he said. "Your sister is out there, the fucking madwoman."

"Celestia is fine." This was a lie. Celestia was heartbroken. But she was not dead, and she would not die today, because the magic of this place told Izara everything. She suspected that was how the kajani knew Lindon and his men had planned a failed infiltration and were now riding in on some wild last stand.

Ico slumped back. Wrapped his arms around his chest. Stared out at the desert. A trio of riders appeared on the horizons, the sand billowing up in a cloud behind them. Izara felt a sharp pang of sadness in her heart, on her sister's behalf.

Ico gaped at the scene playing out before them. "This is insane," he said. "Why is Kjari even fighting this? He wants to disappear out of the world. How is that any different from just dying?"

"It's the kajani," Izara said. She felt numb; her tongue was heavy in her mouth. The palace's magic was speaking through her. She saw things she shouldn't. Felt emotions that weren't her own. "All the kajani have dedicated their lives to protect

Lord Kjari. Right now, he wants to be protected in his death. This is a final gift to them, I think."

"One more battle. Just like old times, huh?" Ico shook his head. "And these madmen are just riding right into it, aren't they?"

"Something's sickened them," Izara said sadly. "Or perhaps it's just hubris. I can't tell."

"For the love of the ancestors, why are we even here? Why don't we just conjure up the Lady of the Seraphine and tell her we found him?"

"We have to bring him to her," Izara said numbly. "She can't come to this place. Just like Xima can't come to this place."

Ico frowned.

"We have to draw him out."

The riders approached, and the kajani waited, magical flames licking at the darkness. And through the haze of magic Izara thought of Lindon as he'd been before at Cross Winds, running the acreage, working in the surrounding forest. Brown-skinned and handsome. She had always liked him well enough. She had always thought he brought out the best in Celestia. But she knew he didn't love her, not really. He loved the title her name brought him.

Still, she didn't want to witness his destruction.

Another tear fell. Another. The drums beat faster. The riders showed no sign of slowing. Their initial scheme abandoned, they were going to ride straight into the line of kajani.

Izara held her breath, waiting.

The two sides moved closer to each other.

Closer.

Closer.

When the riders crossed the boundary of the kajani, Izara's entire body went rigid. A jolt of pain radiated out from her chest and then faded. The drums stopped and there was the sound of screaming and growling, of metal clanging against metal. Ico pressed himself against the railing, the magic lights illuminating his face. Izara closed her eyes and she didn't know if she saw the present or the future—but there was Lindon, slick with sweat, swinging his sword in a wide arc as his horse leapt into the line of kajani soldiers.

The present, she thought. *The magic is showing him to me as he is now.*

Lindon's horse toppled, screaming, and Lindon leapt off in a flying arc, his sword gleaming. He hit the ground at a crouch and then whipped the sword around, fending off attackers. Black kajani blood splattered across his face. He opened his mouth in a scream Izara could not hear, and then he was running, charging at a kajan in black armor.

The kajan deflected the blow. Lindon ducked. Swords flashed, blood gleamed. Lindon moved in a blur, a constant stream of violence.

And then, abruptly, he went still.

Blood streamed from his mouth. His eyes were sad.

A sword jutted out of his chest, and he dropped to his knees, then slid face forward, into the sand. At least the life drained out of his eyes. At least this close to Kjari, death was still a gift to end the torment of violence.

Izara gasped and opened her eyes. The kajani were swarming like ants. Her entire face was wet.

"It's over," she whispered. "It's over."

~

The door to the apartment slammed open, and Omaira walked in, Celestia draped over her arms. The battlefield had already cleared, and the scents of smoke and incense drifted in through the open window. The magic had told Izara that Celestia survived, but Ico rushed over to Omaira, demanding, "What's wrong with her? What happened?"

"Her heart is broken," Omaira said, "and so is mine."

She carried Celestia down the hallway and into her bedroom. Izara trailed behind, feeling loose and falling-apart. Omaira gently set Celestia on the bed. She brushed the hair away from Celestia's face and smoothed it down. Celestia's eyes were closed but her face was blotchy and her shoulders were shaking.

Omaira stepped away and crossed her arms over her chest. She wore battle armor, monstrous twists of steel and leather, but her expression was not that of a warrior.

"Did she see?" Izara asked softly.

Omaira did not take her eyes off Celestia. "No. I failed my trial so that I could protect her from that horror."

They stood in silence. Ico slipped into the room, hanging back. Celestia moaned, drawing out Lindon's name. Izara's heart twisted.

"She tried to stop him," Omaira said. "But he wouldn't listen. He thought she'd been possessed by Lord Kjari."

Izara bowed her head as Celestia let out a harsh, wracking sob. Omaira knelt at the side of the bed and took Celestia's hand, as soft and delicate as a hibiscus when compared to Omaira's steel gauntlets. Celestia rolled over, her eyes fluttering open. She gazed up at Omaira in a way that rippled the magic in the room. Izara took a step back at the strength of it, head spinning. She didn't know what it meant.

"Celestia," Omaira said softly. "You should rest."

"He's gone," Celestia said in a pitiful voice. Her eyes glimmered with tears. "He didn't believe me and now he's gone."

Omaira didn't let go of Celestia's hand. Izara wrapped her arms around herself, trying to squeeze in some warmth of her own. She could have done more, she knew, to stop Lindon from rushing into the fight. She had seen it. She could have stopped him—

How, she didn't know. But she should have tried. Because

she hated seeing Celestia like this, pregnant and curled up on the bed, sobbing into the pillows, a kajan holding her hand.

A bell chimed through the apartments, three notes rising along the scale. Someone was at the door. Omaira and Izara looked at each other.

"Who's that?" Izara asked.

"I don't know."

Izara left the room to answer, but Ico beat her to it. As she approached the door, he pulled it open to reveal a kajani dressed not in armor, as she had expected, but in a dark crimson robe that dragged the floor. He bowed deeply, and upon rising, produced a scroll.

The kajan cleared his throat and unfurled the scroll. "To the Ladies Celestia and Izara," he read in a droning, sonorous voice, "and the pirate Ico—"

Ico rolled his eyes.

"The High Master and Ruler of All Chaos, Death, and Decay, His Lordship Isidore Kjari, has requested your presence in his receiving chamber tomorrow morning when the clock strikes ten."

Izara blinked.

"He looks forward to making your acquaintance," the kajan read. "And discussing those matters which are of upmost importance to you." The kajan rolled up the scroll with deft fingers and slipped it back into his robe. He looked at Ico and Izara with those black, appraising eyes. "My name is Fenis," he said, his intonation less formal now. "I am the Lord's attendant. I shall provide you with appropriate dress for tomorrow's meeting, and will accompany you to the room as well." Without waiting for an answer, he bowed again, his arms crossed over his chest, and then turned on his heel and vanished down the hall.

Ico and Izara stared after him.

"Huh," said Ico. "Didn't expect that."

Neither had Izara. She hadn't seen it in her visions. Lord Kjari had been blocked from her.

Ico closed the door. Izara turned and found Omaira standing in the entrance leading into the hallway.

"She's in no condition to meet with Lord Kjari," Omaira said.

Omaira was right. Izara sighed. "But it may be the only chance we have. The Lady can't come here. We have to bring him to her. We can't let Lindon's death be in vain." She looked Omaira straight in the eye. "Or your own sacrifice."

Omaira studied her, and Izara had the sense she was looking for sarcasm. But Izara had been serious.

Omaira bowed her head in agreement.

Izara was waiting when Ico arrived in the sitting room the next morning. Although she had not styled her hair, she wore a silk dress dyed a dark charcoal gray, with shimmery white ribbons cinched passably well around her waist. A veil was laid out on the couch beside her, and she scratched in a notebook, her brow furrowed in concentration.

"Are you ready for this?" Ico asked when she didn't look up. He wondered where Omaira and Celestia were. He suspected they'd be with each other. He'd seen that kind of thing before. Trauma can tie two people together.

"No," Izara said. She paused to glance over her writing, then frowned, scratched something out, and took to writing again. Ico sighed. At least Celestia would have talked to him.

He walked over to the cupboard by the balcony and pulled out the bottle of sweet infused liquor that he'd been drinking from, steadily, since they'd arrived at the palace. It was half empty at this point, and he didn't bother with a glass, just took a long swig and then shoved it back in the cupboard.

"We need to know what we're going to say."

Ico turned around. Izara was still writing in her notebook. "We'll tell him the truth," Ico said.

"Yes, because that worked out so well with Lindon." Izara's writing grew more fervent, as if she were trying to carve the words into the paper. Ico heard the edge in her voice. It surprised him, coming from her.

"Lindon was blinded by fear," Ico said. He wanted another drink but knew he shouldn't have one. Not this early, not with liquor that strong, not before they were about to go in front of yet another one of the ancestors-damned Airiana.

Footsteps sounded in the hallway. Izara tossed the book aside and stood up just as Omaira and Celestia stepped into the room. It was a shock, seeing Celestia. She wore the same ceremonial gown as Izara, but her face was wan beneath the thin, cascading veil. Her eyes were sunken, her expression slack. She leaned against Omaira, who had her arm wrapped around Celestia's waist. Omaira herself was back in her original leather. Still, it was a sight, the two of them together. Violence and sorrow winding round the other.

Izara rushed over to her sister and drew her into an embrace. Omaira watched them, her expression hidden by her helm. It made Ico nervous, not seeing her eyes. Even after all this time. He ought to trust her. But it was hard.

"Are you sure you want to do this?" Izara said.

"I have to." Celestia kept her gaze downcast. "We have to end this." Her hands dropped to her belly, swelling beneath the net of white ribbons, and Ico felt a sharp twist of pity in his chest. For Celestia, for that baby. For all of them, really.

"Besides," Celestia said, glancing up at Omaira. "I've heard that it's proper, in this place. For Lord Kjari to speak with the—" Her voice trailed off and she pulled away from Omaira, drifting over to the balcony window, her veil fluttering out behind her.

"To speak with who?" Izara cried out. She glared at Omaira. "What did you tell her?"

"The truth," Omaira said. "It is one of the utmost acknowledgments of respect for Lord Kjari to see the widow of one of his enemies."

Izara whipped around in disgust, and even Ico felt the snap of her anger. "May be a bit much for her right now," he muttered to Omaira.

"It won't be too much for Celestia," she answered.

"Stop speaking of me as if I'm not here." Celestia turned away from the balcony windows. Her eyes were luminous beneath her veil. "If you can allow me my grief, then you can allow me my dignity as well." She strode away from the window, toward the front door. They watched her silently. She flung open the door. The hallway outside was empty, no Fenis to be seen. Celestia's shoulders slumped. Ico felt sorry for her—so much for her grand departure.

"We must wait," Omaira said. "So we can be shown the way to Lord Kjari."

Izara snorted. "Just like the Emperor. They're all the same, aren't they?"

Omaira scowled. But Ico wanted to laugh. If they were comparing Lord Kjari to the Emperor, at least Kjari didn't dress him in commoner's clothes and toss him in jail.

They waited for some time, no one speaking. Celestia left the door hanging open, and the torches in the hallway flickered orange against the gray walls. The clock ticking on the wall finally rang out the tenth hour, and, as if he'd been summoned, Fenis appeared in the doorway, dressed in an elaborate silk robe that trailed behind him, puddling on the floor like rainwater.

"Good," he said crisply. "You are all prepared. Follow me."

They walked through the hallways, the sound of their footsteps bouncing off the walls. They went down a single, simple flight of stairs and then followed a labyrinthine path that twisted around on itself, seemingly unending. Ico had no sense of how long they walked, only that the soles of his feet started to ache in his heavy black boots.

"How much longer?" he finally asked. It earned him an angry scowl from Omaira, but he didn't care.

Fenis gave a sharp cough. "Longer than it would have been if you ask me that question again."

This time, it was Izara's turn to glare. "The magic," she hissed, "makes the building larger on the inside. If you don't shut up we'll be walking for days."

Fenis laughed. "Listen to her, pirate." He said *pirate* the way Ico would say *kajan*. As if he didn't quite believe pirates existed. Ico scowled but he kept his mouth shut. Magic. He glanced at Izara, hoped she wouldn't have another fit.

In time, the hallways widened. The stone darkened until it was a rich, velvety black, the same black stone as the outside of the palace. The flickering torches were replaced with magic lanterns that gave off a clear, unwavering white light.

They came to a door, guarded by a pair of the most grotesque creatures Ico had ever seen. He supposed they were kajani, although Omaira was a human beauty compared to them. Celestia gasped and covered her mouth, and even Izara looked away.

They stood nearly seven feet tall, with two-foot horns twisting out of their foreheads. Jagged teeth hung over their lower lips; their jaws jutted out like a warthog's. Their skin looked as if it were carved out of stone. And as Fenis approached they slammed their spears down in unison, blocking the doorway.

Ico clenched the muscles in his arms, ready to fight. It burned like a fever inside of him. Izara tottered at his side, and Omaira reached out and caught her, holding her upright. "Bloodlust," she murmured.

"Yes, bloodlust," Fenis sighed. "One of many spells of protection isolating his lordship from the world."

Bloodlust. Ico could feel it, bubbling beneath his skin. He could feel Omaira watching him and that was the only thing keeping him from losing his mind, the knowledge that she would put him down like a dog.

Fenis bowed to the two monstrous kajani and spoke in a language that burned the inside of Ico's ears. Immediately, the guards removed their spears, and Fenis approached the door and lay his hands on it and began to chant. The sound of it bore into Ico's brain. He ground his teeth together. Images flashed in his head: of death and dying, of blood and disease and decay. The door glowed a silky yellow.

Then it opened, and everything went away. The bloodlust. The pain in his head. The images. Ico sucked in a breath of air and staggered back. Izara was trembling, her skin ashy.

"This way," Fenis said.

They hesitated. "Come," Omaira said gently. "We can't be far now."

"What is all this?" Celestia asked. "This—this magic?"

"Protection," Izara said. "It's how he's stayed hidden all this time."

"Yes, yes," came Fenis' voice, seeping out of the darkness behind the door. "And it will keep the four of you out if you don't follow me immediately."

Ico did not want to pass through that doorway. The memory of the bloodlust stirred in his thoughts, a darkness twisting in his head. But Izara gave him a little shove forward, and he didn't turn back.

With them all on the other side, the door slammed shut with a deep, echoing clank, plunging them into darkness. Celestia shrieked; Izara just sighed. But then a light appeared up ahead, a tiny floating lantern. It drifted toward them.

"I told you," said Fenis' voice, coming from the light, "that you needed to follow immediately."

The light darted forward. Ico trudged after it, aware of the others around him even though he couldn't see them. His skin tingled and he wondered what magic they were passing through this time, if poor Izara would emerge on the other side drained of her life force, or whatever it was that happened to unfortunate magicians.

The light led them to another door, and to Fenis, who stood waiting with his arms over his chest. There were no fearsome guards here. Just a thin, tremulous light that allowed Ico to see the irritation on Fenis's face.

"On the other side of this door," Fenis said, "is His Lordship's personal chambers. You will behave respectfully, or face destruction at my hand. Do you understand?"

Omaira was the first to speak, muttering a "yes, sir."

"I wasn't worried about you," Fenis said, and he peered at the rest of them, his gaze lingering on Ico.

"I got it," Ico said.

"We're only here to speak to him," Izara said. "We have a pressing matter—"

Fenis flicked one hand dismissively. "It really doesn't matter what you want to talk about." And then he pressed his hands to the door and muttered some words in Kajani.

The door popped out of its frame and Fenis pushed it open. One of the sisters gasped, and even Ico thought he might be hallucinating.

The room on the other side was so *ordinary*. Not a throne room, like Ico had been expecting. Not some den of torture, either. But a sitting room of the sort you found in middle class houses, small and cozy. When Ico'd gone straight all those years ago he'd found himself in rooms like this on more than one occasion, usually after he seduced some merchant's wife after a boat ride with her friends.

They filed into the room. Fenis came in last and shut the door and then disappeared down a hallway without telling them to sit or offering a drink. For a moment Ico just took the place in, craning his head back, looking at the paintings on the wall. They were the bland paintings to be expected in a room like this, landscapes of the river and smudgy little captures of a bowl of fruit. The wallpaper was ordinary to the point of ugliness; the furniture was mismatched and worn.

"Should we sit?" Izara asked finally, looking over at Celestia and Omaira.

"I—I don't know," Omaira said. Her gaze caught on an embroidered pillow sitting askew in the arm of the couch.

Footsteps sounded in the hall. Omaira straightened her spine, her shoulders stiff like a soldier's. Izara moved closer to Celestia. Ico braced himself for a nightmare.

An old man stepped into the room. His skin was brown and leathery, his hair the color of snow, a bald patch shining on the top of his skull. He walked with a cane, his spine hunched into a curve. He peered up at them, and his eyes were the inky black of a moonless night, deep and terrible. That was how Ico knew.

This was him. This was Lord Kjari, the Airiana of Decay.

"You aren't sitting," Lord Kjari said, his voice gravelly and rough. "Please, don't stand around like statues. Sit." He waved his cane at the couch. "And you, get up. No need to bow to me."

He was talking to Omaira, who had fallen to her knees, her head dipped down. "My Lordship," she murmured.

"Sit," Kjari said, and then he did, nestling down into a big overstuffed chair. The sisters exchanged glances and draped themselves onto the couch. Ico lowered himself down next to them, senses alert. Omaira stood up after a moment of hesitation. She looked stricken, Ico thought. And why shouldn't she? Her all-powerful creator had turned into a doddering old man.

"I see Fenis was less than hospitable," Kjari said. "Didn't even offer you a drink, did he?"

Only Ico was brave enough to break the stunned silence. "No," Ico said. "Just corralled us in here and then took off."

Izara shot him a furious look, but Kjari merely chuckled. "Sounds like Fenis. He worries. I'll fetch you something. Food, too. Are any of you hungry?" He looked up at them with those unfathomable black eyes. Ico's stomach churned. He shook his head.

"We ate breakfast before we came to visit," Celestia said in a thin voice. Trying to be the prim and proper lady. This was her scene, wasn't it, this room, these rules of propriety? But she wasn't quite herself this morning, either.

"Ah, good. I told my palace to keep you fed and happy." Kjari tapped his cane once against the carpeted floor. Immediately, cups of frothy coffee materialized on the table in front of them. The smell filled the room: earthy and dark and rich. Ico picked up a cup, took a hesitant sip.

"This is excellent," he said, and meant it. Kjari smiled.

"Good, good. I've always had a fondness for coffee. Ah!" Kjari clapped his hands together. "Ladies, I see Fenis forgot to tell you as well—there's no need for veils here. Please, take them off."

The sisters looked at each other.

"We were told—" Izara started.

"You were told wrong. I don't care about such things anymore."

Ico smiled. "And you won't be able to drink any of this delicious coffee with those things."

Just as he'd hoped, Kjari laughed. "Exactly! Your Akuranian friend has the right idea. Please, take them off."

Izara pulled her veil off completely, balling it into her lap, but Celestia only lifted it away from her face. When Kjari saw her, with her ashen skin, her big glassy eyes, he frowned.

"The widow," he said softly.

Celestia didn't move. Ico paused, coffee cup halfway to his

mouth, watching this. He felt more relaxed than he had in months, but he didn't want to see Celestia break down into sobs again.

"Yes," Celestia finally said. "Your kajani killed my husband. Lindon."

"One of my kajani tried to save him." Kjari nodded at Omaira, who tilted her head down into a sort of bow. She hadn't touched her coffee. "A brave act, indeed. And a sacrificial one." He tsked. "Lost your place in my army, did you?"

Omaira frowned.

Kjari waved his hand. "I'll have no need of an army soon enough. I'm afraid you traveled all this way for nothing. But," he smiled. "I do appreciate the gesture. In another life, I would have taken you on."

Omaira bowed her head deeper and spoke in the kajani language. Lord Kjari smiled, spoke back. When she lifted her head, Ico saw tears glittering beneath her eyes.

"Now," Kjari said. "Let's discuss why the rest of you are here."

"And why my husband is dead," Celestia added—rather rudely for her, Ico thought.

"They are not the same reasons," Kjari said. "As you well know."

Celestia didn't say anything. Kjari leaned back in his chair. He seemed to disappear into it. Sitting down, he was even smaller than he had appeared in the doorway. Curling in on himself like a dying flower.

"Your husband," Kjari said, "was here to murder me. Or at least make the attempt. You wish to save me."

This statement was met with silence.

"Of course," Kjari said, "I have no desire to be murdered or saved. I merely wish to leave this world on my own terms." The old man studied them, looking so pleased with himself, like this was some devastating response to everything they'd been through—the journey up the Seraphine, the nights spent in the Emperor's castle, the endless travel through the Atharé Desert. Anger surged up inside Ico.

"We're not here to save you," Ico snapped. The others were looking at him but he didn't give a damn. "We're here to bring you to the Lady of the Seraphine."

Kjari laughed. "So she can try to convince me to stay."

"Yes, so we can save the people of our world. Your dying— or disappearing, or whatever it is you're doing—it's making this world unbearable."

Kjari stared at him with his bottomless black eyes and Ico knew he'd screwed up, that this was the end of him. Those eyes would be the last thing he'd ever see. But he didn't regret it.

"The world needs you," he said. "And that lady lost her husband because of you. So you can do the right thing and save yourself."

Silence rang out in that ridiculous, ordinary room. Izara stared at Ico with an expression of sorrow, of pity. She knew he was dead.

Kjari laughed, a laugh as dry and rough as old dust. "You want to stand up to me? An old man?" He waved one hand around lazily. "In my prime, I would have destroyed you. I would have eaten your soul in one bite. But now—" He shrugged. "I'm not the cruel creature I once was."

Ico knew he should feel lucky. Happy to have gotten out alive. But he didn't. Kjari's confession just made him angrier.

"I'm tired of being evil," Kjari said, before Ico could lash out again. "Tired of being the monster human children fear before they go to bed. River has no idea what it is to fill the role I fill. None of them do, not even my darling twin, Growth—who has retreated away from humans herself, I might add. But that's always been her way. Set things in motion and then fade." He peeled himself out of his chair, his movements shaky and pitiful. If he'd been anyone else, Ico would have felt obligated to help him. He almost felt obligated now.

Kjari picked up his cane and hobbled over to Celestia. She gazed up at him, her veil a dark halo around her face.

"I'm sorry your husband had to die," Kjari said. "Truly I am. This is a testament of how I've changed—once, I would not have cared."

"We came all this way," Celestia said, her voice cracking. "Please, just speak to the Lady of the Seraphine. So we can be free of our arrangement."

"It wouldn't matter," Izara said darkly.

"Wouldn't matter?" Celestia cried. "We'd no longer be beholden!"

"And so we'll be free to suffer with the rest of the world," Izara said bitterly. "The Lady is not going to convince him of anything."

"I'm afraid the mage is right." He leaned back in his chair. "My going to visit with River would not end my retreat. I've put Lord Kjari behind me." He shrugged. "The world despises me. I am so tired of being a monster. It's easier to just fade away."

"But the world is suffering!" Izara cried out. "No one will die, but only because we'll live our deaths for eternity."

Kjari looked at her. "I won't go back to being a monster again." Then he straightened, just a little, and waved his cane. "Finish your coffee. You're welcome to stay in my palace as guests as long as you'd like. But this conversation is over."

He left the room, his cane scraping against the floor. And the four of them were left in that painfully ordinary sitting room, their coffee going cold in its cups.

⁓

Izara sat on the balcony even though there was nothing to see. After their meeting with Lord Kjari, the palace had slipped back into the sand, back into its hiding place in a place like the Aetheric Realm but which was not the Aetheric Realm; this was as if the Aetheric Realm had been undone.

They had been walking through the hallways when it happened; a sudden jolt, a sudden burst of magic. Fenis had kept walking, calling out behind him that there was nothing to worry about.

There was everything to worry about, Izara had thought, as she felt the palace slide into oblivion.

She stared out at the blackness drifting outside the balcony. Occasionally she saw shimmers in the eddies of its movement, but mostly she felt it—a clammy pressure on her skin, a weight in the back of her head. The magic of Decay.

They couldn't stay here. If Kjari finally diminished into nothing, this place would go with him. The palace and the kajani and she and Celestia and Celestia's baby and Ico—all of them would be subsumed into the darkness. But if they left, what did it matter? They had failed in convincing Kjari to speak with the Lady of the Seraphine, and if he was to believed, it wouldn't have mattered even if they had.

Soon they world would be a teeming mass of life. Soon it would be unlivable.

Izara had never been one to succumb to hopelessness. Neither had Celestia, once. But Celestia had come back to the apartment and crawled into her bed and not climbed out of it all day, and all Izara could bring herself to do was sit out here on this balcony and get used to annihilation.

The glass doors scraped open; Izara felt the warmth of the inside of the palace on her back. She didn't turn around. "What do you want?"

"How can you stand to sit out here?" Ico stepped out onto the balcony, his arms wrapped around his chest. "Gods and monsters. It's like looking at a nightmare." He went silent for a moment, and Izara felt a breath of relief; silence she could understand. But then he said, "Do you think this is his way of keeping us prisoner?"

Izara looked up at him. He stared out at the blackness, his face in shadows.

"I mean, it's not like we can just walk out of the palace."

"He's fading away. Removing himself from the world." Izara drew her knees up to her chest. The darkness swirled past. "We're going to have to decide, you know. If we want to leave and suffer, or if we want to stay, and waste away with him."

"For fuck's sake," Ico said. "I came out here so you could cheer me up."

Izara shrugged. She didn't want to talk about this. There was nothing to say. Without Decay, the world would fall out of balance. It had already fallen out of balance. Nature tried to correct itself. And they would all suffer terribly in the process.

"Your sister refuses to get out of bed," Ico said. "So we won't be leaving even if we wanted to. Or could." He turned toward the door, his hands shoved into his pockets, and strolled back inside. Izara didn't move. She wondered if Celestia had said anything since they returned from the meeting with Lord Kjari. Even if it was to Omaira, who had refused to leave her side in the hours that passed. When the kajani servants brought trays of food—ordinary, human food— Omaira had gathered up two trays and disappeared into Celestia's room. Izara hadn't been able to eat. Her tray was still sitting in the common area, the food turning lumpy and unappetizing.

She sighed, stood up. Her muscles ached from sitting. It wasn't good, her sitting out here, and she knew it. It was like when their parents died, when they'd run out of money, and all she had left was Cross Winds and Celestia. How many times had she gone out to the forest and nestled herself amongst the vines and drifted away? And it was worse here.

The magic intoxicated her, left her drowsy and disoriented if she let it.

Izara stepped back into the clean light inside. She closed the door and then pulled the curtains over the glass. The sitting room was empty. She didn't want to be alone.

She went down the hallway, to Celestia's room. The door was cracked open, and she pushed it open. Celestia was a lump of silk blankets on the bed, and Omaira sat to her right, her head bowed. She had changed out of her armor and into a simple dark tunic.

"She's sleeping," Omaira said softly, without looking up.

Izara crept forward. She knelt down on the floor at Omaira's side. Celestia's eyes flicked beneath her lids, and her face was twisted into an expression of sorrow. Izara wondered what her dreams were like, if the magic affected her too.

"I'm worried about her," Omaira said.

"It's not your place to worry."

Omaira finally looked at Izara. Her black eyes blazed. "Don't tell me what is or isn't my place. I didn't want this when I brought you here."

Izara felt a brief rush of shame. She was always doing that without Celestia. Saying the wrong thing, being rude without thinking about it. Her eyes burned and she reached up and swiped at them. She didn't want Omaira to see her cry.

The room fell into silence. The only sound was the staccato beat of Celestia's breathing, the occasional murmur as Celestia whimpered in her sleep. Omaira leaned forward and took Celestia's hand, pressing it between her own. She whispered something in the language of the kajani, and Izara felt a stirring of healing magic, a kind of balm, and Celestia's breathing evened out, and her expression turned placid.

Omaira pulled her hands away.

"It helps with the nightmares," Omaira said, gazing down at Celestia.

"Did you learn that from your family?" Izara asked.

Omaira smiled. "Yes. But I was never so good at magic. I thought I'd be a better warrior. It seems that wasn't to be, either."

Heat rushed into Izara's face. "You saved Celestia's life. I saw it. I'd say that makes you an excellent warrior."

Omaira turned to her. "Kjari said the same thing to me, when we visited him."

They fell into an easy silence. Celestia slept peacefully

"He's hated," Omaira said after a moment. "That's why he's doing this to himself."

Izara felt a bolt of understanding. He *was* hated—as Lord Kjari, but also as the Lord of Decay. Of all the Airiana, he was the most feared. A story used to scare little children.

"Who wants to live in a world where they are hated?" Omaira stared down at Celestia. "It's the same reason the kajani retreated into the Aetheric Realm after the war's end. Why should we live among those who despise us?"

Izara didn't say anything, because she knew if she did they would be the wrong words. But she didn't leave, either. She stayed by Omaira's side, watching over her sister.

~

Celestia's dreams were full of Lindon. He kept dying, over and over, in all the ways her burning mind could imagine: swords slicing off his head, plunging into his belly. His blood spilled hot and sticky over her hands. The baby was gone, in these dreams, her stomach flat again. The baby was Lindon; Lindon was the baby. And both were dead.

Celestia jerked awake. The room was dark and her sheets were twisted around her feet, cocooning her. She rolled over to her side and tried to beat back the sorrow that rose up inside of her every time she was awake. Even with the nightmares, it was easier to sleep.

She dropped her hand to her belly, which was as swollen as it had been before she fell asleep. Dreams weren't real, even in this place.

She was alone. No Omaira, no Izara. She thought she heard voices drifting in from the hallway but she did not care enough to find out. Even calling Omaira's or Izara's name was not worth the effort. Better to close her eyes, to fall back asleep.

But she couldn't sleep. She kept thinking about Lord Kjari, the way he seemed to have faded away into the distance. She wondered how much longer it would be until he vanished completely, a wisp of mist on a warming morning. How much had she given up to come to this place, to pay back a favor that had been murdered in battle? Her thoughts didn't wander to the obvious tolls, to Cross Winds and the acreage, but instead to the trunk of things she had brought with her on her journey and left at the river authority in Istai-Seraphine. Her fine dresses, her twinkling jewelry. It had belonged to another Celestia in another life. Not to her. She had never witnessed anything beautiful in this life.

Pain lanced through her body.

She gave a shout of surprise. The pain was sharp and hot and intense, but then it faded to a dull ache. She lay in the bed, breathing hard, not knowing what to think.

There came another burst of pain, longer this time, and Celestia flopped over onto her back, arching her spine, trying to contain it. She shrieked and pounded her fist against the mattress. Footsteps pattered somewhere far away, and the door burst open.

"Celestia?" Omaira's voice seemed far away, too. "What's happening?"

Celestia stared up at the shadowed ceiling. The pain was fading, but she dropped her hand to her stomach. The baby was kicking frantically.

"It's too early," Celestia mumbled. "Too early. I don't understand—"

Omaira ripped the blankets away. Pain concentrated in Celestia's belly, a kind of tightening. "Something's wrong," she gasped, tears falling out of the corners of her eyes. First Lindon, and now the baby. It was this place. This palace of darkness and decay. She should never have come here. She should never have left Cross Winds. "Something's wrong. Something's wrong."

"Izara!" thundered Omaira. "I need you in here now!"

The pain faded and Celestia felt something hot and wet run down her legs. Blood? She didn't look, only stared at the ceiling, aware of her sister rushing into the bedroom, demanding to know what was wrong, what was happening, aware of Omaira barking instructions to fetch a guard—a guard? Nothing made sense anymore, she was too dizzy with sorrow to try and understand. Her vision blurred with tears.

"The baby is still moving," Omaira said, pressing a cool, dry hand to Celestia's forehead. "He is still alive. He's just early."

"Early," whispered Celestia, and she couldn't make sense of the word.

"I know magic to care for him," Omaira went on. "Your sister can help. And I've fetched the grand mage—her magic will be far more reliable than mine. You'll be fine."

Omaira's voice was like velvet, a softness Celestia couldn't imagine. She tilted her head toward her. Omaira smiled, and in that smile Celestia saw all those moments together, the tea that Omaira prepared, the way she'd tried to save Lindon, giving up her place in Kjari's army in the process. And for a heartbeat Celestia's thoughts cleared, and through her grief she felt a flush of happiness. Maybe not joy. Not yet.

And then pain tore through her body again. Celestia screamed. Omaira pressed her hands on her chest and began chanting in Kajani; the pain lessened but did not go away. Celestia gasped for air and Omaira told her she needed to breathe, that all she needed to worry about was breathing and controlling the pain, but the words rolled off Celestia and she screamed again, not out of pain this time but out of terror. It was too much. Too much death in one day.

Someone slammed into the room. Heavy footsteps, a gruff female voice that reminded her of Omaira but who was not Omaira. "Breathe," said Omaira. Celestia breathed, ragged and shallow. She looked out at the room. Izara was there, with a kajan dressed in flowing black robes, her black hair loose around her shoulders. No Ico. But of course not. This wasn't men's business.

"The baby's alive," the kajan said. "I can feel his heartbeat. Can you?"

Celestia muttered a response—Yes? No? She couldn't feel anything but panic and burning in her belly. But then Izara gasped out, "Yes!"

"Good. You hold on to that. Tell me if anything changes." The kajan knelt down beside the bed. She cupped Celestia's face in her hands and tilted it toward her and looked Celestia in the eye. "I'm going to save your baby."

A mage, Celestia realized with a start.

"Do you know anything about human babies?" Izara asked. Her voice was far away. It seemed to echo. Celestia thought she should chide her for being rude but her mouth was too dry to speak.

"I know more than you," the mage snapped. She was still looking at Celestia. "Your baby will be safe."

"Thank you," Celestia gasped as pain ricocheted through her body again.

The mage began barking orders at Izara and Omaira, a blur of words. Cool kajani hands pressed against Celestia's brow and then pulled her dress away from her legs. The mage chanted and Izara and Omaira joined in, their voices forming a chorus. Celestia gasped for her breath. Pain wrapped around her. *Somethings's wrong something's wrong something's wrong.* This was deep and it was insidious. She screamed at the ceiling. Sweat poured over her face, soaking her hair, the bedsheets. The chanting filled the room, wrapping around her like smoke, seeping into her lungs and choking her. The mage loomed overhead—was she flying, her hair and robe streaming around her?—and Celestia's head lolled back. The world went dark and she smelled flowers. She thought perhaps she had died.

And then Omaira's voice came through the dimness. "Push!" she cried. "Push! The baby's almost here!"

Celestia strained, bracing her back against the soft mattress. The room shot back into sharp focus, the lines of the walls too bright, too angular. Celestia tasted her sweat on her tongue. *Something's wrong.* She screamed. When she tossed her head back and forth, trying to control the pain, her cheek brushed against a bouquet of dead roses, the stems tied up with ropes of silk. Celestia felt the magic emanating from them, a magic of decay and death that would somehow save her child. Even without Izara's knowledge of magic, she understood that.

And then she heard it, a squealing, pitiful wail. The sound caught in the back of her brain, and she held on to it, afraid it was a dream.

"There he is," said the mage. "A boy. Too small but I've got the magic to take care of that."

Celestia lay amongst the tangle of her soaked bedsheets. Her whole body trembled. The mage crawled into the bed beside her, knocking the dead roses aside. "Here he is," she murmured, pressing her head against Celestia's. "You can hold him, just for a moment. He needs magic to survive. Just for a few weeks."

Celestia gazed down at her son. He was tiny and skinny and purple in the black cloud of the mage's robes, and his eyes were squinted shut from his wailing. Celestia gathered him in her arms—he was light, lighter than seemed possible, as if he were made of air, and pressed him to her chest. Birth fluid smeared across her chest and when she kissed the top of his soft damp head it smeared across her cheek, but she didn't care.

"My baby," she whispered.

"Name him," the mage said as Izara and Omaira pressed close. "That helps the magic, if he has a name."

Celestia gazed down at her baby. He was almost unrecognizable as human but he was entirely recognizable as hers. As Lindon's. She hadn't thought about names. That was a decision that was to be made with his father. But now his father was gone. It was only her.

She closed her eyes and concentrated on the tiny flutter of the baby's heart. It was like a butterfly beating against her palm.

"Hurry, my dear," the mage said softly. "He's too young. He needs my magic."

There were a thousand family names she could choose from. The most obvious, of course, was Lindon, but the name soiled on the tip of her tongue before she could say it. And like a flash, she knew—Izar, the male version of Izara. It had belonged to some great great granduncle or another. Now it was his.

"Izar," she whispered, looking down at him, his wrinkled, purpled face.

"Izar," the mage said. "A good name." And then she swept Izar out of Celestia's arms. "You need to rest," she said. "And so does he. I must get him under protection. But you can come see him when you've healed."

She left the room, her robes billowing out behind her. For

a moment Celestia felt a kind of empty nothingness. And then she began to weep, her sadness so dark, so profound, that it was as if she were drowning. "No," she wept. "No, don't take him from me, not after everything—"

Arms wrapped around her, pulled her to a broad, soft chest. "Shhh," murmured Omaira. "He's safe. You can see him soon."

"Yes." Izara slid into the bed beside her and wrapped her arm around Celestia's waist. The three of them lay there, wrapped together. "The magic here tells me things. I can feel her intentions. The baby needs magic to survive. He came out too early."

Izara's words soothed her. Celestia pulled away from Omaira but grabbed her hand and squeezed, not wanting to let go. She rested her head on Izara's shoulder. "I named him after you," she said. "Izar."

Izara laughed. "Oh, Celestia! That's a terrible name."

Celestia smiled. "No. It's perfect."

"I think it's a fine name," Omaira said.

Celestia closed her eyes. Her sadness had passed. So had, in this moment, her grief. She knew it would return. But for now, she was too exhausted to feel anything but a kind of shimmering hope.

⁓

Celestia went to see Izar that night, after she had slept off her exhaustion. She woke to find Omaira asleep in her chair beside the bed, but she didn't wake her, just pulled herself out of bed and dressed. She brushed out her hair and washed her face in the water from the pitcher that sat on the vanity. Then she shuffled into the sitting room. It felt strange to move around. Her muscles were weak and tremulous. But it felt good, too.

Izara was awake, sitting on the couch, reading through a fat book bound in leather. She glanced up when Celestia entered the room. Her eyes widened. "Should you be up?"

"I'm fine," Celestia said. "I want to see Izar." She tottered to the left and braced herself against the wall. Her head spun, and she closed her eyes until the dizziness passed.

"Clearly you're not fine."

Celestia took a deep breath. Opened her eyes. Steadied herself. "I'm fine," she said, more firmly. When she walked over to Izara, her gait was steady and unwavering.

They looked at each other for a moment in the silence.

"Please," whispered Celestia.

Izara sighed and dropped the book onto the couch. "Fine. But we should wake Omaira. She'll know the way."

"I'm already awake." Omaira stepped into the sitting room. "You didn't think you could sneak past a sleeping kajan, did you?"

Celestia smiled at that. "I suppose I did."

"I'll take you to the mage's quarters," Omaira said. "It would be good for you to see that little Izar is safe."

"I can't believe you gave him that name," Izara said, turning back to her book. But Celestia knew her sister well enough to know that it pleased her.

They left the apartment, leaving Ico to sleep away the night. Funny how even kajani had the superstitions about men and pregnancies, about women's mysteries. Celestia wondered if they had borrowed from each other, some transmission of knowledge five hundred years earlier, when kajani and the humans of the Seraphine fought together under Lord Kjari.

The mage's apartment was at the top floor of the palace, in a turret that, Omaira said, always faced south. It was difficult for Celestia to walk up the stairs, all of them narrow and winding.

The mage's door was carved with enchantments that glowed faintly in the darkness. Omaira rapped on the door twice. The enchantments glowed in time with her knocks. Celestia fidgeted with worry—all she wanted was to see her baby, her son, and press him to her breast and know that he was safe.

The door swung open. The mage glowered down at them, but her expression softened when she saw who it was.

"My new mother," she said. "For you, I don't mind being woken in the night. Little Izar is quite well. Come. But only Celestia. You two—" She nodded to Omaira and Izara. "—You must stay. Too many people could weaken the magic."

The mage turned and disappeared into the dark caverns of her room. Celestia took a deep breath, her heart hammering, and followed. The mage's apartment was dimly lit with half-melted candles. It smelled of dead flowers, a kind of sickly sweetness that went straight to Celestia's head. The mage led her down a narrow, dark hallway, into a room where the air made the hair on Celestia's arms stand on end.

"The magic keeping him alive," the mage said. "You may not be able to stay in here too long."

But Celestia barely heard her, because at the center of the room was a cradle draped in black silk and silver sigils, dead flowers hanging upside down above it like a mobile. Celestia rushed forward, the magic filling her lungs.

Izar was sleeping, his skin soft and clean. Celestia's breath hitched in her throat. She reached out with one shaking hand and brushed the top of his head. His eyes fluttered open and he gazed up, not quite looking at her but past her, as if he could see her spirit rising out of her body.

He was so small. Too small, like a kitten curled up in his enormous cradle. But he looked healthy, his eyes luminous and bright, and his skin was smooth and dry to the touch. He reached up with one hand and batted at her finger—his hand was so small in comparison, and it tickled her skin like a whisper. Tears welled up in her eyes. All this hope, all this potential, concentrated in one too-small baby, his vision unfixed above her.

But then Celestia felt a darkness inside her chest. A poison. Izar had no future. Not here, not in the Seraphine. Not if Kjari allowed himself to fade away, stripping the world of the necessity of his presence.

Celestia pulled her hand away. Izar blinked. She was numb and lightheaded. The scent of dead flowers choked her, and little dots of light swam in front of her vision. The room blurred; she thought she saw shapes in the shadows, cities where plants grew so thick and wild they wound around buildings and people alike, and the dead were undying, caught up in the tangle of growth like insects in a spider's web.

"No!" she cried out, and she tasted something bitter on her tongue. She lost her balance and fell—right into the strong arms of the mage, who dragged her out of the room, slamming the door shut.

"I told you the magic would get to you," the mage said.

"I saw—I saw—" Celestia couldn't put it into the words, those images. Already they were fading from her memory. But the sense of them lingered, and she was swollen with an overwhelming sorrow. Tears fell over her cheeks. "There's no point in saving him, not if Kjari won't *listen*."

The mage only frowned, her black eyes glittering.

Celestia whirled away. Izara and Omaira burst into the room, both of them looking ready to fight. "I felt that!" Izara cried. "That magic. What did you do?"

"I did nothing," the mage said crisply. "And your sister is quite fine. The hysteria should pass in a moment. It's a side effect."

"No," Celestia mumbled. "No. Not a side effect. I saw—" And she looked up at Izara. At Omaira, standing a few paces behind her. They would become wraiths, too. And Ico. All of them would face endless suffering because one selfish, bitter old Airiana refused to acknowledge his role in the world.

"I have to speak to him again," she whispered. Izara frowned, took a step toward her. "Kjari. I won't let him—I won't let him turn the world into a nightmare."

"He won't listen," Izara said. "He won't even listen to the other Airiana."

Celestia turned back to the mage, who stood with her spine straight, her arms crossed over her chest so that they disappeared in the flow of her robes. Her expression was unreadable. "You have to help," Celestia said. "If you can save Izar, surely—"

"His Lordship is at the root of my magic," the mage said. "I deal in decay. In death. And yes, I am weakening, as he falls away." She tilted her face down. Her hair fell in a curtain along both cheeks. "He wouldn't listen to me, either."

Celestia took deep breaths. She looked at the door that separated her from Izar. That separated her from her future. "There has to be a way to convince him."

"The Lady of the Seraphine sent you here to convince him," the mage said, after a moment had passed. "I can feel it on you. And she wouldn't have done so if she hadn't thought it possible for you to succeed." She paused. "But I have no way of offering aid. I can save your baby. Perhaps that is the last good I'll do in this world."

I can save your baby. Celestia kept looking at the door. Magic seeped out of it, mingling with the air she breathed into her lungs. She wondered what the magic did to her. She realized she didn't care.

She realized, too, that she had an idea.

FOURTEEN

"**Y**ou want to do *what*?" Ico sputtered.

Celestia was very calm. She was so calm Ico thought she might be insane.

"I'm not giving up," she said. "I'm not holing away in this palace while the world grows like a cancer around us. And I know you don't want to either."

"There's the Lady of the North to think of," Izara added. "Surely you want to see her again?"

Ico fixed Izara with a sharp glare. "Don't talk about her," he snapped. The truth was she was right, but the reality of it was too painful, and he preferred to pretend that nothing had changed, that all he had to do was get out of the palace and he would see her again.

"What do you think of this?" he asked Omaira, who was lurking behind Celestia, her arms crossed. "It's crazy, right? Tell her." He jabbed his thumb at Celestia. "For the love of the ancestors, she just had a baby."

Omaira looked at him, then at Celestia. "I don't want His Lordship to vanish," she finally said. "And I don't have any other ideas."

"It's our ass, though." Ico fumed. "You and me, we're the ones who have to do the really dangerous work."

"Excuse me?" Izara snapped. "You think I can just wave my hands and part the magic? I could bring this whole palace down if—"

"Stop." Celestia stepped in between them, holding out her hands as if to keep them from charging. "Ico, if you don't want to help, then you don't have to. But I'm going down there regardless of how you feel about it." She took a deep breath. She wore the expression of someone about to reveal a secret. Wonderful. There was something she hadn't told them about this madness.

"I'm going down there," she said, "and I'm taking Izar with me."

"What!" squawked Izara, and even Omaira's mouth fell open.

"Celestia," Omaira started.

But Celestia dismissed her with a wave of her hand. "I've made up my mind. He's the key to all of this. The mage has already agreed to help me."

"When did you talk to the mage about this?" Izara cried.

"After you left." Celestia shook her head. "It will be difficult—"

"Dangerous," Izara said. "It will be *dangerous*." She looked up at her sister, her eyes pleading. Ico felt for her. "You're putting your baby at risk for nothing."

Ico agreed. Part of him could understand what she was trying to do. Because sure, she was right: what other options did they have? But to take a fucking baby down there—

"This is motherhood sickness," Ico said, blurting out a

term he hadn't thought about in years. It was something a first mate had told him about, back in his pirating days. "You had your baby and now you're suffering. It's normal, but you need to rest."

All three women glared at him. It was that damn Seraphine hang-up, that men shouldn't have anything to do with pregnancy. It wasn't that way in Akuran and it annoyed him that it was that way here.

"She's putting the baby at risk!" he shouted, throwing up his hands. "What do you want me to say?"

"It's not motherhood sickness," Celestia said, her voice low and icy. "It's desperation. It's the only idea I have."

"Surely we can think of something else," Izara said. "I don't know what difference Izar will make if Kjari didn't listen to us before."

But Celestia shook her head. "You don't understand," she said. "Izar—Izar is what makes everything different." She turned toward the balcony. The curtains were drawn over the window, blocking out the blackness outside. "Izar is the future that Kjari is denying us."

They fell silent. Then Omaira pulled her sword out of its scabbard and jammed its tip into the floor. Ico jumped at the sound. As he watched, Omaira fell to her knees in front of Celestia, her hand wrapped around the hilt of her sword. She bowed her head low. Celestia gazed down at her without speaking, although Ico thought he saw something like awe glowing in her features.

"Lady Celestia," Omaira intoned, "before these witnesses, I pledge my fealty to you and your cause. My sword is yours."

"Please, stand up," Celestia said. "There's no need for all this."

Omaira looked up at her and smiled. "Do you not want my aid?" she asked, a joking lilt to her voice.

Celestia ducked her head down, eyelashes fluttering. "Of

course I do," she murmured. "But you don't need to swear *fealty*. I'm not Kjari." And then she held out her hand to Omaira, who took it, gazing up at her with that teasing smile on her lips. Ico felt something shimmering on the air as their eyes met, and Celestia smiled back, looking in her thin gown and her tangled hair as radiant as a queen. Ico felt as if he were watching something he shouldn't, some intimate moment between two women who had always been strangers to him.

Omaira stood and held Celestia's hand for longer than was needed. When she dropped it, she looked at Celestia only in little furtive glances that Ico didn't think he was meant to see. He wondered if Celestia noticed them.

Celestia turned to Ico. "Do you agree or not? It'll be easier if Omaira doesn't have to fight the guards alone."

"The guards?" Ico sputtered. "What about the magic?"

"I'll take care of that," Izara said. She shot Celestia a dark look. "Although I can't promise I'll be able to protect the baby."

"I told you, you won't have to." Celestia didn't take her eyes off Ico. "Well? What do you say?"

Ico glanced at Omaira. At Izara. At Celestia. All three of them were staring at him, and something in each of their expressions, their stances, reminded him for a moment of Xima. He was never going to see her again. Certainly not if he stayed. And probably not if he went. So what did it matter? At least he could go out trying.

"Fine," he said. "But I want a weapon."

"You'll have all the weapons you need," Omaira said. "I'm not sending you down there unarmed."

"We'll leave tomorrow," Celestia said. "Before the morning bells ring."

No one answered. But Ico knew they all understood.

The palace was as still as death. They walked single-file down the narrow hallways, a magic globe drifting alongside Omaira's head, casting barely enough light for Ico to see by. It was early enough that the torches along the wall hadn't been lit, and Ico could imagine the palace waking up on the floors overhead, heaving itself to life. Nothing had been brought to life down here.

He and Omaira led the way; Izara was behind him, and then Celestia behind her, the baby bundled to her chest in a fabric sling. She wore a crown of dead roses and a necklace of threaded bones; before they'd left the apartment, the mage had anointed her with oils that smelled of dying flowers.

"Keep alert," Omaira said in a harsh whisper. "We're approaching the guards."

Ico tensed and took a deep breath. His heart thumped. He put a hand on the hilt of the sword Omaira had given him and used the other hand to pull out the big fierce knife he'd also finagled out of her. Behind him, Izara muttered in a language he couldn't understand. Protection against the bloodlust. His head swooned, but he didn't feel overcome with the urge to fight, like he had before.

The lantern drifted forward, illuminating the hallway, and then the door, and then the guards.

The guards were unchanged. They regarded the party with blank expressions. Didn't lift their spears into a fighting stance. Ico felt himself relax even though he knew better.

Omaira held up one hand, and everyone slowed to a stop. Then she approached. She didn't pull her sword out and so neither did Ico; she'd instructed him to follow her lead.

Omaira spoke in the tongue of the kajani, demanding they be allowed in.

Ico was aware of the rhythm of his breathing, growing faster. Faster. Faster.

The guards didn't move.

Omaira spoke the same guttural words again.

Nothing.

Ico shifted his weight, unsure what to do. The guards stared out, unblinking. He glanced back at Izara, who was frowning.

"It's not the right language," she said.

Omaira paused. Looked back at her.

"It was a different language," said Izara. "One I didn't recognize."

Omaira sighed. "I know. It was High Kjani. Only those closest to Lord Kjari can learn it." She looked down at her hands. "I never did."

Ico sighed. "I guess the easy route won't do, will it."

Omaira looked at him for a moment. Then she closed her eyes, shook her head. They had discussed this. Ico took a deep breath. Wrapped his hand around the hilt of his sword. The minute he pulled it out, the guards would attack.

Omaira looked at Celestia, who stood with her hands around her baby, her eyes shining in the lantern-light. "Are you certain you want to proceed?" Omaira asked.

"It's our only chance," whispered Celestia.

Ico braced himself.

"Very well." Omaira turned to Izara. "We're ready."

Ico was not ready, he would never be ready, but he kept his mouth shut.

Izara closed her eyes, murmured in that old language.

It was as if a veil lifted from Ico's mind. His blood pumped and he could feel the strength of it, heavy and violent. He yanked out his sword and whirled to face the guards. They were already bounding toward him, and he swung wildly, the sword almost too heavy for him. It slammed into one of the guard's spears. The guard growled. Ico growled back. The bloodlust inflamed him.

The mage had given him a vial of some foul liquid to

drink before they set out; she claimed it would help him focus the bloodlust on his enemies and not his companions. Everything fell away but those two kajani, their jaws unhinging to reveal rows of teeth, their spears whipping through the air. A burst of pain exploded on Ico's left arm but it was instantly consumed by the bloodlust, and he drove forward, sword flying. Everything was a blur of sweat and muscles, blood and steal. His opponent was shrieking in harsh, animalistic barks—and he was howling back. Pain radiated up his left leg and then his sword plunged into something soft. Black kajan's blood splashed across his face, hot and thick, and he swelled with victory. He yanked the sword, felt it lodge in bone. The kajan lashed out at him, still fighting even as Ico drove the sword in deeper, deeper, his face twisting in a grimace. Even when the kajan stopped fighting, Ico pulled out his sword and jammed it again, stabbing and hacking. Black blood flew everywhere. He ran his tongue along his palm, lapping it up, the bitter saltiness of it burning as it went down his throat.

And then, ringing out like a bell, was Izara's voice. A language he didn't understand. She had stood guard as she said she would.

The bloodlust vanished. His sword hit the ground with a clatter, and he retched, spitting to get the taste of the kajan's blood out of his mouth. He was aware suddenly of the pain, of his own blood. He gasped and fell to his knees, clutching at his side. He didn't let himself look at the body of the kajan, which did not look like a kajan anymore, or like a body. Bile rose up in the back of his throat and his guilt threatened to choke him.

"You're bleeding. Let me patch that for you." Izara was at his side, her hands pressing gently at his wounds. Ico sucked in air through his teeth. Omaira was in better shape than him— she could stand at least, although she leaned up against the far wall. Her skin was black with blood, too, and she kept her gaze downcast, not looking any of them in the eye.

A warmth spread along Ico's side, and then Izara leaned away, wiping her hands on the hem of her dress. "There," she said. "You should be able to walk the rest of the way."

Ico got shakily to his feet. He pressed his side, the gauze rough against his fingers. Beneath it was the tingle of Izara's magic.

"Told you we'd need it," Izara said.

"Never doubted you." Ico wanted to bathe. He wanted to dive into cool clean water and never emerge. The blood was drying to his skin, leaving it stiff and uncomfortable. He didn't want to think about what he looked like—a monster. Like the Kozas, when they'd done to the innocents in his life what he'd just done to those guards.

He swallowed back a lump of guilt that rose in his throat. He couldn't think about this now. They had tried to go past them peacefully. He had known this was a possibility.

But where had it gotten them? The door was still closed.

"We should hurry," Izara said suddenly. "In case there are others." Her eyes flicked around the hallway. "Or other traps." Izara took a deep breath. She looked faded and small in the lantern light as she walked to the door, the stone dull and unremarkable. Ico glanced over his shoulder. Celestia stood several paces away, almost in the shadows, her baby clutched to her chest.

He couldn't see her expression, but something about her stance, this mother protecting her young, filled him with shame. Her jerked his head back around. Made sure not to look at the corpses of the kajani.

Izara had her hands pressed against the door, her face twisted in silent concentration, but it wasn't lighting up with magic like it had when Fenis had brought them down here. She dropped her hands to her side and stepped back.

"Well?" said Celestia.

"This magic—I can understand it, but I just can't get *through* it. I can't decipher the formulas." Izara stared at the door while she spoke. Ico trembled. When they planned this ludicrous trip, Izara had sworn that she would be able to handle the magic. If he had slaughtered that kajan for nothing—

"Omaira," Izara said suddenly. "Maybe you can help."

Omaira straightened. Her blood-smeared face dipped into the darkness. "Me?" she said. "I have no skill in this sort of magic."

"You have more than Ico or Celestia. But also, you're a kajan! I think that's why I can't break the seal. Here, come lay your hands on the door."

Omaira paused for a moment, and then trudged over beside Izara. They looked at each other for a moment, and then she reached out one blood-splattered arm and pressed her palm against the door. Izara took a deep breath and did the same. Both of them stood very still. That was all Ico could see, their stillness. When Celestia drifted up to his side, her movement startled him.

"I hope it works," she whispered.

Ico wasn't sure if she meant the door, if she meant this whole decision.

"Me, too," he said.

And then the door began to glow with veins of bluish light. Omaira tensed up, but didn't take her hand away. Izara was shaking, Ico realized, shaking so fast that the edges of her body blurred.

The door sprang open with a crack like a whip snapping the air in two.

Izara collapsed to a pile on the floor.

It was the sound of Celestia's voice that drew Izara back into the waking world. The real world. For a moment all she could see were shapes of light and dark. She thought perhaps she had gone blind, or that the magic had infected her somehow. That was the last thing she remembered—magic. Magic flooding through her body, magic pulsing through the door.

The shapes solidified. She was in a hallway, dim save for her floating lantern.

"Izara!" cried Celestia. "Speak to me. Are you all right?"

"Just a little overcome. It was nothing." Not entirely a lie. Now that she was awake her strength was returning to her exponentially, but this strange dark magic sucked the life from its victims, left them weak and frail. They only needed her to pass through that hallway of terrors, though. If she could ask Ico and Omaira to risk their lives fighting the guards, she could risk her life doing this.

"Are you sure?" Celestia was kneeling beside her, little Izar still strapped to her chest. The magic kept him sleepy, so that he wouldn't cry and draw attention to them. Part of the way the mage was keeping him safe.

"Yes. I'm sure." Izara sat up. Something rang inside her ears, a constant clanging bell, growing softer as she took in her surroundings. The blood-splattered hallway. The lingering smoke of magic resting on the air. And the door yawning open. She stood up, her legs shaking. "How long was I out?"

"Only a few minutes." Celestia frowned. "Omaira and Ico went ahead, to make sure things are safe. They should be back any moment, though. We have to push through."

Izara nodded, then walked toward the door. She side-stepped the massacred bodies of the guards, even though, in this place, there was a magic in their deaths. A strength in their decay. She could feel it pulsing on the air, and as she passed by she reached out, drawing some of that energy in. She'd need it, in the hallway. It made her swoon.

"Izara, wait! I told Omaira we'd stay here—"

"We should pass through and shut the door," Izara said. "In case anyone else comes down here."

Izara heard footsteps and she knew Celestia was following. She passed through the threshold, her skin tingling. Still safe. They hadn't gotten to the hallway of nightmares yet.

Celestia slipped in behind her, skirts swishing. She had worn the ceremonial dress from before.

Footsteps clamored up ahead. The sound of metal on metal. It was only Omaira and Ico, though, when they rounded the corner. Both of their faces were dark with blood, and they radiated the strength of death. Good.

"Everything's clear," Omaira said.

"At least as far as we could see," Ico added. "It gets dark."

Izara grabbed the door handle and dragged it shut. The *clang* sealed them in, a finality like a gong.

"Yes," she said. "I remember."

She took a deep breath and pressed her hand to her chest and concentrated. A ball of light flickered into existence at her side. It wouldn't be enough light for all of them, she knew, but it would be enough for her to lead them through.

"Let's go," she said.

She strode forward, keeping her spine straight and her hands clenched into fists so the others wouldn't see how terrified she was. "Walk behind me," she told Omaira and Ico as she passed them. "Stay close." She didn't tell them that she needed the blood soaking into their skin, didn't tell them that the miasma of death that clung to their spirits would be the weapon that would see them through the darkness.

That was how Lord Kjari's magic worked, she suspected. He fought darkness with darkness.

They walked toward the black hallway. It did not take long

for Izara to feel the prickle of magic in her bloodstream. The scent of the dead flowers Celestia wore grew stronger, until Izara felt as though she were drowning in sugar water. The darkness swarmed around them, thick as ink. Her lantern cast just enough light that she could make out the stones she walked upon; they were etched with runes, the power of which reverberated up through the soles of her feet. Images flashed in her head, the usual things: animal corpses rotting in a field, mushrooms blooming along the branch of an ancient tree. Her bones seemed to vibrate inside her body. It was time.

She pressed her hand to her heart, as if she could reach through her chest and squeeze Iomim's Treasure, as if it were an organ, a tangible physicality. She concentrated. The blood drying on Omaira and Ico became a center of focus, and she walked meditatively, heel to toe, her palm taking in the drumming of her heart.

She was working in the realm of decay now.

The wards in the hallway came crashing down at once, invisible and powerful and stinking of death, but they were met by the dome of Izara's magic. The others said nothing; little Izar didn't even cry out. They were safe.

The wards pressed down on Izara's protective bubble, threatening to crush all of them. Her knees buckled but she didn't fall. Her heart pumped and with each beat she could imagine her magic streaming out between the fingers pressed against her chest. Her whole body trembled. She kept shuffling forward. It was like walking along the bottom of the ocean, all the weight of water overhead. All the weight of dark magic. And she knew if she stopped moving, if she stopped concentrating, it would destroy them all.

The light in the lantern wavered. Izara sucked in her breath, shot out another force of magic. The runes sent lightning running up her spine. She kept walking. They had to be close, the hallway had not been this long before—

Tears streamed out of her eyes, hot and salty. She could hardly breathe from the strain of holding back the wards. Her steps became stumbling, slurred. She almost tripped, and for a half-second she lost her concentration and the wards lurched down, knocking the wind out of her. She gave a scream and pushed back with all her might.

From somewhere in the darkness, she heard Ico ask, "Izara?"

"Keep walking!" she gasped.

She trudged forward—

Forward—

And then she saw it. A pinpoint of light. Her relief bubbled up inside of her and turned to a stream of hysterical laughter. The runes faded away.

They had made it.

They were here.

⁓

Kjari was waiting for them when they came to the entrance of his quarters. He leaned against his cane, his arm trembling. There was a flatness in his washed-out features that sent a wave of fear down Celestia's spine.

He said nothing as they approached, or as they slowed to a stop. Omaira knelt down, her head bowed, and he ignored her. Izara pressed against Ico, her face ashy, her body shaking.

Celestia moved forward between them, cradling Izar's head with one hand. She stopped a few paces from Kjari and for a moment they just took each other in. He was even more faded than he had been before. His hair was thinner, and his black eyes were now the color of stormy seas, as if the color were slowly leaching out of them.

"You are determined," he said in a voice like a frog's croak. "But my answer's still no."

Celestia glanced over at Izara, on the brink of collapse. At Ico, covered in kajan's blood, his expression haunted. And Omaira, still kneeling before a king who only wanted to abandon her.

"I don't care," she said.

His smile was like a fissure in the earth. "You had your baby, I see."

"My baby is why I'm here."

He seemed to consider this, pressing his weight against his cane. His bones jutted out from his skin, which was nearly translucent. His robes hung loose from his shoulders.

"I heard about that baby," he finally said. "It's been a long time since a life has been created inside these walls. Not since I created my kajani, longing to be like my sister Growth. To be as loved as her."

Celestia smothered her shock. He wanted to be like Growth? She glanced at Izara, who seemed just as startled.

He shuffled forward. "May I hold him?"

Celestia hesitated. Izar was still asleep, as the mage had promised—but his protection was contingent on him staying close to Celestia's beating heart. However, perhaps if Kjari held Izar, if he understood what it was to feel the future breathing softly against his skin, maybe then he'd change his mind.

"That magic," he said softly, nodding at the dead flowers. "It's to protect him, isn't it?"

"He was born too early," Celestia said.

"I see." Kjari looked at Izar then, and Celestia felt Izar stir against her chest. His eyes fluttered open. They were still that strange dark blue. Izar made a little burbling noise.

"Did you do that?" she asked, forcing herself to keep her voice steady.

"I will not harm your child." Kjari leaned his cane up the wall. "I am not the monster they say I am."

Celestia heard the bitterness of his words, and without thinking, she slid her arm out of the sling. Izar burbled, blinked his eyes. His body was swaddled up tightly in magic-soaked cloth, and Celestia knew she had to trust Kjari if she was to ever convince him.

Kjari held out his frail, thin arms and nodded at her expectantly. She passed Izar over, her breath caught in her throat.

But Kjari just gathered up Izar as if he were his own baby. He cradled him close to his narrow, sunken chest, and peered down, smiling a little, revealing a row of jagged sharp teeth that made Izar coo.

"Why did you bring this baby all the way down here?" Kjari asked without looking up. "You knew it was dangerous."

Celestia drew herself up. She looked at Omaira, who had risen to her feet and now gave a tiny, infinitesimal nod of encouragement. She looked at Izara, still weak from her magic; at Ico, still covered in blood. They had risked themselves for this, too.

"So you would see," she said, "what you're destroying as you fade away."

The air rang out. Blood rushed in her ears. Kjari rocked Izar back and forth, still smiling, still showing his teeth. He didn't speak for a long time. The silence filled up the tunnel. Celestia squirmed, wanting to say more, knowing that she had said all there was to say.

"You thought a single baby would convince me."

"It's easier to imagine," she said, "a single baby. Easier than an entire world."

Kjari kept rocking Izar, gazing down at him, smiling.

"When you finally vanish," she said. "Death will vanish, too. We will live forever. Izar won't age or grow old. Sicknesses won't die, either. Eventually, he would catch something terrible, some blood fever. And he will bleed and bleed for the rest of existence."

Kjari stared at her. Was it her imagination, or had his eyes darkened?

"We cannot exist without you." She nodded at Izar, her chest tight with fear and apprehension. "Life cannot exist with you. You say you longed to be like your sister Growth?"

Kjari's expression soured, his gaze turning back down to Izar. "To be loved as she's loved."

"But don't you understand?" Celestia cried. "She's only loved because you exist! If she's loved, so are you!"

Kjari didn't move. Were his features stronger, his skin smoother? Was it only wishful thinking?

"If he had come early outside my palace, Niry would not have been there to save him. She's a talented mage. Your sister is almost as talented as her, if she was able to lead you through the black wards in my tunnels." Kjari held out Izar, and Celestia gathered him up, grateful to have him close to her chest again.

"Come into my apartment," he said. "Just you. The others can wait out here." He pushed the door open and went inside. Celestia looked over at the others.

"Go," said Ico. "Don't make this for nothing."

She nodded. She tightened her grip on Izar. She would not fail them. She would not fail the world.

She slipped inside.

The apartment's strange decor had not changed. Kjari had already settled himself into his chair. "Close the door," he told her, and she did, and then she sat down on the sofa in the same place she had sat last time. For a moment they regarded each other over the coffee table. Izar nuzzled against her breast.

"He's hungry," Kjari said. "Feed him, if you wish."

Izar squirmed and made little crying sounds, so Celestia untied her gown and Izar latched onto her. She had not fed him herself since he was born. For the last two days, he had been kept alive by magic.

"Did you really think this would work?" Kjari asked. "Bringing a baby down here, prattling on about how Growth and I need each other?"

"I didn't know what I thought." Celestia kept her gaze on Izar. Her child would survive an early birth only to die because one of the Airiana felt unappreciated. "All I knew was that I wasn't giving up so easily." She looked up at Kjari. "That I wasn't letting my baby suffer because of you."

Kjari did not react to that. "Your people hate me," he said. "They loved me once, a long time ago. But when we lost that war—I've been suffering their hatred for years."

"Your domain is death and decay," Celestia said. "People have always hated those things. It doesn't mean they aren't important."

He laughed, leaned back in his chair. "Yes, and it gets to you, after centuries and centuries of being feared and loathed. Becoming human, leading your ancestors into battle—" He waved his hand. "It was a moment of glory. I've never experienced it since."

"So you'll let the entire world become an endless stream of horrors?" Celestia stroked the soft, downy hair on Izar's head. "Because you can't play general anymore?"

She immediately regretted it—this wasn't the way to win him over. But Kjari threw back his head and laughed. "When you put it that way, it makes me sound like an ass, doesn't it?"

Celestia smiled sweetly. "I'm speaking with a mother's wisdom."

"Apparently you are." Kjari sighed. He looked up at the ceiling. The only sound was the soft suckling from Izar's nursing.

"I have not cared about your world in a long time," Kjari said softly. "Not since I lost the war. It was a humiliating moment for me. For all Airiana. And so now it is time for me to leave."

"You weren't Airiana when you lost the war," Celestia told him. "You said yourself. You turned human. Humans are fallible." She paused. "Airiana are not. Which is why you won't go through with this." With her free hand, she gestured at him, at the absurd room. "This fading away. You know it's wrong."

He watched her. His eyes stormed. They *were* darker.

And she didn't look away, didn't change her expression from calm implacability, even though her heart was pounding. Izar finished nursing and pulled away from her; she covered her breast and held him, staring at Kjari as he stared at her.

"You are correct," he said. "Perhaps my time as a human affected me more than I thought."

"Perhaps," she said. She stood up, her skirts falling around her feet. Izar nuzzled against her, drowsy from eating and the magic keeping him safe. "Perhaps you should consider righting that wrong, so that my baby will have a chance at life."

She moved toward the door. There was nothing more to say to him. She could hope she had allowed him to see the nature of his mistakes. She reached out and put her hand on the doorknob.

"Wait," said Kjari.

She stopped. She didn't turn around.

"If I'm to be myself again," he said, "an Airiana at the height of his power, I should act as one. We need to make a deal."

All of Celestia's body went cold. But this wasn't about a husband. This was about the entire world. And so she dropped her hand, and she turned around.

And gasped, slamming up against the door.

Kjari had transformed. He was no longer frail and thin but

young and imbued with strength and a dangerous power. His skin glowed golden brown; his black hair fell in ribbons around his shoulders. His black eyes bore into her, and he smiled at her expression, revealing those same sharp teeth. Celestia felt dizzy with fear and desire both, a strange darkness that coiled up inside her like a snake.

"This is what you want to bring back into the world," Kjari snarled.

"What deal do you want to make?" she asked, and the words were sharp on her tongue, painful. All this had started because of a deal she had made five years ago—except no, it hadn't. It had started five hundred years ago, for reasons that had no bearing on her, on her life. And yet here she was, affected still by the past.

Kjari walked toward her, loping like a panther. He pressed his hand on Izar's head and a wave of panic rose up in her— *No, I won't give him up!*

"I'm not asking you to," Kjari said. He peered down at her. His proximity made her tremble, now that he was himself again. He smelled like the dead roses she wore, like the coppery tang of blood that had erupted in the hallway as Ico and Omaira had slaughtered the two guards. She forced herself to meet his eye.

"Good," she said.

He smiled. "You pretend you aren't afraid of me. I appreciate the gesture." He slid his hand away from Izar. "Your baby is blessed with magic. What do they call it in the Seraphine?"

"Iomim's Treasure," Celestia whispered, and she looked down at Izar, so small, so weak, and couldn't imagine it.

"Yes. Iomim's Treasure. Like your sister." Kjari nodded. "When he is old enough, he will train in the tradition of my magic—the deep tradition, that which is banned by the human world. He will train in all the magic of death and blood. He will become my acolyte."

Celestia took deep breaths. "That's all?" she said.

"He will be hated and feared for it, and you know it. But yes, that's all. In exchange—I will continue to exist." Kjari sank back down in his chair. He looked, just for a moment, like the old man he'd been. But it was only for a moment. A surge of that strange dark desire twisted up inside of Celestia.

"My son will be hated so you won't be," she said.

"No, I still will be. But I won't be alone in it. He'll have my protection. My blessing." Kjari spread his hands. He looked absurd in his surroundings, the ugly wallpaper, the threadbare furniture. "He was halfway there anyway. He was born in this place, after all. That makes him mine."

No, it didn't, Celestia thought, but if she said yes to this deal, then it would. She looked down at Izar, sleeping peacefully against her breast. She wouldn't lose him, which was what she feared. But she was placing a burden upon him. She was giving him a responsibility he should choose for himself. Yes, he would have magic, and he would have power and protection. But he would be an outcast. He might very well be the last of the De Malena line.

The last of a line, to save the entire world.

"What do you say, Lady Celestia De Malena?" Kjari said. He sat in his chair like the emperor in his throne. Menace radiated off of him. But Celestia knew it did no good to be afraid. Not now. Not anymore.

"I agree to your conditions," she said. Her voice cracked. Tears welled up in her eyes.

But in Izar, she felt a swelling of power, a sharp sting of magic.

In his sleep, he smiled.

FIFTEEN

I t worked.

Izara felt it, a sense of wholeness where there had only been an emptiness she hadn't recognized until now. Something missing was back in its place. It was funny, she thought, how small and significant it seemed. Just a moment of completeness, a lack made clear by its absence.

But then the palace began to tremble.

"What's happening?" Ico grabbed Izara's arm, bracing them both. Vibrations rattled up through Izara's limbs. The walls groaned; dust fell from the ceiling.

"I don't know," Omaira said, pulling out her sword.

But Izara did. It was Kjari's magic. It was growing, strengthening, infusing all the particles of the air. Matter itself rattled around. She grabbed Ico's arm and squeezed as the floor tilted, righted itself.

The door to Kjari's apartment slammed open. Celestia

raced out, her veils streaming behind her, Izar clutched to her chest.

And behind her—

Behind her was Kjari, the Lord of Decay. He was no longer old and decrepit, but at his full strength. His muscles were lean, rippling beneath his skin, and his hair was so black it absorbed all the light. Seeing him Izara felt a blast of power, a kind of brightness behind her eyes. She tottered backward, pulling way from Ico. She couldn't think straight. Her head was full of images slamming through her faster than they ever had before. A parade of death.

"My lord," cried Omaira, as Celestia ran to her side. "You've returned."

"What the hell is going on?" Ico demanded. Izara pressed herself against the wall. She wanted to curse him—he couldn't speak to the Airiana like that! But Kjari only laughed. His teeth gleamed.

"Omaira has the right of it," he said. "I've returned."

He lifted his hands above his head, and immediately the ceiling fell away, chunks of stone slamming into the walls. Izara screamed and covered her head, but nothing hit her. Nothing hit anyone. Then the floor shot straight up. Izara was flung away from the wall, and Ico caught her before she slammed into Kjari, who was gazing upward, his expression beatific. A god returning.

Celestia clung to Omaira, her body turned so that Izar was pressed between the two of them. Izara inched toward her. "Celestia!" she cried, and Celestia turned to her, her eyes damp with tears.

"It's done," she whispered. Izara could barely hear her over the rush of wind.

She flung herself at her sister, pulling her and Izar into an embrace.

"What did you have to do?" Izara whispered, because she

knew there would have been trade. There always was, where the Airiana are concerned.

Celestia looked down at Izar. Her veils whipped around her. Izara got a knot in her throat—*the baby, she has to give up the baby*. But when she looked at Izar, she felt a jolt, Iomim's Treasure recognizing a kindred spirit.

"He can stay with me as a boy," Celestia whispered, "but he'll belong to Kjari when he becomes a man."

The room shuddered to a stop. Omaira threw out her arm to keep Izara and Celestia from falling. A harsh, cold wind blustered across the room as Kjari lowered his arms. They were at the top of the palace. And they were out of that strange netherworld—she could see piercing blue sky in the gaping hole where the ceiling had been.

The stillness of the room was unnerving. Izara kept staring up at the sky. She thought about little Izar, who bore her name—he would have magic, too. But it wouldn't be her magic. It would be the magic of this place. The magic that frightened and disturbed her. The magic that she had learned to control anyway.

"My palace will rebuild itself in the desert," Kjari said. "Already my kajani are amassing. Omaira—"

She jerked her head up. Did not put down her sword.

"Your failure at your trial no longer matters. You have a place in my army."

Omaira stepped forward. Black blood streaked across her gray skin, leaving her looking mottled like a beetle. She went down to one knee but she didn't bow her head as she had before, only offered her sword, the blade resting on the palms of both her hands.

"Thank you for that kindness, my lord," she said, "but respectfully—I give up my place in your army." Her expression was hard and determined. "To live among the humans."

Celestia gasped and covered her mouth. Kjari stared down at Omaira, the wind stirring his hair.

"You want to go with them," he finally said. "With my *liberators*."

There was a mocking lilt to his voice. He peered up at Celestia and smirked. She did not flinch away, but Izara didn't think she would have been so brave.

"Yes," Omaira said. "I understand I won't be able to return."

Kjari waved one hand. "Very well." He gazed at the rest of them, each in turn. "I'm assuming the rest of you wish to leave, too." He stopped at Izara. "You," he said, "intrigue me the most. You learned my magic quite quickly."

Izara shivered. His gaze made her feel cold and hollow, as if she were stripped bare in the middle of the night.

"There's a place for you here," he said, "if you wish it." He paused, and Izara shivered harder, her teeth knocking up against each other. "I know you lost your place in the Academy when River dragged you away to find me. I can teach you." He gestured toward Celestia. Toward, Izara realized, Izar. "And you can join your nephew."

Izara looked over at Celestia, who stared back at her, ashen-faced and trembling. And hopeful. Izara saw it. A glimmer of hope, that her child, her son, would not have to be alone in the world.

"What do you say?" Kjari leaned in close to her and Izara smelled that sweetness of decay that followed her everywhere here. She wondered what there was for her back in the Seraphine. Without a degree from the Academy, she could not practice magic. And there was nothing she wanted more from life than magic.

"I won't be your prisoner," she said.

"Izara, don't do it!" Ico shouted, but Izara ignored him.

"If I want to come and go, I will," she said. "I will not be your servant or your slave." She hesitated. Glanced at Celestia, whose face was shining with tears. She shook her head, but Izara knew she didn't mean it, not really. She had seen that glimmer of hope. And anyway, she wasn't doing this for Celestia, or for Izar.

"You'll teach me everything you can," she said.

"Of course I will," said Kjari, and then he bowed to her, hinging a little at the waist. "It's been a long time since I had a human student." He straightened. Izara felt numb. But she also knew she didn't want to go back. She didn't want to live at Cross Winds, the spinster aunt to a Decay-kissed child. All her life, she had dreamed of magic. Now she had the kind of magic at her disposal that she would never have gained at the Academy.

She turned to look at the others. At Celestia, still weeping, and at Omaira, stone-faced. And Ico, who gaped at her as if she were mad.

"You can't!" he said.

"If you can spend the rest of your days with the Lady of the North," Izara said, "then I'll be fine here." She brushed past him, over to Celestia. She turned and looked over her shoulder at Kjari, who watched her with that stormy expression of his. "May I have a moment?" she said. "Before you send me away?"

"I'm not sending you away," Kjari said. "You're my apprentice. You'll stay at my side. But them," he nodded at the others, "them I'll send away."

Izara turned back to Celestia. Tears streamed down Celestia's face, and Izara felt a sadness welling up inside of her. But she didn't cry. She never cried.

"I'm sorry," Celestia whispered. "I'm sorry."

Izara looked down at the floor. It was coated in dust from the desert, from the ceiling flying away.

"It's my fault," Celestia said. "If I hadn't asked for a husband—"

"Stop." Izara grabbed Celestia's hand and squeezed. They looked at each other. The veil streamed out from the crown of Celestia's head, and her eyes were pink and swollen.

"It's not your fault," Izara said. "You did what was needed. We dabbled in magic I didn't understand. And it always has a cost." She laughed. "I learned that at the Academy, you know. Who knows what I'll learn here."

Celestia smiled, sniffled. She pulled her hand away and placed it on Izar, who was still sleeping, protected by the magic. "Promise you'll visit when you can," she said.

"Of course," Izara brushed her fingers against Izar's soft cheek, and she felt the energy of Kjari's magic, faint and flickering. It would get stronger as he grew. Magic always did.

"I suppose things will be easier than when you were at the Academy," Celestia said.

Izara laughed a little. "I suppose so." Then she threw her arms around Celestia's shoulders, careful not to crush the baby. Celestia squeezed back, Izar nestled between them.

"Goodbye," Celestia whispered.

A hand pressed against her shoulder, heavy as stone. Kjari loomed behind her; she could feel the presence of him, an obstruction of the air.

"It's time," he said. "Time to rebuild."

Izara stepped back, holding on to Celestia's hand as long as she could. Celestia smiled sadly at her, tears glistening in her lashes. Then she looked up at Kjari.

"The baby is still too young," she said. "I need your mage's magic."

"No, you don't," Kjari said. "Your son will survive. I saw to that."

Celestia lowered her eyes in acknowledgment. Omaira moved to her side. So did Ico. Already Izara felt a rift forming between her and the rest of them. A gap where they could never reach her. But that was always to be her lot in life, really.

When she went to the Academy, there had been a rift. She had never been like the others in the Seraphine. Even among those blessed with Iomim's Treasure, she had always been strange.

"Where are you sending us?" Ico asked.

"Wherever it is you want to go," Kjari said. And then he lifted his hands above his head. "Watch, apprentice. Pay attention. This is the magic you'll be learning soon enough."

It was almost like being back in the Academy. Izara concentrated. Already the magic was stirring, churning. The sweetness of decay swept into the room. Celestia lifted her hand in a wave of goodbye.

The magic was like nighttime in the desert, dark and full of shadows, dark and full of dangers. Izara felt it deep inside her chest, where Iomim's Treasure resided.

She was not afraid.

Goodbye, she thought, as her sister and her nephew and her friend were wrapped up in the magic.

~

Ico saw what death was like: an endless expanse of nothingness, a coldness that cut to the marrow of your bones. But then he realized he was only lying in a drift of snow. The sky overhead was not the brilliant blue of the Atharé Desert, but a steady, unyielding gray. *More snow coming soon,* he thought, and then he knew where he was.

He pushed himself up. His limbs kept sinking into the snow, and he was weak from the burst of magic that had sent him here, but eventually he spilled out of the softer snow, onto a more solid pack. Xima's palace glittered up ahead. Blue on white on gray. He laughed, a long trail of laughter that echoed up to the sky. And then he ran. He ran despite the weakness in his legs, despite the cold seeping through his thin clothes. He ran because he had made it out alive.

They had brought Kjari back.

He had completed the task.

The door to the palace swung open, and there was Xima, her long white gown lying close to the curves of her body, her hair falling in waves like the snow drifts rising up around him. "My north wind!" she cried, and she ran out into the snow and that was where they came together, Ico collapsing into her arms. She pulled him close to her chest and he lay there, his cheek pressed against her smooth cold skin as she stroked his head.

"You're filthy," she said.

"Yeah, I know."

She laughed—it felt like years since he'd heard her laugh, and it sparked through him.

"I felt it," she said, "when you succeeded."

"So I'm free?" He almost didn't want to ask it. Almost didn't want to hear that the answer was no.

"Yes, my north wind." She pulled away from him and put her fingers under his chin and tilted her face toward his. Ico was aware of the sweat and dried blood coating his body. But out here in the cold, it didn't matter. "Death has returned to the world."

Then she leaned down and kissed him.

It was a kiss he had traveled through the jungle and across the desert for.

It was a kiss he was never giving up again. Not until the day he died.

~

Celestia awoke from a dream, a long nightmare in which Lindon had died, and her sister had been usurped by a mad man, and the baby had come too soon—

She jolted up, her heart pounding. Not a dream. Not a dream at all. And yet she was in her bed, *her* bed, the bed at

Cross Winds. Except she lay on top of the sheets, and she wasn't in her sleeping clothes but a black gown, a veil twisting around her shoulders. She yanked the veil off and threw it across the room. *Her* room. It was her room, she was certain of it. The curtains were drawn, and sunlight—green, filtered, Seraphine sunlight—streamed in through the windows. She slid off the bed, her body trembling. The baby. Izar. Where was Izar?

She raced out of her bedroom, into the hallway, past the guest bedrooms, the furniture covered in white sheets. She ran toward the nursery because she could not think of anyplace else to go. *He promised,* she thought, anger seething inside of her. *He promised I could keep Izar.* He'd taken Izara and he'd taken Lindon but Izar could stay, that had been his promise.

She slammed into the nursery, the door banging against the wall. And then she stumbled to a stop, breathing hard. The nursery hadn't been prepared for him, but the bassinet where she and Izara had slept was still in there, along with all their old toys. The windows were open here, letting in light.

Omaira stood beside the bassinet, rocking it back and forth. She looked up at Celestia and smiled. It was so strange to see her here, at Cross Winds. A piece of a childhood story come to life.

"Is he safe?" Celestia breathed.

Omaira nodded.

Celestia floated over to the bassinet. She felt lighter than air. Izar lay amid the blankets, his eyes open and bright. He blinked at her, then tilted his head away and gurgled.

"He's stronger than he was back at Kjari's palace," Omaira said. "Healthier. More color." She grinned a little. "More brown in him, like a human."

He did look healthier, Celestia thought. She reached into the bassinet and gathered him to her chest. She could still smell the dead flowers from the mage's protection spells. But he wasn't going to need those anymore, would he? Not until he was grown. Not until Kjari came for him.

She looked over at Omaira, who was still in her blood-splattered armor. She would have to find clothes for her. Have some made at the tailor. It would be difficult to explain, why a kajan had come to live with her. That a kajan existed at all.

There would be talk. She didn't care. She had handled talk before.

"Where did you wake up?" she asked.

"Here," said Omaira. "I think he sent me to protect the baby." She lowered her gaze and her shoulders hitched with a sigh. "It was good for me to leave. I think he wanted it. So I could watch over the child." She paused. "So I could watch over you."

Celestia frowned, ran her hand along the back of Izar's head. "No," she said. "You made the choice." Her breath was tight. "You—you gave up that life. Everything you wanted." She hesitated. "For me."

Omaira looked at her again. Her black eyes were filled with a warmth that made Celestia's heart thrum. She shouldn't feel this way. Not so soon after Lindon died. Not with a kajan. And yet she did.

She did.

"What if he only made me feel that way?" Omaira asked. "It's in his nature to manipulate."

Celestia shook her head. "No," she said. "Your kindness while we were in the desert—" She sighed, looked to the window. "No," she said again, with a kind of finality. "It wasn't him."

Omaira stepped closer. She lifted one hand, and then she placed it, hesitantly, on Celestia's shoulder. Lightning rocked through Celestia's body. *It's too soon,* she thought, and then she thought of Lindon, refusing to listen to her, running into battle. It was too soon. But perhaps Omaira would wait for her.

She hoped she would wait for her.

They stood for a moment, in that ancient nursery, the sun warming Celestia's skin. And then she set the baby into the bassinet. "There's one more thing I should do," she said.

Omaira looked at her, not saying anything.

"I just want to make sure," she said. "I want to make sure it worked."

"You were split apart from Ico," Omaira said. "Wasn't that part of the conditions? That you would be bound to each until the favor was finished?"

Celestia nodded. "But I want to make sure. That's all. Will you stay here with the baby?"

Omaira nodded. Celestia gazed up at her, and she was overcome with a surge of affection and although she knew she shouldn't, although she knew it was improper, that she needed to mourn, she still stood on her tiptoes and brushed her lips against Omaira's cheek. Omaira's eyes widened.

"Celestia," she whispered.

"Thank you," Celestia said, close to Omaira's ear. Then she kissed her again. Again. Again. And then they were kissing one another, soft and sweet. It was not what Celestia would have expected from a kajan.

She pulled away, her cheeks hot. Omaira just watched her. Celestia's body shimmered with desire. Later. She would deal with it later.

She pressed her hand to Omaira's heart. Omaira looked down at it, then laid her own hand over it, and Celestia smiled. Because she could imagine this life. It would be hard, but she could imagine it.

"Wait here," she said, her voice a husky whisper.

And then she left, walking through the empty house, past the shrouded furniture, the covered paintings, out into the front garden. She walked through the trembling grass to the river. The heat beat down on her shoulders, and she sweated in her dark robes. She had forgotten what the heat was like.

When she came to the river's shore, the Lady of the Seraphine was waiting for her. The Lady stood on the water, a glow where her heart should be.

"I asked you to bring him to me," the Lady said in her burbling river voice.

Celestia stiffened. "So you could convince him to stay in this world."

The water of the Lady's body glinted with sunlight. "Which you did yourself, quite admirably." She nodded once. "And so I decided that you had completed the task after all."

Celestia sagged with relief, but she managed to stand upright.

"Decay has come back into this world," the Lady said. The dead will die."

"It's not that easy," Celestia said. "My husband—he was fighting with the Eirenese. They won't be happy to know that Lord Kjari wasn't killed."

"No," the Lady said. "But those are human concerns, are they not? You are free from your debt. What you do now is up to you."

And then she collapsed back into the water with a splash. Celestia stood at the river bank, watching the Seraphine slide toward the ocean. She didn't want to think about war. She didn't want to think about death, about dying. But that was what she had brought back into this world, hadn't she?

The world needed death if it were to keep on turning.

Celestia turned away from the river and followed the path back up to Cross Winds. She was free from her obligation, but the weight of her actions weighed heavily on her.

A figure moved in one of the windows. Omaira, standing in the nursery with Izar, watching as Celestia glided over the grass. And despite everything, Celestia brightened at the sight of them. She stopped, and smiled, and waved.

When Omaira smiled back, it was the opposite of a war. It was the opposite of grief.

And so Celestia kept walking toward this strange new life.

ACKNOWLEDGMENTS

The Beholden had a long gestational period, and many people have helped take it from my initial germ of an idea to the book you now hold in your hands (or which exists in the aether of your e-reader).

Thank you to my critique group, Space City Critters, both in its current incarnation and the incarnation who read and critiqued an early draft of *The Beholden* at my house over brisket: David Young, Kevin O'Neil, Chun Lee, Chrissa Sandlin, Holly Walrath, Michael Glazner, and Tria Wood. In addition, heaps of thanks to my other writerly friends, Bobby Mathews and Amanda Cole. We don't talk much about writing these days, but those conversations were instrumental in helping me with every book I write!

As always, thank you to my agent, Stacia Decker, for her feedback on the manuscript and her work on finding it a home.

Thank you to the team at Erewhon Books: my editor Sarah Guan for her excellent revision notes, which helped to uncover and elucidate exactly what I was trying to accomplish with the book; Martin Cahill for working so diligently to ensure the book finds its place in the world; Kristina Carroll, whose beautiful painting graces the cover of the book; and Dana Li, who turned that painting into a book cover.

Finally, thank you to my parents, for all their love and support over the years.

ABOUT THE AUTHOR

© *Lightbox Photography Studio*

Cassandra Rose Clarke is the author of *Star's End*, *Our Lady of the Ice*, and *The Mad Scientist's Daughter*, as well as several novels for young adults. Her work has placed in the Rhysling Awards and been nominated for the Philip K. Dick Award, the Romantic Times Reviewer's Choice Award, the Pushcart Prize, and YALSA's Best Fiction for Young Adults. She holds an MA in creative writing from the University of Texas at Austin, and in 2010 she attended the Clarion West Writer's Workshop in Seattle. She grew up in south Texas and currently lives in Virginia, where she writes and tends to multiple cats.